The **Frost** of **Springtime**

The Frost of Springtime

Rachel L. Demeter

Black Lyon Publishing, LLC

Our books may be ordered through your local bookstore or by
visiting the publisher:

BlackLyonPublishing.com

Black Lyon Publishing, LLC
PO Box 567
Baker City, OR 97814

This is a work of fiction. All of the characters, names, events,
organizations and conversations in this novel are either the products
of the author's vivid imagination or are used in a fictitious way for the
purposes of this story.

ISBN-10:   1-934912-61-1
ISBN-13: 978-1-934912-61-4
Library of Congress Control Number: 2013954503

Published and printed in
the United States of America.

Black Lyon Historical Romance

For my grandparents,
who shared the most inspiring love story of all.

PROLOGUE

Winter of 1862

Paris could have been mistaken for a ghost town. The night was black, oily and slick as ink. Swollen clouds spread out to the horizon, sealing the heavens off from earth. The only noise for miles around was the wind's mournful cry. It echoed, penetrating the emptiness with an eerie howl.

Winter's first snowfall descended from the bruised sky and hid the cobblestones beneath a lush blanket of white. Somewhere deep in the heart of Paris, a gas lamp flickered as it fought to brave out the storm. A humble and rather inconspicuous structure stood several feet away. Withered and faded with time, *Bête Noire* had been carved into the planks decades earlier.

The brothel's insides were equally gutted and stripped of any hope for warmth. Voluptuous shades of scarlet veiled the windows, while jaded chaises allowed a gentleman to rest his legs. Splintered floorboards were poorly shrouded by the modest Persian rug. And a tarnished chandelier hovered overhead, half of its candles lit—all the teardrop crystals resemblances of human sorrow.

On nights such as these, most gentlemen preferred the warmth of a hearth to the warmth of a whore. Regardless, one man loomed before the chipped counter.

The glory of his body was engulfed by a black frock coat and hidden away like a dark secret. Every stitch of material had been tailored from the finest silks; every inch of flesh was a manifestation of startling male beauty. Heavy boots wrapped his calves, encasing them within a lover's touch. Majestic and striking, the formal coat swept across the panels, equipping him with an authority that dared to be tested. But most notable was the man's askew hat. A stiff rim of velvet crowned his head with the irony of a slanted halo—its sole purpose to shelter his identity from the world.

After a stale moment of introspection, he pounded at the golden service bell with the heel of his palm.

Madam Bedeau appeared almost at once. Ample breasts were drawn together, strung high and fastened tight, overflowing the bodice in ridiculous proportions. Both cheeks were finely sculpted and smothered with rogue, her lips an appropriate devil red.

In youth, Pauline Bedeau had been positively stunning—a goddess amongst mere mortals—and known far and wide as France's most desirable courtesan. Unfortunately, her fall from grace had marked a true descent into hell. Although she'd remained undeniably lovely, her beauty was branded by all those years of fruitless labor. And it was no great secret that Bête Noire had fallen alongside its mistress.

Once upon a time, the brothel had existed as an elite pleasure dome, catering exclusively to society's most precious darlings. But much like the frost of wintertime and spring's delicate harebells, its charm had faded away with the ever-changing seasons.

Madam Bedeau approached the man with a knowing smile and provocative sway of her hips. With a seductive grin and batting hood of sooty lashes, she proceeded to greet her most loyal patron. Indeed—she and the cloaked figure shared a partnership that outlasted many marriages.

Like a mezzo-soprano, the tone of her voice was delightfully low, laced with a huskiness that emptied gentlemen's purses at leisure. "Bonsoir, monsieur. How good it is to see you again." The man responded with a sharp nod. "What do you desire tonight? The usual, I shall suspect?"

The door burst open before he could answer. Wind wailed. Snow blew across the archway in a violent storm. Two dangling, silver bells clapped together as they announced the arrival of clientele. They tinkled in merry oblivion, filling the walls with a short-lived cheer.

A beautiful lady donned in a beautiful gown walked across the threshold. A little girl dressed in rumpled clothing and bruises was dragged close behind; white powder caked her skin in a poor attempt to mask the injuries. She cried out in agony, struggling to match her mother's determined steps.

Madam Bedeau propped a hip against the counter as she watched the wretched scene unfold. Long ago, the girl's gown had possibly graced the finest ballrooms and soirées. Now, countless seasons past its prime, it was closer to rags than riches.

"Oh, please, Maman!" Her voice was haunting. "Please! You mustn't! You mustn't do this—"

"Quiet your insolent whining, little whelp." The mother's face contorted into a scowl that marred all traces of beauty. Speaking through a sneered whisper, she tightened her hold on the flailing creature and hissed like a feline in heat. "You have been quite troublesome enough."

Drowning in tears, the child collapsed to the oak floorboards and vainly attempted to crawl away. Mother latched onto the girl's ankles, muttered a lewd curse, and reeled her tiny body across the ground.

The girl clawed at the worn surface, desperate and astonishingly headstrong, each breath rising in a choked pant. Then her gaze simply widened in rekindled horror. A mane of chestnut curls cascaded over her body with the elegance of a diva's shawl. Breath caught in her chest, she perched onto her knees and stared into her mother's vacant eyes. "Maman ... Maman, please. Why must you do this? Don't you love me?"

The inquiry earned a solid slap to the face. Madam Bedeau winced from her viewing spot, body pulsing with barely restrained anger.

"You best hold your tongue. Wretched bastard. You've brought me misery, stupid chit, nothing more." Impossibly long fingers snatched at the girl's chin, twisting her slim face up and back. "You hear me? I refuse my name to be ruined another instant." The child gave a last tug for freedom. Her words were almost inaudible, which made them all the more deadly. "On my word, I shall break your other wrist. And Lord knows—you will need it from here on."

The next few moments flew by in a frantic and surreal blur. The girl was yanked onto her feet and lunged toward the service desk without mercy. Exhausted from her exertion, clearly unused to lifting so much as a pinky finger, Mother exhaled a melodramatic sigh and smoothed down her skirt's slight imperfections.

"Why, the little imp wrinkled my gown," she said with a shaky laugh, making light of the obvious tragedy at hand. "Imagine that!"

Madam Bedeau mutely narrowed her gaze upon the woman's crucifix. All glitz and glitter, the thing was nestled between thick mounds of cleavage and comically out of place. "You cannot be saved." The words weighed heavily in the air, each one uttered with the gravity of a death sentence.

Mother abandoned her highborn pride and shivered at Madam Bedeau's damnation. "Why ... You shan't be so alarmed. This is simply for the best, you see." She peered down at her child with a poorly worn and plastered smile; it was a smile worn as badly as her faith. "Tell me, madam, how much could you offer?" She coiled a hand through the mass of curls and arranged them over the girl's trembling shoulders. "I can assure you, she cleans up quite nicely."

For the first time, the full extent of the child's suffering slipped into sight. Numberless cigar burns disfigured her malnourished right shoulder. And her left wrist was clearly broken. It hung at her side, cocked at an awkward angle. The girl had suffered unimaginable horrors. There was no mistake of that. And yet, her battered appearance did little to diminish her beauty.

Her eyes were brilliant to behold. They were, in a word, breathtaking. Carved from a pristine sapphire, those eyes were as vast as the ocean, brimming with an unparalleled innocence. And, much like the ocean blue, a foreboding undercurrent seemed to swim through their depths.

Many gentlemen would pay a princely fee to possess such innocence. Madam Bedeau cringed, shuddering at those unorthodox desires. They were desires she'd witnessed on far more than one occasion—desires that spoke of a twisted hunger—a hunger sated by the flesh of a child.

Like herself, the girl would be forever ruined. Forever forgotten and cast aside. Her youth would exist as nothing more than a half-remembered dream, a delicate memory of the deep subconscious.

Patience dwindling and blessed with all the focus of a gnat, Mother scoffed at the whore's indignation and sought distraction. She turned her attention to the cloaked figure drenched purely in liquid black.

"Say, what is the likes of you doing here, monsieur? Why, I could satisfy your desires far better than some sullied harlot." Her tone changed from feline to serpent, words always an inviting purr.

The opposite hand skimmed up and over the swollen rise of her breasts. As if on cue, they strained against the material of her bodice and quivered to bust free. "Mmm, indeed, monsieur. I could milk you of your deepest, most decadent desires. And I daresay you may take me free of charge. Your pleasure would be my pleasure—"

The very target of her seduction latched onto her wrist without warning. A massive gloved hand enveloped it completely. Mother cried out, yelping in a flash of pain and anger. "Why, you despicable—"

"Touch me again and I break *your* wrist with pleasure." The menacing baritone vibrated through silk clad fingertips as he released her. Voice dark and ominous, timbre steadier than a war drum, he resumed, "On my word—utter so much as another breath and I vow it shall be your very last." Alluring, emerald eyes shifted away to focus on Madam Bedeau. She was fishing a sum of francs from her bodice—taking the woman up on her indecent proposal, no doubt. "Not another move from either of you. Am I quite clear?"

Pure silence followed after. It was not a question.

Bête Noire's walls shook as a gust of wind moaned in the distance. Soft and shameful sobs accompanied the ambiance with haunting precision. The child sank to the crutch of her knees—defeated, starved for food and warmth—as if she might escape the world in that way.

Moved by her humiliation far more than he dared admit, the dark stranger removed his bowler hat and crouched to her level. He replaced the hat after running an unsteady hand through his hairline. His chest lurched as the child adjusted the torn tatters of her clothing. Swishing off his frock coat, he draped the material over her body like it was a security blanket.

She grasped the wool with her good hand, plummeted onto her bottom, and pulled both legs against her chest. Her face sank from eye-line as she hid below a fortress of upright knees. Tiny and perfectly helpless, the abundance of thick folds seemed to devour her whole.

"Cold night," he whispered.

"Thank you, m-monsieur."

The man softened at the tragic sight that lay before him; icicles, which had too long clung to his chest, deftly thawed and melted away. He felt an incredible pain, a sincere compassion and aching sympathy, which he'd believed he no longer possessed. Despite his better judgment and a lifetime of indifference, his heart broke.

Damnation. He longed to turn his cheek in apathy and disgust. He yearned to feel numb to the girl's pain and loneliness. He wanted to hate the child—to despise the child—for having invaded his sole sliver of peace: darkness.

Tucked within a foreign part of his heart, only emptiness had ever existed. A terrible and twisted emptiness. And for seventeen of his twenty-seven years, he'd filled that internal void with darkness.

Eyes of emerald locked with eyes of sapphire, each pair searching the secrets of its counterpart's soul. He could sense the girl's will to live, to simply survive the world and all of its cruelties, as if it was a tangible thing. And, within that lucid moment, a recollection from his own childhood emerged. The emptiness eased and lifted. His heart pounded as a montage of horrors resurrected— just barely ...

A whisper of half-sobbed words: "Life is pain. Love is a pretty lie." Empty and burning tears. A seductive glint. Steel, cold and rusted, plunged into a slate of creamy flesh. A distorted prayer: "Do not love the world or anything in it. The world and its desires pass away. But those who do the will of God shall live forever." A moment of silence followed by a pair of beautiful, breathless lungs—

The jumbled tangle of memories disappeared as quickly as they'd come. Once more the emptiness returned. But one truth remained—long ago, something had happened. Something unutterable. Something his conscience and consciousness had chosen to forget.

And then, miraculously, for the first conceivable time in the man's life, a ray of hope shined through his darkness.

Perhaps the girl could help him find himself.

Perhaps two orphaned souls could unite as one.

Consumed by his sudden revelation, the dark figure lifted his hand and attempted to brush a stray curl from her eyes. Jerking free of his touch, she flinched out of his reach—just as he'd expected she might—behaving like a mongrel who'd only known beatings. He retreated with a dejected sigh and shook his face.

"Might I know your name, ma petit?"

"Sofia ..." Her voice was little more than a whisper and a true breath of fresh air.

"Good to know you, my dearest Sofia." The man inclined his head, gave a charmingly crooked grin, and clasped a palm to his heart. Aware that everything had changed, it beat against his rib-cage at a rapid pace, the rhythm hard and strong. "I am Alek."

Aleksender scooped Sofia into his arms and embraced her brid-al style. Tuned into her pain as if it was his own, he struggled not to inflict further discomfort upon her injuries. He cradled the child like one might a newborn babe, instinctively sheltering her from the world.

A strange calm washed over him. It was miraculous. It was beautiful. Within seconds, she'd melted into his arms.

If a moment of kindness could inspire such contentment, Alek-sender caught himself marveling, what would a lifetime of love bring?

And could he ever bring himself to love another?

The question resolved itself as Sofia nuzzled deeper into his warmth, stretched her good arm, and curled each limb into a ball. Soothed like a restless pup, she listened to the melodic drumming of his heart and surrendered to an adorably large bear yawn. She inhaled his scent and committed the distinct blend to memory, locking it within the most precious corner of her soul.

Exotic Persian spices ...

A comforting veil descended as peaceful, dreamless sleep claimed her. Aleksender whispered the eternal vow, his voice beau-tiful and soothing, every word spoken like a lullaby: "You are safe with me, my little Sofia. No harm shall come of you now."

CHAPTER ONE

Spring of 1871
Coast of Normandy

Luminous shafts of orange and red illuminated the limitless morning sky. The horizon was halfway hidden behind a blanket of swirling clouds and still tucked in for the night. It was a breathtaking sight to behold. The world was no more than an artistic canvas, and God had painted a masterpiece. A few stars shined overhead, their glows absorbed by the imminent sunrise. The North Star was front and center. And she curtsied in the sky.

A ship's massive silhouette clashed against the horizon. Cradled by the ocean's tide, the vessel approached its port, skimming across Rouen's leaden waters in slow and steady movements. Heroes of the Franco-Prussian war lounged among the clutter of crates, barrels, and weaponry, oblivious to their defeat … oblivious to the hell in which they were returning. They simply rested in harmonious silence, lost halfway between dreams and reality.

Aleksender de Lefèvre and Christophe Cleef tapped their beer bottles and drank in the sunrise. A mild breeze stirred the ship's billowing sails, carrying them ever closer to home.

◆

Any semblance of peace quickly vanished.

Rouen's central railway station was packed tight that morning and an engine of pure chaos. Aleksender and Christophe shoved through the commotion, tense expressions on their faces and satchels slung over each shoulder. Mon Dieu. There was barely enough space to breathe, let alone walk.

Thick clouds of smoke ascended into the rafters and flooded

Aleksender's lungs. Streams of light poured through the above woodwork, illuminating dust motes that danced about midair. Mourning doves roosted among those polluted ceiling beams, oblivious to the hustle and bustle, devotedly preening and nurturing their young squabs. Aleksender squared the wide expanse of his shoulders and continued his pursuit.

The steam locomotive was hard at work and breathing heavily as it recovered from a recent round-trip. Aleksender empathized with the thing, feeling a strange sort of kindred spirit.

Indeed—within seconds, the agony of the past year had struck him in one fell swoop. Mounting exhaustion claimed every last muscle. A film of sweat gathered above his brow and blurred his vision. Each step burned more than the one before it. And the ground below his feet was painful to the touch. It seemed to be paved with hot coals rather than stones—

"Ah, come now. Look alive, mon ami." His comrade's voice sounded surreal, impossibly distant.

Moments from departure, the locomotive puffed out ribbons of smoke and blared its horn in warning. Aleksender and Christophe muttered a unified curse and picked up their strides.

Anywhere was better than this limbo.

Alas, Aleksender had half-expected to be greeted by Charon, Hades' personal ferryman—the infamous seaman who escorted the souls of the dead into the Underworld. And instead of paying passage with coins of gold, they'd offer two clammy pieces of parchment.

Aleksender blinked away the beads of sweat. Upside-down words, *Chermin de Fer de Rouen—Voiture,* were slightly smudged and damp with perspiration marks. He and Christophe beelined through the maze of swishing skirts and worn helmets, hearts madly pounding, those one-way tickets balanced between their fingertips.

Overhead the silhouette of an eagle emerged from a black haze of smoke. Mindless of his friend's glower, Aleksender stopped dead in his tracks, brushed away his forelock, and marveled at the vision. Colossal wings were curved into two elegant arches as if preparing to take flight. But the creature remained unnaturally still. It was a shadow kissed by coils of smoke, a sinister force that had come with the tenth plague of Egypt, hovering high above the station like the Angel of Death.

Wearing a scowl that could only be described as weary, Christophe socked Aleksender's shoulder and urged him into motion. A set of dog tags dangled from his neck and clashed against the uniform's navy hue. The tags tinkled with the delicacy of tin cymbals, manipulated by each shift in his body weight. The sound irritated Aleksender. It reminded him of nails on a chalkboard. Or, more appropriately, like nails raking against the inside of a coffin—

"Stand there like that and I reckon we'll never see Paris again." The train whistled another warning and pumped out furls of smoke. Christophe scoffed, massaging the arch of his chin in a nervous gesture. "What in the devil has gotten into you? Would you—"

Aleksender silently shoved past Christophe and claimed the lead. He half-expected the eagle to descend from the rafters at any given moment. But the illusion faded away with each of his steps—unveiling that bird of prey for what it truly was. "The Imperial War flag."

Or rather, the symbol of the Imperial War flag.

Christophe rotated in the direction of Aleksender's voice with a grin and arched brow. Murmuring a pained grunt, he adjusted the satchel's strap. The leather was pliable and soft with age, though fully capable of leaving a solid welt in its wake. "Ah. So it is ..." A chuckle rumbled low in Christophe's throat. "Bit of an ugly thing, eh?"

Aleksender said nothing. Firmly rooted in place, he held his breath and surveyed the station in its entirety. For the first time, he really drank in his surroundings.

And the truth was a knife to his throat.

An overall sense of discontentment tainted the air. Hordes of Prussian soldiers infested nearly every square foot, outnumbering members of the French military three-to-one. Aleksender felt strangely out of his element—as if he was intruding upon his own home. He cursed and blotted away beads of sweat with the side of his cufflink. "What horror have we returned to?"

His words were lost to the surrounding din. From wall to wall, a wave of excitement had flooded the station. Men, women and children eagerly huddled about as they contended for a proper viewing spot of the building action. A little boy was lifted onto his father's shoulders, granting him a bird's-eye view as the scene unfolded.

The competition was ruthless. In a single instant, Aleksender had returned to the damn battlefield.

Laying down the rifle and satchel, he extended each limb and inhaled a deep groan. He was more than a bit grateful for the delay. As he'd expected, his comrade flocked to the drama, behaving like some petty spinster rather than a veteran of war.

And what spectacular drama it was. Within moments, the surrounding madness escalated to a full-blown riot. A handsome, young couple was hustled from the train in order to make room for two Prussians. A tangle of protests and empty threats filled the station as France's citizens flocked to the couple's defense.

"My sincerest apologies, madame, monsieur," the guard mumbled without an inkling of sympathy in his voice. He led them down the three wooden steps and onto the platform.

The lady twisted on her fine heels. Her fair complexion flushed deeply, gloved hands strangling the parasol like twin manacles. "You dare turn us out for those savages!? Those ... those common Visigoths!"

"Don't fret, darling," crooned the husband as he caressed her arm with calculated strokes. "We shall catch the next one without delay."

She jerked free of his touch, lips hooked into a fierce scowl and pretty eyes blazing. An arm was propped on either side of her hip as she hotly spoke. "Why, I never took you for a coward till this moment! I suppose Father was right about you, after all."

The faintest blush singed the gentleman's cheekbones. Leaning on his walking stick like an old man, he cleared his throat and shrunk two full sizes. "Now, see here, darling, I simply—"

"How can you be so shameless? Why, I've half a mind to board the first ship out of this wretched place and never look back!"

Suspended above this melodrama was Prussia's black and white flag. Fluttering amongst a smoky sea of ashes, it hung in the midst of France's greatest railway station without a trace of honor.

A true angel of death, Aleksender inwardly mused.

And that blackened eagle had confirmed his deepest, darkest premonition: the war was far from over.

The bloodshed had only just begun.

•

Dawn was almost fully broken an hour later. Flittering street lamps cast rings of light that were lost to sunrays. The long streams oozed through Paris's ancient buildings and monuments, awarding the city with an unworldly quality.

Aleksender and Christophe wandered the cobblestone walkways in uniformed silence. All around them society was waking for the day. The town baker rolled his cart, whistling a merry tune, the bread rolls still warm and steaming. Men and women opened up shop and greeted awaiting clientele. This spectacular show of normalcy was contradicted by countless barricades—a handful of which clogged alleyways and blocked store entrances.

Together, Aleksender and Christophe observed Paris like it was a foreign land. And in a most strange way, it was.

Indeed, a black plague had consumed every inch of Paris since she'd been under siege only months before. The war had left the city isolated from the rest of France and in a state of purgatory. Monarchy was dead, the government virtually useless, and citizens overcome with poverty and despair. Cries of revolution had spawned as the National Guard took charge, enlisting persons of all ages and social classes to stand at Paris's defense. It was a militia created and sustained by the people—and a force that opposed France's formal army.

Early stirrings of civil war had broken out between Parisians and the military of Versailles. And this so-called peace, a sentiment that comes with the ending of war, was nothing less than a mockery of Paris's former elegance.

Blaring signs of chaos were everywhere—the beggars, abandoned buildings, rundown whores, starving children, filthy sidewalks.

Christophe's voice finally broke the pressing quiet. "My shop better be alive and well. I got no chit awaitin' my return. Only a couple knives, saws, an' clamps to keep me warm at night. Be a damn pity to lose the one thing I can rightfully call my own."

A tight and poignant chuckle inflated Aleksender's lungs. "I doubt such a thing matters with the whole of Paris good and dead."

Aleksender drew toward one of the wrecked shops and studied its emaciated and skeletal frame. The windows had been shattered, exposing lightless and gutted insides. Out-of-doors, the red freedom flag hung from the structure's aged planks like a bloody omen. Christophe fondled the scarlet linen, scanning the various nooks and crannies that lay beyond the battered walls.

Observing his friend's silent awe, Aleksender stepped back and adjusted his satchel. Christophe Cleef was thirty-five years old, though a bit of a child himself. Blessed with boyish good looks and the devil's charm, he did not see France's swift surrender as defeat; he rather saw it as an opportunity to inspire much-needed change within his beloved home. Like so many before him, he was blinded by idealistic thoughts and would stop at nothing to see them carried out.

Aleksender certainly did not see eye-to-eye with his comrade's whimsical perspective of the world. He rather thought Christophe's grand ideas were downright ridiculous—the ambitious musings of a deluded idiot. Such passion was both a blessing and curse.

"What a pity," Aleksender mumbled, his voice icy and void of remorse. "The people insist on bringing about their own destruction."

•

Christophe shot Aleksender a look and hastened his steps. As usual, he remained mute and turned a deaf ear to his friend's cynicism. He shook his face and rounded the maimed structure, an all-too-familiar resentment thrumming through his veins. He desperately needed space—a breath of fresh air. The temptation to lash out at his comrade was just too great. And that was one territory he didn't wish to revisit any time soon.

As Christophe continued his investigation of Paris, the street narrowed, enclosing his body between wood and stone. Steam from a nearby workshop fogged his vision and curled around his limbs, urging him forward. His hair grew heavy with condensation as he waded through the dense cloud.

All around him, sunrays speared through splintered planks and illuminated the ornaments that decorated his military coat. The assortment of bronze and silver shone in the early morning light and contrasted against the uniform's deep hue. Lost within a strain of thought, Christophe paused in his tracks and inclined his chin. A burst of pride instantly overcame him.

The bronze military decoration glittered like a beacon, reminding Christophe that France had not suffered true defeat. No—there was still much to be won. And he'd never been one to stand idly by. Distant chatter filled the alleyway and anchored his attention. He trailed after the faint rolling of drums and muffled voices—drawing closer to the sounds, closer …

Soon the melodies climaxed and blossomed into a brilliant crescendo. Just as quickly silence took hold. Only the repetitive clicking of his boots shattered the quiet. Christophe veered down one of the sharp corners and eased into the long, dank alleyway.

A rather impressive and unexpected sight greeted him. Christophe laid down his belongings, knotted both arms across his chest, and observed the action with a rekindled patriotism inside his heart.

Several rows of uniformed men stood single-file, bodies erect and rifles propped over their shoulders. All eyes were staring forward and fixed on the Captain of the Guard. Representing everything that a good captain should be, the figure was stationed front and center, hands tucked behind his dark coat. Almost comically, a coal-black mustache twitched in time with each of his words. "Citizens of Paris! Our National Guard has become a federation—a federation that challenges a government that has betrayed us!"

A chorus of hoots and applause sounded out. Christophe felt his pulse quicken in anticipation. He leaned in closer so as not to miss a word. "Prime Minister Thiers violates our rights! We must unite against this tyranny and exploitation. Long live brotherhood and solidarity!"

Christophe collected his belongings from the pavement and headed back to the boulevard. With each step, the cheers dissolved into an empty and sullen silence. And yet, inside his mind, the message remained loud and clear.

•

Pacing back and forth, Aleksender waited as his comrade sated his curiosity. He felt himself grow increasingly impatient and uneasy. A mounting detachment was steadily forming between him and what was left of his home. Not for the first time, his eyes ran across a placard that was tacked onto the shop's door:

French Republic
Liberty—equality—fraternity
The Commune de Paris decrees all citizens
as a part of the National Guard.

Aleksender scoffed at Paris's insolence and stupidity. It was as though the people longed to suffer. There could be no other explanation for this foolish burst of patriotism.

The war had come and gone, leaving a window of opportunity for the city to rise from its ashes. But no—the people were far too proud to accept defeat.

Wearing a smile that didn't quite reach his eyes, Christophe came into step beside Aleksender. "I believe that's twenty francs to you, ol' friend." He paused, allowing Aleksender a moment to recall their latest wager: whether horrors of the battlefield were preferable to the horrors of polite society. And then that smile successfully reached his eyes—as if he'd convinced himself of his own blatant lie. "It's a fine thing to be home."

Christophe inhaled the musky sea air and curiously looked about. "Yes," he repeated with a new confidence, "it is quite good to be home again. A little time and care and she'll be good as new." He and Aleksender crossed the street, mindful of the omnibuses and horse-drawn carriages rolling by. "Am I right, ami?"

"One would have hoped," Aleksender muttered beneath a stale drawl. He passed a hand over his hair in a slick motion—an overused habit that often marked his distress. "But even a blind man can see the truth. This is the beginning of the end. Nothing more, nothing less."

"Is that right? That how you see it?"

Christophe froze in the middle of the street. People momentarily stopped whatever they were doing and watched the veterans with blank expressions and sideways glances.

An omnibus screamed to a halt, nearly running Aleksender and Christophe into the ground. "Take care, messieurs!" the driver hollered from his spot on the wooden bench. And then he coaxed the two geldings into a steady gait and moved on with his day; the clapping of hooves against pavement resounded once more. With a detached awareness, Aleksender's gaze followed the large block lettering that rimmed the vehicle's upper floor: *RUE DE LA PAIX.*

Christophe slammed his satchel onto the ground and glared at Aleksender with bitterly cold eyes. Aleksender remained in his characteristic silence, quiet as the grave.

"I may pity you more than I pity Paris." Without sparing another word, Christophe collected his satchel from the pavement, whistled down the omnibus, and climbed onto its platform. Aleksender shook his face and joined Christophe with a dejected sigh.

The vehicle harshly lurched into motion. Aleksender and Christophe leaned against the railing, exhausted and spent, chassepot rifles dangling from their shoulders.

•

Established along the Right Bank of the River Seine, Cafe Roux was a true diamond in the rough. By day, it was a charming and quaint restaurant located conveniently on Rue de le Paix—one of Paris's most fashionable boulevards. It stood as a bit of a sanctuary, offering the leisurely ways of the easy life: relaxing for hours on end, catching up on the latest scandals, all while watching the world pass by.

By night, however, the cafe transformed into a watering hole for gentlemen of all pedigrees. It attracted the upper class, the lower class, and those sorry wretches who were squandered somewhere between the two worlds. Due to its close proximity to the up-and-coming Opera Garnier—and the fact it had been designed by none other than Charles Garnier himself—Cafe Roux had earned its reputation as a unique and revered attraction. Within its walls, it was not so uncommon for a pauper to rub shoulders with a prince.

The little dwelling was a wonderful kingdom of idiosyncrasies. The selection of ladies was always most satisfying while the brandies never disappointed. Even well past the wee hours of morning, it remained a rather risqué drinking bar and wenching ground. While it was far from the finest of bars, from nine PM to eight AM, Cafe Roux offered a nice escape from the clutches of one's mistress or madame.

It was within this decadent time frame that Aleksender and Christophe paced inside. Aleksender studied Christophe as his friend's roguish nature took hold. Welcoming the crude atmosphere and stale scents with an open heart, Christophe's grin grew lopsided, steps eager, and tongue heavy with wit.

Arms crossed over his chest, Christophe scanned the room from wall to wall. The place was a damn madhouse. "Dawn has yet to break and the better half of Paris is already drunk out of their wits? Fine thing to see nothin' has changed in the least."

A heated game of commerce occupied the cafe's sole card table. Rowdy jeers and handfuls of sous were traded amongst the men. Reckless wages overlapped in a flurry of excitement, each battling to be heard. Cigar smoke obscured the air in collective white clouds. Seductive barmaids served drinks to loyal patrons, not minding the obscene fondling of their backsides. Between the cinched bodices and wicked smiles, they beamed with the charms of a good whore. And it had been ages since either Christophe or Aleksender had reaped the pleasures of a good whore.

The two veterans seated themselves before Cafe Roux's endless counter.

At once, a strong sense of not belonging overcame Aleksender. Finding no comfort, he settled into the stool and fished a wedding band from his trousers. The trinket was caked with grime and severely tarnished. Christophe scoffed, not bothering to hide his disgust.

"Mmm. Speak of the devil. I see you haven't changed so much yourself. You might've forgotten Elizabeth entirely."

Offering no words of denial, Aleksender rubbed the golden band against his cuff till it came to life with a weak sparkle. "Ah, come now. What in God's teeth are you doin' here with me?" Christophe roared a humorless laugh and shook his face. "For all I know, this wretched pisshole is the closest thing I got to a home. You, on the other hand—you have a warm bed awaitin' your return, a pretty wife to properly tumble." A tense silence passed between Aleksender and Christophe. "Eh, I suppose I could do the job for you?"

Aleksender slid the ring onto his wedding finger, movements lethargic and lifeless, a withheld sigh caught in his chest. "It's not so simple."

Christophe laughed once more, this time feigning no humor. "That's Paris's ol' vicomte for you. Takes a blessin' and shoves it up the ass."

Indeed, Aleksender de Lefèvre was none other than Paris's vicomte. And the very thought disturbed him greatly and to no end. He had no interest in handling the mundane affairs bestowed upon a comte—affairs that had become steadily more mundane over the last decades. Despite the abolishment of aristocratic rights, an unspoken hierarchy still existed. The prerogative of the nobility was as strong as ever, forging a social barrier between titled peers, common citizens, and the bourgeoisie class. And that insufferable gap that separated rich from the poor, fortunate from the unfortunate—was widening with each season.

Devil take it. Aleksender wanted no part in the fate of Paris. He only prayed that his dear father might live to see one-thousand years. Since boyhood, he and his father had been impossibly close. His death would have imparted far more than the curse of a noble title. The death of Comte Philippe de Lefèvre would have devastated Aleksender beyond reason.

Christophe slumped both shoulders in defeat and drew a beaten case of cigars from his coat. Aleksender waved a declining gesture as he was offered a smoke. Nine years ago, he'd quit the habit.

"Ah, yes, that's right. No cigars for dear Alek. Slipped my mind, I suppose ..." After an uneasy silence, Christophe balled his fist and slammed it on the countertop. Aleksender tensed at the sound, startled by the jarring crack of flesh against wood. "Holy hell, what damned horrific service this is."

Cafe Roux's round-faced-jolly-bartender buzzed about, pouring drinks this way and that, his bloated face grinning wide. The prospect of wealth kept his attention at bay as tips were passed into his pudgy hands by the dozens. Tossing a wave in the wretch's general direction, Christophe scoffed and gestured the aloof bartender. "Correct me if I'm mistaken ... but the fool once knew our preference of drink, oui?"

How many nights had Aleksender and Christophe spent in this very establishment, listening to Round-face-jolly-bartender's outlandish conspiracies—both of their faces plastered with feigned amazement?

A particular rambling came to Aleksender's mind: "I tell you, the Revolution was a ploy!" Purely for dramatic emphasis, Round-face-jolly-bartender had tossed a dishrag over his shoulder, propped both hands on the counter, and leaned in close. White whiskers sprouting from his jowls twitched along with the words. In the same breath, his English accent thickened to the point of incoherency. "A ploy to overthrow the crown and church, it was. Good riddance I say to the crown. But as for the church—ah, our Lord and savior ain't so easily duped like them knaves."

Shrugging his sturdy shoulders, Aleksender offered Christophe no direct comment. The tone of his voice was thick and hauntingly composed—much like the calm before a storm. "It is not so great a mystery. A year of war tends to have that retrograde effect. No good comes of it."

"Ha! Imagine that—we bled our souls for these, uh, broken fellows, womanizers, wretches ... and yet, here I sit dry as a bone! Where's the good ol' show of patriotic hospitality, eh?"

"Still blind are you?" Aleksender shot in quick reply. "Paris could not care less. Our sacrifice was moot. The war has not ended. It has merely followed us home."

Christophe heaved a sigh and stroked the curve of his chin. "Splendid. There's a bit of irony for you."

Two glasses were finally passed down the counter and into their hands. Christophe raised his drink to Round-face-jolly-bartender in a mock toast.

Inhaling a generous swig of alcohol, Aleksender closed the topic. "I daresay irony at its finest."

Minutes later Christophe finished off his drink in a single swallow. "Alek, Alek, Alek ..." he said through a constricted chuckle, already more than a bit tipsy. He draped a muscular arm over his friend's shoulder and clenched the cigar between barred teeth. The faint and fair mustache dusting his upper lip strained in triumph. "I must say, you're quite likely to be the Third Empire's downfall. Either that or the Third Empire shall be your downfall."

Scowling, Aleksender shrugged Christophe from his shoulder. "The day France falls will be no fault of mine. I have found my peace. Damn it to hell France shall deny me my liberty." He stared off, mysterious emotions crossing his features by turns. "I have served her well."

"Eh, you serve only yourself. Always have, always will."

Aleksender drew silent as a dull ache tugged at his chest. That look—the disdain in his comrade's eyes—would follow him well beyond the grave. In endless ways, he and Christophe were as opposite as day and night.

Within that moment, a strange question rose inside Aleksender's mind: out of the two of them—he and Christophe—who was day and who was night?

Interrupting his thoughts, Christophe rotated in the stool and moaned an incoherent grumble. A lovely barmaid shimmied by, trotting to the opposite side of the room, moving with the gait of a prized pony. Christophe called out to the chit. He whistled and snapped his fingers, battling for her attention in the rudest ways imaginable. It was certainly no way to win a lady.

But the proud creature was no lady.

"Suppose I should announce we're in the light of the great vicomte, himself?" Christophe complained, pouting like a young tot and mumbling his unhappiness. "Surely I'd have another brandy by now."

The cynicism in his comrade's voice did not go unheard. Aleksender shoved his glass into Christophe's hand, wishing he could impart his noble title with just as much grace.

CHAPTER TWO

It was five minutes till striking eight AM. Salle Le Peletier, the temporary quarters of the renowned Paris Opera, appeared regal beneath the glowing sun.

Once completed, it was rumored that Opera Garnier would dwarf Salle Le Peletier with its massive scale, sophisticated lighting, and sixteen hundred seats. Such mutterings seemed to be remnants of wishful thinking and nothing more. The opera house's construction had been called to a halt ever since Paris had been under siege, and the city's condition was far from improving. Even well before the invasion, Opera Garnier's progress had been painfully slow. One setback had been encountered after another.

As it happened, the opera house had required a much deeper basement than most buildings. As architects and laborers had cut into the earth and gutted the land, the groundwater level was reported suspiciously high.

This first obstacle had led to the discovery of the vast underground lake. Paris's catacombs and underground waterway were found to be intimately connected through twisting tunnels, sweeping archways and haunted sepulchers. Grounded upon death and decay, it seemed that the fate of Opera Garnier had been doomed from the start.

But nearly a decade had passed since the discovery, and the new opera house was on the brink of completion. As it stood, Opera Garnier was already enchanting. Perched amongst the three domes and solitary pediment, the lyre of Apollo was held high and proud as it kissed the heavens, sunlight seeping through the instrument's precious strings of gold. And, on the clearest of days, the towering stone walls resembled Mount Olympus—the home of the twelve Olympian gods. Within this edifice, the God of Music and Light reigned all.

Aleksender stood off to the side and surveyed the glorious monument erected before him. Granted, Salle Le Peletier didn't have Apollo's protection or his godly wisdom. But the place was far from lacking.

The building held a power of its own. Angels carved from stone graced the columns, their features cold and unfeeling, bodies stronger than a warrior's. Epically handsome and still as death, those divine sculptures seemed to echo Aleksender's gaze. Such a thing was beyond unsettling—one might even say demonic. Salle Le Peletier was no Mount Olympus or kingdom of light. Aleksender neurotically threaded fingertips through his hairline and forced his eyes upon brighter pastures.

And then it happened.

A young lady with striking beauty rounded one of Salle Le Peletier's corners in a frantic rush. She clutched at the hem of her skirts and raced up the winding steps, nearly tripping over herself in the process. Aleksender emerged from his shadowy concealment in a swift movement. He grasped the girl's slender forearm and spun her round in a remarkably graceful dance.

Really! She'd half-expected to be tossed into the waltz! Instead, she shrieked and collided with a wall of masculine flesh. Very masculine flesh that roused her senses and smelled vaguely familiar.

An exotic blend of Persian spices.

Sofia fell into stunned silence as the revelation crashed down like a crystal chandelier.

In the same breath, Aleksender shamelessly returned her stare as he examined his ward from head to toe. Mon Dieu. She was slender and fragile—beyond gentle and angelic. Her petite height reached the middle of his chest and came not an inch more.

Curls descended just past the small of her waist in lush ringlets. Her lips quivered as the blue of her eyes flooded with a storm of unshed tears. And those eyes were truly breathtaking to behold. Her sapphire gaze sparkled, shining like twin diamonds, running over his features in pure disbelief.

Aleksender felt something contract inside his chest.

After gathering the slightest sense of composure, Sofia managed to utter all but a single word. "You …"

She splayed a hand over her bosom, entirely breathless. Aleksender's eyes followed the unconscious motion and lowered to the tender swell. Transferring his attention to one of Salle Le Peletier's forsaken stone angels, he cursed himself and averted his piercing stare.

Just who was this woman? She was incredible.

"Sofia ..."

Aleksender whispered the name with unearthly reverence. He dared to step intimately close, drawn to Sofia much like a moth is drawn to the promising heat of the flame. Unsteady hands rose from his sides in a tentative and suave movement. They cupped her cheeks and deftly lifted her downcast face with the pads of twiddling thumbs.

He drew invisible circles along her flesh, worshiping everything that was his beloved ward, tracing down the smooth bend of each cheek and back up again. A solitary tear streamed over the curve of her chin and vanished between her lips. Aleksender's eyes traced the liquid path and settled upon the lush flesh of her mouth. Sparks of awareness coiled through every inch of his body. Clasping Sofia's chin, he gently swiped away her tears and offered a weak smile.

"Sofia," he repeated, stunned by her appearance, adoration lacing all three syllables.

"I thought you for dead. A year and not so much as a word?" She sniffled, surrendering to a smile that melted Aleksender's heart into ashes. "I was sure I'd never see you again." Luscious curls fell across her shoulders as she inclined her chin. "Oh, Alek. How I missed you." She lunged forward and threw her arms around the circumference of his waist, tugging Aleksender impossibly closer. "You—here in my arms." Her lashes fluttered shut. "Tomorrow I shall think this was all a dream."

"A dream we have both shared." Aleksender sighed and inhaled her sweet essence.

Roses and the frost of wintertime.

"You've truly grown up," he whispered, speaking more to himself.

With Sofia resting in his arms, Aleksender felt strangely content. Strangely happy. And the epiphany frightened him half to death.

At nineteen years, she was terribly young and naive. Was she even aware of how she affected him? Did she know of the burning desires that ignited from her soft embrace? Could she sense—Dieu, could she feel—the extent of his passion?

The truth was mind-boggling. The realization was terrifying. And the onslaught of unorthodox urges paralyzed his mind and body in a thick haze. It had taken, damn it, just over a year for the inevitable to happen: his ward had matured during his absence.

And little Sofia was not so little anymore.

Granted, she'd always possessed promising beauty. It could not be ignored then and it certainly could not be denied now. Ever since Sofia's seventeenth birthday, innocent nudges were no longer so innocent. Sarcastic insults had become tentative flirtations. In a way, Aleksender freely admitted to himself, enlisting in the military had been an escape from the inevitable.

Luckily, for him, the pains of jealousy had never fully surfaced. Over the years, Sofia had never expressed the desire to court a gentleman nor seek out a proper suitor for marriage. He'd reluctantly questioned her disinterest in acquiring a husband—and her response had pleased him far more than it should have.

"Oh, my silly, silly, Alek!" she'd exclaimed, ever the actress, clutching her heart with a rather comedic and melodramatic passion. "Why, don't you know? You, mon amour, are the man of my life!"

The man of Sofia's life.

Those playful words had behaved as a rude awakening. Aleksender had known he was in terrible trouble. Whether she'd been aware of it or not, they were trudging dangerous grounds. After all—some lines simply could not be crossed.

The recollection violently tore through his thoughts. On the afternoon of his departure, they had embraced, and he had kissed her. Within the potency of that moment, it had seemed an incredibly natural thing to do—kissing Sofia on her lips. He could have died out on the battlefield, alone and empty, without ever knowing her taste. Only now did he realize the gravity of such a thing.

But then again Aleksender could have never anticipated this.

Where was the little one who he'd taught the alphabet? Where was the weeping child who'd sneak to the de Lefèvre chateau in the middle of the night and toss herself in the shelter of his arms, seeking comfort from her reoccurring nightmares? Where was the bright-eyed child who shuddered at the thought of a snowstorm? And what had ever become of the girl who'd lie in his drawing room—sprawled across the warmed floorboards like a feline—lost within the throes of his elaborate stories?

Gone was the child who he'd once adored. And it was a breathtaking woman who now stood in her place.

CHAPTER THREE

Sofia Rose had first decided she'd marry Aleksender de Lefèvre nine years ago. Such longings were all in good fantasy. Her attachment was to be expected.

The man had rescued her from the endless floggings of her mother. He'd saved her dignity from the life of a whore. He had educated her, cared for her, dressed and fed her, built an entire convent house in the saving grace of her name. He'd fueled her talents and secured her a position in the opera's chorus line. He'd hired none other than Marie Taglioni, the widely adored Swedish prima ballerina, as her private dancing instructor. He had dried her tears and chased away the monsters of her nightmares.

He had been her everything—her hope, her inspiration, and even her despair. Days before Aleksender had left for the war, he'd sworn to write weekly. Months had passed without a single utterance. The grave realization had been soul-shattering for Sofia.

A life without Aleksender? What life? Without his gentle touches, without his guidance and devotion, she could have let Death claim her. And he almost had. Sofia had fallen deathly ill.

By strict order of her doctor, she was pardoned from Salle Le Peletier for bed rest. Aleksender had been her other half. She'd never felt such pain, such indescribable sorrow and heartache. The beatings of her mother had paled in comparison. Endless nights were dedicated to mourning a love she never had. Each waking moment was spent weeping over an internal loss, a painful void, which could never again be made complete.

At the tragic acceptance of his death, Sofia had divulged herself within a fantasy world that began and ended with Alek.

Her Alek.

The characteristic shine had returned to her skin in a matter of weeks. She resumed her role at the opera house and was back on her toes once more. In that time, she'd playfully decided that if Aleksender were to ever return, he'd belong to her and her alone.

Behind her shut eyes and most private thoughts, touches that had always been paternal and protective turned intimate. Wildly possessive. Her white knight mutated into a black knight. Within the impossible realm of sleep, they would merge together as one— mind, body and soul. These surreal thoughts, Sofia had imagined, were a happiness that harmed no one. But now, as Aleksender embraced her to the rhythmic beat of his heart, the line separating reality from fantasy became obscured.

He was her Alek.

"Sofia …" She snapped from her whirlwind of thoughts. The husky accent in his voice sounded foreign to her ears and positively thrilling. It was sultry and rich, smoother than any lullaby. Sofia felt the baritone resonate deep inside her.

Grinning from ear to ear like a pretty fool, she freed Aleksender from her clutches and took a demure step back, moving with the grace of a true ballerina. She kissed each cheek, just below the arch of his chin and the very tip of his nose, concluding her darling ministrations by running fingertips though his coal-black hair.

In spite of all notions of right and wrong, Aleksender found himself mimicking her affection tenfold. His hands were possessed with desire, and they moved on their own accord.

"Sofia, chérie, have I ever told you how lovely you are?"

Her eyes lowered at his praise. Swatting away tears, she blushed. "Now you're just flattering me."

Aleksender slid his fingers through her curls a last time. He balled his hand into a tight fist and brushed his knuckles against her cheek. She smiled, covering them with the creamy flesh of her palm. Returning her warmth, he grasped her hand, entwined their fingers, and laid the united grip over his lips. "My sweet Sofia."

There was no war. There was no duty to his father or homeland. There was no vicomtesse who was sadly awaiting his return. There was only Aleksender and his little Sofia. He sighed, momentarily lost to a world that began and ended with the two of them, a cocoon of happy thoughts, surreal thoughts that harmed no one, an unblemished realm of oblivion.

And for the first time in so many years, Aleksender felt like he belonged.

Alas, all is fair in love and war.

•

Elizabeth de Lefèvre stood on the balcony and absently stared into the gleaming skyline. The lawn glowed, sprinkled with remnants of the early afternoon sun.

Elizabeth was thirty-one years old and perfectly lovely, boasting everything that high society could ever hope to offer. A tea dress of mint green complimented her fair complexion, the abundance of silks and satins draping behind her like a queen's regal trail. Matching gloves wrapped her hands and arms, fastened in place with rows of delicate white pearls. Succulent honey blonde locks were meticulously pinned beneath her hat, the occasional tendril falling across her cheek in a fetching swirl.

Elizabeth sighed and gazed down at her wedding ring. Caressed by the surrounding light, the diamond glittered and gold shined. And yet, her world had never seemed darker than at that moment.

Then everything changed.

Elizabeth squinted and shaded her gaze from the sunrays. A handsome figure was approaching the chateau, the frame of his body appearing tall and sinfully elegant. Could it be? Could it possibly be him? Her heart did a little somersault at the thought.

Aleksender, her dear husband, had written to her on occasion—and she'd treasured both of his letters. True, they had been far from fluffy or romantic. For Elizabeth, the letters had served as much more than some mushy sentiment. Those letters had proved her husband was alive and well. Aleksender's rather impersonal and vague prose had never bothered her much. After all, she was a far cry from a melodramatic and love-struck adolescent.

Or so she'd convinced herself to believe.

A gasp fled from Elizabeth's lips as she gripped onto the banister with growing anticipation. The man's complexion was an unusual and tempting shade—tan and wonderfully sun-kissed. He hardly resembled the Aleksender whom she had known and adored. Both in spirit and form, he seemed quite darker. But there was no question as to his identity.

Aleksender Raphael de Lefèvre had returned to Paris.

•

Aleksender's chest constricted at the approaching image. Elizabeth sprinted over to him, alive and beaming, wearing a smile that was visible across the expanse of the lawn. One hand clutched at her skirts as the other secured a fluttering hat. Aleksender inhaled a deep breath and quickened his stride. Regardless, his was the walk of a dead man.

"Aleksender! Aleksender, mon amour!" she passionately called from afar.

Elizabeth outstretched both arms as they finally came together, their two bodies colliding as one. Her hat blew away, whisked off by the wind like some hostage tumbleweed.

Elizabeth grasped onto Aleksender's shoulders with an impressive force. "Oh, Aleksender! I simply cannot believe my eyes!"

He dropped his satchel with a low groan and embraced his wife. A moment later, he discarded the rifle as if it were no more than an outgrown plaything. He sighed into her hair as a rush of guilt secretly consumed him. Aleksender's body shook while he caressed her waist in tremulous motions.

Pulling back to kiss each of his cheeks, she cried out, "Look at you! You have never appeared better! A proper meal and you shall be good as new."

She embraced him once more, nuzzling, cooing incoherent words into the warmth of his chest. Curls of gold came unfastened by his fingers. They tumbled down and over her shoulders in an enchanting flurry.

"Promise to never leave me again."

"Forgive me." Fatigue strained his voice, making it impossibly tight. Speaking far more than the obvious, he continued in a hushed murmur, "Forgive me for everything."

Elizabeth sighed and brought her lips to his neck. She whispered against Aleksender's skin, the soft brush of air teasing his pulse. "Believe me, dear. I already have."

Aleksender knew he didn't deserve her forgiveness. He'd never been a decent husband. Alas, he'd never been a decent man. Much like himself, Elizabeth was an heiress born to a noble family. Despite the longing to enjoy being young—to relish the simple joys of living, frolicking and causing unnecessary mischief—she was betrothed to Vicomte de Lefèvre on her fifteenth birthday.

Elizabeth had cursed both her family and blood. She wanted

nothing to do with such a thing as marriage. She was a mere fifteen years! She wanted to live. Not love! But everything had changed the moment she set eyes upon her future husband. A curse had quickly transformed into a blessing.

In spite of herself, she'd swooned before the man whom she had passionately sworn to hate. From the bottom of his polished shoes, up to the top of his blackened hair, he'd been the picture of masculine perfection. Elizabeth had stuck up her nose, convinced that she was immune to such a breed of gentlemen. Surely, Elizabeth had vowed with a proud inward smirk, Vicomte de Lefèvre would be no different.

She could not have been more wrong.

It had taken only one dance. The first stirring of lust and love had swelled her tummy from the inside out. Elizabeth had accepted her fate with wide eyes and a maiden blush.

Aleksender had been as stubborn as they come and quite the rake, always throwing caution to the wind and never conforming to society's mold. But his father had seen much more than his stiff exterior. Comte de Lefèvre had purposefully steered his son's wandering eye, declaring Elizabeth Rousseau a proper match. And Aleksender would have done nothing to displease his father.

It wasn't until he and Elizabeth had taken their vows that his resentment surfaced. Did he not deserve the same happiness— the same chance for love and true affection—as his parents had shared?

Any enjoyment between Aleksender and Elizabeth had rapidly faded. On their wedding night, he could not bring himself to consummate their partnership. He'd already stolen her youth. He didn't love her.

As tempting as Elizabeth had been—a vision cloaked in chaste white, a quivering bud aching to bloom beneath his touch—he'd refused to take her remaining innocence.

That fateful evening, however, Elizabeth had recalled a story—a rather saucy story that her eldest sister had shared with her. Covered in a maiden blush, she'd run her wedded fingertip up her husband's trousers seeking that impressive, hidden bulge with daring caresses.

Both hands had settled upon clasps that concealed a mystery— a mystery she was suddenly eager to unveil. Romantic ideas had flooded her thoughts in a thrilling rush. She was about to experience an epic moment, a moment shared between man and wife, a moment that would connect their souls forever.

That moment was shattered. Aleksender had peeled away her trembling fingers, kissed her knuckles, and wished his bride sweet dreams. The vicomtesse turned away from her husband and privately cried herself to sleep.

Mercifully, after a year or so of marriage, Aleksender and Elizabeth had developed a delicate bond. They understood each other. They understood each other's families and the expectations that came with their bloodlines. They understood that they were, in fact, very much alike. And they were almost content.

But time is the most accurate measurement of truth, and, within time, Aleksender's unorthodox ways only progressed. That strange emptiness that had lurked inside of him seemed to expand, engulfing him whole. Something crucial was missing inside his heart. Something foundational. Something existed as nothing more than a faraway dream.

And so, as blackened souls are wont to do, he'd searched for comfort in the wrong places. All of Paris's finest whores couldn't have filled his internal void. His detachment grew over the years, enslaving his spirit—until fate had given him the bright-eyed, lovely child whom he'd eternally sworn himself to. Aleksender had resurrected Sofia from her own ashes. Only then were his visits to Bête Noire less frequent—only then did the emptiness no longer shape his understanding of the world.

Elizabeth breathed deeply as if summoning the courage to speak. With a shallow exhale, she stepped back and stared into his eyes. "Aleksender, there is something I must tell you."

Aleksender's blood froze over. Time seemed to stand still. He could have sworn the wind was weeping. Heart banging against his ribcage, his mind spun.

"Your father ... He fell ill shortly after your leave. He's passed now. It happened only weeks ago—"

Comte Aleksender de Lefèvre collapsed without warning. He clutched at his chest, overcome with a fierce wave of nausea. One hand pushed against the pavement in an attempt to prop up his fatigued body. Elizabeth knelt beside him, caressing his back with delicate, slow strokes.

"Aleksender, please—listen to me. He was so proud of you. He loved you. He died with a smile to his lips knowing you would do great things. Magnificent, great things."

Aleksender was disconnected, perceiving Elizabeth's voice through a strange and glassy filter. The whole world and everything in it seemed to drift away.

Despite being a devout atheist, he understood how Lucifer must have felt when he'd fallen from the bruised skies of heaven. Cold, forgotten and entirely alone. In a single morning, the weight of the world had fallen onto his shoulders.

And the weight of the world was no small burden.

CHAPTER FOUR

The afternoon was full of sunshine and smiles. Golden embers drifted into the air as the hearth crooned and cackled. A dozen or so sweet faces glowed brightly all around, each pair of eyes fixed ahead. Sofia sat front and center, the melody of her voice quirky and animated. The russet strands of her hair glowed, alive with metallic flashes of champagne and bronze.

She felt quite toasty—almost uncomfortably so. Indeed, it was a balmy day in mid-spring, and the fireplace was more for dramatic effect than any warmth.

Sofia was the eldest of the girls and had been ordained as "Sacred Heart's storyteller" several seasons back. And it was a role she'd always been more than happy to fulfill.

Sofia brought the fairytale to life as she read from the faded pages. Reeking of antiquity, each one was tinted yellow and curled at the corners. "The nightingale flew over to the rose tree that was growing beneath the Student's window. 'Give me a red rose,' she cried, 'and I will sing you my sweetest song.' But the tree shook its head." Utilizing her skills as an actress, she shifted her tone to better suit the personality of a wise, old tree. "'My roses are red,'"—as usual, a couple of the youngest girls giggled at the sound of Sofia's comically gruff voice— "'as red as the feet of the dove, and redder than the great fans of coral that wave and wave in the ocean-cavern. But the winter has chilled my veins, and the frost has nipped my buds, and the storm had broken my branches, and I shall have no roses at all this year.'"

Alas, Sofia sounded remarkably like a tree. "'One red rose is all I want,' cried the nightingale, 'only one red rose! Is there no way by which I can get it?'" Her voice hushed to a whisper. As not to miss a word, several of the girls scooted several inches closer. "'There is a way,' answered the tree, 'but it is so terrible that I dare not tell you.'" Eyes wide and beaming, Sofia bookmarked the volume with her palm and addressed her eager audience. "Hmm. Shall I tell you?"

"Yes!" Miriam cried out, hugging her ragdoll impossibly tighter. "Tell me," she protested, quoting the nightingale's precise words. "I am not afraid!"

"Brave little one!" Sofia laughed and leaned forward, pinching Miriam's cherub cheek between two fingertips. Lips puckered into a fierce pout, the child huffed and knotted both arms across her chest. Sofia merely grinned at the great show of insolence. The girl was picturesque and adorable beyond words. And Miriam's genuine affinity was a treasured thing; aside from a select few, it was no secret that the majority of Sacred Heart's residents were resentful of Sofia's so-called "double life."

Spirals of blonde curls cushioned Miriam's pudgy face as she hotly asked, "Aren't ya gonna keep reading or aren't ya?"

"Oh, all right. Yes, yes—I shall continue." Sofia cleared her throat and resumed the story with extra exuberance. "'If you want a red rose you must build it out of music by moonlight, and stain it with your own heart's blood. You must sing to me with your breast against a thorn. All night long you must sing to me, and the thorn must pierce your heart, and your life-blood must flow into my veins and become mine' ..."

She paused, strangely affected by the words. She'd known the tale for countless years, and yet, it felt as though she were reading it for the very first time.

Sofia's heart took flight as she reflected on her reunion with Aleksender. Yesterday morning there had been something there. Like a palpable force, there had been something unspoken between the two of them. It was the way in which his fingertips had caressed her through the veil of fine silks. The way in which his face had bowed forward and carefully inhaled her essence. The way in which his heart had thundered against her own, and his unsteady breaths had brushed against her pulse, grazing her body like some secretive kiss.

Sofia's mind raced at a dizzying speed. Her palms grew hot, humid and clammy. The pages stuck to the moist pads of her fingertips as she attempted to flip them.

Dieu! What sort of girl was she?

She was shaping up to be no better than her mother.

And what would Sister Catherine possibly think?

"Soffffiiiiaaaa?"

Sofia snapped out of her daze and anchored herself in the here and now. Expectant eyes bore into her own. She obliged with a small sigh and continued reading from the weathered pages.

"'Death is a great price to pay for a red rose,' cried the nightingale, 'and life is very dear to all. Sweet is the scent of the hawthorn, and sweet are the bluebells that hide in the valley, and the heather that blows on the hill. Yet love is better than life, and what is the heart of a bird compared to the heart of a man?' So she spread her brown wings and soared into the air. She swept over the garden like a shadow, and like a shadow she sailed through the grove—"

Above the mantle, the cuckoo bird emerged from his whittled home and chimed in the hour. The melody, normally so cheerful and full of life, held an ominous edge. It was something Sofia couldn't quite place her finger on.

"Oh, listen!" Miriam cried out as she clasped both hands together. "He's singing for us! Just like the nightingale!"

Whitney, a girl who was a few years shy of Sofia, threw the child her most condescending glare. "Don't you know anything?" she scoffed, flicking a carefully spun braid over the curve of her shoulder. "That's a cuckoo bird. Not some silly little nightingale."

Sofia narrowed her eyes and shot Whitney a disapproving glance. "Whitney! You must apologize!"

The girl looked away and lifted her chin at a defiant angle. "Who are you to order me about?"

Sister Catherine bustled into the room, cued by the singing cuckoo clock. The thick material of her skirts rustled with every step. Sofia greeted her with a wide smile and delicate nod of her chin. Despite Sister Catherine's severe nature, she'd grown to adore the head nun with a fierce affection over the years.

"Come, girls!" She huffed, smoothing out the grim material of her habit. "You must return to your studies. There shall be time for fun and games later." With a unified groan, the children of Sacred Heart climbed to their feet and flocked into the adjoining school room. "That includes you, too, Whitney." Whitney released an irritated sound and followed suit with mutinous steps.

Sofia laid the book in her lap and surveyed the German cuckoo clock. The creature had vanished back into its home, leaving the rest of the world in lonely silence.

Sister Catherine fetched a poker from the mantel and crouched in front of the hearth. She muttered incoherently beneath her breath, stabbing at the logs with an uncharacteristic aggression. The effect was highly comical. Sofia bit her lip and harnessed back a grin.

"Must they always insist on lighting this wretched thing?" Fiery sparks crackled and ascended into blackness. Sister Catherine sighed and shook her face, burying the embers with the little copper shovel. One by one, they suffocated and lost their customary glows. Beads of sweat formed along the border of Sister Catherine's wimple as she labored. Suspended midair, the crucifix dangled in free-fall, tossing luminous shades of orange and red upon the carved mantle. Sofia gazed at the glowing emblem, strangely transfixed. "On my word, it's close to an oven in here!"

Sofia came to her feet with a laugh and gently touched the nun's shoulder. "Here—allow me." She stole the poker from Sister Catherine and rolled a log onto its side. A solid *thwack* was followed by the groan of splintering wood.

Sister Catherine dabbed at her brow and claimed a seat in the ancient rocking chair. The cozy sound of a repetitive *thump, thump, thump* filled the room, warming Sofia's insides.

"You remember that feeling I had?" Sofia began conversationally. "A couple days ago—about Alek being alive ... being near?"

"Yes. Yes, certainly I do."

Sofia glanced over her shoulder with a beaming smile. Sister Catherine clutched onto her chest as it quaked with lighthearted laughter. A blend of soot and ash shadowed Sofia's nose and cheekbones.

"Come—come here, petit." Sister Catherine signaled Sofia over with a wave of her hand. "My, aren't you a sight."

Sofia set down the poker and knelt beside her. One of the nun's wrinkled hands steadied Sofia's chin—the opposite wetted her thumb pad. A deep crinkle warped Sofia's nose as the soot was washed away.

"Now," Sister Catherine smoothed down her habit and folded both hands in the cushion of her lap. "What was it you were trying to say?"

"My feeling—it came true, Sister Catherine! Alek has returned! He arrived only yesterday."

The nun's eyes widened at the news. It wasn't the first time Sofia had predicted such things. And it most certainly wouldn't be the last.

"Blessed heavens!" She clasped a palm to her heart and crossed herself in a graceful movement. "Day and night, I have prayed for his return." Silence pressed between the two of them.

Sofia felt her chest sink. Worry was cleanly etched in Sister Catherine's brow. "Sister Catherine? What is it? What is wrong?"

"His heart must have broken when he learned of his father's passing."

Sofia nodded as she watched the last embers disintegrate into ashes. "I can only imagine his pain," she whispered, mind elsewhere. "Losing someone you love is one of life's greatest tragedies." Sister Catherine cleared her throat, rose to her feet and smoothed down the hem of her skirts. With a soft smile, she reached out and cradled Sofia's cheek in her palm. "You're truly a dear girl, Sofia. And there's something magical between you and your Aleksender. Something remarkable. Something I can't quite place my finger on." She sighed, shoulders arching into a defeated shrug. "Heaven knows—I have tried."

And, without another word, Sister Catherine departed from the room and left Sofia alone with her thoughts.

•

The morning air was crisp and cool, seasoned by the bitter-sweet blooms of the coming springtime. From the premature flower buds, up to the noisy nest of sparrows that was cradled upon a tree's bough, the world whispered of birth and new beginnings. Golden rays oozed between shuddering branches, while shafts of light illuminated their dew-covered leafs. A sea of tall grass swayed in the wind's breath, moving to and fro, lolling like the ocean's tide. Aleksender surveyed his home as he acquainted himself with the second Parisian morning since his return from the war.

Quiet and tranquil, the veranda was a peaceful sanctuary, far from the city's chaos and disorder. Perched upon a slope, it overlooked the lush and endless gardens that had belonged to the de Lefèvre family for hundreds of years.

Aleksender's thoughts drew ice-cold as he recalled the blood and tears of war. Shattering screams haunted the darkest caverns of his mind ... the screams of death and despair. Those cries had changed him forever. As both a person and citizen of Paris, he would never again be the same man. Out on that battlefield, and along with his father's uncalled death, he'd sacrificed a critical part of his soul. Aleksender's hands were clean, true, but his heart was longtime stained.

Then there was that dark and silent corner of his consciousness, that mysterious, faded moment during his boyhood, a moment that had altered him ever since—a moment that his mind had completely washed away.

Just what was that moment? It was always lodged inside his thoughts like a raw canker sore, irritating and inescapable, reminding him of the emptiness. And only Sofia soothed away the pain.

Aleksender was jolted from his distressed thoughts as Elise, the pretty servant girl, shyly approached him. At only fifteen years, she'd proven herself as one of the chateau's finest caretakers. Aleksender paid her a rather hefty salary—perhaps, one that was a bit too generous—well aware that she was nursing her bedridden mother during her "leisure time." As expected, golden curls were fastened in a customary bun like an old spinster might wear—yet her eyes were wide and brimming with innocence.

"Monsieur le Vicomte shall be arriving quite soon."

Successfully departing from the family nest, his little brother had purchased an estate off the outskirts of Loire Valley months before the war. Aleksender envied his freedom greatly. He was bound to Chateau de Lefèvre by his inheritance. And without the warmth of his father, the halls felt colder, vaster and infinitely more empty.

Elise set down a brunch tray that was near to overflowing. Red wine and a plethora of elegant treats were laid out beautifully, presenting a feast for a king. Aleksender glared down at the food and swallowed his gut. He had no appetite.

"Yes, Elise," he murmured, "that should do just fine."

Elise reached inside her starch white apron and withdrew several newspapers: *Le Figaro, La Gazette,* and several publications of *Le Père Duchêne* were arranged in front of Aleksender, ordered by date.

"Shall you be requiring anything else, monsieur?"

"No, no," he said, throwing a nonchalant wave in her general direction. "You are dismissed." Before departing to the side, Elise curtsied, blushed once more, and straightened out the conservative material of her uniform. For reasons she couldn't begin to comprehend, she refused to meet his gaze.

Aleksender's eyes ran across the blackened words that jumped out at him. His heartbeat quickened as he thumbed through the various newspaper headlines:

*Vive la Commune! Citizens fight for a free and social republic
Latest decree of the Commune: any and all places that favor
gambling and prostitution shall immediately be closed down and
rendered illegal*

*AFTER THE SIEGE
Reclaiming liberty beneath the Commune's red flag*

Mind spinning with the ferocity of a toy top, Aleksender flipped through the most recent edition of *Le Père Duchêne*. His fingers were numb, unusually stiff. Blood rushed into his ears as he stared down at a remarkably familiar caricature.

Parade of the pretenders was centered above a single-file line of six rather absurd looking characters. Prime Minister Thiers headed them at the front, a stupid grin plastered to an even stupider face. Comte de Chambord was squatted at the farthest end and depicted as nothing more than a ball of shriveled flesh. Then came several notable monarchists: Marquees Boury, Baron Rieu and Le Pere Bandigue. But it was the soldier standing directly before Adolphe Thiers who defined the caricature. Muscled arms were crossed over a puffed out chest, an arrogant nose pointing straight to the heavens. *And Comte de Paris?* was inscribed just below his heels.

Aleksender scraped the picture aside with a sharp intake of air. A stinging fear crept into his bones. The newsprint might as well been written in blood. And he could already feel the guillotine's crisp blade slicing through his neck. It would be the Reign of Terror all over again. He stretched against the chair with a groan and downed a generous swig of red wine.

Aleksender couldn't say how much time passed before the playful voice interrupted his concentration: "*Frère aîné!* You look positively terrible!"

"Richard."

"Monsieur le Comte," Aleksender's brother greeted with a small grin.

Richard de Lefèvre really was a spitting image of their father. The resemblance was a difficult thing for Aleksender to stomach. Much like the late comte, Richard was tall with a gentle attraction and kind eyes. A pale mustache peppered his upper lip, awarding him a distinguished and noble presence.

Aleksender came to his feet and outstretched a weathered hand.

"Really—a handshake, Alek? Such formality!" Richard reeled Aleksender into an embrace and patted his shoulder with rough affection. "I see war has stifled you." He stood away and nodded, examining Aleksender from head to toe. "Good to have you returned to us."

The two brothers claimed parallel seats. For several minutes, they engaged themselves in harmless conversation, reminiscing on memories of their father, observing each other with an unmistakable and nostalgic fondness. Elise came forth and placed a brunch tray in front of Richard, filling his glass with red wine. Then she eased back into the shadows, granting Aleksender and Richard privacy.

The tender moment passed by too soon. There was no time for sentiment. Paris had lost that luxury long ago. Richard cleared his throat and gestured to the collection of newspapers. "Conditions in Paris are unfortunate. Worse now than they've ever been."

"This commune—"

"Is expanding as we speak," Richard finished in a pained tone. "Expanding in both size and power. At present, the group is rather unorganized—spread throughout the city. But they are steadily gaining influence. I estimate a matter of weeks before they have all of Paris eating from their palms."

"And their demands?"

"Ah, mostly fancy ideas and radical reforms. The majority of these so-called Communards do seem harmless enough ... even good-natured. But you mustn't be fooled. Many are turning to violence. See, they're in the process of trying to pass a law that requires every person between nineteen and thirty-five years to join the National Guard." Richard suggestively arched a brow, signaling himself. "Present company included."

"Ridiculous."

"I shall try not to take offense to that." Between a heavy sigh and exhaled breath, Richard went on to say, "My advice? Remain on exceedingly pleasant terms with Prime Minister Thiers. The wretch has no conscience and full control of the military. He'd wipe away the Communards without second thought. A hundred or so already have been killed."

"They are really so troublesome? Troublesome enough for Thiers to risk further revolt?"

"Well," Richard began, chuckling beneath his breath, "the Commune damn well drove him from Paris."

Aleksender's mind felt ambushed. He gave a sharp nod as he struggled to absorb the startling information. "I understand the military is stationed in Versailles now."

"Indeed. They've been relocated to Chateau de Versailles." Richard pressed the glass to his lips and downed a mouthful of wine. Then he dug a hand into his pocket and withdrew a case of cigars. He absently toyed with the tortoiseshell casing as he spoke. "The Communards have already taken Baron Rieu and Marquis de Boury into custody. And just this week they threatened to kidnap the archbishop … or whomever might be of value. Poor fellow would be a 'hostage of the Parisian people.' Or so they passionately say. Look here—" Richard fetched one of the newspapers and directed Aleksender's attention to a particular passage:

The government of Versailles tramples the rights of humanity. All persons accused of complicity with the government shall be decreed accused and imprisoned. All the accused shall be hostages of the people of Paris. For every death of a prisoner of war, or a partisan of the Commune, the execution of three hostages shall follow.

Aleksender stared forward, mute and motionless. For the life of him he couldn't find his voice. Richard lit a cigar and slipped it between the seam of his lips, inhaling a long and tasty drag. He exhaled the pasty cloud of smoke and lazily crossed a leg knee-high. "After our surrender, Paris lives in a state of constant fear. Fear of poverty. Fear of the monarchy resurrecting and seizing all control. Fear of losing all liberty. Fear of another revolution ... of Prussia invading our homes and streets once more." Tense silence hung in the air. "Dark times such as these call for a certain measure of diplomacy, so to speak. You ought to make haste to Versailles. I've no doubt you would win Thiers's favor."

"Absolutely not. I've no desire to meet with him."

"Even so, at least you would be safe—"

"I've even less of a desire to run away."

"Then you are making a deadly mistake."

Aleksender scoffed in disgust and shoved a handful of fingers through his hairline. "What would you have me do? Flee to the palace like a damn mongrel, tail tucked beneath my legs? I've already surrendered once," Aleksender spat, referring to the shameful defeat in Sedan—the battle that had inevitably earned Prussia its overwhelming victory. "Mark my words. I refuse to do so again."

"Then your arrogance shall be your downfall." Richard hesitated. "Look at me, Aleksender." Unblinking and unmoving, he leaned forward and locked Aleksender's gaze. "I am asking as your brother, as someone who cares for you deeply. Whether you wish to admit it or not, you're a sure pawn for these men. You've held the title less than a month. They shall expect your protection." Richard hesitated, lowering his tone to a careful whisper. "And Father would have never denied them such a thing. You know this better than myself." Victim to an ominous undercurrent, his voice held a slight tremble. Richard's hands shook as he fisted the tablecloth between strong fingers. "Lives are being threatened. Go to Versailles." His next words were recited with the gravity of a death sentence. "If not, you could be named next."

The meaning was explicit. A fierce chill overcame Aleksender.

"I'll say nothing more on the matter." Richard heaved a long sigh and leaned back in his chair. "Stay here in Paris if you please. Lord knows—this wretched town could use some tender care. Just this afternoon I saw a child's corpse laying in the gutter, thin as bones." Aleksender said nothing, at a total loss for words. "I do hope you come to your senses. In the end, it's your choice and yours alone. I only pray you choose wisely."

"Damnable. Year of war, now this." Then, beneath a hushed breath, "This comes as no surprise."

Richard's eyes ignited. His voice contained a triumphant edge, almost infantile in its glee. "Ah, but you are no longer so inferior nor unarmed. Can't you see? You have the power to restore us. You can clean our streets, regain our people's trust. As comte—"

"And you are beginning to sound as mad and delusional as Christophe," Aleksender scoffed, waving him off. Richard's sudden rush of excitement did nothing for his amusement. Even so—according to this Commune, his "loyal people" desired his head on a pike. Certainly not his guidance or interference.

"Well, I must thank you, then. I've always fancied Monsieur Cleef. A fine gentleman and soldier, if I may say so."

"Well. I advise that you not get too attached," Aleksender dryly said. He leaned back in the chair, stretching his strong limbs with a feline's grace. "Between his outrageous schemes and wagging tongue, the fool is bound to get himself killed. Perhaps worse."

"Yes. Though, his intentions are as honest as they come." Aleksender gave a look. Richard shrugged, defeated. "I suppose his methods are a bit ... err, unorthodox."

"To put it mildly."

"Good to see you haven't abandoned that terrible sense of humor of yours. Paris would have been quite lost without it."

Aleksender betrayed himself and surrendered to a small chuckle.

A considerable silence pressed between the two of them.

"How is Elizabeth faring?"

"Cannot say. Like anything else, I suppose time shall tell."

Richard nodded, cleared his throat, and glanced down. "A lovely creature."

Aleksender paused for a moment, absorbing any possible sentiment of Richard's words.

A breeze stirred, catching the de Lefèvre brothers by surprise. Aleksender watched as the trees swayed back and forth, manipulated by nature's gentler element.

"I should have been at his deathbed." Aleksender's voice was detached and heavy with emotion.

"Father never questioned your love." Richard shook his head and sighed whole-heartedly. "You are an honorable man."

"On and off the front lines, I'm quite finished being noble. Or honorable."

"Ah, come, come—"

"I am done. Finished. *Finis.*"

"Oh, are you now?" Richard shifted his body weight to one side and studied Aleksender with an unwavering stare. "And what, pray, do you plan to make of yourself? Please—humor me."

"Sail away, I suppose," Aleksender said with a small and rather harmless shrug. "I understand America is quite pleasant this time of year."

Richard remained quiet.

"The title is yours, Richard. I am through."

The world stood still. Richard's eyes darkened as he met Aleksender's unblinking stare. Aleksender didn't recognize his brother's voice when he spoke. The tone was deadly and ominous, its timbre equipped with a venomous edge.

"Not another word of that. You hear?"

Aleksender looked away—a harmless gesture that only seemed to infuriate his brother further. "Come now, Richard. It is not so uncommon … a younger heir claiming the family name. And besides—nobility is dead. The title is an item of vanity. Nothing else."

"Need I remind you—our situation is far from common."

"What of our situation? No one needs to know anything. Let it be put to rest with Father."

Tension filled the air in the following silence.

Aleksender could see it. Richard was on the verge of losing himself. Even worse, he was on the verge of losing his pride. And, if nothing else, Richard de Lefèvre was a man of dignified pride and nobility.

"You are a fool. A damn fool to even think I'd put the sanctity of our name at risk—and for your self-righteousness, nonetheless! A fool to think I would risk so much at a time like this! In Father's name, I shall not spit on France's dignity!"

In an even and sinfully smooth tone, Aleksender retorted, "I assure you, her dignity is in far greater peril with me as comte."

"Can you truly think of no one but yourself? Father would turn in his very grave."

"I daresay he is turning as we speak," Aleksender snapped in quick reply, "and, need I remind you, he is your father as much as my own."

"Not a day passes by that I don't wish that were true." Richard massaged his forehead, nursing a migraine. A pang of guilt swelled Aleksender as he witnessed his brother's personal demons materialize.

"Why the need to condemn me to your misery?" Richard's fingertips joined together in the form of a steeple. Shudders raking low in his chest, he convulsed, skittering on the edge of something terrible. "Up for opening all wounds, eh?"

"Richard, I never—"

And then for the first time in over twenty-six years, Paris's Vicomte abandoned his composure.

Richard balled his hands into fists and punched the charming breakfast table with a violent degree of energy. The luxurious tray of food flew to the ground and spilled in a royal mess. Unmovable as stone, Aleksender neither blinked nor stirred a limb.

"Insolent, selfish fool! You are a damn fool—a damn fool and nothing more!"

Cued by the grand crash, Elise rushed over and bent at Richard's heels. She dabbed at the red wine, which looked remarkably like blood, and proceeded to collect the shattered stemware.

"Fool! A year of war does not save Father any more than it makes me a legitimate heir." Richard looked down and took notice of Elise's presence. Not the least bit pleased, he jumped to his feet and towered over the poor child. "Stupid chit. How dare you eavesdrop? You ought to be thrashed from the inside out!"

Elise should have stumbled to her feet with a darling curtsy and attempted to win Vicomte de Lefèvre over with pretty excuses— but she simply could not bring herself to move. She stared up in horrified silence, her tiny form cast beneath the eclipse of Richard's shadow.

Not sparing an inch, he planted a hand on either side of his hip, his strong back straight as an arrow. "I suppose you are a deaf, dumb mute?"

Elise jerked at his vicious tone. She stifled a cry as a monstrous glass shard sliced her palm. A stream of blood ran down her arm and mingled with the red wine.

"Just leave it!" he scoffed. "Leave it and be gone, you daft girl!"

"My a-a-pologies, Monsieur le Vicomte—"

"And you best keep silent! If one word escapes—should you utter so much as a single word—on my father's grave, I swear you shall pay in blood!"

"I-I-I heard nothing! I swear it, Monsieur le V-Vicomte!"

"Idle threats are not becoming of you." Aleksender threw Elise a gentle, almost comforting glance. Still seated and staring into her glazed eyes, he murmured, "Save your breath, child." Twisting back to Richard, "My brother forgets himself."

"Yes, monsieur."

"Come over to me."

Elise obeyed, shuffling forward with baby steps.

"Your hand—let me see the damage you've managed to inflict on yourself." Elise outstretched her trembling palm. It shook midair as Aleksender observed, studying the laceration with an acquired medical eye.

He squinted as a fingertip danced across the surface of her pale flesh. Elise immediately coiled her hand into a little ball. Aleksender straightened out her fingers in a deft touch, lifting her palm to the level of his eyes. "Fairly deep. Quite prone to infection. Go to the kitchens. One of the other servants will surely assist you."

Elise gave a bumbling curtsy and smoothed down her apron before making leave.

Richard sighed and brushed out his double-breasted morning coat. He shook his downcast face, propping both hands on back of his chair. He stared straight into the jaded depths of Aleksender's eyes and spoke to his brother's soul. "You listen to me and listen well. It is a dangerous game you dare play. Though, I do suppose it is easy enough for you, basking beneath your false solace. But you tread dangerous waters, Monsieur le Comte."

Richard spat the formal name with a faint shred of mockery. But his eyes were only sincere; they begged for Aleksender's understanding with desperation and awakened sadness.

"The anniversary of Father's death falls within next month. A memorial has been arranged at Père Lachaise. An informal affair. I knew you would have appreciated a proper goodbye."

Richard fetched the newspapers from the table and fanned through the morbid collection of articles. The fate of Paris passed by in a black and white blur.

"Alek, my dear brother, you disappoint me. One day, I fear your apathy will catch up to you. And, on that day, you shall feel the burn of true loss. The fate of Paris lies at your feet. Have faith in your home, if not yourself ..."

The newspapers fluttered to the ground as Richard freed them from his clutch. They settled around Aleksender's heels, recklessly strewn about, lying in a state of pure disorder.

CHAPTER FIVE

A forest of ancient oaks, locusts and redwoods spread farther than the eye could see. Maneuvering in a graceful dance, two lakes wove in and out of the towering trees and merged together through the waterfall that lay beyond the horizon.

Aleksender wandered Bois de Boulogne's impressive length, hands snugly tucked inside his coat pockets. Located in the sixteenth arrondissement, the park's endless amusements and picturesque setting were adored by everyone. The last streaks of daylight twinkled across the dirt pathways and tugged at Aleksender's imagination.

During his adolescence, wasting away the hours at Bois de Boulogne had quickly become one of his and Comte Philippe de Lefèvre's favorite pastimes. Indeed—fishing, bird-watching, ogling the menagerie's exotic creatures, and wagering on horses were some of his most prized memories.

Home life had been a far cry from flawless. During those rockier days and nights, Bois de Boulogne had transformed into a secretive land—a private sanctuary shared by father and son—a safe and silent corner of the world reserved solely for the two of them. And for Aleksender, Bois de Boulogne would forever remain a place of rest and tranquility.

He absently scaled the surrounding beauty and sought escape. A father and son stood along a glittering water-bank, fishing poles close in hand, sharing stories and laugher. Aleksender pressed his back against a large oak tree. An overwhelming pang of nostalgia bloomed within his chest as he watched the father and son's tender interaction. The mirage of memories took hold without warning—

Learning how to fish for the first time. Father showing him how to balance the pole just right. Father threading the hook as Mother often threaded a bobbin. Father's smile as the line twitched about, moving this way and that, gliding below the lake's glassy surface. Watching Bois de Boulogne's renowned horse races. Asking Father if he might wager on Champion—a rather sorry-looking gelding without so much as a ribbon to his name. Father's smile and gentle laugh, followed by, "A worthy choice, my son! Hopefully he shall live up to his name. You there—twenty francs on ol' Champion, monsieur!"

Aleksender shook away the ghosts of his past and returned to the present. As if on cue, the boy's fishing line began to erratically whiz about. It sliced through the water like some crazed serpent and glided three feet in every direction. Both father and son cried out in triumph and reeled in their catch—an embarrassingly small salmon. And for all the pride on the man's face, the thing might have been a prizewinning marlin. The father rewarded his boy with words of praise and a sturdy slap to the shoulder.

Aleksender turned away. He couldn't bring himself to stomach the sight. And the rest of the world offered only mockery and no comfort. Off in the distance, a couple embraced beneath the bough of an old elm. The gnarled trunk hovered above them, its twisted mass grotesquely deformed and wrought with age. The thing reminded Aleksender of a wounded soldier who'd been blown halfway to hell and was in urgent need of an amputation.

In contrast, the young man was dashing and clearly in the prime of his life. Leaning in close, he clung to his darling's waist, never intending to let go. Beneath a reverent sigh, he whispered sweet nothings and pressed tender kisses upon her brow. A chain of heartfelt laughter was carried by the wind as she reciprocated the affection tenfold. Ever so gently, he cupped her cheeks and lured her into a timeless kiss. It was a kiss she'd remember for years to come—one that whispered a thousand unspoken secrets. In the midst of such dark times, the two adolescents perceived only beauty. Standing below that monstrous elm, they were positively shameless—shamelessly head over heels in love.

Aleksender's lashes fluttered shut as he imagined his mother and father in place of the young couple.

The need for companionship, the sincere warmth of another, violently took hold of him. And remarkably, when he glanced upon the lovers once more, it was not his parents he envisioned.

It was him and his little Sofia.

•

The evening's ballet had concluded thirty minutes earlier. With keen interest, Aleksender had observed as the various performers, stagehands and managers claimed carriages for the night. Each time the ancient door swung open, the expanse of black had been stabbed by a shaft of light. Each time an absurd blend of emotions had welled inside his gut.

And each time Aleksender had been left feeling emptier and more alone than ever before.

Where was she? Where was his Sofia?

Needing some form of distraction, Aleksender paced the length of the alleyway and studied his barren surroundings. Almost all the street lanterns had prematurely burned out, and those that remained shed dismal amounts of light. A deep and not altogether cynical sigh swelled his lungs.

Gas, along with everything else, had become a rare luxury since the siege. "Many weeks were spent in pure darkness," Elizabeth had told him with a shudder. And although the streets shined once more, it was a mere flicker compared to the brilliant lighting of Paris as it used to be.

Indeed. The City of Lights had never been darker.

Aleksender's pensive thoughts were cropped short as the door moaned open. He held his breath in suspenseful anticipation. Two of Salle Le Peletier's corps de ballet dancers appeared—one of whom he immediately recognized as Sofia.

She'd always held a strange calming effect over him. It was a phenomenon that he'd never been able to put into words. Something which betrayed logic. Something he couldn't fully understand nor intended to. In the midst of his personal agony, the mere sight of his ward was balm upon his soul. Dark feelings and even darker thoughts were replaced by a faint ray of hope. And the bitterness that had grown to be an integral part of himself miraculously faded away.

Standing at the stairwell's landing, Aleksender propped a hand on either side of the rail, cocked his head, and intently observed his ward. Sofia's girlfriend tugged at her cloak and whispered some nonsense into her ear. Blue eyes pierced the black as melodious laughter flooded the alleyway.

Aleksender exhaled, releasing a breath he hadn't known he was holding. His heart raced at breakneck speed. His palms grew clammy, weighed down with buckets of sweat. Perspiration formed along the lining of his gloves, plastering silk to flesh. And the metal railing was unbearably cool ... a startling contrast to the current state of certain nether regions. Disgusted with himself, Aleksender groaned and adjusted his posture.

Dieu—what was happening to him?

•

Sofia fell into silence as she gazed at Aleksender's dark form beneath the rim of her hood.

Butterflies fluttered inside her tummy and tickled her with their silky wings. He was a vision to be reckoned with and handsomer than sin. A double-breasted coat wrapped his impressive body like a glove, the top hat camouflaging with a multitude of thick waves to perfection.

And he was her Alek. Her dark knight and eternal protector.

Sofia's eyes came to life as a smile stretched her lips from ear to ear. Grasping the elegant folds of her cloak, she rushed down the five cobblestone steps and threw herself into Aleksender's arms. He weakly returned her embrace. Every inch of his body was coarser than stone. She felt his chest tighten as he glanced down at their joined bodies. Long, inky lashes shadowed his cheekbones with delicate crescent moons. They were a sensual contrast to the golden hue of his skin.

"You're here." Sofia sighed and nuzzled against his cravat, increasing the pressure of her hold. She swung both arms around his neck, perched onto her ballerina tiptoes, and pressed a kiss just below the arch of his chin. Day-old stubble pierced her lips at the contact.

A deep sigh resonated within Aleksender's chest.

"Say, why the big reunion?" Aleksender muttered beneath an airy chuckle. His hands were painfully gentle as he grazed the material of her cloak.

Coming to his senses, he outstretched both limbs and held Sofia at a proper arm's length. An oversized hand crashed down on either side of her shoulders, firmly rooting her in place. She giggled and swayed, struggling against the iron clasp.

"Oh, just couldn't contain myself, I suppose." Sofia closed the space between them and took Aleksender within her clutches once more. "I've just never felt anything more wonderful than having you back in my arms." Delicate fingertips grazed his cloak in a tentative and experimental touch. She sighed and laid her cheek across his chest, inhaling the exotic blend of Persian spices that was uniquely Aleksender. "I've missed you more than I can say." Sofia's head teeter-tottered as his body rose and sank with deep, soulful breaths.

"Alek?" Her voice was swallowed up by the material of his coat and barely coherent.

"Hmm?"

"Your heart is beating so fast."

Those words sobered Aleksender.

He inhaled a shaky breath and took several generous steps backward. The softness of Sofia's body slipped away and made the streets of Paris feel remarkably colder.

He pried the top hat from his hair and passed a hand over the glossy strands. They were heavy with perspiration, soaked through and through. His fingertips skirted across the top hat's velvet rim as he replaced it.

The girl cleared her throat, sufficiently yanking Aleksender from his haze.

"Oh! Heather! Forgive me. This … this is le Comte de Lefèvre."

Heather looked Aleksender up and down, folding both arms across her breasts. A sly and almost knowing smile tugged at her lips. She eased forward, the flaming mass of red curls rivaling her attitude. "So, you are Sofia's Alek?"

Aleksender angled his chin and glanced at Sofia who was singed by Heather's words, her cheeks flushed a severe red. She groped at her skirts without conscious effort and twisted the material between two slender fingertips. "Yes. This is him. This is my Alek. He is my guardian."

Something in her voice made Aleksender's heart skip a beat. Then she stared into his eyes and it skipped several more.

"You have a carriage?" Aleksender asked Heather.

After a speculative glance, the girl nodded, lifted her hood, and vanished into the shadows.

A heavy silence descended.

Sofia eyed Aleksender's elegant dress from head to toe, a subtle grin plastered to her lips. She tugged at the folded cravat with a playful smile, blue eyes shining like beacons. "Look at you, monsieur, so very formal. Off to the races, I suppose?"

Aleksender slipped the cravat from her fingertips. Smoothing the material into place, he sprawled a hand across the small of Sofia's back.

"I've a coach waiting."

Sofia grinned. "Oh, I see. Goin' to wine and dine me in Paris's finest, are you?" she teased, arms propped onto either side of her hips. Then her form shook with happy and heartfelt laughter. She laughed for no apparent reason. She laughed just for the sake of laughing.

The sound was beautiful and brimming with life. The bleak alleyway seemed to lighten the slightest bit.

A wink was Aleksender's sole response as he further expanded the mystery at hand. Together, they wandered down the slim alleyway in silence until reaching Salle Le Peletier's carriage house.

De Lefèvre and a coat of arms were printed across the vehicle's black lacquered door. Aleksender tentatively outstretched his hand and helped Sofia into the coach. A magnetic spark flared between Aleksender and Sofia's fingers, sending currents of awareness shooting through their bodies. Blushing deeply, Sofia cleared her throat and lifted her skirts. Heart beating like a bunny rabbit's, she settled against the fine upholstery and awaited her dashing escort. He propped a hand on the archway and studied her with an intense, unwavering gaze. She felt his eyes bear deeply into her own, drinking her in.

"So wherever are you taking me? I must say—the suspense is nearly too great."

Aleksender shot her a crooked grin. He turned away, directing his response at the driver who was perched in the box seat. As usual, the portly gentleman wore a powdered wig, elaborate garb, and a pensive scowl. "Voisin of Rue Saint-Honoré."

The driver dipped his head in understanding. The walls seemed to shrink as Aleksender tugged the door shut and claimed a seat beside Sofia. After a moment, he pounded the rooftop with his fist and sent the coach rolling into motion.

Scone lanterns flashed across the scarlet walls, bathing the lush interior with gentle glows. The wide expanse of Aleksender's shoulders filled the space with ease. Each bump in the road connected their bodies together—and each collision made Aleksender's cheeks a flaming red. He adjusted his posture, attempting to erect a barrier between him and Sofia without luck.

Dark curls tumbled down and over her shoulders as she pulled back her hood. Aleksender studied her beautiful profile, allowing a comfortable silence to fill the coach.

Sofia swept the curtain aside and glanced into the empty and dimly lit streets. Beyond the coach's scarlet curtains, a father and son waded through the darkness in a protective huddle. Mindful of their seedy surroundings, the man shielded his boy with a watchful eye and sturdy hand to the shoulder. Sofia eased against the upholstery. A cloud formed within the pit of her chest and shadowed her heart. She bowed her head, aching with multitudes of pain. Unbeknown to her, the subtle motion sent a tear rolling down the slope of her cheek.

"Sofia?"

"Yes?"

Aleksender closed the space between them without a moment's hesitation. He lightly touched her chin and rotated her face toward his own. Worry creased his brow as his eyes deepened in concern. His thumb pad massaged the arch of her chin in slow, tentative circles. "What is it, ma petit? You know it pains me to see you cry."

She smiled at Aleksender's words and took his hands in a solid grasp. She stared down at their united grip, thumbs drawing invisible circles along the cool silk of his glove.

"My Alek, I … I'm so sorry." She smiled though her tears and continued to caress his hand. A whirlwind of curls slid down her shoulders, framing her body with the elegance of a gossamer shawl. "You know that I loved your father dearly. And you meant the world to him."

Aleksender wrapped an arm around her slender shoulders and tugged Sofia firmly against his body. "You truly are an angel."

She peered up at him. Their faces were intimately close—mere inches away—mouths sharing the same intakes of air. "All those months I thought I'd lost you." Sofia gazed into her lap as her complexion turned a ghostly white. "Our parting was nearly my death," she confided through an unsteady whisper.

Aleksender swallowed and shook his face. "You could never lose me. Never."

Sofia tightened her grasp on Aleksender's hand. "Sometimes I fear I shall wake up and you'll still be gone." Freeing him, she turned away and stared into the black of night. "And when I imagine what you went through, the things you must have seen ..."

Aleksender settled against the backing with a low groan. He removed his top hat and laid it in the cradle of his lap. Meddling absently with the stiff velvet, he said, "I had lay awake many of those nights, thinking of you. What you were doing. Whether you were safe. Being so far away—knowing that Paris was under siege, that I had no way to protect you—it was easily the worst part."

Sofia smiled at his words and fiercely swiped at her tear-stained cheeks. "Well. I daresay Sacred Heart was one of the safest places in all of France."

Aleksender nodded and exhaled a sigh of relief. "That's what I'd depended on."

"So in a way, even though you weren't here, you still had protected me."

Sofia's palm slid across the upholstery. Her pulse leapt to life as she threaded their fingers together. Beyond the window, the world crept by in a steady blur. And, for the two of them, the light of Paris appeared brighter than ever before.

CHAPTER SIX

Although Rue Saint-Honoré lay on the outskirts of the city, it seemed to be a whole other world away. Gas lamps flickered, their lights strong and sure, bathing the cobblestones with collective glows. More ladies and gentlemen were stationed outside of Voisin's doors than throughout the whole of Paris put together. Within this corner of society, the starving children, grief-struck insurgents, and shady rat sellers were nonexistent ... nothing more than a distant nightmare.

The coach rolled to a jarring halt. All at once, a hush descended as the ladies and gentlemen turned their attention to the rich vehicle. Unused to such excitement and crowds, the horses whinnied unhappily and pawed at the cobblestones.

"Ah, here we are. Monsieur, mademoiselle," the driver announced. "Voisin of Rue Saint-Honoré."

Wary of his sweeping six-foot-two frame, Aleksender inclined his head as he stepped from the coach. He fished a hand inside his coat and deposited a healthy amount of francs into the driver's palm. "I suspect we shall be an hour. Two at the most."

An indulgent grin formed on the man's chaffed lips. He nodded and pocketed the coins. "Yes. Of course, monsieur. Take all the time you require."

Aleksender returned to the coach's door, straightened the askew rim of his top hat, then reached through the portal. Delicate fingertips wound about his hand as he guided Sofia into the street.

"Oh! I remember this place!"

Aleksender chuckled, charmed by her enthusiasm. "Yes. I imagined that you might. Come."

Together, they crossed the threshold and entered one of Paris's finest eateries. The lush surroundings were intoxicating. An exotic blend of rich scents mingled in the air. Twin chandeliers glittered on either side of the restaurant, romanticizing everything beneath the illuminations. From a far corner, the faint hum of music swelled Voisin's walls and breathed life into the establishment. A moderately sized dance floor occupied the middle of the room. Reflecting a swirl of colors, its floorboards were brilliantly polished and alive with countless embracing couples.

Bending into a slight bow, the meticulously attired maitre d' stepped forward to peel away Sofia and Aleksender's garments. The man's wig was powdered a pristine white and slickly combed back without a strand out of place. With a muttered pardon, he handed Aleksender's hat and coat to the nearby footman. Then gloved fingertips stripped away the material of Sofia's cloak, exposing two smooth slates of porcelain flesh—one and then the other.

Aleksender instantly hardened at the vision.

"Monsieur le Comte, Mademoiselle Rose," the maitre d' said through a genuine smile, "how wonderful it is to see you again. Would you prefer a seat by the window?"

Aleksender cleared his throat, wrenching his eyes from Sofia's bared flesh. "That shall do just fine."

Sofia tensed as Aleksender rested a hand across her lower back. His fingers spanned the entire length with ease. Aleksender increased the pressure of his touch and guided her in his footsteps. Her entire body broke out into goose flesh … every last hair stood attentively erect. His hands were large and strong, roughened from his labor out-of-doors. She could feel the warmth of his skin through the thin barrier of silks that separated them. Thumb and forefinger curled against the small of her back and sent chains of awareness surging through her veins. There was nothing inherently intimate about the gesture. And Aleksender had certainly touched her in this way half a million times, and yet something was different.

Undeniably and frightfully different.

"If you two would care to follow me."

Sofia was jolted back into the moment as Aleksender gently urged her forward. They shadowed the footsteps of the maitre d', bodies connected in a transient, barely-there touch. Sofia's heart fluttered as she basked in the pleasure of his nearness. She felt remarkably safe, secure and complete.

A wave of silence crashed down as they wandered past the endless rows of patrons. Her flesh tightened at the burn of over three dozen scrutinizing eyes. And, for a horrifying instance, she swore all of Voisin could read her thoughts.

She and Aleksender settled into parallel seats and exchanged the briefest of glances. The maitre d' unfolded a napkin with a suave flick of his wrist and laid it across Sofia's lap. *Voisin* and flowered swags were embroidered in the damask, awarding the linen with a hint of elegance.

Sofia played with the fringe, unsure of how to act around Aleksender, unsure of exactly what to say. She ached to ease his pain, but was clueless how to do so. The situation was delicate and demanded a gentle approach. Indeed, it required wisdom well beyond her nineteen years. Would he favor a distraction? She cautiously wondered. Or, perhaps, he'd prefer meaningful conversation—the opportunity to express his sorrow and voice his burdens?

"Your server shall be with you in but a moment," the maitre d' announced, interrupting her thoughts. "In the meantime, allow me to fetch drinks? A finely aged wine, perhaps?"

Aleksender nodded. With a last smile, the maitre d' drooped into a bow and departed from sight. A pregnant silence filled the air. Only the cheerful rhythm of clinking silverware alleviated the quiet.

Then light chatter and the melodic drumming of hooves wafted from the window, each sound carried by a mild spring breeze. Tickled by the wind, an abundance of lacy curtains twitched against the wooden pane. Enticed by the sensuous sounds, Sofia gazed outside and into the star-filled sky. Beyond Voisin's walls, the night was an oily black and entirely moonless.

"You are so beautiful." Aleksender's words were sultry and soft—little more than a whisper. For an instant, Sofia wondered if she'd imagined them. Her eyes snapped from the window and settled upon his strained features. A distinct, pained passion embedded his gaze.

No, his expression quickly confirmed—she hadn't imagined those words.

Silence swelled between them like a palpable force.

"Th-thank you," Sofia awkwardly stuttered.

Aleksender offered no response. The corner of his lip merely quirked into a subtle and almost shy smile.

"Mademoiselle, monsieur ..." The maitre d' shuffled forward and interrupted the moment. A slender bottle of wine was cradled in his hands and held at a slant, allowing light from the chandelier's crystals to illuminate the scripted label. "*Cidre de Normandie.* Compliments of the house." He poured a serving for Aleksender and Sofia, filling the hollow glasses with waterfalls of chilled wine.

Then he withdrew a pair of menus from his apron and arranged them atop the embroidered cloth. "Enjoy your supper. Au revoir." With a quick nod, the maitre d' departed from the table and continued on his way.

Sofia's stomach growled as she eyed the delectable columns of entrees. Aleksender cocked his brow, which caused her blush to significantly deepen. "We're not a moment too soon, I see. Err, I hear."

Sofia gasped and leaned forward. Eyes beaming, she drew back her arm and swatted Aleksender with the menu. He laughed at her teasing and dodged the assault by sheer inches. The robust sound filled the room to its rafters and warmed Sofia's insides. Seduced by the playful banter, several patrons exchanged murmurs and glanced over their shoulders.

More laughter bubbled inside Sofia as a fond memory came to mind. Shoulders rolling in a fit of giggles, she pressed a palm to her lips to better stifle the sound.

Aleksender studied her with keen interest, his own smile quickly forming. Such laughter was contagious—and he was far from immune to his ward's charms.

"What, pray tell, is so amusing?"

"Oh, I was just thinking. When I was a girl—remember what I'd do to your poor dinner guests?"

Aleksender stretched against his chair with a small chuckle. He cradled the wine glass and gently swirled it, stirring the liquid to life. "Mmhm. How could I forget? You, chérie, were always right on cue. Alas, as soon as Grace would begin—"

"I'd slip beneath the table—"

"—and fasten the guest's shoelaces together. Each and every time," Aleksender finished with a sly wink, tipping the wine glass against his lips.

Sofia felt her cheeks warm as she eyed the sculpted skin of his mouth. It was lush and full with the slightest hint of a smile. A few beads of wine clung tantalizingly to the flesh. "I suppose I deserved a proper flogging," she admitted, the flush rapidly spreading down her neck. "But you'd never hear of such a thing—even when Elizabeth insisted otherwise. Why is that?"

Aleksender lifted his shoulders with a dry shrug. He worried his bottom lip between his teeth, sucking away the rivulets of wine. "You were happy. Not to mention adorable. And besides, such antics never harmed anyone."

Sofia shrank against her chair with a guilty smile. "Expect for that one time."

"Ah, yes, that one time. Those damnable knaves wouldn't step foot in the de Lefèvre chateau ever again."

Sofia sipped at her wine. She hid a growing smile behind the stemware. "Well, how was I supposed to know the knot would be impossible to unfasten, and that they really couldn't stand each other's company? Goodness. How could a husband and wife loathe each other with so much gusto? Why, I thought binding them together would force them to kiss and make up!"

Aleksender chuckled and folded both arms over his chest. "Innocent little thing, you were. You assumed every match was made purely from love."

"Well, it served the old toad right, anyhow. He just wanted to scurry on back to his mistress." Sofia smiled once more, her delicate shoulders rolling with giggles. "Your father got quite a kick out of it. More than once he caught me red-handed, you know. Oh, I was quite afraid of what he might do, but he simply lifted the tablecloth and winked at me. He winked, all while his snobby guests were ready to blow their tops. Can you believe it?"

Sadness and pleasure crossed Aleksender's features by turns. Then his lips lifted into that rare, crooked grin. It was a grin that warmed Sofia's insides—a grin she had come to love nine years before. "Indeed, I can," he whispered. "Sounds like him."

"He was an exceptional man. And I see him in you. I always have."

Aleksender swallowed as something remarkable stirred within his chest.

Sofia absently gazed forward, a nostalgic smile curving her lips.

When she spoke, her voice quavered with emotion and fond memories. "But what I'll always remember most is the stars."

"The stars?" Aleksender echoed, transfixed.

"When I'd wake up from a nightmare, you'd point out the constellations and tell me each of their stories," she whispered, locking his eyes. "You showed me peace, showed me that beauty could be found within darkness. You, Alek, gave me reason to be happy."

"I wouldn't have had it any other way." Lightening his tone, he cleared his throat and poured himself another helping of wine. "And I hope that hasn't changed. You're still happy? Still at peace?"

Sofia nodded, though her eyes subtly flickered in disagreement.

"And you? Are you happy?" The simple question rendered him speechless.

"I have my moments."

"Such as now? Such as this moment?"

He responded with a sharp nod. Then he cleared his throat once more and nudged the menu aside. "So. Tell me. How is Salle Le Peletier? I take it things have been faring well?"

"Yes—" She briefly hesitated. "For the most part things have been quite well. In fact, I made prima ballerina just last season," Sofia said as she took a delicate sip of wine.

"And you deserve nothing less." Aleksender's crooked grin transformed into a true smile. Romanticized by the surrounding candlelight, the gesture reeked of sensuality. "In all these years, you've never ceased to amaze me." Aleksender raised his glass in a silent toast. Sofia followed suit and clapped their stemware together. A sweet chime rang out as the glasses shared a kiss.

Sofia's cheeks heated, blushing a shade of red that rivaled the table's vase of roses. Then she glanced into her lap and neurotically toyed with the napkin.

"Sofia? What is it, ma chérie?"

She sighed and shook her downcast face. "Oh, it's nothing worth speaking of. Really." She fetched the menu and buried her face behind it. "Mmm … roasted lamb? How wonderful that sounds right about now!" she mindlessly babbled, nose crinkling in time with her words. "You know, last Christmas, during the seige, they served animals from Bois de Boulogne's menagerie. Poor things. Can you imagine it?"

Aleksender chuckled low and hooked two fingers around the

menu's border, yanking the makeshift shield from her grasp.

"You know you can tell me anything," he said. She smiled and gave a hesitant look. "So? What's on your mind, ma petit?"

"Sometimes ... sometimes it feels as though I'm trapped between two worlds." Aleksender nodded as she spoke, understanding deepening his eyes. "At Sacred Heart, I'm one person, and at Salle Le Peletier I'm someone else entirely. It's a strange thing. The future is so obscure."

Indeed, after Sofia had been rid of her mother's abuse, Aleksender had sheltered her from society's cruelty and malice. He'd spent a small fortune building Sacred Heart, one of Paris's most prestigious convent homes. Sofia—alongside dozens of other young girls, many of whom had been orphans—were raised within those conservative walls. Such a thing had proved to be both a blessing and a curse. Aleksender had yearned to gift wrap the world and all of its possibilities for her taking. He'd kept her safe within Sacred Heart's walls, brought the prospect of God into her life, and cleared her way to stardom.

Unfortunately, within the Paris Opera, the road to success is often paved with ridicule and disdain. Prostitution and the performing arts were considered to be close equals. If not for Aleksender's loyal patronage and social standing, Sofia would have never been fit to set foot in a place such as Sacred Heart.

"Be true to yourself," he whispered, settling against the seat. "That's the best any of us can do."

Lost in thought, Sofia shook her head and breathed the words without taking notice. "But only with you do I ever feel most like myself."

The waiter came forth at that precise moment, which proved to be a small mercy for the both of them. His face was long, lean and severe. Sofia was overcome with the temptation to make him laugh. "Bonsoir. Are the two of you ready to order? Or would you care for a few more moments?"

"No. No—we are quite ready," Aleksender replied.

"Wonderful. For you, mademoiselle?"

Aleksender and Sofia ordered their dinners: two servings of tossed greens, plum pudding and roasted lamb. Afterward, the waiter departed from the table, leaving them alone once more. Sofia demurely lifted her glass in a toast. Aleksender followed suit as the grin returned to his lips.

"To many more moments such as these," she declared with passion, tapping their glasses together.

"Many more moments."

All at once, a lively melody swelled the bistro. Hand in hand, couples ventured to the dance floor by the dozens, sending a colorful swirl of skirts whirling across the room. Sofia's eyes brightened in anticipation. Setting down her stemware, she rose to her feet and held out a hand for Aleksender's taking.

He cocked a stubborn eyebrow and crossed both arms across his chest. "You're sorely mistaken, ma chérie. In no way shall I be dancing tonight."

"Oh, come now, you stubborn mule of a man. It would do you some good." Sofia gave his shoulder a firm yank. "Please?" Relentless, he stayed rooted in his spot. "Oh, fine then. You'll know where to find me." Sofia gave a small sigh of defeat and spun on her heels, making way to the dance floor. She stood off on the sidelines and watched the happy couples with a faint smile.

After a few moments, a handsome young man approached Sofia and offered his forearm. Smiling wide, he arched into a chivalrous bow. "Would you care to dance, mademoiselle?"

"Why, yes. I would adore it!" And without another word, she was swept into the gentleman's arms and across the brandished floorboards.

•

Aleksender sulked from his spot in the corner. That boy—that foppish peacock strutting as a man, his mind amended—was holding Sofia far too intimately. And she appeared to be enjoying herself far too much. The two of them waltzed this way and that, laughter beaming from their eyes, dancing like a pair of bunny rabbits during breeding season.

Boasting locks of gold and elaborate garb, the boy resembled a cross between Prince Charming and a cherub figurine. Something that felt remarkably like jealousy blackened Aleksender's insides. He latched onto the neck of his stemware, erupting with the need to destroy something.

Instead, he bellowed a low grunt, downed a mouthful of wine with mutinous fervor, then chased the burn with two more helpings. Aleksender shoved the forelock from his eyes as he surveyed the display with an unsettling intensity. A curtain of chocolate tresses fanned in the air as Sofia was tossed into a spin.

Much to Aleksender's horror and disdain, their bodies re-aligned once more and shuffled together. Enraptured by Salle Le Peletier's prima ballerina, many of the patrons paused their dinning to watch the apparent show. Damn it to hell. Aleksender had been afraid to accept Sofia's dance proposal. He'd been afraid to get too close to her.

But this was exceedingly worse.

The young man slid a palm down Sofia's back in restless pursuit ... stopping a few meager inches from the curve of her bottom. Aleksender bit back an obscenity and scrubbed a hand over his face. The suitor dared to tug Sofia closer. If that wasn't quite enough, he swiped a swarm of curls from her neck, bent forward, and whispered against the rim of her ear ...

Aleksender could only guess what those words had been.

Enough. As if charging straight onto the battlefield, he leapt to his feet and crossed the room with determined steps.

"Pardon me," Aleksender muttered as he cut in, his form towering above the two of them with ease. "I think I'll take it from here." None too happy, the young man stepped aside with a chivalrous bow and vanished into the crowd.

Sofia's face broke into a triumphant grin. "Why, whatever happened to me being sorely mistaken? I thought in no way shall you be dancing—"

Her words dissolved into silence as Aleksender reined her into his arms.

◆

Despite being a seasoned dancer, Sofia felt very clumsy and unsure of herself. She stumbled over Aleksender's feet as he whisked her to one side—then stumbled again when he swung her body full circle.

"You are dancing like a circus monkey," he muttered against her neck. Her pulse jumped to life at the words. Coming from Aleksender's lips, they sounded like an endearment rather than insult. His deep baritone stoked her imagination, igniting a fire deep within her soul.

She chided him with a playful slap to the shoulder. Feigning injury, he released one of her hands and groped the material of his dress shirt. "The pain. The agony!"

"Oh, come now!"

Aleksender's broad chest vibrated with mirth. He tugged Sofia back into his embrace and held her jarringly close. Chills swept through every inch of her body. Thick cords of muscle flexed and tightened beneath Sofia's touch. One of his brows curved into an arch that begged to be challenged.

Sofia tapped her bottom lip in contemplation. "Perhaps, it's you and not me."

"Hmm? What's that?"

"Who's at fault for this dreadful dancing."

"Ah, I see. Is that so?"

"Precisely. You're not at all an agreeable partner."

He perked a brow in amusement. "So ... I'm the monkey?"

Sofia splayed a palm across Aleksender's chest and threw her head back, body rolling with laughter. "No, not the monkey," she corrected, simultaneously catching her breath. "The circus monkey."

Intoxicated by the surrounding euphoria, Aleksender and Sofia lost themselves within the crowd and laughter.

Aleksender wrapped Sofia in one of his arms and swept her across the polished floorboards, fighting at every step to keep up with the waltz's dizzying pace. His hands were firm and strong against her back, sending a chain of shivers down to Sofia's tiptoes and then up again. An abundance of curls nearly brushed the ground as he lowered her into a deep curve.

Everything fell away. A rare sliver of happiness flooded her entire being. In the same breath, the music slowed like a dying heartbeat and settled into an intimate tempo.

Aleksender came forward until their two hearts beat as one.

Poetic words from a familiar story flooded Sofia's thoughts ...

Press closer, little nightingale, or the day will come before the rose is finished ...

Sofia settled against Aleksender's warmth and successfully molded their bodies together.

The Nightingale pressed closer against the thorn till it pierced her heart ...

His breaths fanned across her forehead, branding her forever. She leaned in closer ... closer ... closer still ... letting the moist flesh of her lips ghost across Aleksender's skin. Jet-black hair fell in thick waves, curling a few inches above the meticulous folds of his collar.

Bitter was the pain ... wilder and wilder grew her song, for she sang of the love that is perfected by death ... Love that dies not in the tomb.

They were no longer ward and guardian. They were a woman and man, two lovers in the midst of a groundbreaking revelation.

And indeed—the truth had bloomed before daybreak.

•

Aleksender gazed out the window as the coach calmly maneuvered through Paris's sleeping streets. The various monuments and buildings resembled monsters crouching amongst shadows.

The blunderbuss knocked against his thigh, parroting the coach's unsteady movements. Aleksender absently skirted his fingertips across the musket's polished wood. The silver barrel shone beneath the moonlight like a beacon, illuminating the engraved words *de Lefèvre*. Aleksender traced each letter with a stinging ache in his heart.

Ready to ward off any dangers, he secured a fist around the blunderbuss's finely carved handle. Alas, he would gladly kill for his ward.

Sofia was presently nestled up against his shoulder, all softness and overwhelming femininity. Her presence was intoxicating ... wondrously calming. Lustrous shafts of moonlight bathed her slumbering form and highlighted the delicacy of her features. Aleksender studied Sofia's profile in admiration, in awe of how much she'd matured in so short a time. He struggled to see the little girl he'd once adored. But too much had changed.

God above, everything had changed.

A few erratic curls twitched in her sleep as they were manipulated by deep and dreamy breaths. Aleksender gazed down at her, filled with a startling awareness. She looked so beautiful in her sedated state. So content and so very precious. A cluster of freckles dusted the bridge of her upturned nose. Aleksender balled his hands into two fists whilst he fought the excruciating need to acquaint himself with each and every one.

He sobered as she stirred the slightest bit. Rosebud lips parted in speech—only to mutter a volume of unconscious nonsense.

With all of his heart, Aleksender wished the carriage ride would never come to an end. Minutes later, his insides darkened as Sacred Heart Convent slipped into view.

Aleksender arched his shoulder and nudged Sofia from her dreams. She stirred once more, buried her face in the crook his arm, and gave a defiant grumble. Persistent snoring filled the coach. Aleksender smiled to himself. He'd never heard a more charming sound.

Brushing fallen locks from her eyes, he leaned forward and whispered against her forehead, "Come, come. Time to wake, chérie."

A lush hood of lashes fluttered open, exposing the piercing blue of her eyes. She rubbed her nose till it glowed a delightful pink. "Hullo." Her lips lifted into a lazy smile as their gazes merged together. Aleksender was enraptured. "You know … I was just dreaming about you."

Aleksender cleared his throat. His fingertips slid from her scalp and landed in the safety of his lap. "Ah, is that right?"

Her smile melted away within the following silence. Tiny fists crawled up the length of Aleksender's chest and lost themselves within the coat's thick folds. She gave an urgent tug, drawing him several inches closer … closer … dangerously close.

The heat of their bodies mingled as one. With each breath, Aleksender drank in the sweet essence of roses and wintertime. His mind swam with unorthodox visions and desires. He inclined his head, lost to the power of her nearness, entranced by everything that was his beloved ward.

"Alek, my Alek …"

Each word infused Aleksender with a delicious and undeniable warmth. Intoxicated by roses and wintertime, he found it difficult to speak, difficult to think. Breathless, he swallowed and met the haunting blue of her eyes.

"Please," she dreamily murmured, "I want you to kiss me again."

CHAPTER SEVEN

Several days had passed since Aleksender and Sofia's improper encounter, each one blurring seamlessly into the next. And he found that the nights were no different. Alas, it seemed that Aleksender's existence had transformed into a single, suspended moment.

Lavished in scarlet curtains, rich upholstery and rosewood furnishings, the master bedchamber was fit for royalty. Decked with exotic perfumes and dazzling jewels of all shapes and sizes, a vanity was centered before the grand oversized mirror. A solitary candle glowed, encircling the countertop in a ring of light, painting the walls with its wavering shafts. Elizabeth sat in front of her lovely reflection, looking every bit like a porcelain doll.

A solemn and bloodless porcelain doll.

With a distant look beaming from her eyes and a subtle frown at her lips, she stroked her shiny hair and hummed beneath a hushed breath. Long streams of candlelight complimented her beauty to perfection. The illumination outlined her curves while a sheer chemise hugged her body like a lover, leaving very little to her husband's imagination.

Aleksender sat on the edge of the large canopy bed. A pair of leather suspenders dug into his skin, straining against a firm slate of muscle. Fitted trousers hugged each thigh and a cream-toned dress shirt swallowed up the cummerbund waistline.

Studying the glamorous reflection with a haunting attentiveness, Aleksender watched as Elizabeth embarked on her nightly ritual.

He surprised himself and thought of his mother.

Comtesse Victoria de Lefèvre had tragically passed away during Aleksender's tenth year. Her death had been painfully sudden, though he could recall nothing of the accident. According to his father, a spooked mare and unhinged carriage wheel had been to blame. Aleksender, too, had been in that carriage—and had survived the incident by some twisted stroke of luck. Even in Victoria's absence, Philippe had expressed an endless devotion to his late wife. First hand, Aleksender had witnessed the transcending power of love, a fidelity that knew no boundaries, time and again.

Aleksender shook away the memories and returned to the moment.

Within Elizabeth's emptiness he saw himself. And the cause of her heartache was no great wonder. Yet, here she sat—radiating with the innocence of a girl, daring to steal a glance of him every few brushes. Mimicking all of the correct movements without any inspiration, she was a stunning shell of a human being.

With a heavy heart, Aleksender imagined Elizabeth brushing her hair, just like this, night after night ... staring at herself with a vacant and faraway look in her eyes.

Elizabeth surrendered to an uncertain smile as their gazes came together in the mirror. A light blush tinted her cheekbones and steadily crept down her neck.

Lowering her pale hood of lashes, she spoke through little more than a sweet and serene whisper. "Come now, Aleksender. Must you be such a stranger? Why ... you've hardly said more than a few words these past days."

Cued by her voice, Aleksender rose to his feet and came to the mirror. She gasped as the heat of his body pierced her chemise. He towered over her seated form, impossibly close, shrouded beneath penetrating silence and wavering shadow.

He stole the comb from her hand and swept it through the long and lovely tresses ... admiring the way in which they tumbled down and over her slender shoulders, curling just past the small of her back.

Her eyes whispered shameful secrets and forbidden longings. Things she dared not pursue. Indeed, despite their fifteen-year partnership, she and Aleksender had laid together only a handful of times. Their lovemaking had always been consistently passionless—and the mutual intention to produce an heir had been the sole driving force.

Elizabeth's eyes twinkled as she smiled at him. And, a moment later, a devious grin crept to her mouth. "I thought you were dead, you know. Thought I would never see you. Never touch you again."

Aleksender remained in his characteristic silence. He continued the intoxicating ministrations, brushing out the glory of her hair—gently, slowly, tremulously—eyes never parting from her reflection.

And when Aleksender at last spoke, the words were a tender and light caress. "Sleep well, Elizabeth." With a dejected sigh, he set down the brush, pressed a kiss upon her brow, and went to bed for the night.

•

Chapel Saint Leonard's bells tolled out, ringing their timeless melody as they announced Sunday mass. The humble dwelling was one of the only places of worship that hadn't suffered considerable ruin from the siege and revolutionaries. Two shattered windows and a jarring occurrence stood as the sole traces of Paris's demise. Over the last months, most churches, chapels and sanctums had been torn apart from the inside out. Roofs were ceremoniously caved in, windows broken, and the interiors thrashed to high hell. And the greatest damage had resulted from the citizens' hands rather than Prussians'.

Never had a group of people felt so abandoned by God. It was no coincidence that a large number of the Commune's insurgents held a fierce hatred for religion. Spoken prayer had been outlawed at many of the funerals. In pained silence, mothers had wept as the caskets of their veteran sons were lowered into that eternal dirt.

Chapel Saint Leonard's priest had been greeted by a rather unforgettable sight one morning. The altar had been crudely vandalized, and the spectacle resembled a caricature straight out of Le Père Duchêne's pages. There Jesus hung, dressed in the garb of Versailles, a pipe dangling from lifeless stone lips. And ever since that time, a fragile calm had blanketed Paris to the point of suffocation.

Inside Chapel Saint Leonard's walls, Aleksender, Elizabeth, Sofia, and Richard sat side-by-side along one of the pewter benches. Light poured through the shattered window and illuminated the chapel in a flawless cylinder. The priest's voice swelled the building to its rafters, each word infused with haunting passion.

"We live in a broken world that is filled with sin."

Ever since boyhood, and for reasons Aleksender couldn't fully grasp, religion had always unsettled him. Mind pacing, he turned from the altar and sought distraction. The priest's words transformed into a steady drone.

"As Catholics, we have been challenged to live as people of faith during these dark and unforgiving times."

Roosting pigeons cooed in agreement as the flap of their wings resonated. Aleksender cocked his head and observed the pair of frolicking birds. They playfully dove in and of the wooden beams and rafters, perfectly content and oblivious to the cryptic atmosphere. And in his mind's eye, it was the silhouette of an eagle that loomed above him—the Angel of Death, an ever-present and sinister force …

A strange envy overcame Aleksender as the pigeons escaped through the shattered window. He stifled a deep groan and adjusted his posture. No escape or comfort was to be found. Alas, the pewter bench seemed to be carved from solid rock rather than rosewood … and the surrounding walls resembled bars rather than planks.

"I would like to begin today with a passage from Matthew: 5. Blessed are the poor in spirit, for theirs is the kingdom of heaven."

Aleksender warily glanced at his brother's profile. Richard's head was bowed, both eyes fastened shut. What he was reflecting on was no great mystery. The death of their father was one wound that would never heal. A sharp pang of guilt overcame Aleksender. Their luncheon on the veranda only added insult to injury. Neither of them would ever live up to their father's legacy. Richard was too full of self-loathing and set in his ways, while Aleksender was far too damaged.

"Blessed are they that mourn, for they shall be comforted."

Next to him, Elizabeth blankly stared forward. But her eyes betrayed the show of outward calm. The delicate bond they'd shared for so many years had begun to unravel. There was no denying it. Elizabeth suspected something between him and his ward. Of that he was certain.

Anyone with half a mind could see it.

"Blessed are the merciful, for they will be shown mercy."

As for his little Sofia …

Her nearness was intoxicating. The warmth of her body radiated, filling all five of his senses with roses and wintertime.

"Blessed are the pure in heart, for they shall see God."

After their night out, it was Sofia's breathless plea that had opened Aleksender's eyes to the truth. *Alek, I want you to kiss me again.*

That kiss had sealed their fate. And his immediate self-defense had been to blame the Voisin's "finely aged wine."

At first, silence had been his reply. And then gently, carefully, and ever so tenderly, their lips had come together in a chaste kiss. In itself, it had been quite harmless—proving to be little more than a kiss shared between ward and guardian. But it had whispered of irrevocable repercussions.

Aleksender's lashes had blinked shut in an attempt to escape from his longings. But the bridge had already been crossed. And every barricade, every emotional defense and logical fortress, had burned to the ground.

A decent man would have pulled away. A decent man would have corrected the poor girl's delusional thoughts and straightened her thinking.

But Aleksender was far from a decent man.

Instead, a pair of trembling arms had enveloped her waist. He'd tilted his head and reverently bowed his face, inhaling her femininity. Gathering her to his chest, he'd tugged her impossibly close, never intending to let go, allowing their two heartbeats to consummate as one—

"Blessed are those who are persecuted because of righteousness' sake, for theirs is the kingdom of heaven. Amen."

A moment of silence descended over the patrons of Chapel Saint Leonard. Aleksender conformed to his surroundings and followed suit, bowing his face in personal grief rather than prayer.

•

Sunday mass concluded two hours later. Needing urgently to speak with Sofia, Aleksender had inquired Richard if he'd mind escorting Elizabeth back to the chateau. "I should say not," he'd replied, meaning each word. "It would be a pleasure." Aleksender had winced, stung by the bitterness that tinted his brother's voice.

Remnants of suffering and despair hung amongst Place de la Concorde like a bad omen. Ensuring they'd not have to look upon the invaders, black coverings had been draped over the statues' faces during the siege. Months later, the linens still remained, now sun-streaked and faded.

Sofia and Aleksender quietly stood at the center of the Tuileries Garden. In the nearby distance, the Vendôme Column towered against the sky, Napoleon's likeness scraping at the heavens. Over a hundred of the column's spiraling bronze plates were rumored to have been constructed from captured cannons. And each one stood as a sentiment of the military's power and might. Elaborately dressed in Roman garb, Napoleon's statue symbolized France's greatness and immorality.

The Tuileries Garden had remained the city's most popular leisure spot despite its recent torching. Vivid plant life and brimming ponds textured the premises in an array of colors.

But nothing could have alleviated the storm cloud that hovered over Sofia and Aleksender. Nearly a week had passed since their kiss. And now Aleksender could feel his doomed fate closing in on him like a palpable force. He was sinking into the blackened depths of despair. And those faceless statues reminded Aleksender that those closest to him were very much in jeopardy. Damn it to hell. He'd sooner slit his throat than bring Sofia down with him. And if things remained in their present condition, such a thing would be inevitable.

Aleksender distracted himself with a boyish fantasy. Perhaps he would purchase a ship with a generous sum of his inheritance. For sentimental reasons he would name the vessel *The Nightingale*—a shameless homage to a story he'd often read to Sofia. He would rule as the ship's captain, and—if the fool played his cards right—Christophe would serve as his first mate.

And Sofia, his lovely and sweet ward, would bunk with him each night and absorb the sunrise each morning. Maybe from the crow's nest, should he successfully rid himself of his fear of his heights. The evenings would be dedicated to ravishing the holy temple of Sofia's body, much like the loyal servant ravishes his goddess. Aleksender would become a legendary pirate king, the ruler of the high seas, Poseidon in the flesh. From coast to coast, the three of them would sail the world in silent harmony. Naturally, they'd make a brief stop to America where Christophe could find a fiery wench to tame.

Perhaps Aleksender would deny his destiny and fate would no

longer claim the upper hand.

"Alek ..." The surrounding tension might have been severed with a blade. Standing mere inches apart, Sofia draped a hand over the ragged arch of Aleksender's shoulder. He jerked from her touch as though it had burned. "Alek? What—"

"We can't see each other anymore. Not like this. Not for a while."

Sincere confusion crossed over her features. She tucked a loose curl behind each ear and shook her face. "What? What are you even saying?"

Aleksender inhaled a strained breath. "The other night at Voisin—it was a mistake. An impulsive mistake. We mustn't go any farther down this road. We weren't thinking clearly. And it's my fault and mine alone. Sofia ... I should have never come to you that night. I was lonely and—"

Sofia fought back tears as the slender expanse of her chest shook with evident shudders. Aleksender gripped onto her shoulder blades and aligned their bodies. She stared at the pavement below her heels, unable to meet his eyes.

"God, I ... I'm so stupid. I thought—"

"Sofia, you did nothing wrong. Please, you must understand—I care for you. I care for you far too much." Aching from her nearness, Aleksender reached out, attempting to stroke the smooth bend of her cheek.

Sofia flinched out of his grasp with a strange and strangled sob. "No. Just ... don't."

The vast blue sky seemed to darken as clouds overhead swelled and dimmed. The serene backdrop had been painted over and wiped clean out of existence.

Likewise, Sofia's lovely face mutated into a mask of agony. Aleksender felt his heart clench as various degrees of pain crept over her muddled features. The sapphire of her eyes became tarnished, abandoning their customary glow, her ivory complexion whitening to a ghostly pallor.

She fought—bless her dear heart, she fought like a true flesh and blood warrior—to hide her emotions and conceal her pain.

Aleksender searched her eyes for answers, for hidden secrets of the heart. The truth was cleanly etched in her gaze. She believed they could be together. And Aleksender could only assume that he was to blame for her skewed perception of the world. He had raised her on the enchanting romance of fairytales. Now, as Sofia stood before him, the genuine prospect of hope flickered from her blue eyes. And, much like himself, her head was bursting with fantastic thoughts and romantic ideas. Things that could never be.

Sofia trembled from head to toe, shuddering like a leaf in La Havre's summer breeze.

Aleksender stroked her arm with an exquisite deftness as he attempted to sedate her nerves. But she found no relief in his caresses. His touch only burned. And she found that it ignited her spirit with a multitude of flares.

She freed herself from the circle of Aleksender's arms. His fingers slid away, almost in slow motion, that green gaze alive with feeling. Destined tears pricked the corners of her eyes and threatened to spill down her cheeks. She summoned an inner strength, holding them back.

"Sofia? I—"

"Please—no. Just don't touch me. It's too much ..."

A guttural sound erupted low in her throat. Sofia swallowed, cupping her heart in vain. Alas, the very source of her affection was strong and willfully determined against her palm. It thundered in a deafening roar. She inwardly cursed herself, convinced that he could hear the godforsaken drumming. "You promised. Only days ago you said I'd never lose you."

Aleksender inched toward Sofia, both palms outstretched as if he were coaxing a spooked horse into submission. "Sofia—"

She continued to slink away.

He was closing in on her. Their fate was closing in on the both of them. A glorious landslide of possessed emotion was destined to crush their souls. And what more was a landslide than the accumulated pressure of stress and time?

Two steps later and Sofia slammed against one of the garden's stone columns. Aleksender hovered high above her, all darkness and torn emotion, the magnificent curve of his form casting her within shadow.

"I have waited for you. In my heart, I have waited." Her voice was nearly inaudible. "And I know it's wrong. It is wrong and sinful in every way, but I can't shake this feeling. And I know that you feel it, too."

Fate had brought them together. Now fate was to keep them apart.

The epiphany, the full extent of their inability to be together, burned Sofia's soul. The fantasy had been shattered. And now, she would forever be lost—lost with no hope of returning to the life she'd once known and loved.

And yet on the day of Aleksender's departure, as the ship had whistled impatiently and women wept their goodbyes, he had kissed her. He had *really* kissed her.

He had kissed her as though he'd loved her.

"I love you as my ward," was his soft answer to her thoughts, "nothing more." Aleksender swallowed. "And she deserves better." His voice was composed and smooth, yet bore a jagged edge. Sofia dropped her chin and braced herself for the inevitable. "I've already hurt Elizabeth far more than I can bear to live with." Aleksender glanced elsewhere, unable to stomach the sight of her heartache.

She nodded and knotted both arms over her breasts. "I must go."

Pinning her body against the column's cool alabaster, Aleksender blocked her steps and prevented any hope for escape. "Please." He rested a hand upon the slope of her neck, willing himself not to tremble. Visibly battling some inner demon, he gave in and caressed her skin. Her eyes blinked shut at the hypnotic ministrations. "I care for you. I care for you so much. And saving you that night." Their gazes locked, souls consummating. "Was a godsend."

"I … I don't know. I'm not so sure."

A fat tear rolled down her cheek and dampened Aleksender's hand. It burned, striking him like holy water. But he was possessed with demons that could never be exorcised.

"What do you want me to say? What can I say?" Silence followed. Only the wind's breath penetrated the quiet. Indeed. There was nothing left for him to say. In a single instant, their stars had realigned. And nothing could ever again be the same.

"Nothing. I understand." Sofia tucked a chocolate curl behind her ear and smoothed down the delicate material of her skirts. "Farewell, my dear Alek."

CHAPTER EIGHT

Few things are worse than being stripped of everything you hold dearest.

Drunk out of his mind, Christophe pondered this stale sentiment as he stared down the sweltering remnants of his home. His chest clenched at the sight. Alas, the vision was uglier than any battlefield. More disturbing than any number of dismembered limbs or decapitated heads. Christophe medicated himself with a generous swig of alcohol, chased the liquid with his cigar, and swept unkempt locks from his eyes.

Mon Dieu. When had he last bathed? Days ago? A week? It was impossible to say. But one thing was vividly clear—the stench was inescapable and Godawful. He reeked of filth, sweat, sex, and brandies. Near to suffocating and disgusted within himself, Christophe unbuttoned a row of clasps on his blouse and urged the spring air to clear out the musk.

What was that ridiculous saying? Ah, yes, some English fool—the great Sir Edward Coke—had once said that "a man's house is his castle and fortress, and each man's home is his safest refuge." How very ingenious were the English! Neurotically gnawing at the tip of his cigar, Christophe looked upon the tangled mass of blackened planks and fluttering debris—the half complete rosewood furnishings and whittled keepsakes, the gutted ashes of his home.

Everything was burning. And all that remained of his past was a rusted Prussian dagger and a mangy pair of dog tags.

A handful of Versailles soldiers were to blame for the destruction. Christophe was certain of it. Yes—the National Guard and France's formal "defenders" had been exchanging bombs within yards of Christophe's humble abode. One of the damned shells had slipped and tore through the walls. Thanks to Christophe's patriotism—thanks to his personal collection of chassepot rifles and gunpowder kegs—the explosion had proved to be quite a spectacle. The very things that had kept him alive out on the battlefield—those precise things that had once served France's formal military—had inevitably destroyed all he held dearest.

Aleksender's words invaded his mind. *I daresay irony at its finest.*

And where was the great Comte de Paris now? Sitting up in his castle and fortress, locked away in a safe haven, a refuge—oblivious to Paris's destruction. Comte Aleksender de Lefèvre had served "her well" and wanted nothing to do with the war. And his wish had been granted on a silver platter.

And what of his comrade, Christophe Cleef? What of himself? He'd gone bankrupt weeks ago (after all, few people purchase writing desks and wooden benches during a siege) and had hit rockbottom ever since.

What were Aleksender's words? What were those sparkling words of wisdom? What else had Aleksender said in Cafe Roux on that fine Parisian morning?

The war has not ended. It has merely followed us home.

The war had followed Christophe home, yes—all while Paris's noble comte blissfully hid himself away.

Alas! Had Christophe not been at the local brothel the previous night, tucked snugly between the legs of some exotic whore, he'd exist as nothing more than a pile of rubble and ashes.

And death was a welcoming thought.

His head spun out of control, drowning beneath a fiery lake of alcohol and bitter thoughts. What absurdity! What spectacular wisdom! This man's house was a hellhole—and the only refuge to be found was at the bottom of this bottle! Irony at its finest, indeed! Christophe laughed at the fantastic turn of events until his stomach ached. He laughed until tears rolled down his cheeks ... laughed until he retched straight into the dirt ... and he continued to laugh until those tears lost all of their mirth.

•

The next afternoon Aleksender arrived at Cafe Roux fifteen minutes shy of one PM. The lunch hour was as dead and as quiet as the grave. From wall to wall, the place was empty and void of life. A small cluster of Prussian soldiers were seated along the windowpane and engaged in heated conversation. A masterfully sketched map occupied the whole table, its parchment wings fully spread. Across the top, *Carte de Paris* was inscribed in elegant calligraphy. At the opposite end of Cafe Roux, several National Guardsmen drained a coffee pot, the morning's edition of Le Père Duchêne sprawled open across the tabletop. The situation at hand was almost comical. Here sat Prussians and Frenchmen in civilized silence—both of whom had spent the last year slaughtering each other.

Round-faced-jolly-bartender kept to himself as he whistled a dull tune and wiped down the bar with a faded dishrag. Heavy with sweat from his brow, the material was soggy and in need of a good wash. And that round face of his, normally flushed and beaming, was anything but jolly.

Aleksender scanned the expanse of the room for any trace of Christophe Cleef. His chest sunk at the sight. The silhouette of his comrade was tucked in the furthest corner and cloaked in darkness. And all of Paris's shadows couldn't hide the fact that he was stinking drunk and teetering on the edge of sanity.

Clearly in the midst of some disagreement, the Prussians' argument escalated to a steady roar. Christophe rotated in his seat with an irritated groan. The chair creaked in defiance, manipulated by the pull of his body weight.

He interrupted the Prussians. "*Sie müssen nach Rouen bahnhof fahren, von dort kommen Sie nach Versailles.*" They exchanged a glance, stunned into silence by the Frenchman's flawless German tongue. "*Die Fahrt wird einige Stunden dauern.*"

Aleksender's mouth ticked at the corner. Christophe had prepared to work as a spy shortly before the war broke out, which had been one of many short-lived aspirations.

Aleksender released a long breath and crossed the room.

"Ah. So you made it. How very good of you." Christophe said in a dry slur. Aleksender narrowed his eyes and examined his friend's disheveled appearance from head to toe. Each thread of his coat was covered in dirt and only God knew what else. The auburn waves of his hair were unkempt and weighed down with grease. His grin, normally bright and brimming with good humor, was no longer starch white but tinted yellow. But hardest to stomach were his eyes. Rid of their customary gleam, they were cold, insipid and vacant.

The Prussians folded the map, climbed onto their feet, and stood next to the table. Christophe downed his alcohol and tossed a hand in the air, waving them off. They muttered a weak "merci" before proceeding on their ways.

"Christophe. What'd they want?"

"What do you think? Directions to Versailles, of course. Now come take a seat. We've much to talk about."

Aleksender straightened out his morning coat and warily sank into a parallel chair. He folded both hands together in the form of a steeple before he spoke. "You look like hell and you smell even worse."

Christophe barked a humorless laugh, which resembled a hollow cry, and inhaled a mouthful of brandy. With a strained chortle he swiped the dribbles from his mustache. "Charming as ever, I see. Wish I could say the same 'bout you." Christophe traced the rim of his glass in contemplative circles, staring into the liquid. "But you were right. We haven't returned home. We've merely traded one battlefield for another."

Aleksender tensed at his words. The shift in his friend's attitude was alarming. Little red flags emerged inside his mind. "What did you expect? We were under siege only months ago. Give it time. You—"

"I'm not talking about that." Christophe sobered and met Aleksender's eyes. "I'm not talking about Sedan or Wissembourg or even the camps."

Aleksender paralyzed. Ah, yes, those damn camps. He cleared his throat—feeling a blade buried deep inside his flesh. A chorus of cruel, mocking laughter echoed his mind—

Christophe banged his bottle against the tabletop and startled Aleksender from his trance. "Alek?"

"A civil war. You're talking about the beginnings of a civil war."

"No. No, not a civil war." Christophe shook his head, lips hooking into a grin. "A new revolution."

Aleksender's eyes darkened. "What you call a revolution I call anarchy. And what you claim to be 'justice' Adolphe Thiers claims to be punishable by death."

"Some things are well worth dying for. Now don't you agree?" Christophe slid his brandy across the table and ushered it into

Aleksender's hand. "Here. I believe you may need this as much as myself."

Aleksender nodded his gratitude and downed a mouthful. The brandy coated his throat with a soothing, slow burn. The glass skittered across the counter as he returned it to Christophe.

"I wanted to tell you ... ah—" Christophe's voice broke off mid-sentence. Unable to meet Aleksender's eyes, he scratched at his neck and stared into the bottle. "I'm not good with these sort of things." Christophe took a swig for courage. "Damn. I'm sorry 'bout your father."

"You and me both."

"Paris could've used him right 'bout now."

"To hell with Paris. To hell with all of France. I'm finished with her. And you ..." Resentment boiled inside of Aleksender. His head pounded, eyes seeing red. "You didn't call me here to wish your condolences. That much is obvious. So I suggest you stop wasting our time. From the way of things, we may be on limited supply."

The chair creaked as Christophe leaned against its wooden back. Unblinking, he crossed both arms across his chest and studied Aleksender. "What a fool I was, thinking you might give a damn." Christophe smirked and shook his head once more. "Of course. Why should you care? You've never cared for anything. Never have had any reason to."

His voice rose in volume with each word. The National Guardsmen halted their conversations and narrowed their gazes upon Christophe.

"Christophe—you are creating a scene."

Not seeming to hear Aleksender, he uttered a curse and slammed his fist onto the table. "There's nothin' of your father in you. You only enlisted because you couldn't deal with your own desires. Ain't that right, mon ami? You wanted that dancing ward of yours." A severe smile framed his lips. "Ah, don't look so surprised. It was obvious enough between your stories and the letters. Come now. I'm not that foolish. Tell me—what's her name again? Hmm? Sidney, Cecilia ... No, no. Those aren't right."

"What do you want from me?"

"Take a guess. Go on." Silence. "Ah, you never were one for games. Truth be told ... Paris is in great need of your great and humble charity, Monsieur le Comte." Each syllable dripped with mockery. "Lives are bein' stolen." Christophe paused before continuing. A look of severe pain marred his features. He adjusted his posture and scrubbed a hand over his weathered face. "People are losing everything that matters ... their homes, loved ones—"

"A pity." Aleksender absently stroked a hand through his hairline. "But not my concern."

"Damn it, Alek. You could turn this around. I'd likely be shot to high hell if I stepped within a mile of Versailles. But you ... you are different. You have the one thing that everyone else lacks. A worthy name."

Aleksender's lips curved into a cold, almost triumphant smile. "That's where you're wrong. None of us are worth a damn." Aleksender pushed back his chair as he prepared to stand.

"Sure, you're all high and mighty now," Christophe stuttered. "But just wait. Wait till your darling wife is raped up against a wall, till your chateau is burned to the ground and your father's grave is pissed on—all while your little Sofia whores herself for a loaf of bread." Aleksender tensed at the sound of his ward's name. "This has always been your answer to everything. Run away ... run away and hide like a damned coward. So very noble of you, monsieur. Your father would be most proud."

"We're done." Aleksender rose to his feet, signaled to Round-faced-jolly-bartender, and threw a handful of francs onto the table. One of the coins rolled across its counter and spun in dizzying circles. Through Aleksender's eyes, it was Champion, Bois de Boulogne's sorry-looking gelding, putting around the racecourse. It was Sofia Rose, Salle Le Peletier's beloved ballerina, mesmerizing everyone with her delicate movements. "And Christophe." Aleksender grated as he gestured to the coins. "Here's my charity."

•

Sacred Heart's dormitory was exceptionally cozy if not a bit cramped. A dozen or so wooden beds lined the plastered walls, each one centered below arches and hanging crucifixes. Sconce candles gently flickered and cast dancing shadows across the cracked floorboards. Like all other nights, the convent was quiet and unnaturally still.

Sofia lay stiffly in her bed, mind racing and unable to sleep. Her cot was stationed in the farthest corner of the dormitory, which allowed her privacy from the other girls. A moderate-sized window hung nearby. On most evenings, she'd gaze into the star-filled sky and lose herself within the constellations. Tonight, however, no stars could be seen. The night was black and cold—a bottomless, unforgiving void.

Sofia tossed onto her side as worry furrowed her brow. Left alone with her thoughts, she reflected on her past and considered her future. The dormant feelings she'd longtime held for Aleksender had become amplified, and could no longer be ignored nor written off as mere fantasy.

The drapes lazily fluttered under the wind's breath. The windowpane jingled, thrusting back and forth in steady movements. A mild breeze whispered across Sofia's cheeks in a pleasant and transient caress. She inhaled deeply as the scent of fresh blooms stirred all five of her senses to life. With Paris in such poor condition, leaving the window undone was undeniably dangerous, but it was a risk she'd always been more than happy to take. Countless nights, Sofia had imagined Aleksender climbing through that slim portal. He'd come and spirit her away, whisking her off to some distant land.

Like everything else, the fantasy was short-lived. Most evenings, light footfall followed by the click of a latch jarred Sofia from her thoughts. Indeed—Sister Catherine often locked the window once she believed Sofia had fallen asleep.

Sofia flipped onto her stomach and hooked both arms around the pillow. Tears sprang to her eyes, threatening to dampen the material. Nuzzling deeper into the cotton, she inhaled a strangled sob. She couldn't help it, couldn't stop the tears. Soft cries shook her body. The pillow muted the sounds and grew heavy with moisture. She missed him. She missed him more than she could say. It seemed he'd returned only to disappear once more. It was a year ago all over again.

Why? Why did things have to change so suddenly? And why must Aleksender force them apart? She understood his reasons, of course … just as she understood they could never be together. As both a husband and citizen of Paris, Aleksender was wedded to his duties.

His words from the Tuileries Garden haunted her mind. *We can't see each other anymore. Not like this. Not for a while.*

Did he truly think her so cold—so unloving and cruel? She

could never turn her cheek from his pain and agony, especially now.

The question rose in her mind like a dark storm cloud: what was to become of their delicate bond? What was to become of her—and what of Aleksender?

Her choices were barren at best. A loveless marriage was something she could never endure. And she was confident that Aleksender would not force her into a marriage of convenience—the same sort of partnership he shared with Elizabeth.

During her nineteen years, Sofia had known only two homes: Sacred Heart Convent and Aleksender's arms. If she could no longer be with Aleksender, she'd remain at Sacred Heart forever. She would likely leave the stage and take her vows.

And yet, despite her adoration for God, she had no desire to spend her existence as a nun. She yearned for romance and unbridled passion—two things that would become entirely forbidden. She yearned for children, the comfort of a family. But, above all things, she ached for Aleksender's love—something that had always been, and always would be, forbidden to her …

Despite her rather strict religious upbringing, despite the knowledge that such desires were built from sin, despite Aleksender's words from only days ago, *I love you as my ward … nothing more,* Sofia couldn't shake the feeling they were supposed to be together.

Resting on that thought, the thumping window transformed into a soft, rhythmic chime as sleep finally came.

CHAPTER NINE

They demand answers. They take a perverse delight in taunting my willpower, teasing me, waving a dagger before my eyes. The tarnished blade drips, coated with blood—the blood of my fallen comrades. The evidence of my fellow men's suffering only empowers me. I do not answer.

I invite their tortures with a low and sardonic chuckle. They oblige, plunging the rusty blade deep into my back. The pain is excruciating. Even worse, it is degrading ... humiliating. I'm unable to suppress a choked cry. I cringe in spite of myself and bite down on my lip till the metallic flavor of blood floods my jaw line.

As always, they share a rough laugh and demand my cooperation in clumsy French. But all I ever offer is bitter silence and a more bitter grin. I raise my head with feigned pride. My parched lips curl into a chilling smile. Blood seethes from between my teeth, leaking down my chin—dripping onto the muddy ground below. Muttering vile curses and promises of pain, the dagger is mercilessly twisted—lodged inside my flesh, buried to the hilt—crucifying my soul ...

Christophe's frantic pleas slice through my consciousness: "Hör auf damit! Hör auf damit ..."

I shall not allow them the pleasure of my agony. I do not stir a limb. I detach soul from body—thinking of her. My grin widens as one of the men cross themselves in a rushed motion: in the name of the Father, Son, and the Holy Spirit—

Aleksender woke with a violent start. Mon Dieu. The nightmare had been painfully vivid. He could feel the blade impaling his flesh, hear the cruel, mocking laughter, and smell the rancid stench of sweat and blood.

Near to suffocating, Aleksender tore through the bedchamber's double-doors and stepped onto the balcony. The night was black, bottomless and empty. Above, a storm of clouds maliciously shielded the moon from his gaze. A strange fog blew in all directions, blanketing the walkways beneath a thick and milky haze. Rain drops fell from the sky and filled the ground with bruised puddles.

Strange. Stormy weather was unusual for spring. An impending sense of doom was inescapable, and Paris seemed to be weeping for her fate.

Aleksender stole a backward glance of Elizabeth's reclined silhouette. She was slumbering, appearing wonderfully peaceful in her sedated state.

Yet her tear-stained cheeks told a quite different story. His chest contracted at the sight of her pain.

He swallowed and returned his gaze to the bruised sky. Despair, guilt, and sorrow swelled all four chambers of his heart. The material of his cloak flowed behind him, whipping fiercely in the wind.

Not far in the distance, a cloaked figure broke through the rolling haze. It approached the chateau at a vast and remarkably graceful stride. Aleksender exhaled a shaky breath, passed a hand over his hair, and summoned every ounce of his noble courage.

Both of them would need it.

•

Aleksender crossed the chateau's front lawn at a steady pace. In response, the cloaked figure also increased its speed, reaching a sprint then a fierce run. Standing inches apart, Aleksender and the cloaked figure came together after some steps. Both remained perfectly still, perfectly silent. Their breaths penetrated the air, misting in a unified cloud.

Aleksender was the one who took a swift step closer.

His six-foot-two frame towered over the delicate figure with ease. The thick navy-blue hood hid the stranger's face, sheltering his or her identity from his eyes. And yet he knew. Out on the balcony he'd felt her very presence.

His icy voice split the darkness. "I told you—you have no place here. You were supposed to keep away."

A growl rumbled low in his throat as he tossed back the hood. For both of their sanities, he'd planned to be ruthless and cold, cruel and unfeeling. Aleksender's courage instantly faltered. The vision enchanted him beyond words. His malicious intent dissolved into affection—the indescribable need to shelter Sofia from the world ... to shelter her from himself.

Her eyes, so blue and deep, struck him like a whip. Tears swam down her porcelain cheeks and descended in a waterfall, mingling with the falling rain. Freed from the hood's snug confines, a whirlwind of russet curls flowed behind her in a fierce flurry. They danced freely in the breeze, mocking her enslaved spirit.

"I'm sorry. I know I wasn't supposed to come. It's just ... I—I had a nightmare," came her soft confession.

Indeed, Sofia had been plagued with recurring nightmares for years. In sleep, her mother would return along with the pain of her former life. The burns, blasphemy and humiliation ... within the darkness and solitude of her thoughts, all of the horrors would return. And Aleksender's arms had become her safe haven ... an escape from the ghosts of her past. Ghosts that would never be laid to rest. His touch chased away those monsters that came for her during the night. His words had always been a breath of fresh air and a token of courage.

Aleksender replaced her hood with a reverent touch and gathered Sofia to his chest. "I would never let harm come of you. And no matter what happens between us ... I shall always be there." He pressed two fingers below her chin and tilted her face back. "You know that, don't you?"

Sofia said nothing. She spoke with her touch. Her fingertips grazed the nape of his neck and clawed at the rugged flesh, forcing him dangerously close. Sofia laid her cheek across his shoulder and inhaled an uneven sigh.

The heat of her breaths impaled his dress shirt and warmed the depths of his soul. Not thinking, not caring anything for propriety, Aleksender aligned their two bodies. Their heartbeats touched, echoing an undeniable affection, whispering things they dared not say. And so he simply allowed himself to feel.

Aleksender inhaled a sharp breath and deftly grazed her upturned cheek with the back of his hand. The opposite ran through her hair and fanned the precious satin. Against his roughened flesh, every bit of Sofia felt impossibly vulnerable. The texture of her curls was spun from exquisite velvet and sinfully soft.

Lowering his lashes, he gazed down and marveled at the sight of their joined bodies. A peaceful smile graced Sofia's lips. Pressed against his much larger form, she looked small and perfectly helpless. Safe, secure and completely at home within the circle of his arms.

A warm sensation pierced Aleksender's chest as her tears ran anew. Sofia groaned aloud at her weakness and shamefully hid her eyes within the folds of his dress shirt. "I told myself I wouldn't cry."

"Ah, ma chérie ..." He cradled Sofia in his arms, rocking her to and fro, back and forth, as one might a babe. With every movement her tears faded away until there was only the two of them. "Why must my angel weep?"

When she spoke, her voice was a husky and unusually deep mezzo, its timbre dipped within a vat of unfilled longings. Neither of them recognized it as her own. Each of her words fluttered against his cheek like a kiss. "Tell me this is not all in my mind." Aleksender felt his heart skip a beat. And then he felt it skip two more. "Tell me." Their eyes united in a single, powerful gaze. The heat of her words fanned across his face in an enticing tease, transient and tempting. Her breath smelled sweeter than nectar from the honeycomb. "Tell me you feel what I feel."

Silence was his reply. He answered with his touch. Gently, carefully, and ever so tenderly, their lips came together in a kiss.

Sofia's face bent forward as if in prayer, sapphire eyes lowering to the ground beneath her feet. Both she and Aleksender were left breathless, resembling a couple caught in the midst of passionate lovemaking.

Sofia tucked her head beneath the arch of Aleksender's chin as a discrete smile stretched her lips. Content and happy, she relaxed within the protection of his arms.

A feeling of completeness claimed the both of them. It seemed they'd waited a lifetime for this moment, for this sense of security and comfort, this mutual tenderness and appreciation.

"No. You are not alone," he carefully breathed into her curls. "Dieu. I ... I feel the same."

In an unexpected movement, Sofia lunged forward and grabbed onto the material of Aleksender's cloak. She twisted it neurotically between her tiny fingertips—fearful that she would too soon awake—fearful that he would vanish from her grasp.

"Stay with me, Alek."

He rested a palm against the middle of her back and gave a gentle push. Sofia's fingers slid up his chest in an intimate and experimental touch—up the strong column of his throat, then back down again.

Raw desperation empowered her touch, while primal longings allowed Aleksender to accept it. Sofia's slim arms circled his hips. Her hands slid up his waist in a shy and painfully slow motion. He'd bedded handfuls of whores and mistresses—countless whores and mistresses—without a trace of shame. He'd lain with women whose sexual appetites would make even a seasoned harlot blush. And yet, this was the most intimate moment of his entire life.

Sofia's tender and virginal touch was more than he could bear; it was nearly his undoing. Aleksender groaned against her neck. Her curls quivered, manipulated by his heavy and erratic breaths. They tickled his cheek with the caress of a butterfly's silky wings. His manhood simultaneously twitched, swelling to painful proportions behind the confines of his trousers.

"Please, please ..." he implored—though he knew not for what.

Please don't do this to me ... to us, his mind shouted. *Complete me, make me whole*, his heart simultaneously pleaded.

But words were unneeded. Sofia read into his deepest and most sincere of thoughts. "I've been so empty without you."

He swallowed at her confession. "So empty," he confirmed, defeated and at her mercy.

Empowered, Sofia's hands crawled around his body and slowly inched up the impressive length of his back. Her fingers clawed at the cloak's thick material—digging at the covered terrain in hopes of discovering some unknown treasure.

A treasure she felt the greedy desire to possess.

And then she simply relaxed in Aleksender's embrace. A mass of chestnut curls cushioned his chin as she tucked her face into his chest. She was shaking—from fear or the cold, he could not say. Aleksender gathered his cloak and wrapped their bodies within the material, constructing a makeshift cocoon. Both Sofia and Aleksender savored the newly found sanctuary, never wishing to abandon this warmth. The absolute warmth of each other.

After a moment, Sofia raised her head and chanced a look at Aleksender. Their lips were dangerously close, mere inches apart, the cloak tying them together in a snug bundle.

"My Alek, so many nights ... endless nights I dreamt of you." She hesitated and paused her brazen confession, allowing a maiden blush to polish her cheekbones. "I dreamt of you in my arms, my bed ..."

Aleksender swallowed and tightened against her, both hardening and softening in one breath.

Sofia's eyes descended to his lips—full and beckoning lips that framed a beguiling mouth and were sculpted with the purpose to tell pretty lies.

"I dreamt of you, Alek."

"Sofia," he hoarsely warned. His voice was a rich and sultry growl, music to her little ears. And his desire was unmistakable. She could feel the source of his physical affection pulsating against her. And the evidence of his passion only fueled her longings tenfold—empowering her beyond recognition, equipping her with a startling audacity.

"I dreamt of you. All of you. Your touch. Your kiss. I—"

Aleksender swallowed the very last of her words. With an urgent sweep of his tongue he parted her mouth and wedged between the moist seams of her lips. Sofia obliged with a soft and wildly feminine sigh. Body and soul, she surrendered to the onslaught of his passion. His heart did a quick turn, spun by the sweet sounds which fluttered from her throat.

The rain fell in harsh streams, showering the two lovers. Neither Sofia nor Aleksender felt the assault, completely lost within each other. Entirely lost within the beauty of the moment. They were a royal mess, resembling a pair of frolicking adolescents. Sofia's russet curls were glued to her cheeks. She looked wonderfully attractive in her disheveled state. Likewise, Aleksender's white shirt was plastered to the chiseled contours of his chest and nearly transparent.

The seasoned lover, the adulterer, and murderer had vanished away. In that moment, Aleksender de Lefèvre's innocence had been preserved. He trembled within Sofia's arms, standing before her as no more than a helpless and lost boy.

Sensing the sudden reluctance that claimed his body, Sofia's hold tightened, wordlessly reassuring Aleksender. He was slipping away. Sofia doubted that she could bear losing him again.

"No ... no. Don't do this." Tentative words from only moments ago were spoken once more: "Stay with me."

As a veteran of war and the son of Philippe de Lefèvre, he knew there existed one quality and one alone that measured a soldier's greatness: the courage to sacrifice.

"Come. I best return you to Sacred Heart."

CHAPTER TEN

The carriage house was stationed in the farthest corner of the chateau's magnificent seventeen-acre property. From the side door, it opened to a breathtaking pasture that stretched on forever. Sweeping greenery engulfed the dwelling and shrouded it from wandering eyes. The gardens towered nearby in a lush array of manicured hedges and decorated trellises. Off in the distance, Chateau de Lefèvre dominated the horizon with its dark facade and even darker secrets.

Several rows of parallel horse stalls lined the small structure. From wall to wall, an intricate blend of hay, rocks, dirt and twigs blanketed the flooring. Long streams of moonlight slanted through splintered panels and illuminated the dust particles that drifted midair.

Wary of his sweeping height, Aleksender ducked as he entered. Sofia trailed behind him at a steady pace. With each step, she fought to keep her chin high and face proud. Enough tears had been shed. Far more than enough.

Aleksender gazed at her through lowered eyelashes.

Dieu. Sofia's nightdress was sopping wet. It conformed to the delicious curves of her body—the body of a prima ballerina—wrapping her with the intimacy of a lover's touch. The rise of her breasts gently rose and sank, manipulated by her strained breathing. The nightdress's material was borderline sheer, its neckline weighed down from the rain. It puckered forward in seductive invitation, exposing the tempting swell of her cleavage. In restless pursuit, a solitary raindrop rolled down the crevice and vanished into the valley of the Promised Land.

And Aleksender knew he was not fit for the Promised Land.

He dropped his gaze and muttered a slew of vulgar curses. "You should not be here." The timbre of his voice was low and brutally sharp. An exotic blend of desire and agony laced each syllable.

A tense silence stretched between Aleksender and Sofia. Only the drumming rain could be heard as it caressed the structure's rooftop in a provocative and relaxing melody. Aleksender swiftly moved past her. His eyes were purposefully fixed ahead, steps quick and determined. He needed to ignore his ward. He needed another female.

And so Aleksender made eyes at Juliet—his lovely and ever loyal white mare. Sensing the arrival of her master, she popped her head over the stall's inner door and nickered a friendly hello. Almond eyes beaming, Juliet pawed at the ground and bobbed her face from side to side. Sofia's lips broke into a subtle smile. Seduced by a melody of giggles, Aleksender peered at her—enchanted by the dimple that had embedded her cheek.

Looking away and fondling Juliet's velvet muzzle, he crooned, "Easy, ol' girl, easy."

Sofia came forward—wildly jealous of a horse—looking every bit like a charming young lady. Aleksender stiffened as the warmth of her body impaled his back. Her nearness called to him, engulfed him whole, caressed him with an intimate, inviting touch.

"Remember me, Juliet girl?" Juliet's head bobbed once more. Yes, she seemed to answer. "And do you remember tossing me from your back?" Juliet remained perfectly quiet, perfectly content. She dared not answer, Sofia very well assumed.

Sofia draped a hand over the stern rise of Aleksender's shoulder. He hardened beneath her touch as she gave a tender squeeze.

"Alek ..." More silence. "Why are you betraying your heart?"

Aleksender shook his face and exhaled a breath he hadn't known he was holding. "It's wrong, Sofia. I should have never acted."

Aleksender swung past the wooden gate and crossed Juliet's stall. The ancient closet rattled and moaned as he tugged it open. An assortment of combs, feed and woven bridles lined the interior in meticulous fashion. Careful not to disturb their order, Aleksender jumbled through the various items and settled on a brush. With a soft exhale, he averted his focus back to Juliet.

Gently, softly, he combed out the creature's flowing mane. She whinnied lightly and nuzzled his chest, basking beneath her master's tender affections. Aleksender caressed her with a haunting deftness, stroking her smooth sides, whispering sweet nothings into her perked ear, peppering tiny kisses upon her muzzle …

"You mustn't seek me out again." Aleksender's voice broke the quiet. His words were soft and airy, barely audible. "I forbid it. The streets are no longer safe. And you shall not put yourself in danger for my sake."

He tensed, absorbed in a strain of deep thought. Juliet tossed Aleksender's hand into the air and gave an impatient whinny. Snapped back to reality, he resumed the ministrations. "Impossible girl," he murmured against her smooth muzzle.

Sofia gazed through the panel's slim openings. Clouds shifted in the night sky and unveiled the glory of the moon. She summoned her bravery, folded both arms over the weight of her chest, and took a tentative step toward Aleksender.

"It wasn't wrong." Her muted footsteps approached. Aleksender's hand froze midair. "Following your heart can't be wrong. Not really. I know that—"

"You know nothing." Any sliver of peace fled as quickly as it had come. Aleksender slammed the brush down onto the floor; cushioned by the lush hay carpeting, it landed with a muffled bang. In a harsh and unexpected movement, he spun around full circle and latched onto Sofia's shoulder blades. Nearly crumbling at the seams, she winced as her body was bunched between his fingertips.

"Alek, please!"

"Why are you doing this? What do you want from me? What? I have nothing. Nothing to offer you!"

His mouth was mere inches from her own. The molten sting of his breath bit her cheek as she twisted her neck up and back. "But know this—I will destroy you. I'm no good for you, for myself—for anyone. Damn it, Sofia. I was only at Bête Noire that night because I was looking to bed a damn whore."

"Yes. And that was nearly ten years ago. You are not the same man! You—"

Aleksender shook her body without thinking. Her bones reverberated, rattling and rolling beneath his chilly fingertips. She was limp as a ragdoll, paralyzed in a sudden burst of terror. A lifetime of torment seemed to fuel his anger.

"Damn you, Sofia. Foolish girl. Don't you see? I am precisely the same man."

Sofia cried out as Aleksender shoved her backward. He stalked over to her, moving like a predator, his pace slow and achingly steady. Sofia inched away from her guardian, overcome with disbelief and mounting despair. In spite of herself, she was trembling. Each breath rose in a choked pant. His awakened madness was a palpable, terrifying force. Never had he spoken to her in such a way.

She was not daft. He'd killed numberless men during his time at war. And ever since she could remember, he'd always possessed an inhuman strength. Though, he'd always used it to protect and shield her. Certainly not to scare her from her mortal skin.

"Please, Alek. Please, whatever you are trying to prove, stop it."

"Just forget me. Forget me, ignorant child!"

"Child? I'll have you know, I'm far from a—"

One step later and Sofia slammed up against the structure's wooden panels.

Aleksender towered above her, all heartache and torn emotion, smoldering eyes staring down. Sofia shrieked as he ensnared both of her wrists and enveloped them completely. In a harsh movement, he lifted her slender arms sky-high and pinned her flush against the wall with his strong body. Wiggling within his grasp, Sofia cried out and struggled in vain. There was no escaping. She was imprisoned, trapped within a cage built from sinewy muscle and brawn. Dusty cobwebs tangled around her ankles, their eight-legged widows infesting the silk. The panels creaked and moaned beneath the fragile pull of her body weight. Jagged splinters gnawed at her skin, chewing through her flesh like teeth. There would be blood. She was certain of it.

"A woman, are you? What? What do you wish to hear? Speak!" His eyes burned. She had to look away.

"No! Don't you dare turn from me!"

Aleksender's free hand wrapped her chin in a rough motion. He twisted her face back, forcing Sofia to meet the potency of his glare. Brilliant specks of gold flickered and flashed, contrasting against those jade irises. He was branding her with his own inner torment. She was sure there'd be bruises in the morning. They would be branded upon her heart, if not flesh.

"Yes, ma chérie. I am the Comte de Paris and you ... you are unworthy of me! Satisfied?"

"Let me go." Her voice was no more than a hushed and shaky whisper, nearly inaudible.

"No," Aleksender roared, "you let me go."

God help him—she would know him as a man. Sofia would know what she claimed to love. His grasp tightened as she squirmed, fighting to break free.

"Please. You ... you are frightening me!"

"Since my nobility forbids you as my comtesse ... care to settle as my mistress?"

"Do you wish me to fear you? To hate you?"

Her words passed through him. Aleksender heard nothing save for his racing heart. He was lost within a desperate haze of pained passion.

"Pray tell, should I take you as my own—here and now in this very stable? Mount you like a primitive beast? No?"

She struggled against his grasp, shamed and humiliated, cheeks reddening to a scarlet. Aleksender chuckled. It was a low, haunting sound that massaged her entire form. A viscous stream of chills shot through her small body. It surged down to the tip of her ballerina toes and back up again.

His hold constricted on her wrists, cutting off her blood flow.

"Come, come. No time for maiden blushes. You cannot fool me. I know you, Sofia, far better than you know yourself. Your body aches for my touches. Even now, you quiver for me. Indeed you fear me just as the common devout fears and submits to his God."

Amused, he snickered as she flinched at his blasphemy.

"But," he contemplated darkly, "one question remains. Before I make you mine forever, do tell ..." Hissed into the tender hollow of her ear, he purred the ugly words, "Should I take you like a harlot?"

"Stop ... stop this."

"Ah, you wouldn't be my first whore, you know." Aleksender pressed the length of his rock-hard body against her, mercilessly grinding, forcing Sofia to endure his prominent desire.

Eyelashes lowered, he murmured a dry afterthought, "Nor would you be my last." His following words impaled her heart. "In fact, had I not saved you that night, I daresay I could be taking you right now."

"You are breaking my heart, Aleksender de Lefèvre." He ignored her detached whisper. "You told me I was not alone. You told me you felt—"

"Lust. Desire. Filled with need."

"You are lying to me. You are lying to yourself."

"I have done things, terrible things ..." His words were a sensual caress. "Things that would make your skin crawl. And I don't mean on the battlefield." His madness was escalating. The sheer force of his vocals radiated from his chest and abdomen, rubbing Sofia's entire body. "Damn you! You look at me! Look—look at what I am!"

"First say you do not love me."

"I do not love you! Insolent child! You hear me, Sofia—I do not love you! No! You are my poison." Her eyes flew open. "I do not love you!"

His tone dropped several octaves—reaching a rich and demonic bass. Sofia scarcely recognized his voice. Her spine stiffened to impossible limits. Her flesh constricted, strangling the ivory of her bones. From head to toe, her body convulsed in a chain of violent shivers. "Never."

Aleksender released her wrists and stepped backward. Sofia winced and spun in place, rotating toward the splintered wall. The moon glowed through the wooden cracks and slight imperfections, bathing Paris beneath a peaceful light. But Sofia only saw darkness. An inescapable and immovable darkness.

Aleksender turned Sofia's slim form within his arms, aligning her to his chest. He collected her wrists and held them tight. They were red, inflamed and severely irritated. His throat sank into his gut.

Dieu. What had he done?

Sofia flinched as he massaged the sore flesh, caressing her skin with gentle circular motions. A powerful combination of sorrow and self-loathing burdened his stare. Muttering a curse, Aleksender pressed his lips against the underside of her wrist. The hiss of damp, cool air was morbidly invigorating. Her nerves stirred at the subtle contact and pulse jumped to life.

"Forgive me. This was never my intention for you ... for us."

"And what was?"

"I don't know." He gathered Sofia in his arms and pulled her against the beat of his chest. "I am lost." His hands caressed her delicate waist, savoring all that was Sofia, inhaling her delicious scent. Roses ... wintertime. "I know I do not love you."

Aleksender leaned forward, crushing Sofia with his body weight, burying her against the wall.

"I do not love you."

His lips crashed against Sofia's in a movement he was utterly unable to control. Both hands broke through the material of her cloak in a jarring whoosh of air, grazing her shoulders with his icy fingertips.

Riding up and over the curve of her hips, speaking into the dewy heat of her mouth, "I do not love you." Rough, weathered hands skimmed over the tender swell of her breasts and worshiped every inch of her beauty. His tongue dueled with her own, drinking Sofia deep, sucking in her spirit. Her kisses were sweet as nectar, dripping with pure seduction and a virginal sensuality. "I do not love you." Aleksender's quivering fingertips tangled within the mass of damp, russet locks. He gave a gentle tug and reeled her closer. "I do not love you."

Both hands swept down the elegant column of her throat and enveloped the thin shaft. Aleksender tenderly cupped her face within his palms. His thumbs stroked her cheeks and drew invisible circles along the slates of porcelain flesh.

Sofia knew he was a broken soul ... more so now than ever before. No, she was not scared. His cruelty was entirely wasted. One look in his eyes had confirmed her every thought. He'd never harm her. Although, for reasons she couldn't fully comprehend, he wanted her to believe otherwise.

But Sofia saw past his rugged façade. And her heart only constricted for his pain. She felt so helpless, so very trapped. How she ached to heal him! She ached to kiss away all of his scars—internal and external, old and new. She ached to rescue him from the blackened depths of despair—just as he'd done, all those nine years ago. No. She could not stop herself. Sofia sighed and slanted her lovely face, deepening their kiss to new limits.

Yes, Sofia's heart screamed, she could heal him. He needed only to open his arms, mind, body—

Aleksender forced himself away. Sofia's eardrums thundered, slamming against her consciousness in a deafening roar. She could hear her own pulse. Her heart swelled to painful proportions, threatening to burst free.

Aleksender and Sofia harmoniously panted as they struggled to catch their breaths. Eyes blinking shut in despair, Aleksender pressed his temple against Sofia's. Nestled within the safety of her arms and speaking for the both of them, he recited the tragic confession. "I cannot love you."

CHAPTER ELEVEN

Hooves clinked against the cobblestone streets as coaches arrived by the dozens. Greeted by the countless footmen, ladies and gentlemen stormed up the grand staircase and entered Salle Le Peletier in an elaborate and eager herd. Excited chatter and warm smiles swelled the air. It was as though the city had never been under siege, as though the alleyways were not stained with blood and littered with bodies of the martyrs. Tonight, the horrors of the last few months existed as nothing more than a distant nightmare. All of Paris had been flung into a state of euphoria. Everyone was simply high on life.

Alas, tonight was no ordinary night. Tonight was the debut of La Sylphide, Marie Taglioni's very own masterpiece.

A team of four strapping horses halted in front of Salle Le Peletier, their magnificent bodies regal against the black of night. Hushed whispers stirred in the air as everyone anchored their attention upon the newest arrival. The de Lefèvre crest was emblazoned across the coach's black lacquered door. The coat of arms was an intricately detailed design, featuring a roaring lion, fleur-de-lis, and white dove. After a breathless moment, the comte and comtesse stepped down from the vehicle, arm in arm, joining the hustle and bustle of high society. The crowd parted like the Red Sea, entranced and charmed, every pair of eyes fixed upon the striking couple.

Indeed—Paris's new comte was devilishly handsome, though his entire demeanor scarred from war. Those emerald eyes were cold, acute and unwelcoming. They brimmed with cynical mirth as he scanned the surrounding faces. In contrast, Elizabeth presented the perfect picture of aristocracy. Silks and satins draped her body as the elegant knot of her coiffure sensually fell across her neck. Two footmen bent into shallow bows as the comte and comtesse passed through the great doors.

Chandeliers soared high above and illuminated the ornate foyer, luminous shafts pouring through their teardrop crystals. Angelic visions of heaven were painted across both the walls and ceiling, each trimmed with gold. Gleaming beneath the intimate lighting, the marble floor reflected everything and everyone.

Aleksender briefly thought of Chateau de Versailles's elaborate entrance and grandiose hall of mirrors.

Outside of the auditorium he came to a halt. Elizabeth stared into his eyes, looking delicate and infinitely lovely in her dark evening gown.

"Elizabeth, why don't you get seated?" With expertly masked hesitation, he continued, "I ought to greet Sofia before the performance. She'll be delighted to know we're in attendance."

Elizabeth gripped onto his forearm with a surprising force. When she spoke, her voice was shaky and unsure, bearing a desperate edge. "But after the performance we can greet her together—all of us! Why, you cannot possibly venture backstage! It simply wouldn't be proper. Sofia is no child."

Aleksender peeled away her fingers and chuckled low. Pressing a kiss to her knuckles, he smoothly murmured, "I'm well aware. No worries. She shall come out to see me."

"Oh. Oh, I see. I suppose I should visit her, too?"

Aleksender shook his head.

"It's far too crowded in the hallway, I'm afraid. And besides—I wager Richard has already arrived. Go on, chérie. Go and get settled into our box. I shall join you shortly."

Elizabeth nodded, a hint of despair knotting her chest. "Bid Sofia well for me."

•

Aleksender stood paralyzed outside of Sofia's dressing room. The prima ballerina's dressing room. A surge of pride and nostalgia flushed through his body. He was truly in awe of her accomplishments.

What, pray, was he doing outside his ward's dressing room? Aleksender cursed himself to the deepest circle of hell. It was no use. He was drawn to Sofia with an irrational attachment. Over the past nine years, she'd become an integral part of himself. He had loved her as his wide-eyed ward, a dear friend and student. It was only within the last few years that his affection had mutated—a phenomenon that had corrupted their bond forever. With a desperate longing, Aleksender ached to perceive her as a child once again. If he could somehow sway his wretched desire, they could be together.

Aleksender knew he should turn away. But first he needed to make things right.

His gloved fist melodically rapped at the door. It wrenched open almost at once, exposing a servant's bright and youthful face.

Helena, Salle Le Peletier's lead chambermaid for several seasons, stepped into the hallway and flexed at her heels. "Oh! Monsieur le Comte! Bonsoir! You are here for Sofia, I should suspect?"

"Please. If she's not too consumed."

"Why, 'course not. She'll be overjoyed to see you! She's presently getting into her costume. But, if you care to wait, I'm sure she can visit with you in a few moments."

Aleksender's chin sank into a curt nod. "Of course."

His pulse surged forward, reaching a breakneck speed. Vats of sweat welled inside his gloves. And yet, to the outside observer, Aleksender knew he was the pretense of flawless composure and self-assurance.

•

With a twirl of her skirts, Helena shut the door, returning to the dressing room and its withdrawn occupant. She'd encountered handfuls of noble figures over her few years of service. And yet nothing could have prepared her for le Comte de Paris. He'd seemed more warrior than a stuffy aristocrat, more beast than man. Overwhelmed by the masculine presence that towered before her, her features had flushed at the very sight of him. He was a powerful and menacing vision, drenched purely in the blackest of black.

Inside the dressing room, Helena was plagued by a haunting combination of awe and sympathy. She eyed Sofia who was calmly seated before the vanity and combing out her hair.

Costumed as La Sylphide's mystical sylph, the opera's enchanting forest spirit, the prima ballerina was beyond ethereal. Airy, white silks hugged the tender curves of her body, the flowing hem scandalously short. An abundance of delicate lace and pearls deco-rated the chaste material, enhancing its angelic charm. The neck-line hung off the shoulders, flaunting the creamy swell of Sofia's breasts. Shimmering wings sprouted from her back. And a wreath, woven from pale pink roses, crowned her dark tresses.

Sofia was unaware of Helena's presence as she stared at her reflection. In fact, she seemed to be unaware of everything. Her blue eyes vacantly gazed forward, searching the smooth glass, struggling to find some lost part of her soul within the mirror … within herself. Weighed down with a distinct despair and sadness, the fairy wings appeared to wilt. Sofia was tragically in character, resembling the ideal star-crossed lover.

"Mademoiselle," Helena said, approaching the mahogany van-ity, "you've a visitor."

"A visitor?"

"Monsieur le Comte—that is, your foster father—wishes to greet you before the performance! Isn't that grand?"

The brush tumbled into Sofia's lap as her grip faltered. She stammered, breathless and wide-eyed. Her porcelain complexion turned unnaturally pale and borderline sallow. "Alek is not my fos-ter father, Helena. You know that."

In spite of herself, Helena blushed, flustered by the sound of the man's Christian name. Then she flustered once more—feeling wildly uncomfortable with Sofia's strange reaction.

"Course he's not. Do forgive me. I mean to say, your Alek wishes to greet you."

Sofia's chest vibrated with an evident shudder. Her eyes squeezed shut. A mass of curls flowed down and over her shoul-ders as she dropped her chin.

"Oh! You poor dear," Helena cried. "Are you feeling quite all right?" She stood behind Sofia and gently grazed her shoulder. So-fia glanced up at Helena, wearing a smile that didn't reach her eyes. No sound came forth when she attempted to speak.

"Why, you look positively ill!" Helena softened her tone to a whisper, mistaking Sofia's muddled appearance for stirring nerves. "Shall I send him away, mademoiselle? I'm sure he'll understand—tonight being La Sylphide's debut and such."

"Oh, no, Helena. That won't be necessary," Sofia breathed. "Of course I shall see him."

◆

Aleksender awaited Sofia in suspenseful anticipation. He leaned against the archway and loosened the cravat from his throat. Damn societal Paris and its conventions. The wretched thing had been strangling him like a Punjab lasso.

Illuminated by rows of glittering sconce lanterns, the hallway was slim and sensually cozy. Such a place was an ideal hideout for an intimate rendezvous between two lovers. And the frolicking couple, which lurked only feet from Aleksender, vividly confirmed his assumption.

A buxom, raven-haired temptress was pressed up against the wall, her coiffure wildly disheveled and reckless. Her voluptuous body was wedged between wood and flesh, quivering within the arms of her lover. And the plunging neckline of her gown left very little to her suitor's prowling hands and imagination. As Aleksender turned away a deep, wildly feminine moan echoed the hallway.

The air thickened. Aleksender's head spun out of control. Fate had failed him once again. The pale and bejeweled hand of his former mistress was tugging at his shoulder.

He rotated on his booted heel and stood face to face with the lovely Joanna Rosalina. As always, she appeared remarkably exquisite, lavished in Paris's finest fashion and glowing with a raw sensuality that equaled his own.

"Ah, so it is you!" Joanna's dark gaze provocatively examined him from head to toe. "Yes. Yes, it is, indeed." She drank in the tanned flesh at his throat and exhaled an appreciative sigh. Stepping closer, her well-endowed bosom brushed up against his chest in a tease. Fully aroused nipples grated his upper body, battling their velvet confines. Unwanted and regretted memories paralyzed Aleksender, flooding his mind in a gloomy haze—torrid memories of heated nights, whispered demands and dripping, tangled limbs.

"Delicious, as always," she praised, speaking through a tone which was designed to drive men mad with desire. And, years ago, her voice would have done just that. Such a voice would have worked wonders upon Aleksender's mind and body. Joanna had brought him to his knees, and far more than once.

Running fingertips down his torso, she breathed in a husky voice, "I see war agrees with you, my golden Apollo."

I see war agrees with you.

Those words infuriated Aleksender. Blood-lust pumped through his veins and hardened his bones. Both hands clenched into deadly fists—lest he submit to his desire and strangle the vixen. Seething, he glared down at her wanton caresses. He couldn't recall a time when he'd been more fit to kill. In the same breath, the absolute shallowness of his former lifestyle was brought to light. No, he was no longer in awe of Joanna's exotic beauty. Instead, Aleksender only saw himself—the heartless, crude shell of a human being.

"Don't reckon with me, Joanna." His green irises flickered. "Don't reckon with the devil."

Vixen that she was, Joanna Rosalina misinterpreted his threat. "Aw, fret not. Do you really think me so very cruel? Why, I don't intend to tease." Her hand traveled over the front of his trousers and cupped his groin within a clenched palm. "Oh, Aleksender. I'm terribly, terribly wet for you." She massaged the hidden bulge of flesh, eyes overflowing with wicked intentions and intense promises. "In fact, I've been wet for you for a year now."

Aleksender grasped onto Joanna's hair—handling her as if she were nothing more than a bitch in heat. She yelped in pain and stifled a vile curse. Her bosom madly heaved, busting from the sweeping bodice in absurd proportions. A few more breaths and the seams would surely give way.

Both eyes narrowed into cunning slits. She was a viper ready to strike. "How dare you, you vile knave!" she hissed. "Why, I ought—"

"Ah, chérie, to shame." Aleksender dryly stated, gesturing her neglected suitor with a nonchalant wave. "You seem to have forgotten your good Christian etiquette."

The young man in question adjusted his cravat and smoothed down unkempt hair, cheeks flaming. He made a bumbling exit and muttered something vile beneath his breath.

Joanna sobered and returned to her flirtatious nature. A sly grin stretched her lips from ear to ear, racy and decadent. "Now, now, Aleksender," she playfully scolded, fingers meddling with the dangling cravat. "You shan't be jealous. If you're feeling jilted ..." She leaned into his heat, eyes never leaving his. "Well, I am more than willing to compensate for my wandering eye. How 'bout I share you with one of my girlfriends? Hmm? As I recall, last time there was plenty of you to go around."

The husky accent of Joanna's voice dissolved into silence.

The semblance of a smile curved her lips as she glared over Aleksender's shoulder. "My, my, what have we here? A dazzling, little forest nymph?"

Indeed, his scandalous ways were widely known through Paris. All of France knew precisely who and what he was. And Aleksender had never cared a thing for his reputation—instead, he'd always enjoyed his fiery liaisons and exploitations with a cynical sort of satisfaction. In the carriage house, he'd tried to unveil his inner demons to Sofia. And now the very thought of Sofia witnessing the truth of his character was unbearable. Aleksender could have wept with the shame of a lad who'd been caught with his hand shoved in the cookie jar. Aleksender slowly rotated his body, overcome with a wave of nausea.

His mouth instantly went dry. Joanna ... the opera ... Elizabeth and his brother—his ability to draw a coherent sentence—everything—faded away.

Sofia was breathtaking. His eyes drew to her lush bosom, behaving on their own accord. Mon Dieu. Indeed, between the shimmering fairy wings and plunging neckline, the costume was a paradoxical blend of scandalous innocence. The urge to fondle her creamy skin—to cup those magnificent breasts within his palms, to feel the weight of her derriere pressed in his clenched hands, to wind all ten fingers through her private curls, to join their bodies in the most primitive of ways—was almost too much to bear.

Sofia's widened eyes sobered Aleksender, anchoring his senses.

Why? Why was he doing this?

Jealously was the very least of Sofia's feelings. Such a thing was far too petty of an emotion. How could he be so cruel? So heartless? Was this just another way to illustrate his ruined soul? Another method to drive her away? Was his outburst in the carriage house not enough?

"Alek!" Joanna piped, arms knotted over her breasts, nerves growing visibly restless. "Why, your daughter is even more adorable than you had described her to be!" Joanna gushed in her most condescending tone. Sensually stroking the rise of his shoulder, she melodically chimed, "To shame! Where have your manners gone to? Aren't you going to introduce us?" Joanna gasped as Aleksender spun round in a harsh and unexpected movement. His eyes were cold, ruthless and unfeeling. In spite of herself, early stirrings of fear bloomed inside Joanna.

"Leave us." The deep baritone of his voice filled the slim hallway. Joanna stubbornly knotted her slender arms and gave an adorable pout. "Leave us now, or, on my father's grave, I shall make you sorry for ever crossing me."

Joanna coiled a rather possessive hand around Aleksender's neck and brought her lips against the rim of his ear. "You may play the 'good and chaste comte' to your heart's content. But, at the end of the day, you and I both know who and what you really are. A hungry wolf in sheep's clothing. Nothing more, nothing less."

Those words troubled Aleksender more than Joanna could ever know.

Joanna took a delicate step back and bowed her head. "It was a pleasure. I must say you are positively charming. Quite unfortunate that your foster father here insists on cutting our meeting short. Perhaps you can pound some sense into him. Lord only knows, I have ..."

With a last smile, Joanna strutted down the corridor and out of eyesight. Aleksender watched the vile creature vanish with a burning hatred inside his veins.

"Sofia, I—" The words came too late. Aleksender's voice was absorbed by Salle Le Peletier's rosewood door.

•

Dangling beneath a swirl of clouds and paisley blue, the grand chandelier shined like the sun. It was twenty minutes into the second act when a colorful swarm of ballerinas skirted across the wide stage. Each dancer appeared more poised than the last, and the collective ensemble was a breathtaking vision to behold. A soothing and mystical melody swelled the rafters to their limit.

All of Salle Le Peletier was entranced. Eager to get a closer peek, ladies leaned over the railings of their boxes and balanced whispering fans between fingertips. Nodding in appreciation, gentlemen filled their lungs with smoke, juggling cigars and spectacles by turns.

Richard glanced over his shoulder at the sounds of creaking wood and footfall. Aleksender inclined his head as he entered box two and nodded his greeting. Nothing had changed. The tension from their luncheon still weighed heavily in the air. Neither Aleksender nor Richard dared to utter a word for several moments.

Elizabeth also remained static and soundless, both eyes fixed on the spectacle below. A delicate, lace fan was sprawled across the cushion of her lap, entirely disregarded.

"You nearly missed her variation," Richard muttered beneath a hushed breath, cautious not to disturb Elizabeth. "What in God's teeth kept you so long?"

"Nothing," Aleksender replied as he claimed a seat between his brother and wife.

"Nothing?"

"Business affair in the parlor." As if assessing his alibi, Elizabeth stole a glance of Aleksender from her peripheral vision.

"Ah." Richard gave a curt nod and flashed a pristine smile. "Very well, then." He crossed both legs knee-high and leaned into Aleksender after a brief silence. "Speaking of propositions," Richard drawled into Aleksender's ear, his words nearly inaudible, "Mademoiselle Rosalina made me a rather indecent offer not one hour ago. I was searching for you in the parlor when she approached me."

"Cunning whore."

Elizabeth's head snapped up, alert to the direction of her husband's curse.

"Yes. Yes … I must say—I share in your sentiment."

Richard gazed at Elizabeth and admired the delicate silhouette of her profile. His heart ached at the vision. He never could understand Aleksender's rakish ways nor his fascination with creatures such as Joanna, and his brother's sudden disdain for the wretched woman was less than satisfying.

Surely, there would be another mistress to fill her shoes.

As for Elizabeth, her pain was palpable. Painfully so. Could Aleksender not feel it? Was he truly so blinded?

What emptiness, Richard secretly pondered, was Aleksender attempting to fill?

Without warning, the stage cleared and darkened for the second act variation. A collective hush swept over Salle Le Peletier as the prima ballerina claimed centerstage. The spotlight illuminated Sofia's limbs, drenching her beneath an immaculate shawl of gold.

A distinct sadness radiated from each of her movements. Aleksender's body visibly tensed. Each hand gripped onto the armrest with the force of a manacle. Unblinking, he leaned slightly forward, eyes never parting from Sofia.

Richard shook his head, seeing nothing but his own tangle of inner thoughts.

He would have given everything for Elizabeth's love.

CHAPTER TWELVE

The streets hollowed out as the ladies and gentlemen steadily retired to their homes. Silence descended and Paris was returned to her sedentary state once more. Cloaked beneath the fall of night, Aleksender paced outside of Salle Le Peletier's backstage exit.

He couldn't part from Sofia on these terms. During the third act climax, just before the sylph's wings had crumbled and fallen away, Aleksender had muttered a pitiful excuse and prematurely departed. "Elizabeth ... forgive me. I must wrap up a business affair in the parlor," he'd stupidly offered. The devastation, the utter heartache that had radiated from Sofia's performance, would haunt him forever.

Salle Le Peletier's ancient wooden door swung open to reveal his ward in all her loveliness. No longer the sultry fairy of an hour ago, she was dressed conservatively once again. An abundance of curls was tied back in an elegant knot, a dark cloak wrapped her body, and both cheeks were rosy from hours of exertion. Aleksender thought she'd never looked more beautiful than in that moment. Roses and wintertime flooded his senses as she whisked by.

Distracted and unaware of his voyeuristic presence, Sofia took no notice of Aleksender. Trembling within the bitter cold, eager to free herself from thoughts of *him*, she tightened the cloak about her body and rushed down the five cobblestone steps.

She did not get far.

By the second step, she knew she was far from alone. By the third step, she heard the muttered whisper of a cloak. By the fourth step, a masculine figure emerged from the shadows. The lean frame of his body blocked her pathway with ease. Sofia tilted her head as her eyes ran down the man's form. The pounding of her heart returned to its normal pace. He was a complete stranger.

A top hat crowned his head, the fine material cushioned by a bountiful swarm of blonde curls, the burgundy smoking jacket striking in the night. Sparkling, green eyes bore deep into her own. The bulge of his Adam's apple bobbed about like a buoy at sea as he swallowed.

Sofia cleared her throat and arched her fine brow. "Pardon me, monsieur."

"Oh! Do forgive me," he squeaked, awakening from some trance. Graceless and pitifully awkward, he removed the hat, curled it against his chest, and dipped into a slight bow. When he finally spoke, he stumbled over his words, sounding far more boy than man, eyes glowing with star-struck awe. "Mademoiselle Rose, I am quite possibly your greatest admirer."

"I'm flattered," Sofia said with a smile, complete sincerity in her voice.

"If I may say, I watch you as often as I can. Never could quite find the courage to make an introduction. But, after tonight ..." He inhaled a long sigh and boldly inched closer to Salle Le Peletier's prima ballerina. "Tonight, I knew I had to meet you. I would have never forgiven myself. I confess—your performance sent me to tears."

"Thank you, monsieur. You are most kind." Wearing a smile that could only be relief, he took Sofia's hand in his own and guided her down the fifth and final step.

"I am Manuel. Manuel Dumont." A new confidence empowered his voice. Manuel shuffled both feet as his fingers curled around the rim of his top hat, absently bending the luxurious velvet. "I was hoping, that is, if I may ..."

Sofia smiled reassuringly, well aware of what he was about to inquire. It was charming. The young man's declaration warmed her heart and temporarily lifted her from the prison of her thoughts. And no matter how fleeting, such freedom was a beautiful thing.

"Yes?"

"Mademoiselle," he firmly proclaimed, the pale hue of his complexion reddening impossibly more. "Might I call on you sometime?"

"No."

The single syllable resonated. Uttered from beneath a low, slick bass, it seethed with an authority that dared to be tested. Manuel merely rolled back his shoulders—perhaps in an attempt to gain an inch or two—and fumbled toward the lurking shadow. "Now, look here, monsieur—"

Sofia grasped onto his forearm and vainly struggled to lure him back at her side. It was no use. "Please, no—I beg you to forget him."

"Leave us," growled the disembodied voice, "now."

Manuel straightened out his lapels and extended a pointer finger. As if compensating for some other deficiency, he angled his chin ridiculously high. "Say, I don't know what you're about, monsieur, but your interference is quite uncalled!"

Reluctant admiration welled inside Aleksender's gut as the young man refused to back down and stupidly shuffled forward. Such valiancy would have made any mother proud.

"You speak big words for a little boy." Aleksender's shoulders quavered with dark humor.

Sofia wedged between the two males, movements uncharacteristically clumsy, as she attempted to erect a flesh and blood barricade. Aleksender's erratic breaths misted the air, shrouding him in a fierce cloud. "Alek—please. Just stop this."

Aleksender latched onto Sofia's slender arm and moved her aside.

"Now, listen here, monsieur!" The boy took a moment to secure his top hat, lest it tumble into the gutter. "Unhand the good lady or I shall inform the gendarmes!"

Pure, impenetrable silence.

Then Aleksender surprised the both of them and did the unexpected. He laughed. Alas—he tossed his head back and roared out his amusement, stabilizing himself with the banister. He laughed till tears blurred his vision, and then he laughed some more.

"You are a monster." Sofia's whisper sobered Aleksender, anchoring him back into the moment. He brushed away his mirthful tears and inched over to the youth.

"Insolent, stupid, child."

Manuel eased backward, one of Aleksender's steps matching three of his own, skirting away like some unfortunate hermit crab—a poor hermit crab who was about to be boiled and poached—immediately regretting his gallant show of chivalry.

"Why, did you not hear? Nearly a fortnight ago a whore was

gutted and thrown into the Seine without your gendarmes so much as blinking an eye."

"What? No. I—I was unaware—"

"Please. By all means—go inform them. Inform them that the noble comte is about to take Paris's precious ballerina against a wall."

"How dare you!" Exasperated and pushed beyond her limit, Sofia held nothing back and full-on attacked Aleksender. Two tightly wound fists plummeted into his chest, one after the other—

"Are you quite through with your tantrum?"

Sofia fought to catch her breath and reclaim the slightest sliver of composure. She was far too angry to form a coherent sentence.

"And you," Aleksender said, continuing to advance on the boy. "Where's your bravado gone to so suddenly? Shall I take it you are through making a fool of yourself?"

Sofia grabbed hold of Aleksender's cloak and twisted the wool between her fingertips. A pinnacle of emotions ignited her soul. "Stop! You hear me, Alek! Stop it now! Stop this, or I shall never forgive you for your cruelty."

One step later and the youth found himself pinned up against the stairwell. The comte's final worlds were nearly a whisper, making them all the more ominous. "Go. Go inform the gendarmes. Better yet, go inform the entire military of Versailles. Inform them and see if they give a damn." Aleksender latched onto the scruff of Manuel's shirt and hurled the boy onto the ground like a pup. He slammed into the cobblestones face first. A ring of blood blossomed, encircling his left knee and sullying the trousers' fine material. "Now get the hell out of my sight."

Sofia sank beside Manuel and draped a hand over the curve of his shoulder. The rugged broad cloth was ruffled and severely torn beneath her fingertips. Sofia took a breath and counted to ten.

God above, she'd never been angrier.

"God, I am so sorry for this. Are you badly hurt?"

"I'll survive." Retaining as much dignity as he could possibly muster, Manuel picked himself off the ground, collected the prized top hat, and smoothed out his smoking jacket. He swiped away a stream of blood with his cufflink. "You, mademoiselle—you will be all right?"

This—this—was the sort of man who was worthy of her love.

Kind, patient and gentle.

"Mademoiselle?"

Still seated, Sofia glared at Aleksender and answered Manuel's inquiry. "Yes. I'll survive."

"Very well." Manuel was swallowed up by the shadows as he departed, each of his steps leaving Aleksender and Sofia a little more isolated.

Aleksender outstretched a hand after a moment of stillness, offering Sofia his aid. The stale gesture only irritated her further. Aleksender—a gentleman? She scoffed at the very notion. He was far from gentle! And much more monster than man. "No," she spat, shoving a swarm of loose tendrils from her eyes, "I need nothing from you."

She rose to her feet and stepped dangerously close to him. Their breaths consummated in a duel of swirling clouds.

Aleksender reached out for her cheek only to have his hand whacked away. "Do not touch me. Don't! Don't you dare touch me!"

"Sofia—"

"You have no right! I am not ten years-old any longer! And I'm most certainly not some shiny toy, some porcelain doll, which you can play with at your leisure whenever the time happens to suit you best."

Aleksender speared his fingertips through his hairline before attempting a reply. "I'm sorry. I didn't intend for Joanna to be there. I only wanted to speak with you."

"You have done more than spoken. Now, I ought to be on my way. Do pardon me—" Aleksender blocked her body with his own, preventing any escape.

"I have tried to shelter you, God, I have tried to shelter you from everything, from myself. I—"

"Perhaps, I don't wish to be sheltered! I tire of you elevating me onto this pedestal!" Aleksender stared at Sofia as if she was speaking in a foreign tongue. "I am sorry if this kills you to hear, but I am not the delicate, little Sofia that you fantasize me to be. I am not a butterfly whose wings will crumple and fall at the slightest touch."

"He wanted you in his bed," Aleksender growled. "Damn it to hell if I would allow such a thing."

"That is hardly your concern. You have no special claim on me. I am not yours to command. And besides, not all men are after the same thing." The words were a painful jab and devastating for Aleksender to stomach.

"Ah," was his cool reply—the figurative mask securely in place. His body slinked forward till their chests rubbed together. "But you are. Have you forgotten? I am your guardian and you my ward."

"No. You know what you are? Jealous!" A long silence followed after. Sofia shook her head and inhaled a strained breath. "You are hurting me, Alek. I can only bear so much. Being around you. Seeing your face. Hearing your voice. I care for you. I care for you more than anything. But I can only endure so much." The last of Sofia's words died on her tongue. "As you said, things have changed between us. And you ..." She took a step forward, voice lowering to a compassionate whisper. The heat of her breath fanned against his cheek. "I know you. You are better than this."

Aleksender gazed deeply into her eyes, entranced and unable to turn away.

"What you'd said about Versailles—that was the first time you've mentioned the war since your return."

"Some things are best left forgotten."

"Forgotten? How—"

"I try to remember the war as a distant nightmare."

Sofia's fury equaled her pity, and her love overshadowed her hatred. She clasped onto one of his hands and brought it up to her cheek. He'd begun to tremble. "You cannot do that to yourself. You cannot shut out the world. It will only destroy you from the inside out."

"You think I don't know that?"

The timbre of his voice dripped with pure mirth. She flinched as Aleksender snapped his hand away, his emerald eyes blazing.

As if overcome with sudden agony, Aleksender stepped backward, swept a hand through his hair, and cleared his throat. "It grows late. They shall wonder where I am. And you'll be expected back. I—"

His eyes said everything.

"Come—come with me."

Aleksender shot her a questioning look.

"Please?" Sofia smiled, took hold of his gloved hand and ascended the stairs. The wood creaked beneath the soles of her feet, echoing in the night. A stream of light split the black as the door creaked open. "I want to show you something."

•

All of Aleksender's worries momentarily fell away as he ventured through the theater's widely spread wings. The hustle and bustle was strangely intoxicating and, even more, wonderfully distracting.

Beyond the stone walls and bleak alleyways, Salle Le Peletier was alive with activity. Countless stagehands, carpenters, riggers, seamstresses and maids buzzed about, sharing stories and laughs as they labored. Voluptuous furls of steam rose into the air, spewing like the breaths of a fairytale dragon. Men whistled in harmony and drained their beer bottles. A flock of spinsters delighted in the latest scandals, cackling amongst one another with the audacity of hens. Towering, faux trees were wheeled aside as La Sylphide's forest gradually transformed back into that of a plain stage.

But there was nothing plain about Salle Le Peletier.

Smiling wide and shouting greetings here, there, and everywhere, Sofia appeared to be entirely in her element. Every so often a crew member would call out to her and offer his congratulations. Indeed—for all the attention Aleksender was paid, he might have been a ghost rather than the noble comte. And he could not have been more satisfied with such treatment.

Many single-stemmed roses were strewn about, carpeting the brandished floorboards in a colorful array, each one representing a patron's adoration. In light of the prima ballerina's stage name, roses had predictably become the most common token of gratitude over the last season.

Sofia knelt to the ground and fetched several of the fallen flowers, tucking them inside her cloak. Aleksender leaned against one of the wooden columns and threw her a curious sideways glance. "Don't mind me." She blushed a shade of scarlet that rivaled many of the roses. "See, I like to collect them after performances. They make lovely bouquets and just smell beautifully."

"I wouldn't have ever guessed," Aleksender wryly stated as the surrounding aroma overwhelmed his senses. Sofia came to her feet, edged onto her tiptoes, and tucked a yellow rose behind Aleksender's left ear. The brilliant hue was magnificent against the deep black of his hair.

"How very dashing you look!"

"Glad you think so, chérie." Aleksender harnessed back a grin, removed the rose, and tucked it within his coat for safekeeping.

Salle Le Peletier's cheerful nature disappeared in the following silence. The commotion of the theater finalized for the evening as the men and women each took their leaves. One by one, the gas sconce lanterns winked into darkness, footsteps faded, and quiet descended. An eerie calm washed over Salle Le Peletier as only a few lights and laborers remained for the night.

Body heat radiated all around as Aleksender stepped intimately near to Sofia. He bowed his face and allowed his breath to waft across her cheek. "Sofia," he murmured in a low tone, "tell me— why are we back here? Where are you taking us?"

"No questions." Warmth surged through her veins like a wildfire. She ignored his inquiry, pushed past his body, and continued to stroll about. "See, I've made it a bit of a habit, gathering flowers after the curtain call. I do admit I've managed to earn the nickname 'flower girl,'" she said with a faint blush. Losing herself in a wilderness of ghostly props and shadows, Sofia inched deeper backstage and signaled him to follow. A wooden stairwell lined the furthest wall, its slim frame ascending into pure blackness. The thing looked dangerously flimsy and anything but dependable. Sofia slowly turned to Aleksender. She offered her hand and an achingly sweet smile.

He took two generous steps back. A flash of pain creased his brow. Only two people knew of his fear of heights. Sofia was one of them and the other was dead. "You know I cannot."

"Of course you can."

Aleksender glanced up and stared into the dark void. The black seemed to go on forever. "The roof," he breathed. "You mean to take us to the rooftop?"

Sofia lightly placed a hand on his forearm and gave a gentle squeeze. "Please, Alek. Just trust me."

And so they ascended the winding stairwell, climbing higher and higher, soon reaching the rafters, catwalks, elevated platforms, endless flies and wooden beams. On either side of them the massive curtain was securely tucked in for the night, the heavy drapes mimicking a pair of colossal, scarlet wings. Aleksender and Sofia continued to venture upward as the combined weight of their bodies shook the opera house from its nightly slumber. Aleksender felt seasick as the stairwell swayed back and forth, the ancient car-pentry manipulated by the slightest of movements. Low moans, groans, grumbles and creaks resounded with each step they took. The building seemed to possess a life of its very own, and it was an angry beast waking from a long hibernation.

"Can you hear it?" Sofia drew to a halt nearly thirty feet up. "The theater—" she exclaimed, imaginative as ever. "She is speaking to us."

"Is she now?"

Aleksender glanced down and came close to losing his breath. Beneath his heels, the theater was clearly visible through the wood-en cracks. A million miles away, it glowed softly and surely beneath them. And they were not getting any closer. There was no turning back. For better or for worse, wherever this twisted pathway may lead, there was nowhere to go but onward.

Sofia and Aleksender continued their endless ascent in silence, with only the theater's laminations for company. Every few steps, she glanced over her shoulder and offered Aleksender a reassuring smile. The small gesture empowered him far more than he dared admit.

"Almost there," Sofia said as their destination finally slipped into view.

CHAPTER THIRTEEN

Salle Le Peletier's rooftop was the ultimate hideaway and sanctuary. The frail lights of Paris winked against the horizon, peppered amongst a sea of inky black and shining like constellations. Aleksender and Sofia breathed in the crisp, spring air and wandered near to the rooftop's edge.

Aleksender gazed down at the quiet streets below without hesitation. His fear of heights had miraculously melted away. On this night, within this moment, he felt empowered and invincible. The nightmares, Christophe's disdain, the war, his father's death—they all faded away. Placed high from society's reach, he and Sofia were perfectly alone, yet far from lonely.

And so Aleksender was in no way surprised when Sofia murmured, "I often come up here when I need to clear my thoughts. And sometimes, if I close my eyes and concentrate hard enough, I feel as though I'm on top of the entire world."

He stood beside Sofia, taking delight in the serene smile that had claimed her lips. Moonlight danced across the material of her cloak, brightening the dark hue to various shades of gray.

A gust of wind swept away her hood and sent an abundance of auburn curls flowing behind her. In the same breath, the breeze parted Aleksender's dress shirt and exposed one of many scars. Jarred by the sight, a faint gasp emerged from Sofia's lips. She turned to Aleksender, aligning her body with his own, and carefully traced the slight indention with an index finger.

When she at last spoke, her voice was soft, serene and overflowing with compassion. "They say the Prussians captured Napoleon's entire army at Sedan—seventeen thousand men died on that battle, and those who survived were taken as prisoners. Only after the siege were they to be returned home."

Aleksender swallowed. He nodded and returned his stare to the night sky. High above, Orion floated against the endless horizon, ready to ward off all evils, his bow drawn into a taut arch.

"You were there. You were at Sedan." Sofia reached for Aleksender's face and gently cradled his cheeks. Day-old stubble pierced her palms as the tips of her fingers drew invisible circles along his weathered skin. She followed the stubborn curve of his chin, caressed each cheek, brushed the forelock from his eyes. "You were a prisoner of the war."

Aleksender considered her words for a moment. "We were all prisoners of the war. And none of us have yet to be freed."

Sofia's hands slid away and fell despairingly to her sides. She withdrew a scarlet ribbon from her cloak and thoughtfully meddled with the fabric. She wound it about her fingertips till they grew white from a lack of circulation. She was visibly wrestling with herself—aching to comfort Aleksender, but unsure of how to approach such a delicate issue. Finally, she eased into conservation by reducing the matter to small talk. "Tell me. What was it like? At the war?"

Aleksender shook his head in silent contemplation. A shiver coursed through his body as both eyes squeezed shut, remembering ... reliving. "Lonely. Long. Not much to be said."

Sofia tucked the ribbon back into her cloak. She aligned their bodies and ran her fingertips down the length of Aleksender's torso, deftly brushing the folds of his cloak aside. She paused on top of the dress shirt's golden claps. Their gazes came together. She questioned him with her eyes. His face dipped into a subtle nod. Swallowing, she deftly unfastened the row of buttons. Aleksender's breath hitched. The beat of his heart thundered beneath her fingertips. Each snap sounded unnaturally loud within the quiet din.

She peeled the material aside, exposing a slate of sculpted muscles. Spanning from neck to abdomen, every inch of Aleksender was peppered with black hair and reeking of masculinity. And, as she'd expected, faint scars wove in and out his flesh. Unshed tears clouded Sofia's vision. She covered the middle of his chest with her palm.

The simple gesture was beyond beautiful—beyond moving. Aleksender felt something open up inside his heart.

As if reading his thoughts, she tentatively murmured, "Let me in. Let me take some of your pain. You don't have to be alone, don't have to be lonely. Let me help you heal." A gentle smile curled her lips. "Let me be there for you as you have been there for me all these years. Please, Alek, just free yourself."

Aleksender stepped intimately near to Sofia. Lost in her closeness, he curved his hand and gently stroked the side of her face. A wisp of air escaped from her lips as she dipped into his touch. Aleksender felt his heart skip several beats. He removed both gloves and set them atop the stone banister. Free from barriers, he touched Sofia once more, allowing his callused skin to slide across the smooth surface of her flesh. His fingertips trembled in time with his racing heart.

Sofia swallowed, eyes sparkling with deep emotion. "Alek ..." She cocked her head back the slightest bit, causing their lips to align. They shared the same intakes of air, mouths mere inches apart.

Dipping into a bow, Aleksender surprised Sofia and outstretched his hand. "Care to dance, mademoiselle?"

With a defiant pout, she folded both arms over her chest. "Dance? Why, I thought you had no desire to do such a thing," she teased, referring to their tender evening at Voisin.

Tension furrowed Aleksender's brow. He swallowed and hung his face in despair. "I had my reasons for distancing myself."

"And now?" Sofia finally gripped onto his hand, eyes never parting from his steady gaze.

"Now I'm afraid I could never have it any other way."

Without another word, Sofia smiled and stepped onto his toes, wrapping Aleksender within her embrace. He swayed back and forth, to and fro, carrying her body in sync with his own. Smooth baritone spilled from his lips as he sang into Sofia's ear. Her heart grew heavy with nostalgia and warm memories; it was the precise lullaby he'd often sing when she was a child:

"Sleep, my child, peace attends thee ...
All through the night, Guardian angels God send thee ...
All through the night, while the weary world is weeping ...
Love, to thee my thoughts are turning ...
All through the night, though a sad fate our lives may sever, our

parting shall not last forever ...
There's a hope that leaves me never ... all through the night ..."

Everything fell into place as they held each other beneath the eternal sky. Sofia dropped her chin a few inches, leveling her lips with the arch of Aleksender's chin. She pressed a kiss against the rugged flesh, then rose a centimeter and kissed the corner of his mouth, his cheek—one and then the other.

A tortured groan emerged from Aleksender's throat. Their lips crashed together in a movement neither of them was able to control. Sofia grasped onto Aleksender's shoulders as her nails dug into the muscles that sculpted his forearm. He slanted his face and deepened their kiss to impossible limits, drinking in her very spirit.

And then it all ended.

Aleksender pulled back, breathless, head spinning. He deftly lifted Sofia off his feet and raked a hand through his hairline. "Damn myself. I'm sorry. Wasn't thinking. Again." Face sunken, he spun on his heels and gripped the banister. Frustration and a potent self-loathing pumped through his veins. The cold stone was coarse beneath his fingertips—a powerful contradiction to Sofia's warmth and delicate beauty. He steadied his body weight with his palms and glanced at the stars.

Roses and wintertime whispered against Aleksender's back. Sofia joined him at the railing and folded both hands atop the stonework. She pointed at the sky, gesturing the brightest star to be found. When she spoke, her voice was soothing and wonderfully calm. "Many think that Venus is just another star. But she's so much more than that."

Aleksender finally managed to catch his breath. Finding comfort in her peace, he gazed at Sofia's serene expression. "I see. And who is she?"

"Why, the goddess of love and beauty, of course."

Aleksender had known the story longer than Sofia had been alive. Regardless, he feigned a look of surprise. Sofia played along in turn, her consciousness fading into fantasy. Within her mind's eye, she was sprawled before a hearth and relaxing in the arms of her guardian's voice.

"There was only one more exquisite than Venus. Her name was Psyche and she was a mere mortal ... earthbound. Throughout the land she was revered for her beauty. Forgotten by the people, Venus's temples quickly fell to ruin. Jealously twisted her soul and warped it into something monstrous." Aleksender leaned against the banister and studied Sofia's bright and beaming face. It had come to life with her storytelling. "So, she called upon the services of her son Eros, the God of Love. Venus ordered that he strike a monster with one of his golden arrows and sentence a demon to fall in love with Psyche. But even Eros was swept by her beauty. He'd often gaze upon Psyche from afar knowing they were from different worlds, knowing they could never be together."

Sofia brushed the voluptuous material of her skirts aside and knelt to the ground. She patted the empty space beside her, gesturing Aleksender to take a seat. He obeyed. An aura of warmth swept over Sofia. His nearness stirred all five of her senses to life.

"Where was I? Oh, yes—amidst Eros's infatuation, one of the arrows fell forward and pierced his heart. Panicked, he soared back to his home. Time passed and Psyche was still immaculately beautiful, still praised by everyone. Burning with vengeance, Venus stranded Psyche on top of Mount Olympus, waiting for either a demon or Death to claim the poor girl. But Eros spotted Psyche from the skies. Cloaked in the dark of night, he took her into his wings flying her into the heavens—"

Sofia paused as Aleksender stripped away his cloak. Each movement sent muscles straining against the material of his dress shirt. Claiming a seat, he smoothed out the wool and arranged it across the cold flooring.

"Do continue, ma chérie," he said, ushering Sofia down onto the makeshift blanket. "You have me quite intrigued."

Heart banging against her ribs, Sofia scooted close to his body. Tension flared like a tangible force. Moonlight caressed the raven locks of Aleksender's hair with enchanting highlights.

"Eros and Psyche soon wed. But he would visit her only in the darkest nights. She pleaded that he reveal his identity. Psyche was with child and longed to know her husband more than ever before. But he sadly shook his head and explained how 'his home was her home, and that he loved her dearly.' See, if she were to look upon him before their child was born, the baby would grow to be mortal. Within the darkness, Psyche came to be very lonely."

Sofia's storytelling stalled to a halt. A sigh fled her lips as she reclined on Aleksender's cloak. Head cradled in his lap, she stared at the immeasurable night sky. A mild breeze swam through her hair and tossed flurries of curls against her cheeks. Fingertips lingering against her flesh, Aleksender deftly tucked them behind each ear. Sofia swallowed and gazed into the haunted depths of his eyes.

"Psyche was lonely, you say?"

"Yes, she loved her husband, but missed her mortal sisters terribly. Eros took pity on his wife and allowed them to visit one evening. They grew jealous of their beautiful sister—jealous of her wealth and her heavenly home, her husband. They formed a plot, finding a way to take Psyche's lover and fortune as their own. They warned that she was in great danger and needed to know her husband's identity, that he must be a demon—having come only in the night and never showing himself. And if he was indeed a demon, Psyche must kill him before he killed their babe."

"Ah. That's women for you." Sofia balled a hand into a fist, reached behind herself, and blindly socked Aleksender's torso. He caught her wrist in a suave motion. Before lowering it to the ground, he awarded her flesh with a small kiss.

Sofia continued the story with a laugh. "Terrified, Psyche decided to act on the advice of her sisters. One night, Eros slept, spent from their love. Psyche lit an oil lamp, knife in hand. She was determined to know the truth—prepared to plunge the knife deep into her lover's sleeping chest. But what she saw wasn't a horrifying demon. No. It was a beautiful young man, donning wings of gold."

Aleksender absently ran his fingertips through her curls and sifted the fine silk with reverence.

"Taken by the immaculate sight, Psyche forgot about the lamp and spilled oil onto Eros's shoulder. He woke in pain. Saw his wife had betrayed him. The God of Love left Psyche. She was heartbroken. Having learned of her son's love for Psyche, Venus took the girl as a slave. Psyche obliged, praying it'd win back Eros's trust. But she was sent on a death quest into the Underworld, where Venus demanded that she fetch a small box. Psyche arrived and found it with little trouble. But a sly demon beckoned her to open it, saying it held beauty remedies. Unable to resist such temptation, she opened the box and descended into a deep and unnatural slumber. Eros vowed to find his love, looking everywhere—even the Underworld. His divine touch woke Psyche. Eros flew her into heaven, begging Jupiter to make her immortal so they never again could be forced apart."

Aleksender leaned forward just as the last word of Sofia's words faded.

He split the upside-down seam of her lips with his tongue. Sofia obliged with a soft sigh, matching each of Aleksender's thrusts with one of her own. Large hands grasped onto her face and cradled the curve of her cheeks inside his palms. Delicious chills shot up and down Sofia's spine.

He tipped Sofia's face ever so slightly, drank in her essence, and deepened their kiss. She moaned inside the dewy heat of his mouth and floated into oblivion. Aleksender's hands slid down her cheeks, wound through the mass of curls and ventured down the elegant column of her neck, slinking over the cloaked rise of her breasts.

He parted the material, exposing the swell of her cleavage to the elements.

The feeling of absolute security, true happiness and belonging was undeniable. Their hearts burned with an overwhelming affection, which felt remarkably like love.

It was a relief unlike any other, and difficult to ignore. Defeated, entirely at her mercy, Aleksender shook his head. Inhaling a shaky breath, he traced crescent circles upon Sofia's flushed cheeks and lost himself in her eyes. He curved his neck till their foreheads gently pressed together. Wisps of his breaths fanned against Sofia's skin, caressing her. His words were barely audible and spoken more to himself: "This is how I can heal."

Aleksender knew that his fate lay entirely in Sofia's hands. She held the power to destroy him forever, should she so much as please. Though, he doubted she was capable of destruction. Sofia's unabashed innocence, her unconditional if not blinded faith, did wonders upon the tattered depths of his soul. Aleksender gathered Sofia's arms and angled them behind her reclined form. One by one, he guided her hands below the material of his dress shirt and wound them about his torso.

The realization sliced through Sofia.

Tears instantly spilled down the slope of her cheeks. "No, no. What did they do to you?" She trembled, flooded with a violent degree of anger. He'd been branded by cruelty. She could feel it. His scars—those scars—were deep and gruesome. By comparison, the injuries on his chest were mere scratches. The epiphany was a knife in Sofia's heart. He'd been tortured. Brutally tortured.

"What did they dare do to you?" Sofia demanded once more, choking on sobs and staring into his eyes. Anger coiled through her body like a palpable force.

The broad expanse of Aleksender's back inflated and deflated beneath her fingertips ... inflated ... deflated ...

For countless moments, only the faint breeze and Sofia's weeping could be heard. When Aleksender finally spoke, his voice was cryptically monotonous and dry as if the very topic bored him to tears. "We'd been in the camp for weeks. As you said, those who survived at Sedan were taken as prisoners."

Aleksender crawled from her arms and hugged onto his legs, every inch of his body convulsing. Sofia saw the memories buried within his eyes. Gunshots. Screams. Rolling cannons and the faded cries of despair. They lodged inside Aleksender, battling for his soul.

Sofia rose from the ground and tentatively crouched behind him. Remaining silent, her hands sunk below the material of his dress shirt and encouraged him with gentle caresses.

"Disease and death were everywhere. Men with boils and rashes the size of saucers. Anyway, we almost managed to escape. It was a good mile away that we were spotted. They were corrupt soldiers, nothing but hungry dogs with a taste for blood-lust. We were tied at the wrists and ankles, crammed inside a tent. Whether it was days or weeks, I cannot say." Scoffing under his breath, he spat, "The fools demanded answers. They demanded our plans. Strategies. We refused each time. Even so none of us knew anything."

"Oh, Alek. Why didn't you tell them? To think you could have avoided so much pain."

His shoulders lifted into a dry shrug. "I suppose we took a morbid delight in their frustration." His voice was icy and harsh and void of all emotion. "And besides—it was the prospect of whipping information from our skin that kept us alive. But we were eventually returned to the camp. Bloodied, battered and burned—but alive." Aleksender passed fingertips through his hairline. "Till this day, I have no idea what changed their minds ..." Aleksender sighed and gave an afterthought, "Word had spread of their rather unorthodox methods, so to speak. According to rumor, they'd paid dearly."

"I pray they burn in hell," Sofia gasped. "Every last one of them!"

Aleksender laughed, amused by her goodhearted blasphemy. "Ah, Sofia, ma chérie. You do wonders for me." And then a sudden thought came to his mind. "Christophe was there with me."

"In the tents?" Sofia murmured, her heart reaching out to both heroes.

Aleksender merely nodded.

Although she'd never had the pleasure of meeting Monsieur Cleef, his name inspired a strange twinge of nostalgia inside her gut. Aleksender had often spoken of his dear friend—a rather admirable man of big ideas and too little restraint. From what she knew of the roguish skirt-chaser, she'd always admired him very much.

"Such wonderfully brave men," she crooned, caressing one of many scars. "You have a soldier's heart."

Cloaked beneath the darkness, Sofia's fingertips moved over his back in hypnotic motions, not leaving an inch of him unloved. "Do they pain you much?"

"No," he hoarsely answered, "they are no bother." His body trembled within her arms. "Not any longer."

Between tentative kisses and muffled sniffles, she whispered, "To think of the pain you endured. The cruelty—your suffering."

Aligning their two bodies, Aleksender cradled Sofia's face between his palms and sweetly stroked her skin. Sofia's toes curled against the barrier of her slippers. It was intoxicating. By far the sweetest moment in her nineteen years of life. With a last kiss, he whispered into her mouth, "Pain is in the mind. And, in my mind, ma chérie ... I was with you."

CHAPTER FOURTEEN

Sunlight bathed the ground in dancing shafts. Curving in and out of the various trees, rosebushes, and trellises, the cobblestone walkway offered a path through paradise.

Arm in arm, Aleksender and Elizabeth strolled through the chateau's gardens at a leisurely stride. Apart from his detachment, everything was bright, brilliant and wonderfully full of cheer. And Elizabeth was no exception.

Shielding her complexion from the dreaded sunrays, Elizabeth clutched onto her parasol for dear life. Laughter beamed from her eyes. A silk bonnet fluttered atop her curls, fondled by a gentle breeze, its fine material accenting the delicate arch of her brows.

"Oh, dear me ..."

Aleksender bellowed an exasperated groan. Somehow, someway, they'd wandered into the infamous hedge maze. How could he have been so distracted? Aleksender blamed Elizabeth's constant chatter. Near to fuming and not in the mood for infantile games, he glared at Elizabeth and bit back a curse.

Did she dare to smile?

"Elizabeth—"

"Bet you cannot catch me!" she exclaimed, eyes sparkling with mischief. Tossing Aleksender a playful backward glance, she chucked the parasol over a hedge and hiked up her skirts. "Come on now," she cried over her shoulder, "whatever are you waiting for?"

Mesmerized, annoyed, and a bit perplexed, Aleksender observed as her bonnet was swept away. An abundance of golden curls was freed and tossed about by the wind. Elizabeth ran from him, her slender form appearing smaller and smaller with each step. Robust laughter filled the air. "Come and get me, Alek!"

Aleksender paralyzed, questioning his own sanity. He blinked once. Twice. No, it was not an illusion. Elizabeth appeared to be fifteen years-old. Indeed, the mature curves of her body had been replaced with gangly and undeveloped limbs.

She was fifteen and very immature, he quickly concluded. She'd vanished from his sight to dart around one of the maze's clever corners.

Aleksender reached the spot of her disappearance in a few quick strides. He encountered an endless pathway around the bend. Parallel rows of hedges went on forever, stretching into eternity.

And yet Elizabeth was nowhere to be seen. The phenomenon betrayed the laws of logic.

Damnation—it betrayed common sense.

"Impossible," Aleksender muttered under his breath. Such a thing simply could not be. Had he finally gone mad? The notion certainly held a twisted appeal. In a way, madness was a sort of luxury.

A delicate hand interrupted his thoughts before he could further contemplate his questionable state of mind.

Ah, Elizabeth ...

He turned to the soft touch.

Aleksender swallowed a generous intake of air. She was dressed scandalously—inconceivably so—donning no more than a flimsy nightgown and wicked smile. And those curls were loose and wild, draping over the tempting curves of her breasts like two sensual waterfalls. She had the decency to blush beneath Aleksender's hardened stare.

"Sofia? How—"

She pressed an index finger to his lips. "Hush now." For the life of him, Aleksender couldn't stir a limb. Couldn't speak. The irrationality of the moment became moot. Her simple touch inflamed his mind and body. From head to toe he was coarse as stone, behaving like a randy lad ravenous with lust.

"My dear," Sofia purred, "we really mustn't have her suspect anything."

"You should not be here." His menacing voice vibrated against her nude fingertip.

"Silly Aleksender," she chided, wagging her finger in mock

scolding. "Don't you see? This," gesturing the towering hedges, "is a maze. Finding a way out is near to impossible. Just give in."

The flesh of his mouth grated her finger with each word. "Ah, but you are wrong, ma chérie. You see, this is built as a labyrinth. It has but a single path—nothing more. It's only an illusion. An illusion designed to appear as a maze."

"Well. Even so ..." Her lips widened into a grin as her eyes brazenly peered southward. She stepped closer till her bosom skimmed the expanse of his chest. Her thumb absently traced over Aleksender's lips. The opposite hand cupped his groin—fondling his rigid arousal through the trousers.

"N-No. You—" his objection broke off into a pitiful stammer. "You must not—" Aleksender hissed between clenched teeth as she increased the pressure of her caress.

"Aw, why so?" Eyes fallen to half-mast, he studied the pale arch of her shoulder. Near to bursting, he fought an excruciating desire to nip at that delectable, ivory flesh. As if she'd been denied her after dinner sweets, Sofia's lips drooped into an adorable and almost childish pout. "Is my touch truly so abhorrent?"

"You know damn well—" Pressing down on Sofia's wanton hand and shamelessly grinding against her palm, he moaned. "That I burn for you." The words were spoken between sharp thrusts and choked breaths, rasped and guttural. Sofia's eyes glittered, taking a perverse delight in Aleksender's loss of control.

"Tell me, amour. How many nights have you lain awake and aching, fantasizing about my lips, my touches? How many nights have you seduced your body, imagining my caresses? How many whores—how many mistresses—have you taken in my name? How many times have you made love to your wife thinking of me?"

She began to unclasp the front of his trousers, her voice lowering to a husky alto. Aleksender gave a hard moan as her fingers brushed over his swollen flesh. "Tell me—how many nights have you dreamed of this moment?"

A painful ache settled inside Aleksender's chest. Where was his sweet, wide-eyed ward? Where was his little Sofia? No. This was neither his dream nor heart's desire.

This was nothing more than another shade of his reality.

Panting and gasping for air, Aleksender stumbled backward and speared all ten fingers through his glossy locks. "Play with fire, you get burned." Trapped and entirely alone, he scanned the fortress of hedged walls, vainly searching for some way out. It was useless. Without knowing the correct pathway, even a labyrinth could imprison a man.

Just give in …

Sofia's nimble fingers teased the fastenings of her nightdress, unbuttoning each one, working at a maddening pace. With a sensuous moan, her pink tongue swept across her bottom lip, moistening the fleshy seam. She provocatively pried her nightdress open and bared her breasts to Aleksender, revealing herself inch by inch. "Then let us burn."

He woke with a violent start. His hands trembled like that of an addict's, temples slick with perspiration. Revolted with himself, Aleksender spouted a curse—discovering that other regions also felt damp.

He threw back the coverlet. Reality and his dreams had collided once more. Indeed, shameful proof of his suppressed passion had invaded his marriage bed. Down below, his nightshirt bore a large slick spot, branding the region that he'd come to despise most. How humiliating. At thirty-six years, he was nothing more than a little boy who'd wet the bed.

Deeply shamed and ridden with guilt, Aleksender flipped onto his stomach with a groan. Beside him, streams of moonlight danced across Elizabeth's unconscious and tranquil features. All the time-burdened imperfections seemed to melt away, leaving the unblemished innocence of a fifteen-year-old girl in its wake. Staring down, he tucked a loose curl behind her ear. "You don't deserve this—any of this."

Aleksender turned away and buried his face in the mattress, unable to stomach the sight.

•

Bête Noire's sleigh bells tinkled in greeting. The room shrank three full sizes as a shadowy figure crossed the threshold.

The place had undergone very little change since Aleksender's last visit. Years had passed, and yet the floorboards were still splintered, windows veiled, and the chandelier weeping. And Aleksender felt strangely at home.

Business was clearly slower than it had ever been. A handful of whores were spread out on the two chaises and immersed in mindless chatter.

Aleksender pounded at the golden bell, cringed at its sleazy melody, and nodded when Madam Bedeau finally appeared.

"It has been a long time, indeed, monsieur." Flat and painfully tight, her voice had lost nearly all of its innate sensuality. "Tell me—what is your desire tonight?"

Aleksender signaled to one of the whores—an appealing, slender brunette. She was young and bright-eyed, likely in her early twenties. Her bodice was a deep red, astonishingly low cut, and overflowing with the swell of her breasts.

"A worthy choice, monsieur." Madam Bedeau offered a smile and called out to the girl. "Esther. Kindly show this gentleman to the rooms."

"Yes, madam." Esther threw her friends a small grin before departing to the counter. Her fingers curled around Aleksender's arm as she led him down the darkened hall. "Come along. This way, monsieur."

•

The match came to life with a hiss. Esther lit a pair of candles, bathing the room with gentle glows. Regardless, the surrounding shadows remained thick and impenetrable, obscuring everything.

Esther inhaled a sharp breath as her client's broad form stalked behind her. He came intimately near. Strong hands wrapped the shaft of her neck in a feathery and teasing touch.

Indeed. Most of her patrons were either drunks or homely-looking fellows—more often than not, a little bit of both.

But no—not this man.

This man's eyes were clear and pristine, every inch of flesh handsomer than sin. It was strangely unnerving. His finely tailored clothing and distinguished accent suggested that he was a gentleman—and Bête Noire hardly received gentlemen. Granted, Esther had been working only a few months—but she knew the establishment had lost its prestige many years ago. Like the rest of Paris, it had fallen victim to the shadow of despair.

The features of the man's face were hidden by an askew hat and impossible to decipher. And that voice …

His voice was an instrument of pleasure—a low rumble, rich and sultry. "Take down your hair."

Esther untied the coiffure, her nimble fingers unusually clumsy.

Dark ringlets fell down her back in vast waves, creating a satin barrier between her and the mysterious man. She shuddered as elegantly long fingers brushed across her temple. A cluster of curls were swept aside, exposing her nape to the elements. The heat of the man's breath drew close, wafting against her in a molten sting. The other hand found the ties of her bodice and loosened them one by one. Within moments, the front of her dress puckered forward, wide and gaping. Each sleeve slid away from her shoulder, exposing smooth slates of flesh.

The heat of his body shifted. Esther glanced over her shoulder. Apparently he'd found a moment to remove the hat. Hair, blacker than the night, shone beneath the illumination. He stood at the foot of the bed, dark, menacing and purely male.

"Come here." He waved his hand in a suave and elegant gesture.

Esther obeyed. "Onto the bed." Staring into his eyes, she eased onto the mattress. The whole affair—everything about this gentleman—was strangely discomforting. His slow sensuality, transient touches, deep gaze and hypnotic, lukewarm voice.

"This really isn't necessary, monsieur," Esther said. "I—"

"Shh. Don't speak." Every muscle tensed as he settled next to her. A deep crater indented the mattress as it was manipulated by the pull of his weight. "Don't look at me." Esther turned her eyes away. His lips descended in one, sweet swoop and skirted across her neck—down one side and up the other. His hands—those strangely gentle, callused hands—discarded her bodice.

He rolled away in an urgent movement. An unbearable pain lined the depths of his eyes. A single word was chanted beneath a choked breath. Sorrelli ... no, no—Sofia? Did he whisper Sorrelli? Or had it been Sofia? Esther wasn't sure.

"Monsieur? Are you all right? Is ... is something amiss?"

"I must go."

He replaced the hat, dug a hand inside his cloak and laid a fistful of francs upon the pillow. Without a backward glance, he vanished into Bête Noire's shadows.

•

Lost in silent contemplation, Aleksender stood before the hearth as he absorbed its heat. He bowed his head and wrapped his hand around the meticulously carved mantel.

Tonight, the truth had emerged. He could no longer lie to himself. He'd been forever changed.

Sofia had touched something deep inside his heart, which he'd believed was longtime dead and buried. Her beauty, her kindness, their unified and kindred spirit ... had awoken a dormant tenderness within his soul.

And now he was falling deeply in love with his ward—hard and fast. Such a thing was inevitable. He'd always felt more alive and worthy in her presence. The emptiness didn't seem to matter as much with Sofia by his side. Or, perhaps, the dark void had merely been filled with light and laughter.

Unblinking, he stared into the flames as the firewood perversely crumbled, split and blackened.

Now, only one question remained. Could Aleksender protect Sofia from himself?

CHAPTER FIFTEEN

March 26, 1871

Once upon a time, Paris had been a renowned mecca of art and culture. Now, the alleyways whispered tragic secrets. Suffering souls of all ages infested each corner. Barricades obstructed many of the streets, reinforced by restless members of the National Guard and Commune. Mountains of wrecked debris and broken carriages stood as Paris's sole defense, pitifully warding off attacks from the army of Versailles. Without a sou to their name, many homeless Parisians were forced to consume sewer rats or worse, lest they go hungry.

For Christophe, starvation wasn't an imminent concern. He'd managed to secure a handful of odd jobs, most of which were given to him out of pity, and had taken residence at some dumpy inn. Mining coal was a taxing affair. Most evenings he lost himself within a drunken stupor, tumbled a whore or two, and rolled onto the god-awful plank that was his mattress.

But tonight was no ordinary evening.

Christophe wandered the length of the Rue de la Paix, hands tucked inside his ratty pockets. A cannon glared out from its barricade as he rounded the corner. Christophe cocked a brow and peered straight down the throat of its muzzle. A fierce shiver coursed through his veins. The thing was black and bottomless. A mouth into hell. A small cluster of National Guardsmen stood nearby, rifles and cigars in hand. Taking notice of Christophe, they exchanged mumbled words and tipped their navy-blue caps in greeting.

One of the men propped the rifle over his shoulder and stepped forward. "You're headed in the right direction, monsieur." Christophe responded with a curt nod.

With growing uneasiness, he continued down the pathway at a quickened stride. Everything was hollow and silent. A plague of death had steadily devoured the sleepless town and tragedy had taken its course. Thick shadows crept over the cobblestone walkways, manifesting in the form of demons. Relief flooded Christophe's body as he finally reached his destination.

Newspaper leaflets danced all around him, harmoniously tossed about by the wind. Whirling and twirling, they skirted in front of Café Roux, carried by the spring air. Muffled talking could be heard within the walls. And a placard was tacked upon its door:

Vive la Commune! Come one, come all!
For a democratic and social republic!
Commune meetings and election tonight.

Christophe was disturbed greatly by the sight. All life had been sucked out of the beloved cafe, and in its ashes stood a morbid crypt. The atmosphere was grave, thick with sorrow, and gloomier than a funeral parlor. Every person appeared to be in attendance. From wall to wall, men, women and children were solemnly strewn about.

Hundreds of bodies filled the moderate space. Members of the National Guard, the barber and the baker, the village gossip and renowned rake. Even their damned children were present.

For many, it was the birth of a revolution. For the others, it was a premature death sentence. For Christophe, it was nothing. Everything had been turned down since his return. Being kept as a prisoner of war and losing everything tended to have that effect.

A cluster of gruff-looking men was huddled about the bar, none of them drinking and all of them focused on the speaker who was seated before them. Christophe drew his eyes to the rough faced boy leading the discussion.

He was seventeen years going on forty. A cigar was clenched between his teeth, bobbing up and down as he passionately lectured. Christophe had once known this boy—this Elliot Francois.

His mother had been scandalously murdered, he gravely recalled, and within the same year, his father had drunk himself into an early grave. Elliot had always idolized him—Lord only knew why.

It was quite tragic. Within the course of two years, all of Elliot's youth and boyish charm had been spirited away. Far more than a little rattled, Christophe shook away his thoughts and wandered to the bar. Stinging alarm flushed through his body. Every voice hushed to a whisper. Every pair of eyes was attentively fixed on him.

"Messieurs," Christophe greeted, "as always, a pleasure."

"Sweet Mother Mary! If it isn't the great Christophe Cleef." Grinning ear to ear, Elliot hopped down from his stool and slapped Christophe's back in an elaborate show of masculine affection. "Fine thing to have you returned to us in once piece."

"Ah, afraid that's a bit debatable."

Elliot smiled wide and signaled to one of the prettier barmaids. "Be a dear and help Monsieur Cleef to his brandy." Wearing a decadent smile, the barmaid smoothed out her apron and did as commanded. She slid the glass down the counter once it was full and brimming. It was a true brush with death. In ridiculously seasoned style, Christophe caught the drink mere seconds before it flew from the bar. Amused with the veteran's suaveness, her lips curved into a smile. "Nicely done," she praised, a hint of seduction tinting the words.

Christophe's eyes twinkled as his lips lifted into a beguiling grin. "My lady." He raised the glass in a mock toast.

Elliot seated himself next to Christophe, straightened out both suspenders, and cleared his throat. "You are quite an important man here in Paris, Christophe. We can expect great things of you, yes?"

"Ah, Elliot, Elliot, Elliott. I am no nobler than the common wretch." Winking at the barmaid, Christophe finished with a sly afterthought, "Save your praise to swoon a maiden and lift some skirts."

Cafe Roux resurrected. Several men wolf whistled at the rather lewd remark. Somewhere far off in the crowd, a mother gasped in horror and cupped both hands over her child's virgin ears. Elliot merely chuckled. "You always were the charmer, eh?" All business, his tone flattened and rid itself of all humor. "No nobler than the common wretch? Now that is debatable. I daresay you're far nobler than any of those self-righteous puppet masters."

Christophe swallowed an impressive mouthful of brandy. "You speak of the monarchs?"

Elliot nodded and erupted into passionate speech. Christophe traced the rim of his glass in repetitive circles. He'd heard renditions of these words, time and time again. Revolutionaries were an admirable breed of people, though rather infamous for repeating the same errors and miscalculations.

This time, things could be different. With the de Lefèvres' charity and aid, the gap between the bourgeoisie and nobility could be annihilated once and for all. But everything had changed since Comte Philippe de Lefèvre's death. Like himself, Aleksender had returned from the war as a troubled and embittered man. And he would not bend so easily, nor be eager to inspire change.

Elliot's voice rose with a regal authority. He walked the length of Cafe Roux, speaking with pride and unbridled passion—sounding very much like a preacher in the midst of a sermon. "We speak of those rich in name and poor in soul. We speak of the religious heads, barons and comtes. The nobility and the traders have had their day. Now, the hour has come for the working man to rule."

Choruses of hoots and hollers chimed out as a chant filled the room. "*Vive la Commune! Vive la Commune! Vive la Commune!*"

"Versailles is finished. Prime Minister Thiers is dead!" Elliott shouted over the roar of excitement. "Enough—enough of this wretched, rotten life. Enough, I say! We don't earn enough to eat or feed our children! This is no way to live. We must fight, or we starve! *Vive la Commune!*"

Christophe studied the eager and beaming faces. They were uniformly fixed on Elliot and savoring every word—eyes swollen with renewed hope. And, when improperly yielded, Christophe knew that hope could become a dangerous force.

Grown men were placing their faith in the hands of a mere boy. Such desperation unsettled him to no end. Paris needed a true leader, not a child. She needed the guidance of her noble comte. Not Elliot Francois.

Elliott regained his seat as a rush of excited chatter flooded Cafe Roux. "Ain't that right?"

Christophe was not listening. Instead, he found himself absorbed in a strain of nostalgia. Speaking more to himself, he muttered, "Alek was my comrade and a fine, fine soldier. A good man who might have been great." Weighed down with a sudden sadness, his head dipped forward. "He was my friend." He sighed, took a generous sip of brandy, and wiped his mouth dry on his sleeve's crisp cufflink. Through an airy chuckle, he went on to say, "Indeed. Quite the fool, that Alek. Took a bullet for me, you know."

Elliot remained in silence, his brows inquisitively drawn together.

"Aleksender de Lefèvre," Christophe drawled. "Comte de Paris."

The boy's face lit up in epiphany. He grinned at the circle of men, eyes alive with emotion. "Well, well! First-name basis, are we? Why, you may have more pull than we'd ever imagined possible."

Christophe tensed and adjusted his posture, suddenly very uneasy. "How do you mean?"

"You've seen and lived the bloodshed. You are the best of us."

Christophe snorted and downed a last swallow of brandy. "Christ, boy! Would you cut the teasing and get to it?" He glanced around, seeking answers. Nothing. The surrounding faces were blank slates. Christophe met Elliot's unreadable gaze, as empty and clueless as before. "Tell me—why have I been called here?"

An ominous silence consumed the cafe and everybody in it.

"We want to elect you as leader of the Commune."

CHAPTER SIXTEEN

The open field was empty and as silent as a grave. Sparse, tall leafs rustled as they were frantically parted by two men.

Christophe and Aleksender raced through the vast and untamed wilderness, panting, clutching onto their precious chassepot rifles for dear life. Thick clouds of smoke poisoned the air, mingling with heaps of dust and the bitter musk of sweat.

Had they escaped death? Or were they still being pursued?

After several critical moments they stopped to catch their breaths. Their navy coats were a stark contrast against the brittle morning light. But there was nothing frail about either soldier.

Exhausted and drained, they propped their bodies against one of the few trees. The stench of death weighed heavily in the air. Both faces were bruised a vivid purple, a thick haze of dirt obscuring their features. They looked like they'd been to hell and back. Within the lingering silence, they recalled the horrific turn of events of only moments ago.

Had they really witnessed the dismembering of half a dozen comrades? Had they truly defied death?

"Damn them! Damn 'em all! Our entire platoon—blown to hell!" Christophe glanced above his head, abandoned his lingering adoration for Christ, and scolded heaven with humorless irony. "Now'd be a mighty fine time to shed your mercy!"

Aleksender's gaze roamed over the field. Paranoia surged through his bones. They were being hunted. There was no doubt of that.

Christophe muttered a slew of profanity and dug a hand into his filthy pocket. Eyes falling shut, he clutched his rosary beads and clung to the faintest ray of hope.

"Hail Mary, full of grace, the Lord is with thee. Blessed art thou among women, and blessed is Jesus, the fruit of thy womb." The vain prayer passed over Aleksender's conscience. His attention was lost to a greater, all-consuming despair. "Holy Mary, Mother of God, pray for us at the hour of our death."

Silence hung in the air like a bad omen. Christophe's eyes flashed open as he muttered, "Amen."

Aleksender shifted closer to his comrade, sensing imminent danger.

It happened in a flash. Aleksender thrust himself in front of Christophe—*bang!*—and threw his head back in a roar. A fountain of blood seethed from his shoulder. He instantly lost his breath and collapsed on top of the intended target. Christophe propped up Aleksender's body, stunned silent—oblivious to the snapping twigs and approaching steps.

"Alek? Alek! Can you hear me?" Christophe rotated with a curse and scanned the dark void. A piercing wail split the air in half, jolting his eyes back to Aleksender. A curved dagger had been plunged into his upper back, blade buried to the hilt. A chilling scream resonated as the metal was swiftly withdrawn, slipping through layers upon layers of flesh, blood, and muscle. Christophe stared forward in mute horror—virtually paralyzed—unable to stir a limb. A demonic chuckle echoed the hollowness. It served as a morbid accompaniment to the sounds of guttural ripping and shallow breaths. Aleksender's back was impaled once, twice, three times, before Christophe regained his composure.

Aleksender hissed through clenched teeth as the dagger was freed from the bloody pulp of his back. Struck by sudden realization, the Prussian soldier fled in a vain attempt to preserve his own hide.

Christophe swore an oath and carefully laid Aleksender into a reclined position. Bile seared his stomach and rose inside his throat. Degraded to nothing more than a heap of sweat and blood, his dear friend was thrashing and crying out, clutching onto his mangled body.

Detachment flushed through Christophe, empowering him with a fierce blood-lust. The rosary slipped from between his fingers and spiraled to the ground. Blood encircled the beads in a morbid ring, drowning the trinket in an unholy sea of red. Christophe looked away from his rosary and secured the dagger in a tight and merciless grip.

All sense of Catholic goodness was forgotten. His breaths were erratic, eyes narrowed in distaste, head pounding like a war drum. The symbol of the Prussian army—a light gray iron cross—was engraved in the sullied hilt. It seared the callused flesh of his palm, igniting an inferno deep inside his soul.

Christophe paced forward, stare harder than nails as he pursued the cowardly shadow. Their steps harmoniously quickened, each man appearing as no more than a graceful, phantasmal silhouette.

Christophe reached the Prussian soldier in a few swift strides. The nemesis spun around in a fluid movement and aimed his rifle. A dull shot rang out and pierced the night. At lightning speed, Christophe latched onto the barrel and urged it downward. A bloodcurdling scream resounded as the Prussian soldier blew off his own foot. Pitiful and on the brink of tears, he limped away—the poor excuse of his foot dragging unceremoniously behind.

Further enraged and oddly amused, a sardonic chuckle inflated Christophe lungs. "Ah, determined wretch, aren't you?" Christophe said, speaking in a German tongue. He emitted a satisfied grunt and plunged the dagger deep into the Prussian's neck. Flesh gobbled up the blade with fervor, swallowing it to the hilt. The grotesque ambiance of anguished cries and sputtering veins came as a welcoming sound. Alas, it was music to Christophe's ears.

Rid of all pride, the Prussian soldier toppled to his knees and clasped his sullied hands together. They trembled in time with his falling tears. "Mercy—please! I—I heard ya! I heard your prayers! I know you are a man of God! I implore your forgiveness—"

"Such pleas would have worked wonders mere moments ago," Christophe drawled in lazy German, lips lifting into a smile. "Unfortunately, for you, your villainy has made me godless." Christophe sank down to the crutch of his knees.

Throbbing with pain, Aleksender observed his comrade from the grass. Christophe's normally animated features were constricted and void—each line tightened into an unfeeling mask of apathy. "I fear my heart has turned to stone," Christophe mumbled. "And feeling nothing is ... strangely liberating. In a way, you are a godsend."

"Please, good monsieur," the Prussian blubbered. "I've a child at home. A lil' boy! He is but a wee babe."

Christophe stroked the curve of his chin, absorbed in apparent contemplation. The Prussian exhaled and whispered a silent prayer of gratitude at the gesture. He'd been saved.

All hope fled as quickly as it had come.

Dislodging the dagger with a deep sigh, Christophe clucked his tongue and dryly murmured, "Tsk, tsk, tsk. You disappoint me. Pitiful. Just look at yourself—beggin' on your hands and knees, weeping like some jilted lad. In Christ's name, will you not die with a shred of decency? You shame your family." For all the calmness in his tone, he might have been discussing the weather rather than questioning the very legitimacy of God. And, a moment later, he did precisely that. "My, my. I do believe a chill has descended."

Christophe tilted his head back and stared at the bruised sky. A shaft of light broke through the fortress of clouds. "Looks like rain." Thunder growled in the distance, confirming his assumption. Christophe slapped his knee with a hooting chuckle, his voice wry. "Were I superstitious, I'd take that as an ill omen."

Leafs crackled and twigs snapped as the Prussian attempted to crawl away. Christophe rose to his feet, dusted off his uniform, and straightened the brim of his askew cap.

When he spoke, his voice was flat and cold, free of all humanity. "An eye for an eye, indeed."

The Prussian panted and increased his pace, slithering through the grass like a wounded snake. Christophe kept up stride with an embarrassing ease. He leaned forward and lowered the dagger in a harsh movement. Suspended in time, the blade gleamed like a beacon, brilliant and almighty, bright against the surrounding black. Vomit and blasphemous curses oozed from the Prussian's lips as his flesh was impaled ... again and again and again.

•

A chorus of chilling screams jolted Elizabeth awake. She flew from the bed and stared down in a mixture of horror and bewilderment.

The devil had been unleashed.

Trembling and murmuring a volume of incoherent nonsense, Aleksender thrashed between the bed sheets, looking every bit possessed. A thick film of sweat beaded from his forehead and trickled down his golden skin. His raven hair was damp, heavy with perspiration, and plastered to throbbing temples. The rivulets glistened like tears beneath the frail moonlight.

"Lord, have mercy!" Elizabeth crossed herself in a clumsy motion. She tentatively curled a hand around Aleksender's rigid shoulder and gave a gentle, reassuring shake. "Aleksender, do wake up," she carefully whispered. "It is a dream, dearest—just a dream."

Aleksender leapt to his feet with a war cry. Both hands fastened about Elizabeth's pale swan-neck. His grasp was lethal. Snug as the hangman's noose. He panted between heavy intakes of air and fumed like a caged bull. Elizabeth cried out in utter horror and fought to break free. Guided by some primitive instinct, Aleksender's hold simply constricted and cut off her desperate pleas.

His grasp was intended to kill.

"Please," she managed to choke out. "Please no."

Aleksender's eyes widened in horror as the realization dawned. Quivering, he freed Elizabeth in a harsh motion.

No bombs. No gunfire. No dying men. No tortures.

But it had been so real. So painfully real.

Elizabeth breathlessly collapsed to her knees. She clutched onto her throat and massaged her half-crushed vocal chords. Her entire body shook with strangled coughs.

The powerful expanse of Aleksender's back rose and sank, manipulated by his strained breaths. Sweat pooled inside the grotesque trenches that disfigured his flesh. Every muscle twitched. Every scar stung like a brand.

He was on fire and burning. He was in hell.

"Elizabeth! I—"

"No! Do not come any closer! Please—just ... keep b-back! Stay away from me!"

The nightmares were evolving. They were becoming more and more lucid—steadily crossing the threshold of reality and dreams—no longer refrained to the realm of sleep.

They were turning deadly. Aleksender could no longer hide inside of himself. Sofia had been right; it was only a matter of time before his agony swallowed him whole. And, aboard this haunted ship, he was drowning and taking everyone down with him.

He would never heal.

Elizabeth skittered away, attempting to escape Aleksender's

madness.

"God. I harmed you." It was not a question.

"No," she whispered, gracelessly staggering to her feet. "I ... I am quite fine." But her eyes had already contradicted the words. "Please—I beg you, just keep away from me."

CHAPTER SEVENTEEN

All of Salle Le Peletier's one-thousand seats were empty and silent. Stale remnants of perfume and whispering fans hung in the air, lingering from the previous night's performance. And those ghosts from evening's past seemed to amplify the auditorium's stillness.

The stage, however, was very much alive.

Marie Taglioni stood before Sofia as the tight coils of her coiffure fell sensually across her frame. All beauty and grace, she floated across the stage, demonstrating a series of complex bends, pirouettes, soubresauts and jeté jumps with ease.

Mind racing, Sofia studied her teacher's footwork with a detached awareness. She inwardly chastened herself, struggling to anchor her attention upon the task at hand.

But thoughts of him filled her mind, body and soul. Ever since the rooftop, she'd become a ghost, barely present, her mind constantly a million miles away.

This is how I can heal.

Had he spoken truth? Could she heal Aleksender—just as he'd healed her, all those years ago? Her heart grew heavy at the thought of his despair. Much like herself, he was severely scarred—inside and out.

Pain is in the mind. And, in my mind, ma chérie ... I was with you—

A startling thwack resonated as Madame Taglioni's walking stick crashed onto the floorboards. "Come now, child! You really must try and focus! Now, back in position."

Sofia blushed at the scolding and arranged her feet into first position. "Forgive me, madame. It shan't happen again."

Madame Taglioni arched a fine brow and circled Sofia with a

hawk's astuteness. *"Rond de jambe en l'air ... oui,* excellent display, Mademoiselle Rose ... *grand rond de jambe ...* and finally—*grand rond de jambe ..."*

But it was no use. Sofia's thoughts took flight within moments. All at once, a strong awareness overcame her. She arched her chin and glanced up—up into the blackened depths of box two.

•

Salle Le Peletier was cloaked in darkness an hour later. Aleksender lounged in box two as a gnawing sorrow consumed him. In the midst of the chaos and heartache, this little corner of the world had become his sole escape over the last few weeks. Being in Sofia's presence was cathartic and wonderfully calming. Only after seeing her face did the ghosts of his nightmares no longer haunt him. Years ago, Aleksender had found a semblance of comfort in the arms of countless whores.

But now everything had changed.

Mon Dieu, they both had changed. When she danced, he saw it—a distinct sadness weighed heavily upon Sofia's spirit, a sadness that wasn't so different than his own. She wore it like a morbid badge. And he ached to lift the burden from her shoulders. He yearned to replace those shadows with light.

The door knob lightly jingled and rattled. Delicate steps resounded, escalating to a steady drum roll. Somehow, someway, Sofia knew he was here, and had come for him. Aleksender tensed against the seat's plush backing and fastened both eyes shut—confident his mind was playing him for a fool. Or that he'd finally gone mad.

Nimble fingertips whispered along the expanse of his shoulders, one and then the other. They kneaded the strain in his muscles, replacing discomfort with pleasure, melting all of his troubles away.

Aleksender exhaled a soul-deep groan and relaxed beneath the hypnotic ministrations. Two delicate hands joined together at the base of his neck, slipping down, down, down—passing over each side of his body and then back up again. Erratic breathing wafted at his nape in an airy tease.

It was a fantasy. It had to be a dream, another cruel dream from which he would too soon awake. Her tentative touches, the scent of roses and wintertime ... the sweet tone of her voice as she reassured, "My Alek, I am here. I am here for you."

I am here.

Aleksender swallowed and inclined his head against the seat rest. "Sofia?"

"Shh." Ever so slightly, she bowed forward, brushed away fallen hairpieces, and pressed a kiss to his forehead. Her lips lingered upon his brow as she cradled either side of his face. "I want you to just relax."

He stared up and muttered a helpless sound. Sofia closed his eyes with a sweep of her palm. Her fingertips eased over his chest in soothing, calculated strokes. The erratic beating of his heart was fierce beneath her hands.

Hesitantly his eyes blinked open. He was afraid she'd fade away, afraid she'd transform into a dark shade of reality like in his dream.

"Sofia?" His beautiful voice was laced with varying degrees of pain. "What are we doing?" He swallowed and shook his face. "What are we going to do?"

The slightest grin formed on her lips. She gazed into the haunted depth of Aleksender's eyes and reached for his soul. "Be true to ourselves." A silence overcame them both. "Don't you know? That's the best that any of us can do."

Aleksender reflected her smile, yet the agony in his brow only deepened.

Sofia straightened her posture and eased to the door. A beacon of light stabbed the box before the soft sound of footfall faded away. Wrestling with his thoughts, Aleksender stared into the surrounding blackness, numb and alone once more.

Yes. This was how they both could heal.

•

A sunset lit the vast sky, wrapping Paris within a gossamer robe of blood red. Aleksender admired the spectacle as Elizabeth lingered close behind him, her figure wedged between the balcony's two double-doors.

It had been several nights since the traumatic episode of his nightmare. Elizabeth's fears had gradually faded away and dissolved into a determined compassion. His suffering had penetrated her soul as she'd lay awake each night, witnessing the tragedy of war before her eyes.

As much as she desired, after that terrible occurrence—a true brush with death—she dared not disturb him again. And, during their waking hours, neither Elizabeth nor Aleksender mentioned the recurring dreams that continued to plague them by night.

"Oh, Aleksender, mon amour ..."

"Elizabeth." A satin robe was fastened around her chemise, its elegant tail trailing behind.

"Won't you come to bed?" A dull silence swelled the air. "What is it? What is on your mind? Please. Will you not open your heart to me ... or at least try?"

Aleksender's posture visibly tightened. Elizabeth sighed and stepped onto the balcony. She came beside Aleksender, demurely folding her hands atop the stone banister.

"Forgive me. I've been terribly restless."

"Yes, I've felt the same," Aleksender said.

"The evening is still quite young! We could take a stroll through the gardens. If I'm not mistaken, the roses are in full bloom. Or, if they aren't to your fancy, we may—"

"Hush now." Aleksender collected Elizabeth's hand and brought it up to his lip, pressing his mouth on the underside of her wrist. Her pulse leapt beneath his touch. "Just find some rest."

Tonight, he'd be true to his heart.

•

A drifting haze obscured Aleksender's vision, transforming the simple walkways into something hauntingly surreal. He surged Juliet forward at a steady gait, in tune with every curve, twist and bend. Draped beneath a heavy cloak and the fall of night, he appeared as just another shadow ... just another tragic secret.

Aleksender held his breath as the dwelling seeped into eyesight. Resembling a storybook cottage, the structure was beautiful in its bare simplicity. A little white fence rimmed the border, its tattered pickets swaying in the wind. Swollen streams of smoke ascended from the chimney. And every foot of the premises had been designed by none other than Aleksender—a phenomenon that had emerged from the tenderest depths of his imagination.

In the front yard, a charming water garden buzzed with life. Nature's music filled the air as the bullfrogs croaked, crickets sang out their merry songs, and fishes waded beneath the glassy surface. They darted in a playful dance, gliding in every direction.

Aleksender dismounted and tethered Juliet to a nearby tree

branch. An oversized crucifix was bolted to the front door. *Sacred Heart Holy Convent and School* was carved just below the emblem. Aleksender stared at the lettering as his gloved hand rapped at the wood.

Muffled footfall resonated from within the home. Sister Catherine appeared after a brief wait. At the ripe age of sixty-five, she ruled Sacred Heart with a quite strict and severe disposition. Aleksender had always fancied Sister Catherine. Despite a rather stern façade, she possessed an unparalleled kindness.

"Monsieur de Lefèvre! Many a night I've prayed the good Lord would embrace you in His safekeeping." She paused to cross herself in a graceful motion. Her eyes grew heavy, weighed down with a mixture of sympathy and admiration. "Monsieur, I am deeply sorry for your loss. We have all mourned le comte's passing, blessing his soul to the heavens." Sister Catherine stepped forward, offering her comfort with a tentative touch to his forearm. "I am overjoyed to see you safe and well."

"You have my gratitude." In truth, Aleksender felt far from gracious. Her condolences unsettled him. And all at once, a dark memory shadowed his mind.

Be not afraid, my child, of those who kill the body. Fear him who destroys both body and soul in hell.

Aleksender cringed at the distant imagery, fearful that the truth was finally fleshing out, fearful that the emptiness would soon be replaced with an unimaginably dark revelation.

What, precisely, had happened all those years ago?

Heart and mind racing, he searched his surroundings for distraction. "I am pleased to find the premises in such fine condition. I take it the young ladies have been progressing well?"

"Yes. Wonderfully so." Sister Catherine pressed a hand to her breast. Her eyes fell shut as though absorbed in prayer. "Your humble charity, your kindness. You have blessed their lives in every way. You, monsieur, have given them a true gift."

Growing increasingly uncomfortable at her praise, Aleksender cleared his throat and raked a hand through his hairline. Sister Catherine's gaze fluttered open. Tears filled her eyes as a gentle smile touched her lips. She observed Aleksender's hardened features with a small, almost knowing grin. "Well. I suppose you should like to have a visit with Sofia?"

"If she is not in prayer."

She appeared minutes later. Aleksender stood paralyzed as he drank in the immaculate sight that stood before him. How beautiful his ward looked, dressed in a chaste white dress, her porcelain skin glowing beneath the moonlight. Lush, brunette curls were fastened back, tumbling down and over her slender shoulders, cascading to the very small of her waist. A scarlet ribbon was knotted about her hips, its material tied into a voluptuous bow. The shade presented a charming contrast to the tea gown's creamy tone. And Aleksender longed to tug the bow loose and unwrap Sofia like a present. Pale lace, as delicate as the wings of a butterfly, outlined the gown's edges, equipping her with a haunting degree of femininity.

And the modest cut did nothing to curb Aleksender's desires. He could not bring himself to move. Alas—he could barely bring himself to draw breath. She was nothing less than an angel. And, tonight, she would be his. Once and for all, completely and utterly his.

A powerful intimacy pressed in the silence. Aleksender's heart sank. She resembled a bride.

Sofia stared up at him beneath her lashes, completely infatuated. Drenched in varying shades of black, his tall form camouflaged with the night, those green eyes glowing with unmistakable passion. She scanned the impressive span of his height in wonderment. Aleksender was handsomer than ever. His breeches were deliciously snug as they framed the lean muscles of his legs. Provocatively draped over his backend, the tail of his double-breasted coat fluttered about in the breeze, accentuating the tender curve. And a cloak hung from the crook of his arm—its lush material folded up like a blanket.

Sofia paid a quick glance over her shoulder and admired the convent—the only true home she'd ever known. Her stare returned to Aleksender. Beautiful and grave, he resembled a dark angel.

This is how Lucifer must have looked just before he fell, Sofia mused in good faith. She approached him, feet carried by her soul, drawn to Aleksender in spite of all notions of right and wrong.

A soft smile ignited her gaze. Sofia outstretched an arm and tentatively reached for his face. "You're here. You came for me."

"I had to." Aleksender dropped his eyes as his manly cheeks

blushed a deep red. Sofia merely returned his innocence tenfold, a light tint searing the shaft of her neck. "You are beyond lovely."

Her head lowered at his praise. "Please. False hope is something I cannot bear—"

"False is a far cry from what I feel for you."

Aleksender finally grasped onto her. He marveled at her brittle delicacy—the way his hands spanned the entire circumference of her waist, the way her eyes darkened at each little caress.

A moment later she was lifted up and onto Juliet's back. She stroked her mane, in awe of the creature's mystical beauty.

Aleksender mounted in back of Sofia and swung onto Juliet with heroic style. He leaned forward, the sweltering heat of his breaths scorching her sensitive skin. The hairs upon her nape stood at full attention. He gathered the tethered reins and deposited them in the cushion of her lap. She tensed as his arms claimed her, enveloping her body from behind and wrapping her within his essence.

Fingertips lingering, Aleksender swept away a swarm of russet curls and whispered low against her neck—making love to Sofia with the sultry accent of his voice. "Tonight, I am yours and you are mine."

CHAPTER EIGHTEEN

A violent rain began to fall by the time Sofia and Aleksender reached the de Lefèvre carriage house. Inside the small structure, the swollen planks harmoniously gaped and moaned as they were assaulted by the storm.

Sofia clutched onto Aleksender's cloak and absently fingered the thick wool. Heaving a deep sigh, she wandered over to one of the walls. Out-of-doors, Chateau de Lefèvre stood in full view, appearing proud and impressively aristocratic. It towered against the bruised sky, a fortress of coarse stone ascending into blackness. Sofia cringed. On this night, it resembled the bastard child of a haunted house and medieval castle. A bolt of lightning split the night into two and set the monument aglow.

Sofia couldn't help but despair. The brutal weather felt akin to an ill omen. Thunderstorms were wildly uncommon during the month of May. She trembled as fat raindrops clubbed at the rooftop, banging with the audacity of defiant fists.

"Most peculiar weather."

Distracted and tending to Mademoiselle Juliet, Aleksender merely grunted in reply. Sofia glanced over her shoulder. Amused, she watched as Aleksender was bombarded with tosses of Juliet's muzzle, which demanded her master's affection. He obliged with another irritated grunt. Sofia couldn't suppress her grin. For the life of him, he was unable to resist the charms of a pretty female.

"Why, Juliet! What a naughty girl, using your feminine wiles on Alek!"

Aleksender couldn't contain his chuckle.

Sofia turned back to the chateau with a small and triumphant grin; she'd almost made him laugh.

Familiar warmth played upon her back as Aleksender wrapped Sofia in the circle of his arms. He laid his cheek across her hair and fondled a loose, silky curl. The charming barrettes gleamed in the moonlight, clashing against the darkness of her hair.

Guilt swelled Sofia's chest as she thought of Elizabeth. "Do you love her? Elizabeth—do you love her?" Aleksender's hand froze midair, the curl slipping between his fingertips.

Silence seemed to stretch on for an eternity. Realizing her error, she stiffened against Aleksender and inhaled a long and unsteady breath. Her head was spinning. She inwardly chided herself. She was cruel to ask such a question. Aleksender was clearly ripped at the seams—torn between loyalty to his home and loyalty to himself. Unlike the rest of the world, she would not force him to choose. In the end, she knew it would break her heart. And it'd be a sacrifice she'd gladly spare for her Alek.

"Forgive me. I—"

"Tonight, mon amour," came his smooth, hypnotic voice, "there is only us." Jolts of pleasure shot up and down her spine as Aleksender's lips ghosted across her nape.

"Us," Sofia echoed the magical word with breathless wonderment.

She rotated in his arms and gazed deeply into the depths of his eyes; she felt as though she was seeing him for the very first time. In a painfully tender movement, she swept fallen hairs away from his eyes and unveiled the windows to his soul.

"You miss your father terribly."

Saying nothing, Aleksender peered through the panels and gazed at his chateau. Sofia perched onto her tiptoes and soundly kissed his cheek. Aleksender inhaled a sharp intake of breath as her lips lingered.

Slender arms encircled Aleksender as Sofia pulled him against her chest. She warmed his skin with her bittersweet words, "You are like ice."

The simple comfort she offered, her genuine compassion for his loss, affected Aleksender far more than he dared admit. Since his return, no one had expressed any form of sincere condolences—not Elizabeth, not even Richard. Cradled in Sofia's embrace, a vulnerability overcame Aleksender that he hadn't known he still possessed. The superficialities of his noble lifestyle vanished away, leaving his true identity and spirit in its wake.

"I can only imagine your pain. I could never endure losing you."

Aleksender stepped back and out of her reach, his entire demeanor darkening. "I am not your father, Sofia," he fiercely snapped.

"No. No, you are not. You are my teacher ... my guardian ... and my best friend." Sofia continued after a slight hesitation, a blush brightening her cheeks. "You ..." Her elegant fan of lashes lowered, casting decadent shadows upon her pale skin. "You are my love." Her gaze rose—brazenly consummating with the heat of Aleksender's stare. "My lover."

Aleksender's final defense broke. He would no longer deny himself. Sofia collided into the wooden panels as she was thrust backward in a jarring motion.

He was upon her. Each of his arms were fully extended and propped on either side of her face, encasing her between sinewy muscles.

Those wondrous, green eyes haunted her every dream—glittered in the darkness. They burned with passion and pent-up desire that equaled her own. The heat of his stare impaled her soul as Aleksender's mouth descended, almost in slow motion, tasting the tingling flesh of her neck at a leisurely pace. He took his sweet time indeed. He would savor every moment to its absolute fullest.

Sofia's thoughts trailed as she fantasized about a rather scandalous story she'd once managed to get her hands on—Polidori's *Vampyre*, the notorious tale of a Lord who delighted in seducing maidens, drinking their lifeblood from their very necks.

She gasped aloud, weak at the knees, shamelessly leaning against the wall for bodily support. Aleksender's lips crawled up her neck, pausing only to tease at her throbbing pulse. She squirmed against him, hissing between her teeth and near to bucking.

"No," she yelped, "s-stop that!"

She felt it. Aleksender was grinning against her skin. "Forgive me. I'd forgotten your neck was ticklish."

"Lying is a mortal sin, monsieur."

He kissed one of her cheeks then the other—stopping mere inches from the dewy heat of her mouth. Their humorous exchange transformed into one of deep emotion.

Sofia broke the spell and raised her defiant chin in an aggravating gesture. She moved her lips out of his reach, smiling from ear to ear. A primal sound rumbled inside of Aleksender's throat as his teeth gritted in frustration.

"Sofia, please."

"I've waited three years, Monsieur le Comte. I daresay you can wait a moment or two."

Three years?

Mild panic rose inside of his chest. She had desired him since she was sixteen? This was wrong—terribly wrong. And yet, as she playfully shifted from the wall and moved away in a sly motion, he pursued her.

Aleksender matched each of her footsteps with two of his own, mesmerized and seduced. Body and soul, he was drawn to her like a moth to a flame. This seductive and teasing side of Sofia had been quite foreign to him. And now he found it be quite intriguing.

"Don't you know that patience is a virtue?" The door emitted a hollow creak as the curve of her bottom pushed against the aged wood, propping it wide open. "Indeed. Patience is passion tamed."

"And you, ma chérie, are a walking proverb."

Sofia discarded Aleksender's cloak in a swift motion. She flung it over his head as if he were nothing more than a coat rack. Tangled and trapped inside, he battled the thick material in vain. Swallowed up by the wool, his muffled curses barely reached Sofia's ears. She clutched onto her tummy, shamelessly enjoying the spectacle and unable to suppress a fit of giggles.

"My poor, poor Alek!"

After some moments, he managed to unwind himself from the cloak's confines. He tossed it to the hay flooring and exhaled an exasperated pant. His eyes were steadily fixed ahead, glaring down the amused female.

Sofia gasped, alarmed and enticed by the gleam in his stare. She hiked up her skirts and bolted out the door. The fine material flowed behind her as she fled the carriage house, a wide, nostalgic grin stretching her lips. In her younger years, she and Aleksender had occasionally frolicked in this way. Those moments were some of her most treasured memories. But now, she found that their game was exceedingly far from innocent.

Glancing over the curve of her shoulder, Sofia stuck out her tongue and sprinted across the lawn, giggling at every step. "Slowpoke!"

Sofia sighed and gradually slowed her pace. She tilted her head back, marveling at the endless, bruised sky that lurked high above. A shaft of light broke through the clouds without warning, illuminating her like a diva's spotlight. She spun in place, laughing merrily and perfectly happy. Not minding the falling rain, she danced within the ring of light, performing for an audience that only she could see.

Aleksender remained silent and still, paralyzed by her beauty. He watched her graceful movements in stunned silence. His heart quickened at the breathtaking sight that unraveled before him. She was lost within her element and entirely at peace.

Sofia had been born to dance.

And Aleksender saw within her. He searched the crevices of her heart with an astute and pristine awareness. Through his eyes, everything about Sofia radiated. Her flesh was no more than a pretty package that covered an even prettier soul. He yearned to unwrap the precious treasures of her heart. He yearned to make her a part of himself forever.

Twirling, she lifted both of her slender arms above her head and grasped at the sky. "Oh, look, Alek! God is weeping for us!"

White cotton was soaked through and through. It clung to Sofia's flesh, molding over her exquisite form and nearly transparent from the rain. Sopping, dark curls flattened against her cheeks and neck, presenting a stunning contrast to her ivory skin.

And then a miracle happened as Sofia came to an altogether stop. A smile—a genuine and true smile—tugged at Aleksender's lips.

Joy swelled Sofia's heart. She couldn't recall a time when he had smiled.

Really, truly smiled.

Sincere laughter filled his eyes—boyish, carefree laughter that softened his rugged beauty and reflected the delicacy of his soul.

Sofia peered at him beneath her lush fringe of eyelashes and drank in his presence with a greedy eagerness. Cherishing his contentment, she absorbed the serene vibes that radiated all around him. His tranquility was palpable. Like a true flesh and blood soul mate, she could feel his shifting emotions, all of his inner doubts and guarded insecurities. And she took an unbridled pleasure in his newly found peace. She observed as his stiff exterior slowly dissolved away, exposing him in his most vulnerable and lovable form. And his grin—that roguish, sinfully charismatic grin—could only be described as infectious. She returned his smile without thinking.

Alas—despite the pouring rain and thundering skies, he was content.

Despite his disheveled and frightfully unruly appearance, he was content.

Despite the fact that Comtesse Elizabeth was presently sleeping—oblivious to his betrayal and deceit—he was flushed with pure content.

And Sofia decided that contentment agreed with Aleksender remarkably well.

His thick, raven hair was plastered to his flesh like melted drinking chocolate. He'd apparently found a spare moment to remove his coat; the crème dress shirt was entirely in sight. It, too, was plastered to the expanse of his chest—molded against his form with perfection. He was painfully handsome, displaying a fascinating blend of boyish appeal and exquisite masculine beauty. He was a wonderful paradox she could never fully solve—nor intended to. He was an illusion that could never be fully realized. She could not tear her eyes from him.

Flustered by his unwavering attention, Sofia flexed at her heels, graceful and delicate, and treated her invisible fans with a curtsy. In response, Aleksender's mouth quirked at each corner and lifted into a crooked grin.

"Hmm." Sofia tapped her lips in deep contemplation. Propping an adorably saucy hand on either side of her waist, she hotly spouted, "I hate to inform you, Monsieur le Comte, but you're not nearly as coarse as you like to believe yourself to be."

His grin grew at her remark. The emerald hue of his eyes transformed as they darkened with desire. "And I hate to inform you, mademoiselle, but you aren't as entirely prudent as you believe yourself to be."

But she was certainly not too prudent to understand his rakish intentions. Aleksender was taunting her, she gathered—testing her, she knew, playing a wicked game with her, she saw.

Sofia's tongue seemed to take on a life of its own. Feminine pride overflowed her mind and body. She was utterly startled by her own audacity.

"Maybe so," she retorted, absently twirling one of her ringlets, returning his flirtation. She openly challenged him, eyes shimmering with mischief. "But that was when you knew me as a child." Sofia took a graceful step forward, hips swaying in a complimentary rhythm. Her voice was husky and unmistakably desirous. Aleksender could scarcely recognize it as her own. "You've yet to know me as a woman."

Those words sealed their fate.

Aleksender lunged forward with a beastly growl. Their damp bodies molded and sloshed together as he captured her torso between his arms. He swept Sofia off her feet—quite literally—his interlocked limbs settled beneath her bottom. Ignoring her fiery and uncharacteristic protests, he tossed Sofia over his shoulder with the ease of a ragdoll. Her legs wildly kicked midair as solid little fists thumped against his back. Swallowing back a chuckle, he heaved a melodramatic sigh and headed for the carriage house.

Her long curls hung like a curtain and nearly swept the ground. "If you think I'm through with you, monsieur—well ... you are sorely mistaken!"

Aleksender merely swatted her adorable, upturned backside—a gentle, playful gesture—and chided her with a mock scolding. A grin spread across his mouth as she audibly pouted, accepting her defeat.

"Surrendered, I see?"

"I shall take great delight in my vengeance," she warned, attempting to blow hair from her face with a shallow puff of air. Soaked from the storm, it remained plastered to her cheek. "Oh, I swear to it."

"Sounds like a challenge," he dryly murmured, enjoying the banter with an immense pleasure.

The splintered door creaked as Aleksender kicked it open with his booted heel, carefully depositing Sofia onto the ground.

He silently cupped her cheeks, caressing the satiny flesh with his gloved fingertips. He gazed deeply into her eyes. Aleksender hushed her with an index finger as her lips parted in speech.

"You've nothing to fear, Sofia," he gently crooned, stroking her skin in tantalizing and hypnotic motions, "I would never let harm come of you." Aleksender glanced away, praying his words were not a lie. "I want you to know, no matter whatever happens I shall be there for you. Always."

She swallowed and silently nodded. There was an ominous edge to his voice, a foreboding undercurrent, which he didn't bother to hide. Something warned Sofia that this would be her last chance to protect her heart from breaking. But alas—she'd already abandoned herself to Aleksender long, long ago.

And now they stood as two martyrs of love, their sacrifice within arm's reach.

CHAPTER NINETEEN

Aleksender collected Sofia's pale hands and suggestively laid them across his chest. His heart thundered beneath her palms, strong and unmistakable. The simple gesture was overwhelmingly beautiful; it was as if he was making a present of his soul.

"Just trust me," he whispered

Sofia smiled softly into his eyes. "I always have."

She was troubled. He could see it in her distant stare … could feel it deep within her skin. Aleksender inclined his head and murmured softly against her cheek. "What? What is it, chérie?"

An eternity of silence drifted by. When Sofia finally spoke, her voice quivered with emotion. "Why is this happening?" She hesitated. "Why is this happening to us?"

Aleksender swallowed and shook his head. "I don't know. I don't know."

"Are you scared?"

"Yes." Both hands descended from her face and fell despairingly to his sides. They tightened into two clenched fists as he prepared to fight off his personal demons. "Very much so."

Sofia's gaze drifted over his troubled features. His rigid posture, haunted stare. Her face sank forward. She was disturbed greatly by the sight. All of his inner torment had surfaced. Sofia knew he had survived terrible, inconceivable tortures during his absence at war—and perhaps even during his childhood.

And she knew that he was battling his passion—struggling to see her as the little girl who he'd once cared for.

She wandered forward until the front of her gown skimmed his chest. Aleksender held his breath and peered down at their two bodies. They were dangerously close, intimately close. Soft and painfully tempting, the rise of her breasts was clearly visible through the soaked cotton.

"Alek." Sofia craned her neck and met those bottomless, infinitely lovely eyes. "I'd never let harm come of you, you know," she vowed with the faintest touch of a smile. "Just trust me." An unwavering, deep sincerity wallowed beneath her playful tone. The implications, the fortifying strength of her words, paralyzed Aleksender beyond comprehension.

Having so much to sacrifice, having so much to lose, was a terrifying thing.

Aleksender brushed past Sofia and collected his cloak from the ground. Its wool flapped about with the audacity of a flag as he smoothed the material across the flooring. Perched on his knees, he turned to Sofia and beckoned her over with the raw magnetism of his eyes.

Sofia came to him until she stood on the outskirts of the cloak. Her smile slowly seeped away, replaced with a startling awareness. His stare was breathlessly hot and powerful—indescribably passionate. She could feel him looking into her very soul. He could see inside her. And the realization pained Sofia. She saw his vulnerability and restlessness—and nothing more. She thought it was quite selfish of Aleksender, denying her access to his soul.

Aleksender coiled his hand around her ankle, enveloping it completely. His sultry eyes never abandoned Sofia. Savoring every inch, his fingers slid up her tingling flesh in an antagonizing slow motion. The cool leather of his glove scorched her skin, branding her with infernal touches. She watched in breathless awe as his hand disappeared, vanishing beneath her gauzy skirts. His opposite hand lifted from the ground and ascended to his mouth in a smooth motion. He nipped at the slick leather and clutched it between his lips, unsheathing himself as he provocatively removed the glove with white teeth.

Aleksender's bared hand sank below her skirts. Sofia's mouth fell open as she gasped at the intoxicating touch. The simple feeling of his callused skin moving against her own was maddening. With each caress, she descended into a state of pure euphoria.

His gloved hand withdrew completely. Slowly he raised the material of her gown. Aleksender's gaze crept down her body and settled upon the creamy flesh of her thighs. He murmured some words in a foreign tongue. Then followed suit in two more languages. Deaf to their meanings, Sofia instantly wished she was more cultured. Though, his sultry accent suggested they were not suited for a lady's ears. Rather than being offended, she inwardly blushed—realizing she didn't oppose to being scandalized.

"Sofia, you are exquisite." He eased her skirts up several more inches. Removing the other glove, his voice husky and trembling with desire, "Nothing short of divinity."

Aleksender clasped onto her slender thighs and worshiped the velvet skin with his fingertips. "I apologize. My dreams have not done you justice." A gasp fled her lips as he cupped the curve of her bottom. He murmured a long, low groan of satisfaction. His groin tightened as he pawed Sofia through the pantalettes and groped the lush weight of her derriere.

Just when she believed he would ravish her whole, Aleksender's hands fell away.

"You are precious to me," he whispered with an uncontainable ardor, staring down at the hay flooring, chest rattling with strained breaths. "You have always been so precious." With an unfathomable degree of humility, he stared up into her eyes and breathed the confession, "Before you, I was nothing. I wanted nothing. I was empty. And now I want everything."

"Alek—" Clutching her bottom once more, Aleksender tugged Sofia impossibly close. He was helpless to resist her beauty, craving a sense of completeness. He quickly freed his last shred of propriety as he reclined on top of his cloak—taking Sofia down with him. His movements were smooth and elegant, executed with a panther's regal grace.

Sofia found herself sprawled across the length of his strong body. She shivered at the feel of him. From head to toe, he was coarse and as hard as stone. And his arousal was no exception; it was dangerously prominent, straining against the fabric of his trousers. Their lips were mere inches apart, tortuously close. They shared the same breaths of air, inhaling each other's exhales. And Aleksender's mouth was remarkably beautiful. It quivered for her kisses, withheld dark secrets, and whispered sweet nothings.

"Sofia ..."

Those magical hands continued their ascent as Sofia's eyes fluttered shut, hooded with intense pleasure. They rode up and over her tender curves—up, up, up, skimming the tea-gown's lacy fabric. Aleksender arched his hips and ground his erection against her soft and pliable body, craving some sense of relief.

"My desire for you is painful."

An exotic blend of Persian spices ...

Roses and the frost of wintertime ...

The two distinct scents entwined as one.

The world seemed to fall away as Aleksender lifted his face and sought her mouth with determination. She surrendered to the insistent probing of his tongue. Beguiled by the rhythmically suggestive thrusting, she cooed a melody of sighs and parted her lips, granting him full entrance. He moaned into her mouth, consuming everything that was Sofia. Her fingers wound about his neck and tugged with a desperate urgency, knotting within the glossy strands of hair. What had begun as a tremulous and almost shy kiss turned entirely breathless. Aleksender devoured Sofia, feasting upon her mouth like a starved man.

"Give me everything. Your heart. Your body. Your soul. Give me yourself completely."

"I am yours and you are mine. Only yours, always yours."

Aleksender made a sound of deep satisfaction. Both of his hands inched up her swan-neck and tangled within the flurry of damp curls. He captured them between webbed fingertips, reverently sifting the damp silk. Aleksender closed his eyes as the heavy locks fanned through his parted touch. Somewhere, lodged inside of the back of his mind, he was aware that their intimacy was forbidden. Yet, as he inhaled Sofia's intoxicating femininity, he succumbed to the man within.

Never breaking their kiss, Aleksender bellowed a beastly groan and rolled Sofia onto her back. He forced himself away and tore their mouths apart, gazing at her flushed features from beneath his lashes. He savored the decadent sight of her slender figure wedged beneath his own. Her soft curves molded him to perfection, fitting his body like a glove. She appeared so delicate and impossibly fragile—an ideal counterpoint to his rugged masculinity. The paradoxical contrast and alikeness, which was shared between their two forms, seemed worthy of Shakespeare's prose.

A thick mane of chestnut curls swirled about her face and cushioned her head. Her sapphire eyes sparkled liked a pair of twin diamonds, staring up. Aleksender propped his weight onto an elbow and worshiped her with tentative touches. He caressed her cheek with the back of his hand, knuckles gliding across the lush and rosy flesh at a maddening pace.

The enchanting blue of her eyes blinked shut at his attention. His fingertips stroked the delicate curve of her chin, swept her hair aside, brushed over her fluttering eyelids and traced her parted lips. In response, her lashes twitched, tickling the pads of his fingers. He studied the pert bridge of her nose with an unblinking attentiveness, counting the adorable cluster of freckles, acquainting himself with each and every one.

Almost shyly, his hands rested atop the front of her gown. A fierce shudder shot through his body as he nuzzled her hair and pressed a kiss upon her forehead. Aleksender's fingertips teased the gown's modest neckline, hot breaths fanning at her neck.

"Please," she softy implored, "I need you."

With her blessing, the clasps of her gown were slowly released. Each snap resonated within the darkened carriage house, unnaturally loud, as if competing with the rainstorm. After what seemed an eternity, the pearl clasps were fully undone. Sofia shivered as Aleksender's cool fingertips dipped beneath the lace and provocatively parted the material, prying it open to the elements. No bodice, no corset. Instead, his smoldering gaze was aroused by the sight of Sofia's cotton chemise. And that flimsy undergarment stood as the final barrier to her flesh.

Aleksender fought back the excruciating need to tear the wretched thing from her body. After he regained a sliver of composure, his fingers triumphed, nimbly skirting across the heaving swell, exploring the trembling valley between her breasts, tracing the circumference of her rosy nipples in slow, lazy circles.

More, more, more, she yearned to scream. The tremulous nature of his affection drew an impatient groan from inside her throat. She didn't want gentleness. She wanted to be ravished.

Sweet, soft moans escaped her lips—wordless pleas for his unbridled touch. She descended further into euphoria as he peeled away his dress shirt, exposing the breathtaking sight of his bronzed chest. His body was chiseled and artistically formed, a flesh and blood testament of his time on the battlefield.

"Oh, Alek. You are beautiful." Sofia raised a trembling hand to his nipple and plucked the hard tip between two fingers.

Sofia's hands slid down the column of his neck, venturing to his back, up and over his scars.

Aleksender rasped a soul-deep moan and gathered the material of her gown, slipping it over her curves.

The carriage house was snug and cozy, though the night air held a biting sting. He prayed that Sofia would not catch a chill ... then nearly laughed off his concern—noting the delicious heat that steadily wallowed between their bodies.

Disposed of her garment, Sofia lay beneath Aleksender, donning nothing but her damp chemise and charming blushes. His manhood immediately jerked in appreciation, beguiled by the heavenly vision. He was bursting—throbbing—to the point of pain. Never had he been so aroused.

"Beautiful," he whispered, tracing the curve of her cheek, the curve of her breast.

He hovered high above her like a magnificent bird of prey, body propped onto each elbow, eyes glazed with desire. Thick strands of hair hung over his jade eyes in a black veil. Rainwater mixed with perspiration as sweat rolled down the slopes of Aleksender's quivering muscles.

Sofia tensed as Aleksender swiped away her mass of curls, exposing the pale arch of her right shoulder. His green eyes darkened and narrowed into blinding slits. He glared down at the countless cigar burns that marred her body. Familiar anger infused Aleksender; it pumped through his veins, pulsating with the beat of his heart.

His lips descended, ghosting across the warped flesh in featherlight kisses, tentative and determined. "She was not your mother," Aleksender growled against her skin.

He held Sofia close and whispered sweet nothings into the hollow of her ear. "I care for you so much," she cooed in reply. Her lashes swept over his neck as her eyes fluttered shut. "There's nothing I would not do, nothing I would not give."

Aleksender's mouth descended in a fierce swoop as his lips brushed insistently against her own, back and forth, commanding her complete surrender. As always, she obeyed him without thought, expressing her submission through coos, sighs and wildly feminine moans.

Aleksender gathered her to his chest. He pressed deep, ravenous kisses down the delicious arch of her neck, feasting upon her flesh like a starved man.

With Sofia resting so freely in his arms, all of Aleksender's rational thoughts and self-restraint were lost to a primitive hunger. It was a hunger to possess what was rightfully his. He ravished Sofia without restriction, allowing his darker side to take over. He kissed her with every ounce of his suppressed passion. He kissed her with the intention of winning her soul.

He could not contain himself. In the back of his mind, Aleksender feared that his passion would startle Sofia. But desire made up for inexperience, igniting her heart, body and soul with a natural sexuality. And the result was exquisite. Never had Aleksender witnessed something so beautifully reckless. So primitive and so erotic.

She rubbed against him with a raw desperation, grinding herself against his flaming erection. Each movement further inflamed his groin. His deep, husky chuckle rumbled against her abdomen. He steadied her swiveling body and bellowed a rough growl.

"Easy, chérie, easy, or you shall be the death of me. It would be a rather pleasant death, but death, nonetheless." Kissing her forehead, the heat of his words wafted against her neck. "I intend to savor each and every moment." His lips pressed against her earlobe, breaths unbearably hot and ticklish. "I intend to savor you." His lips skimmed her flesh, ghosting across the smooth porcelain, moving southward.

His tongue swept over her throat, lapping up Sofia's heavy pants—settling on the erratic beat of her pulse. It tasted light, airy, and bittersweet, much like the melodic thrumming of a butterfly's wings. Teasing love bites were branded upon her skin.

He stared into her gaze as poetic words poured from his soul. "Your eyes—they are a rare sapphire, like the frost of wintertime … clear as La Havre's morning sky and deep as the ocean."

Aleksender ghosted kisses down the column of her throat—down, down, down—swirling his tongue over the creamy swell of her breasts. One then the other. She tasted of rainwater and roses—delectable. Both of her dusty nipples were painfully erect, echoing the very state of his swollen manhood. And, much like the source of his physical affection, they jutted forward in sinful invitation—tenting the material of her chemise. The thin layer of silk clung to her like a second skin. It was a most delicious skin, waiting to be shed. Head inclined, he latched onto a hardened bud and tugged the coated flesh between his lips—suckling her straight though the chemise. A masterful hand kneaded Sofia's opposite breast, caressing and fondling—cupping the voluptuous weight in a holy grail. She tossed her head back and moaned.

"Alek. Let me touch you."

His reply was muffled. Aleksender lowered his head until his dark hair wisped against her, tickling the sensitive skin beneath her chest. As he spoke, he tongued the undersides of her covered breasts and dampened the fine material. His words were husky and slicker than sin. "I want to worship you, all of you, as a servant worships his goddess."

Sofia instinctively arched against his hot mouth—unable to speak—weak moans oozing from her lips. She met his every demand, craving a foreign relief, an unnamable relief ... a relief only Alek could provide. He shuddered against her, steadying those maneuvering hips with a low, tortured groan. Then his mouth descended once more. His tongue drew invisible circles, sliding over each swell, teasing her with wicked intentions and pleasurable promises.

"Dancing nymph," he murmured against her sweat-slickened chest. The raspy baritone made her senses simmer and churn with pleasure. An acute ache pooled between her legs and coiled around her nerves—making her desperate for something ... something she could not fully understand nor grasp ... something so close, yet out of her reach.

The feeling intensified with each little tug, each caress and whisper. Soon, it seemed to splinter her very bones.

"Oh ... I ... I need—"

"I know precisely what you need," came his throaty reply. "And I shall give it to you. Again and again."

She quivered at the vow. The force of his conviction sent shivers up and down her spine. Aleksender curled his fingers beneath each strap. "I must see you," he gasped, slowly dragging the chemise down and over her curves, her hips, inch by glorious inch.

Sofia crossed both arms with a blush, hiding her bare breasts in an adorable, maidenly gesture. Aleksender wordlessly shook his head and unraveled each of her arms. "Do not hide from me. Let me see all of you."

Her breasts were true works of art—luscious, full and finely sculpted. And Aleksender had always been a connoisseur of fine art.

He licked one of his fingertips and lowered it to a pebbled nipple, tracing the tender mound of flesh, delighting at how it tightened beneath his touch.

"You could shame Aphrodite," he praised in breathless admiration. Aleksender dipped forward and replaced the fingertip with his tongue—swirling it around and around the taut tip. Sofia clawed at his nape, blinded by overlapping emotions and sensations. Then he inhaled deeply and pressed his lips against her heart. Sofia nearly wept from the gesture.

Between his deep kisses, Aleksender rasped in a guttural tone, "May I tell you the first time ... the first time I knew I loved you?" He pressed a kiss to the crook of her neck and nuzzled her skin, inhaling her essence. "The first time that I knew that I couldn't live without you?"

Aleksender stared into her eyes. "I saw your smile. After I had taken you under my protection, after I had become your guardian."

Her eyes fell shut as she relived the memory.

"No. No, Sofia, no. Look into my eyes. Let me know you are here with me." She did as commanded. "That first night I saw your happiness. Happiness I had given you." Her lips parted in wonderment. "I adored and cherished you, very much so—as a father does his child. But you matured as did the very depth ... the very core of my affection for you."

"Alek, just love me."

His response sent her soaring.

Sofia shivered beneath him, lost in the throes of passionate ecstasy. Aleksender growled into the tight chamber of her throat, dominating her with an erotic possessiveness and raw desperation. His hand slid between her lush thighs and went in search of her very core. A clever fingertip skirted across the thin barrier of her pantalettes, tracing the lips of her feminine folds through the damp material.

Aleksender tore away her slippers and threw each one aside, allowing them to join the ever-growing mountain of discarded clothing. He buried all ten fingertips beneath the waistline of Sofia's hosiery, held his breath, and freed her from the wretched garment. The apex of her thighs was slick with desire and want. Aleksender gasped in appreciation as he centered himself above her body.

He paused for a moment and pressed a gentle kiss to her lips. Then he pulled back—shocked to find that her cheeks were damp with tears. "Sofia?" he whispered against her skin. "What is it?"

"To think you've shared yourself in this way all those times. Your body, your—"

"Yes. My body. You understand me? I love you, Sofia. I love you as I've never loved anyone."

Aleksender propped up his weight and studied her from head to toe. "But such a thing cannot be undone."

"I need it to be you. Only you, always you. Alek ..." She smiled and reached for his face. "Let me have you in the most intimate of ways, let me give you a part of myself that no other man may touch. Make me yours forever."

Aleksender responded with his caress. Broad, weathered hands skimmed over the valley of her curves as he traced each and every bend. He pressed a wet line of kisses down her neck, her torso— felt a sharp intake of breath as he ventured lower ... lower ...

She squirmed beneath the weight of his body, fingertips tousled in his hair.

Aleksender parted her intimate curls and circled the sweet bud in repetitive and loving strokes, stabbing in and out of the moist heat. He angled his lips and drew the tip into the hot cavern of his mouth. Long, teasing sweeps fell across the hardened tip, delicate pressure was applied ... a little more ... more ... just enough ...

Moans shook Sofia's body from head to toe. He steadied her hips as he suckled, drinking her in. She cried out in a burst of pleasure, swept with pure euphoria, every inch of her flesh tingling and on fire. Spasms quaked through her body. As they subsided, Aleksender slid up her body and claimed her lips in a powerful caress. He grasped onto her pale hand and guided it down the front of his trousers. She massaged him through the material, wrenching a tangle of moans from inside his throat. He felt harder than steel and impossibly large. Slender fingertips molded around the hidden length, massaging, moving up and down ... down and up ...

"Dieu. Sofia," he panted between heavy intakes of air as he

wrenched her hand away. "It's too much. I'm going to take you now."

Aleksender stripped away his trousers and freed himself with a groan, rejoicing at the feel of Sofia's smooth skin against his own. Legs entwined together and mouths connected, he centered himself in front of her heavenly gates. For a weightless moment, a re-kindled rush of guilt consumed his mind.

And then everything vanished—leaving only the two of them and their mutual affection for each other.

Sofia submissively angled her chin forward. Aleksender cradled it in his moist palm, lifting her eyes to his powerful gaze. "I love you, Sofia Rose. And I won't pretend that I am deserving of you."

She nodded her love, voice stolen from her breast. Parting her velvet folds, he slowly slid inside Sofia. He quivered from the painful anticipation and promising release to come. Sweetly kissing the top of her forehead, he sighed, "Forgive me."

And in a single, fluid motion, they were made one. Tears swelled her eyes at the deep burn. Aleksender carefully maneuvered in and out of Sofia at a steady pace, in and out, as he allowed her to grow accustomed to the sensation and his size.

She grasped onto the uneven terrain of Aleksender's back, holding him firmly to her breasts. Her heels dug into the hay carpeting as the uncomfortable, raw ache gradually transformed into something magical. Pain was replaced with a spine-tingling pleasure ... a pleasure only Aleksender could reward her. He increased his speed and pressure with a hoarse grunt of effort. A thick film of sweat gathered above his brow and shone in the moonlight. With each thrust, her body gripped onto him in an unyielding clasp, forcing them back as one. Aleksender curled his face into the crook of her neck and held her tight. He murmured words of love against the fine cartilage of her ear, "*Amour de ma vie ... ton image hante mes nuits, me poursuit le jour, elle remplit ma vie ...*" Love of my life, your image haunts my nights, follows me all the day, fulfills my life.

Strong, muscled arms hooked around her torso, elevating her the slightest bit. Remaining connected in the most intimate of ways, he sat on his haunches and lifted Sofia against his chest. She ground against him in instinctive and intuitive movements ... brushing back and forth, swiveling her hips full circle—one direction than the other. Aleksender raised a hand and gently trailed a fingertip down her body in a feather light caress igniting her skin from breast to bellybutton. Like a true dancer, she varied her tempo and movements in a creative, soulful rendition. Aleksender angled his chin back and propped both hands onto the cloak, lost to pure ecstasy. Encouraged by his deep moans, Sofia gained a steady momentum as she made love to Aleksender with her heart, body, and soul.

"Oh, Alek, I—" Sofia was rolled onto her back just as the sweet force of her climax curled her toes. Unparalleled jolts of pleasure overcame every pore, every nerve, every fiber of her being. Joining in her release, Aleksender buried himself deep inside her body and threw his head back in a wild roar. Pulse racing, he held her against his chest, lost to an exquisite feeling of oneness.

After it was done, they fell asleep in each other's arms, hearts and bodies still entwined.

CHAPTER TWENTY

Elizabeth woke to darkness. Smoke from a deceased flame swirled in a mystifying cloud, its long white ribbons pasty against the black expanse. Eerie and ominous shadows crawled up and down the bedchamber's walls like living things. The melodic thumping of rain caressed the chateau with devious touches. Outside, trees blew fiercely in the wind, their branches clawing at the windows. On this night, they resembled the nails of demons fighting to come inside, burning to drag Elizabeth to hell.

"Alek," she called, "Aleksender?"

Elizabeth sat up and squinted. Her chest ached. A terrible premonition gathered inside her gut. She turned to Aleksender's side of the bed and fondled the cold sheets. On top of the end-table, a sliver of white caught her attention.

It was a note.

Elizabeth rose from the bed, snugly fastened her nightgown's sash about her waist and collected the parchment. She positioned herself near to the double-doors, using the moon's gentle glow as light.

Dearest Elizabeth,
Richard and I have been invited for brandies and cigars with fellow gentlemen. I am sorry to have left you. I had no intention to disturb your sleep. You looked so peaceful.
Yours, Aleksender

Elizabeth gazed at the moon in thoughtful silence. She was caught in a dilemma—forced to choose between the better of two evils. Should she sulk back into bed with feigned oblivion? Or should she unveil the truth she had known all along and had deliberately chosen not to see?

A beam of light poured into the study as Elizabeth squeezed inside. It was a magnificent room, boasting rich mahogany furnishings, a Persian rug, low-hanging crystal chandelier and towering bookshelves.

Arms hugging her torso, Elizabeth slipped deeper into the study, praying she would not be discovered by some nosy, wandering servant. Summoning her courage, she made haste and swiftly approached the elegant writing desk. She turned the knob of a kerosene lamp, shedding a ring of light upon the polished surface. Her fingers slid across the desk's smooth wooden counter in appreciation.

Muffled thunder growled in the distance. Returning to the task at hand, Elizabeth shivered and yanked one of the drawers open. She rummaged through the various odds and ends with only a slight tinge of guilt, searching for anything that might prove—or hopefully disapprove—her unorthodox assumption. If any such proof did exist, surely it would be packed away in his study. Between his thirst for knowledge and love of writing, Aleksender had always valued this room above all others. It was bound to harbor his deepest, darkest secrets.

Elizabeth searched through the other three drawers with no luck. Documents, spectacles, silver seal and wax … fountain pen—

The Bible. How perfectly strange.

Elizabeth hesitated before fetching the massive book, her fine brows propped into questioning arches. Aleksender was many things. Religious was certainly not one of them.

She flipped the Bible open without further thought. Her eyes widened in awful realization. What she found was far from holy.

This was no Bible. It was a trick, a hidden compartment box. Countless letters were packed inside, each one fastened together with a scarlet ribbon. Heart pounding, she collected the stack and flipped it over, studying the coarse and slightly faded parchment. Trembling fingertips tugged at the ribbon. She unfolded a letter dated May 9, 1870—marking it as the oldest of the bunch.

Dearest Sofia,
 I hope you can forgive me for not writing sooner. Know that your

letter was a much needed breath of fresh air. The days have been too long and nights far too short. There is no escaping.

In my free moments, I find myself lost to deep thought. In spite of myself, I feel compelled to share them with you. You had found the courage to open your heart. You only deserve the same from me.

I have convinced myself that my feelings for you start and end at infatuation—the smitten thoughts of a randy lad, no doubt of it. After all, you have grown to be very beautiful.

Taking a bullet opens one's eyes. I was destined for death, Sofia. Dying is a beautifully surreal experience ... much like falling from oblivion, when you are caught between sleep and waking. At the risk of sounding terribly cliché, it was an introspective moment. I could no longer hide from myself nor my feelings. And, within those fleeting moments, I found myself in confession.

Strange that I should spend my final breaths before God, after having spent a lifetime avoiding Him.

Sitting there in mock confrontation—a cruel purgatory, indeed— I concluded that infatuation is the very least of my affection for you. But I am empty. I have nothing left to give.

For all our sakes, forget these words. Forget our kiss. Do not wait for me. Life is too precious, and your soul too lovely to be wasted on an old fool in love.

Always yours, Alek

Tears streamed down Elizabeth's cheeks. Witnessing the truth gave her no sense of closure nor bittersweet serenity. Instead, she felt only heartache. They were letters from Aleksender to Sofia, remnants of her husband's scorned soul, all expressed through eloquent prose.

And all of them were unsent.

•

Juliet slipped through the streets at a gentle and steady gait. Her hooves rhythmically clinked against the cobblestones, filling the darkness with a therapeutic and soothing melody. Snuggled against his chest like a soft kitten, Sofia was bundled in Aleksender's cloak and cradled within his lap. Basking in her nearness, he massaged her slumped shoulders and rubbed heat into her bones.

Sacred Heart seeped into view thirty minutes later. Aleksender dismounted in a reluctant and painfully lethargic movement. He tethered Juliet's reins to a weeping willow and withdrew a bronze skeleton key from deep inside his pocket.

The convent's wooden door moaned as he entered. The house was deathly still, every foot draped in heavy shadows, every woman and child lost within sleep. Aleksender wandered through the blackened halls like a ghost—graceful, silent, and discrete—Sofia's body safely against his chest.

He paralyzed outside the dormitory. He couldn't stir a limb. A dull ache lodged inside his throat. His heart thundered against his chest, well aware he was about to betray it.

Aleksender inhaled a shaky breath and stared down at the slumbering angel with a haunting attentiveness. Her bosoms gently heaved, manipulated by long and sleepy breaths. Its slow, seductive rhythm mesmerized and comforted him. She looked so peaceful. So beautiful and so trusting. He vainly battled for an inner courage he no longer possessed.

Aleksender ripped away his glove with a curse. His fingers reverently fanned through her chocolate curls, submitting their silky texture to eternal memory. The cruel gravity of their fate fell upon his conscience. And the feel of her body cradled to his chest was crushing his soul.

Aleksender lifted Sofia and slowly bowed his face, pressing a chaste kiss upon her brow. He could have held her in his arms forever, just like this, and died the happiest of men.

But it could never be. Alas—only weeks ago, his personal demons had nearly killed Elizabeth. In the end, keeping Sofia for himself would destroy her. No, he would not disappear completely—he could never abandon Sofia. The world was too cruel a place and she was much too fair a creature. Without a doubt, its weight would crush her spirit.

He would always be there for her, he inwardly vowed, distant and unseen—her silent protector and dark guardian—a lighthouse amongst the jagged sea cliffs, guiding her destiny. But first, Aleksender would have to divide their two souls. And he knew it would destroy him from the inside out ... a sacrifice he was willing to make. She would survive. She would flourish.

Sofia was young and impressionable. In time, her perspective of the world would be reborn. He would exist as a half-remembered dream, no more than a delicate memory of the deep subconscious.

In truth, their separation would be a blessing. It would be a godsend.

Yes, she would become a beautiful, distant star—faded and shining amongst the horizon of his despair, placed far from his mortal grasp. It proved unfortunate that he loved the girl; it would have been easy to keep her as his mistress.

Aleksender's head sank forward as his lips ghosted across her pale cheek.

For the last time, he inhaled her unique scent.

Roses and the frost of wintertime.

After a moment, he exhaled a rasped breath and surged forward, slipping soundlessly into the dormitory.

Aleksender's blood froze as he stopped dead in his tracks. A pale hand was coiled around the rise of his shoulder.

He spun around in a startled motion and instinctively clutched Sofia nearer to his body. Sister Catherine's ancient features glowed before him. Nearly unreadable, they were wrinkled and winsome, illuminated by a wavering flame. Anger and frustration overcame Aleksender. This would be Sofia's infinite ruin.

Without a doubt, her "scandalous" behavior would cast her from the convent. As it was, her unusual lifestyle was already in question—the odd combination of dancing and living in a convent home.

And the people of Paris—those malicious creatures whom delighted in scandals—were not ignorant of her origins. The ugly truth was widely known, though scarcely spoken. Sofia was a scorned bastard child, the shunned daughter of a lewd and arrogant woman, and destined for the life of a gutter whore. But, above all the things, she was a remarkable dancer and the beloved ward of le Comte de Paris. And that had always outshone her beginnings. Like himself, it seemed that Sofia had been born from contradictions.

And now, her dignity would be destroyed. His weakness—his desperation, reckless obsession, and installable need—had corrupted the one thing he loved more than anything else. Ladies had been damned for far less.

This time he wouldn't be able to rescue her.

Yet, Sister Catherine's eyes held no scorn, anger nor condemnation. Instead, Aleksender only found a deep compassion and understanding. A soulful blend of wisdom and sadness radiated from her stare. Gazing down at Sofia's smiling, sleeping face, she bowed her head in a regal motion. In that moment, Aleksender knew that Sister Catherine saw everything. And she shared in their tragedy.

Aleksender's mouth parted in speech. Sister Catherine pressed an index finger to her lips, demanding silence. She signaled him to follow with a graceful nod of her head. Clutching the silver candleholder in her palm and lighting the way, long shadows and solemn silhouettes were cast upon the plaster walls. Only the faint rustle of Sister Catherine's matronly skirts penetrated the din. Aleksender wondered where she could possibly be leading them—though dared not ask.

Sister Catherine paused in front of a wooden door. The latch gave a defiant moan as she lifted the metal and nudged it open. She gestured Aleksender inside with an insistent wave of her hand. He entered the cozy chamber, obliging without further thought.

He nearly lost his breath, in awe of the room's pure and simplistic beauty. Several prayer candles had been placed atop the nightstand, bathing the walls with their collective, orange glows. The humble bed was meticulously turned down. Heaps of cotton had replaced the stiff covers. And a porcelain vase of fresh blooms was centered nearby on a small end table, each rose vibrant and full of life. The revelation was remarkable.

Sister Catherine had planned for this moment. He nodded in silent gratitude as she slipped into the shadows.

Aleksender inched toward the bed and spread Sofia's unconscious body across the mattress. Glancing down, he pulled up the coverlet and carefully tucked her into bed—just as he'd often done when she was a girl. A wave of nostalgia weighed heavily on his heart.

This was no child. Aleksender tentatively sunk to his knees and crouched at the bedside. Sofia's complexion was wonderfully rosy, curls unruly, and lips swollen from his kisses. She was exhausted, the poor dear, and wildly disheveled—flushed from the throes of their recent passion. Every curve of her body was bathed by the candlelight. The slight arch of her bottom. The delicate curves of her hips. The endless length of her dancer's legs …

His stare settled upon her tranquil features. She looked so young, so angelic. Propped on both knees, he inched closer to the bed and its offering.

"Sofia, I want you to know ..."

An onslaught of tears clogged Aleksender's throat. His speech was constricted, overflowing with emotion. His head fell forward as his voice shattered. Aleksender turned from her with a strangled sob and pressed a balled fist against his mouth.

Both eyes blinked shut as he imagined a life without Sofia. Without her, the emptiness would return.

"I cannot endure losing you. I cannot ..."

He grasped at his heart and massaged his chest, attempting to ease the pain within. His other hand brushed over her array of curls, stroking her head in repetitive and soothing motions.

"I love you. I love you so much."

Shaking his head, he leaned forward and tremulously whispered, "I care for you, painfully much ... far more than myself. For that reason ... for that precise reason I must let you go. I must ..."

Aleksender draped his cloak over Sofia as he tentatively rose to his feet. His body was languid and unsteady. Clutching onto the bed-frame, his gaze rose to the vanity. In the reflection, he locked eyes with himself. It was a powerfully introspective moment. Moonlight bathed his features and gentled his appearance. Regardless, the truth of his character remained illuminated.

"You deserve much more, so much more than I could ever give." He tucked the cover beneath her chin and tentatively leaned forward. His lips brushed across her forehead in a transient caress.

His emerald gaze descended to her lips. Her mouth parted—murmuring some dreamy nonsense. She was smiling softly in her sleep, relaxed and content, lost to the beauty of her dreams. In contrast to her serenity, Aleksender's breathing was labored, harsh, and uneven. Every emotional barrier, every defense and every barricade, had crumbled.

Aleksender freed his soul. For the first time in years, he let himself cry. Tears cascaded down Aleksender's cheeks without shame. He sank to his knees and sobbed into the auburn silk of her hair, drenching them with his unrequited tears. He wept for the both of them. He wept on behalf of their star-crossed love.

For the first time in countless years, he wept.

"I shall watch over you always." Aleksender stroked her ivory skin in a reverent touch. His lips pressed against the hollow of her ear, whispering upon the fine cartilage, entire body convulsing. "Even though you won't see me, I will be there for you. And that shall never change. Never. I have nothing to offer you. Nothing but my protection."

His eyes drifted shut as he whispered the eternal vow against her skin, voice beautiful and soothing—words spoken like a lullaby. "Goodbye, my little Sofia ..."

Tears blurred Sister Catherine's vision. She watched Aleksender and Sofia's exchange from the shadows, much like she had done for the past nine years. Sister Catherine inhaled a shaky breath and mumbled a prayer from the archway:

O, God, whose love restores the brokenhearted of this world, pour out your love, we beseech you, upon those who feel lonely, abandoned, or unloved. Strengthen their hope to meet the days ahead; grant them courage, bless them with the joy of your eternal peace. Amen.

Aleksender had committed adultery. He'd taken a young girl's innocence—the innocence of a girl who perhaps stood on the precipice of nunnery. And yet within their shared adoration, she perceived only beauty. Without another backward glance, Sister Catherine brushed away her tears and vanished into the shadows.

CHAPTER TWENTY-ONE

"I sleep but my heart is awake. Listen! My beloved is knocking: 'Open to me, my sister, my darling, my dove, my flawless one. My head is drenched with dew, my hair with the dampness of the night.' My beloved thrust his hand through the latch-opening; my heart began to pound for him. I arose to open for my beloved, and my hands dripped with myrrh, my fingers with flowing myrrh, on the handles of the bolt. I opened for my beloved, but my beloved had left; he was gone. And my heart sank at his departure."

— Song of Songs 5

A strong pair of arms held her tight. Lips whispered sweet promises into her ear. Fingertips sifted through her curls, deft and tremulous. An uneven heartbeat drummed against her ribs. Shallow breaths wafted over her flesh. Warm tears fell upon her cheeks, mingling with her own.

Her dark guardian stood before her, blending into the blackness of night. His silhouette sank into a deep curve as he arched over her form. He whispered a soft goodbye against her cheek.

A sob was wrenched from her throat. "No ... please do not leave me." Sofia's arms thrust forward, grasping at emptiness.

Her protector turned away in a fluid motion and vanished into the night. His cloak fanned out in a divine spectacle—appearing as no more than two blackened wings.

Sofia woke with a start. Smoke from the candle's flame swirled about, pasty against the expanse of black. The events of the previous night rushed through her thoughts as she fought to regain her composure.

Sofia blushed at the memory, palms cradling her flushed

cheeks. But where was she now? It was dark as pitch. Regardless, Sofia knew she'd been left alone. She would have felt Alek's very presence.

Had it all been a dream? No more than some wicked fantasy? No—her body confirmed, sore and aching in her most feminine areas. She had been branded by his affection forever. And their union was something she'd never regret.

At the opposite end of the chamber, faint shafts of moonlight shined through a window. Sofia stumbled from the bed and eased toward the teasing illumination. Sweeping the curtain aside, her eyes widened with a sudden epiphany. Indeed, this room was Sister Catherine's chamber—a bit overly lavished at present, but unmistakably the head nun's sleeping quarters.

Sofia clasped onto her heart. Her lashes blinked shut, harnessing back tears she refused to shed. Behind shut eyes she saw him, heard his voice. Somehow, someway, Aleksender's parting words echoed the chambers of her mind.

I care for you, painfully much … far more than myself. For that reason, for that precise reason, I must let you go. I must …

He was gone.

◆

The drawing room was cloaked in silence. Aleksender sat in one of the oversized armchairs, posture straight as an arrow, resembling a king before his throne. His mind was numb as he stared into the blazing hearth. The fireplace seemed to mock his infernal misery. It chanted incoherent curses, whispering promises of eternal damnation. Demonic manifestations flashed across the crimson walls, welcoming Comte de Lefèvre into hell.

But he was already in hell.

Aleksender clutched onto his half-empty bottle of brandy, dangerously delirious and teetering on the edge of sanity. Despite the hearth's warm blaze, he felt cold, lifeless, entirely alone.

Aleksender's mind reeled, thoughts garbled and pensive. He was drunk on brandy and despair. From head to toe, his body trembled with pains he hadn't known to exist. Alas, the horrors of war were incomparable to this agony. Letting her go had been the most painful thing he'd ever endured. Sacrifice was no easy feat.

Aleksender chuckled low as he sardonically praised his fallen comrades, "I applaud you, my good men."

You have a soldier's heart ...

No. He had nothing.

He jolted to his feet and stormed to the hearth. "Damn! Damn it all to hell!"

Aleksender hollered an animalistic cry. The bottle broke into a million little pieces as it was chucked into the fire, shattering against the logs. The flames brilliantly exploded—fueled by the alcohol and Aleksender's madness. Unable to sustain his weight, he groaned and collapsed to the crutch of his knees. Aleksender vainly hugged himself, aching for comfort. Glazed eyes stared forward as he rocked back and forth, to and fro, behaving like a frightened and forgotten child.

•

Manipulated by the invasion of masculine body weight, Elizabeth tensed as the mattress dipped inward and sank into a heavy curve. Every inch of the bed trembled. Aleksender was quivering from head to toe, his teeth chattering like tin cymbals. She felt his ragged breaths draw intimately close. They wafted across the back of her neck, piercing the air in strained clouds.

An abundance of heat radiated all around, molding the contours of Elizabeth's body. It seared the barrier of her lacy chemise—an unpleasant and unwanted assault upon her senses. A damp hiss of air impaled her neck, her back, each of her shoulders ...

"Elizabeth ..." Aleksender's voice was no more than a tragic whisper and nearly inaudible. "Please, I need you."

A powerful humility and desperation laced every syllable. Elizabeth almost found herself pitying the lovesick fool.

Almost.

"Cold," came his detached murmur, "I feel cold. So ... numb." Yes—Elizabeth knew all about that coldness; it was a coldness that was unshakable and bone-deep, over fifteen years in the making. Deft fingertips wisped down and over the inside of her thigh. "Please. Just hold me."

In wordless response, Elizabeth latched onto Aleksender's trembling hand and forced him away with a dark pleasure.

CHAPTER TWENTY-TWO

Comte Philippe de Lefèvre's memorial fell upon an overcast Sunday afternoon. The sky was bruised and tucked beneath a blanket of lush clouds. Hiding beneath finely carved wings and ornate alcoves, stone angels wept as they shed mortal tears. Shafts of sunlight pierced through the tall oaks and maples, offering slim portals into heaven.

Filling the air with conspicuous whispers and sideways glances, Parisians of all pedigrees infested the winding cobblestone walkways. They huddled nearby Comte de Lefèvre's mausoleum, standing as close as the gendarmes permitted. Hilts of brilliant silver, which adorned the gendarmes' swords, clashed against their navy uniforms.

Ravens perched atop swaying boughs and cold tombstones, staring down, slickly attired in their black mourning coats. Stationed upon a hilltop, Richard, Aleksender, Elizabeth and a few others stood before Comte de Lefèvre's grandiose mausoleum. The glorious stone structure dwarfed everything in comparison.

A pastor read from *The Bible* in a monotonous tone, "The Lord is my shepherd. I shall not want. He maketh me to lie down in green pastures. He leadeth me beside the still waters ..."

The drawled words were entirely lost to Aleksender. His head bowed forward, thoughts consumed with his recent losses. And, alongside each of those dark thoughts, he felt the penetration of Elizabeth's eyes.

•

Respectfully dressed in a black frock coat and gloves, Christophe maneuvered through the nosy crowd as he shoved past highborn ladies and obnoxious dandies with growing cynicism. Determination filled his heart and carried his feet.

Alas, he was stronger and healthier than he'd been in weeks. It wasn't over yet. Hope clung to his chest like an icicle, quickly melting away. Dawn was coming.

Christophe tensed and hung his face. An unavoidable resentment stirred within his chest. Every few steps a slanderous comment—whispered mostly on Aleksender's behalf—reached his ears.

" ... better off servicing his whores ..."

" ... a no good, scarred veteran of war with a particular taste for schoolyard blood ..."

" ... seen sniffing round the skirts of his ward as of late ..."

" ... corrupted by the stage, indeed ... has the breeding of her promiscuous mother ..."

" ... not fit to lick the heels of his father's boots—God rest the poor soul ..."

And so forth.

Unable to see past the elaborate swarm of top hats, Christophe followed after the pastor's emotionless drawl. "Yea, though I walk through the valley of the shadow of death, I will fear no evil: for thou art with me. Thy rod and thy staff comfort me. Surely goodness and mercy shall follow me all the days of my life, and I will dwell in the house of the Lord forever."

A stunning vision lurked not far in the distance. The hem of the young lady's mourning dress billowed all around her, carried by a mild breeze. Buried within an abundance of russet curls, the veil's lace filtered her stare. She twisted a faded, red handkerchief between her fingertips, occasionally blotting away a fallen tear. Yet, her gaze was not fixed on the old comte's mausoleum nor the pastor. It was on Aleksender.

Christophe and Aleksender's eyes came together at that very moment.

"Amen."

The memorial concluded a half hour later. Aleksender lurked beneath a weeping willow, back ranged against its massive trunk, both arms crossed over his chest. His eyes fell shut as a wind chime tinkled overhead. The melody was as soft as the wind's whisper, filled with the sorrow and nostalgia of a lullaby. Every limb stiffened as Christophe appeared behind him. Aleksender sensed his presence. He made no effort to turn.

"Bonjour, mon ami." Leaves crunched beneath the weight of his boots with the audacity of breaking bones. "I must say, your stories did her justice. Indeed. Sofia is quite the beauty."

Aleksender's throat tightened. "You are never to mention her name."

"Anger, Alek?" A sardonic chuckle sounded out. "Good God! Was that possibly anger?"

Aleksender pushed away from the tree and moved toward his comrade. He said nothing. His eyes dared Christophe to continue. "A bit refreshing, I must say," Christophe dryly said, "knowing that you are still capable of feeling. I was beginning to doubt that."

Christophe stroked the curve of his chin. Then he sighed and gave an off look. His eyes rose to Elizabeth. She immediately adjusted her bonnet and glanced away. It was no great mystery that she wore the stripe of a lover scorned.

"Ah. I suspect your faithfulness is not quite as noble as your title, eh?"

Indeed, Christophe knew of Aleksender's unorthodox liaisons better than anyone. But the tone of his voice suggested severe implications—a far cry from a typical debauchery. It spoke of an infidelity that went well beyond flesh and blood—an ultimate unfaithfulness to oneself. A crime even Christophe, a rather notorious skirt-chaser of his time, wouldn't dare commit.

Christophe shook his face. "Elizabeth saw the demon in you. Now I as well. And I daresay your father is turnin' in his very grave right beneath our feet—"

Aleksender lunged at him without warning. He grabbed onto Christophe's cravat and slammed his back against the tree trunk with a brutal force. Aleksender stared daggers, breaths erratic, raven hair wildly tousled. He grasped onto the material of Christophe's frock coat with steel fists, eyes blazing.

"You best learn to hold your tongue, Cleef. You and your insolence tread a thin line. Men have been guillotined for far less."

The threat slid from Christophe's back. His feathers remained unruffled. In contrast to Aleksender's madness, he was perfectly cool and collected.

"Gah! Take care! You'll ruin my best frock. And, unlike you, I haven't the luxury nor francs to buy another."

Christophe's eyes drifted to the horizon. Sofia was nowhere to be found. Aleksender released him with a look of sheer misery. The faintest trace of shame embedded his gaze—as if he knew just who Christophe sought.

Christophe seized onto Aleksender's vulnerability. "She's a little girl, Alek. A little girl and your puppet! It is all rather amusing—a child of God, harlot—what, pray tell, shall the noble Comte desire next?"

"You know nothing."

His lips curled into a slick smirk. "Better to know nothing than to be nothing. To feel nothing." Then, through a tense sigh, he added, "Paris—she is angry. How long do you think you can ignore that? Ignore your duty?" Only silence. Christophe scoffed, cursing beneath his breath. A fierce resentment was forming deep inside him. His comrade's indifference was bone chilling.

"To have so much potential for power, for change … to throw it all away is unforgivable. Unredeemable." More silence. "Don't you understand? The people of Paris are starving. Children are born in gutters, only to die. Honest women, virtuous schoolgirls, are whoring themselves. Men are making dinners of flea-ridden sewer rats. All while you hide up in your fancy chateau—regarding everything and everyone with your damn devil-may-care charm."

Christophe swore that a look of shock had creased Aleksender's brow. But it was gone as quickly as it had come. His face had settled back into a mask of unyielding apathy.

"You best be on your way, Christophe." Gesturing one of the imposing gendarmes, not bothering to hide his grin. "If not, I can surely arrange for you to be shown out."

"Pitiful." The threat was as hollow and cold as Aleksender's green eyes.

"You fool no one. You are every bit the self-righteous, holier-than-thou knave you claim to loathe. Only much worse." A sad and mocking smile formed on Christophe's lips. "You are no more than a disgrace. A disgrace to her. A disgrace to Paris. A disgrace to me and your father."

Christophe awaited the wrath of Aleksender's unleashed fury. It never came. Instead, the comte swallowed with a curt and almost humble nod. "I'm afraid I must bid you adieu, Monsieur Cleef."

He stepped forward as Aleksender turned away. Christophe's

emotions bested him as he trembled from his anger.

"I am not you. I shall not stay silent. This ... this is far from over. You hear me, Alek? In spades, you shall pay for your apathy! On my word, 'ol friend ..." His final words dripped with mirth and an ominous edge. "Do take care. The both of you."

Aleksender eased toward him, stride slow and steady, eyes blazing. But Christophe never met his glare. He was focused entirely on the darkening skyline.

"You listen and you listen well," Aleksender spat through a clenched jaw and gritted teeth. "I shall warn you only once: do not underestimate my power."

"Been listening with a deaf ear, have you?" Christophe slapped his thigh, head tossed back in a hearty chuckle. "Ah, mon ami, you amuse me so." After a moment, he leisurely straightened out the rumpled cravat and regained his composure. A feeling of weightlessness descended whilst eyes of cognac locked with eyes of emerald. "Indeed. I underestimate many things about you, Monsieur le Comte. But no—never your power."

•

Sofia hadn't stirred a limb, though the memorial had been over for a good hour. The onlookers had more or less cleared out, plunging the cemetery into eerie silence. Needing privacy and peace of mind—unable to stomach the sight of Aleksender and his relatives a moment longer—she'd wandered away from the memorial. Angelic monuments and towering mausoleums filled her vision. A raven's call mated with the whispering wind as the trees gently swayed, sweeping a sweet fragrance into her nostrils.

How strange it was, being surrounded by death. She scanned the jagged, grave-filled horizon with an ache in her heart. Many of the tombstones were overgrown with weeds, long forgotten by their loved ones. She crouched to her knees, seated herself in front of a rather sad-looking grave, and brushed away a tangle of wild greenery.

Sofia picked one of Père Lachaise's native roses and laid it atop Dumont's stone. The inscription's simplistic wording spoke for itself. Maurice Vincent Dumont had died a lonely man.

Sofia inhaled a dejected sigh and came to her feet. Her thoughts shattered as a breeze stirred, wrenching the crimson handkerchief from her fingers. The wind playfully tossed it about, throwing it this way and that, spiriting away the beloved silk. Its scarlet material brilliantly clashed against the baby blue sky. She picked up her skirts and surged forward. A soft protest left her lips as she pursued the precious keepsake.

Her eyes followed its lazy descent as it fluttered to the ground with a somersault. A second later it stilled, barricaded against a gentleman's polished boot.

He lowered gracefully to his knees and fetched the handkerchief, brushing away nonexistent specks of dirt. "My lady."

He was very handsome, boasting a broad, dimpled chin and wholesome good looks. But something warned her that he was every bit rogue.

She frowned and chewed absently at her bottom lip. An ugly scar disfigured his cheek—the one blemish to an otherwise startling face—stretching from ear to mouth. Sofia tore her stare away, inwardly cursing herself. Really—she, of all people, ought to have known better.

The gentleman surprised Sofia and only grinned. Outlining the raised flesh with a fingertip, he murmured in an easy drawl, "A knife wound." Her lips parted in speech but no sound came. His grin widened to impossible limits. "No worries. I'm of no danger to you, I assure—far from a pick-pocket or alleyway brute." A brief silence pressed between them. He stared up at the setting sun and exhaled the sigh of a tired man. A man who had seen and lived unthinkable tragedy. "I recently returned from the war."

His lips lifted into a dashing, crooked smile. He stared down at his gloved hand, fondling the handkerchief's faded material. After a moment of apparent contemplation, he passed it to Sofia.

"Thank you, monsieur. I would have been positively lost without it."

"My pleasure, Mademoiselle Rose."

Sofia pursed her lips together and studied the smooth stranger from head to toe.

"Pardon me, monsieur," she inquired, "but have we met before?"

"Ah, I am afraid not, chérie. Consider me a dedicated admirer. One of many, I'm sure."

An oddly strained laugh escaped her. Of course. He recognized her from the stage. She forced a smile that didn't quite reach her eyes.

"You are lovely, mademoiselle. Almost impossibly so. And even lovelier up close. 'specially when you smile."

She blushed a deep crimson, both feet shifting uncomfortably beneath her skirts. His flattery was too strong for her liking ... but something about him radiated. She stepped forward and lowered her dark lashes, appreciating the mere comfort of another human being. The full extent of her loneliness and solitude dawned on her. "Thank you. You are very kind."

The gentleman threw a sideways glance, studying her features with an astute awareness.

"It seems I'll be withdrawing from the opera quite soon." Sofia held her tongue as heat rose to her cheeks. What was she thinking? "Oh, I am not sure why I told you such a thing. I haven't been myself lately."

"I understand." He stepped forward with a small grin. "Better yet, I relate."

Sofia smiled softly, believing his words, aching for the companionship he offered no matter how fleeting it may be. "Go on, chérie. I'm all ears," he encouraged. "Unburden yourself."

"Oh, thank you—but there's really not much to be said. I'm at a bit of a crossroads, you see—deciding whether I should take my vows or not."

He arched a fine brow and thoughtfully stroked his chin. "Hmm. In that case, mademoiselle, I am afraid I must object."

"Object?"

"—to this taking-of-the-vows ordeal. It seems an unfortunate waste—a beautiful, talented lady living as a nun."

Sofia smothered a laugh with her palm. "Ah. But you are biased, monsieur!"

Wearing the impossible look of angelic innocence, he raised both of his hands in a harmless shrug. "Naturally so."

Their playful exchange disappeared with a silence.

"Were you acquainted with the ol' comte?"

The sudden inquiry startled Sofia. Her eyes jerked up to him as she held his leveled gaze. She swallowed and glanced at the grass beneath her feet. "Yes ... I am a friend. A friend of the family."

He chuckled, the rich and charming sound filling the grave emptiness. "Why, of course you are—being le Comte's ward and such. How very daft I must seem."

Blood drained from her rosy cheeks. When she spoke, her voice was shaky, words unconvincing and almost silent. "Not at all, monsieur."

The gentleman furrowed his brow and frowned. "Are you quite all right? You look unwell. Perhaps—"

"Please, don't mind me. I'm only tired."

His head dipped forward and sank into a slight nod. "Have you an escort? I daresay a cemetery is no place for a young lady to venture alone."

"Yes," she quickly fibbed. "A carriage is awaiting my return, parked just down the pathway."

Exhaling a sigh of defeat and straightening his gloves, her stranger grumbled, "Very well." He stuffed both hands deep into his pockets and smiled. "I should like to call on you sometime. With le Comte's blessing, of course."

The blunt request rendered Sofia speechless. Beneath the lace of her veil, her sapphire eyes widened, appearing bright and luminous. She shook her pretty head, as if in stunned disbelief, neatly tucking a wild curl behind each ear.

"Forgive me, monsieur, but I don't even know your name."

"I suppose I am a brute, after all." He threw his head back as the broad expanse of his chest rumbled in a wonderfully masculine laugh. "I fear I abandoned my sense of etiquette out on the battlefield." He scratched at the stubble on his chin, murmuring a dry afterthought, "That, amongst other things ..."

The harshly spat statement raised little red flags, shooting chills up and down Sofia's spine. In a single heartbeat, everything seemed to suddenly darken. Père Lachaise, the afternoon sky, her dashing gentleman—they all mutated before her very eyes.

Sofia suppressed a shudder. The man's stare was dangerously perceptive. As he allowed the mask of his façade to slip away, she knew that his kindness had been a masquerade and nothing more—a fact that left Sofia feeling oddly disheartened.

"Ah, I see that I have made you uncomfortable."

"No. No, I—"

"As well you should be," he interjected with only a hint of mockery. Auburn eyes flickered with a devious flare. "After all ... the souls of the fallen are known to wander cemeteries."

What a peculiar and disturbing thing to say.

"I ... I don't believe in such things."

"I present to you, *my little Sofia* ..." The stranger outstretched both arms with a rolling laugh and signaled himself. "Flesh and blood proof before your eyes."

"Tell me who you are," she breathlessly demanded.

He stepped back, a grin plastered to his face. The horribly sardonic expression twisted the scar, transforming his disfigurement into something diabolical. She feared for herself.

"I'm a friend of the family, you could say." Dipping into a shallow bow, he collected one of her fair hands and pressed a kiss upon her knuckles. The gesture of mock propriety sent more chills up and down her spine.

His opposite hand fell out of vision, brushing down and over the side of her body, skirting across the handkerchief's faded material.

Sofia remained ignorant of the gesture.

"Till our paths cross once more, my fair lady, I bid you adieu."

And then, like a true phantom, he was gone. Sofia stared after her mysterious stranger, plagued with a reluctant empathy. She watched as his elegant form weaved in and out of the cold tombstones and sculpted angels, the tail of his frock coat fluttering like wings, wondering just how it felt to fall from grace.

CHAPTER TWENTY-THREE

Nine years earlier ...

The hearth chirped and crackled as its flames warmed the sleek floorboards. Lost within the soothing rhythm of her guardian's voice, Sofia lay close to the fire, bundled up in oblivion. In mere moments, her bright blue eyes fell to half-mast and her heart set sail. She exhaled a shallow sigh and settled into the cocoon of her inner sanctuary.

"'No red rose in all my garden!' he cried, his beautiful eyes filled with tears. 'Ah, on what little things does happiness depend! I have read all that the wise men have written, and all the secrets of philosophy are mine, yet for want of a red rose is my life made wretched.'"

A melody of giggles escaped from Sofia's lips. As always, Aleksender shifted his tone, playing the part of each character with a delightful accuracy and exuberance. On nights such as these, he transformed before her very eyes. The harsh and cold façade he wore during the daytime was nonexistent. Within her presence, something inside of him blossomed to life. It was as though his spirit had once withered away, and now had been nurtured back to health. And it was a phenomenon she, too, often experienced at his side.

Whenever Alek was in arm's reach she felt most alive. She smiled for no reason at all and settled deeper into her daydreams.

Aleksender peered down at Sofia, taking pleasure in her awakened happiness. Although she'd been in his care only weeks, a strong attachment had already formed between them.

Many of the cuts and bruises were still fresh and gleaming. Her left wrist was secured in a Velpeau bandage—a clever contraption that had been fashioned together by none other than the renowned Dr. Alfred Velpeau himself. Her arm slung across her chest in a sort of hammock, keeping the broken limb immobile and sheathed.

"The young student continued to weep, feeling very much alone. 'Here at last is a true lover,' said the nightingale. 'Night after night have I sung of him, though I knew him not. Night after night have I told his story to the stars, and now I see him. His hair is dark as the hyacinth blossom, and his lips are red as the rose of his desire. But passion has made his face like pale ivory, and sorrow has set her seal upon his brow.'"

Sofia thoughtfully propped her elbow onto the floor and cradled the curve of her cheek. With an intuition well beyond her ten years, she observed Aleksender's dark hair and the lines of anguish that had come to burden *his* fine brow.

What made her guardian so very sad? After all, he was simply the handsomest, kindest, gentlest, most intelligent, most caring gentleman in the whole wide world. He deserved only happiness—nothing less.

The rustle of parchment broke the quiet as Aleksender turned the page. Clearing his throat, he resumed, "The young Student looked up at the sky and murmured, 'If I bring her a red rose she will dance with me till dawn.'"

A strange and unnamable awareness chilled Sofia's body. In the span of a heartbeat, an ominous haze seemed to envelop the entire drawing room. Aleksender's voice softened to a delicate whisper.

"'If I bring her a red rose, I shall hold her in my arms, and she will lean her head upon my shoulder, and her hand will be clasped in mine. But there is no red rose in my garden, so I shall sit lonely, and she will pass me by. She will have no heed of me, and my heart will break.'"

Aleksender carefully shut the book and marked the page with a red handkerchief. Sofia sat up with a visible pout as an array of dark curls tumbled down and over her shoulders. He chuckled low, reading into her thoughts.

"I daresay it is long past your bedtime."

"Just a bit longer? Pleeeaaase?"

"Non, non. We mustn't tire you for tomorrow's lesson."

"Oh, poo!" Sofia rose to her feet. Tiny shoulders drooping, her lungs expanded with a sigh of defeat. "All right."

"That's a good girl. Now go run along, ma petit, and one of the servants shall ready you for bed."

Sofia gracefully skipped over to him, smiling from ear to ear. She was positively delightful—a charming mass of uncontainable energy. And yet, as much as he enjoyed her company, he knew the chateau was not a proper home for Sofia. There were too many things he simply could not provide her. And then there were those haunted moments of self-loathing, pain and confusion—things a little girl should never have to bear witness. Yes, his mind concluded, he'd have to arrange other housing arrangements. Decided on the matter, Aleksender shook away his thoughts and eyed his darling ward.

Sofia primly folded her good hand behind her back, just as her governess had instructed she should, and awarded his chin with a tiny kiss.

Aleksender lifted a hand in a suave gesture; it vanished behind Sofia's left ear for no longer than an instant. When he withdrew, a red rose was wedged between his thumb and forefinger.

Magic.

"A red rose!" she cried out, sounding very much like the Nightingale. "You found one!"

Aleksender laughed with the entirety of his heart and tucked the bloom behind her ear. "And now that you have your red rose, ma petit, you may sleep soundly."

"I promise! Bonne nuit, Alek!"

"Bonne nuit, little one."

A foreign sense of worth and contentment flooded Aleksender. Deep in his heart, he knew that saving Sofia had preserved him. And the revelation was a beam of light inside of his soul.

Ah, on what little things does happiness depend!

•

The tender memory faded away as each cord of beauty twisted into something terrible.

The windowpane's rhythmic thumping. An unhinged latch. The subtle creaking of wood ... approaching footfall. The whispered breeze of a frock coat. A weak protest, a silenced cry. The embrace of a gloved hand snaked around a slender throat. Applied pressure—the threat of crushed vocals cords. The splash of hot tears. A hissed command and unveiled threat. *"Ferme la bouche ..."*

The brilliant glint of a knife. A chuckle—devious, rich and full of mirth. A damp handkerchief, red and faded, coiled into a tight ball and draped over flesh. One last cry.

Darkness—immovable and inescapable.

·

Rue de la Paix was packed to its limits. The square was a perfect viewing spot for such destruction. The Vendôme Column was front and center, Napoleon's lifeless stone features etched with blissful oblivion. Ladies hung out of their balconies and chattered amongst themselves. Days earlier, they'd coated the windows with paper and paste to help numb the shattering blow to come.

Down in the street below, newspaper and pastry vendors rolled through the congestion, handing out goods as if they were party favors. A multitude of red flags lined the inside of the square, branding Place Vendôme as a place of liberty and freedom.

The thunder of drums shook the ground. National Guardsmen from various battalions throughout the city had come together for this exceptional occasion. They stood at the foot of the column, passing cigars back and forth as the last preparations were carried out. Workmen drove wedges into the column's sawed crevice, loosening the incalculable weight from the base.

Members of the Commune arrived at the scene in heroic fashion. Propped on horseback, the men stationed themselves in a single-file line at the front of Rue de la Paix's alley.

It was Christophe Cleef who gave the signal.

A number of marching bands issued the drum roll. In the midst of the excitement, a rather courageous man shoved through the crowd. He came beside Christophe and yelled over the music and jeers. "Can't you leave it alone?" His plea was lost to the din. The horse gave an irritated whinny as the man tugged at its hanging bridle.

Christophe narrowed his eyes and stared down at a face that wasn't a day under sixty. "What are you doing? Out of the way! Guards!"

"The column—can't you leave it alone?" he repeated, a knot of desperation in his voice. "It has cost us all so much."

Christophe's broad shoulders shook with laughter. "Yes—yes, it has, indeed. It has cost millions of lives. Now step aside if you care to keep your head." Defeated, the man hung his face and did as commanded, vanishing back into the crowd.

Christophe squinted against the blaring sunrays. On all sides of the monument, ropes were held by over seventy sailors. Muscles strained beneath the afternoon light as the greatest match of tug-of-war in the history of the world took place. As calm and as sure as ever, Napoleon gave a slight sway and glanced down at his executioners. The drums reached their crescendo and faded into a patriotic melody. Minutes later, applause erupted as the column gave way and crumbled at its seams.

The Commune struggled to chasten their horses as Napoleon Bonaparte met his inevitable doom. He crashed down, smashing the cobblestones into rubble—lying before his people in a miserable wreck. In the force of his fall, an arm was amputated and his head cleanly severed from his body.

Women spat upon the heap of stone that once was Napoleon's face and cried nasty obscenities.

In a single Monday afternoon, the Commune had sealed Paris's fate. And now the entire world was crashing down.

Christophe surveyed the riot and escalating madness. His heart triumphed. It was the birth of a new revolution.

Caught in the excitement and flushed with power, he joined in the chanted cry: "*Vive la Commune! Vive la République! Vive la Résistance!* Death to the Empire!"

CHAPTER TWENTY-FOUR

May 21, 1871
La Semaine Sanglante, Day One
"The Blood Week"

Sounds of war shook Aleksender awake. He leapt from beneath the thick coverlet, panting and drenched in buckets of sweat. But alas—for the first time, the booming cannons and roaring firearms were not mere sentiments of his nightmares. He was not trapped within that twisted, internal limbo—that purgatory in which all soldiers go to die. These sounds of war were real.

Very real.

The army of Versailles was upon them. Civil war had finally claimed Paris.

Aleksender stared off at the billowing drapes as he fought to catch his breath. Beside him, Elizabeth continued to sleep in peaceful oblivion.

No, his mind confirmed. The rolling cannons didn't inspire images of dismembered comrades, nor did they take command of his mind, tricking him to believe he was back in those bloodstained battlefields.

No, it wasn't war that claimed his thoughts. It was something much worse and inconceivably more disheartening.

Bile seared Aleksender's lungs and rose inside his throat. He could feel it. He felt it within his very bones. She was in terrible danger.

•

A resonating knock filled the chateau hours later. The sound was jarring within the silence. The first footman, who was presently disheveled and in his nightgown, greeted the horse messenger. Visibly jumping at the occasional explosion, he bristled to the front door with an uncharacteristic clumsiness.

"Bonsoir," the rough-looking messenger drawled, speaking before the footman could offer any greetings. "I hope le Comte may forgive me for bargin' in at such an ungodly hour." One of his hands vanished beneath the riding coat and withdrew a bundled piece of parchment. The footman glanced at both the messenger and his horse—absorbing the fact that neither was adorned with a proper delivery satchel.

"Who sends you, monsieur?" the footman hesitantly asked.

The man merely cleared his throat and continued with his objective. "I've a letter here."

Brows drawn together, the footman nodded and accepted the parchment from the messenger's callused fingers. "Very well. I shall deliver it to him personally."

"See that you do. Tonight." An unsettling grin stretched the messenger's swarthy complexion as he mounted his horse. "I am told it's of great importance." He kicked the creature's flank with a booted heel and tugged on the leather reins. "Dire importance."

◆

Aleksender hovered above his writing desk, the magnificent curve of his back slumped into a tight arch. Both hands were propped onto the counter, stabilizing his languid bodyweight.

Alas, the world had tipped off its very axis. Tears he refused to shed stung his eyes and blurred his vision. The crinkled parchment was unfurled like two gaping wings, its unholy contents unveiled. Aleksender's gaze ran across the familiar and nearly illegible writing for the hundredth time: *Feel nothing? — C.C.*

Sofia's red handkerchief had been pinned to the words. And the sentiment was drenched in blood.

"Something told me I would find you here." Elizabeth's voice broke the silent din and startled Aleksender from his haze. "The letter—"

"Is of no concern to you."

"On the contrary," she spouted in quick reply. "It takes you from our bed." Elizabeth fastened her nightgown's sash and shuffled closer, careful and cautious. "What does it inquire?" She raised her hand, readying to sweep the raven locks from his eyes.

Aleksender averted his face from her touch, every muscle tense and aching. "Let me alone."

"Why, Aleksender!" she gasped in disbelief. "You are crying!"

He heaved a sardonic chuckle that made her skin crawl. "I keep convincing myself," he absently rambled, speaking to no one, "that it is not my fault."

"What? What are you—"

" … cannot stop … replaying our parting words. Indeed. Those words shall follow me everywhere … into the grave … beyond the grave …"

He laughed a terribly sinister laugh—the laugh of a true mad-man—and groped onto his chest in agony. "Far, far beyond the grave."

Elizabeth's spine stiffened, chilled from the coarseness of his voice, the strange and animalistic detachment of his stare. "Please! I beg you. Stop this—"

"Death is no escape," he hissed between clenched teeth. "No! There is no escaping." Aleksender proceeded to pace back and forth. He groaned like a wild, caged beast and neurotically speared fingertips through his sweaty hairline. "I shall have you know, it is far better to know nothing than to be nothing."

"Stop this!"

"Feel nothing."

"Listen to yourself!"

"Yes. The fool was right in that. I feel nothing. Nothing."

Aleksender's body sagged against the wall as he exhaled a strained breath. Struggling to shut out the world around him, he pinched away the tears that burned his eyes.

"The nightingale pressed closer to the thorn … closer … closer till it pierced his bleeding heart." Aleksender raked his fingertips through the vast waves of his unkempt hair. He rocked back and forth, back and forth, tugging at his scalp with an escalating mad-ness and desperation. Black threads were plucked with each little pull—as if he was testing his very ability to feel.

"Bitter, bitter was the pain … wilder and wilder grew her song, for she sang of the love that dies not in the tomb … a love perfected by death."

"You are mad."

His hands fell away and descended down to his sides. They

curled into two clenched fists. Elizabeth eyed his predatory stance with a jolt of renowned fear. A flash of white teeth gleamed in the darkness as he smiled wide.

Elizabeth knew that he was far from amused.

"Ah, I am afraid madness is one luxury I've been denied."

A stream of blood ran down his cheek as it seeped from a cut on his forehead … a cut he'd inflicted upon himself only minutes ago. Aleksender turned to stone, exhausted from his self-mutilation.

Elizabeth's pulse raced as he stared blankly forward, unblinking and unmoving.

She struck Aleksender across the face in an attempt to reel him back into reality. The beginnings of a thick beard stung her palm. The sickening crack of flesh against flesh resonated within the silence.

Aleksender didn't stir a limb.

"Only one person could draw such agony from you. Your little whore!" Aleksender caught her wrists midair as Elizabeth made for another strike. His long fingers coiled around her skin like twin serpents, eyes seething.

Her voice was perfectly calm, a grim and knowing smile tugging at her lips. "I will scream. I shall gladly wake every servant."

She gasped as a low growl reverberated against her. His hold intensified, strangling her very blood flow. Heavy breaths fanned against her flushed cheek, branding her forever.

"I defy you to say her name." The tone of Aleksender's threat mirrored the serenity of her voice. But his words bore a jagged edge.

Aleksender enveloped her wrist impossibly tighter; Elizabeth flinched free with a cry. Her eyes fell to her trembling hand. She absently fondled her wedding finger and caressed the cold trinket. "How I had tormented myself! So many nights I'd lie awake, imagining you with all those whores … wondering where I went wrong."

"And now?" His voice was a deep, tentative whisper.

"I pitied you then. Always distant, never complete. I pity you now … an old fool in love." Aleksender tensed as she recited the very words from his letter.

She shook her head. "But even more I pity myself for believing you might have changed." Elizabeth collected the note from the writing desk's sleek surface.

He shook his head as a rush of guilt overcame him. "I wish I could change. For fifteen years, I've wished for it every day. Even more, I wish I could be the husband you deserve."

"Yes, well, more often than not, I fear wishes are wasted breaths." Fingering the sullied material, Elizabeth laughed beneath a strained breath. "Sofia's handkerchief? She truly was made to dance. I would often watch her from our box, completely taken away. Beautiful. Strangely incomplete." She set down the note and gazed into the haunted depths of Aleksender's eyes. There, she found the remains of a long-suffering soul. After a moment, she took his hand with a weak smile. "I see now. You are both equally trapped. And *I wish* it were in my power to free you."

◆

Aleksender returned to his study, brandy in hand. Memories bombarded his consciousness as he slowly slipped into a blissful, drunken stupor.

But he found no peace. There was no sleep. No dreams. There were only nightmares. Within himself, a symphony of soul shattering screams and bombs exploded behind his shut eyes, *a wailing babe, the hum of a distorted prayer ... the seductive glint of a knife.*

Then he simply descended into black oblivion. Tucked inside that darkly comforting void he was silent and complete.

CHAPTER TWENTY-FIVE

May 22, 1871
La Semaine Sanglante, Day Two

Countless bones and skulls were piled on top of each other, col-lectively forming a gruesome wall endless in length. Composed of winding tunnels built entirely from death, such a hell was not for the faint of heart. The underground catacombs were an astonish-ing and grotesque work of art—constructed from over six million human skeletons—residing as a labyrinth of ultimate despair. A warning to ward off trespassers was engraved across one of the low archways: *Beware the Empire of Death!*

The drone of repetitive dripping echoed, chilling and naturally amplified. Clutched within the grasp of a bloated hand, a lantern swayed midair, highlighting each of the grinning skulls.

Heavy steps resonated as the man entered a makeshift holding cell. The illumination came to an abrupt stop and glowed like a diva's spotlight; it encircled a prisoner who was cloaked in shadow and slumped against a far wall. At the sound of steps, the man's face lolled forward and eyes squeezed shut. The bruised line of his jaw seethed blood. A formal cassock robe fluttered around his form, the abundance of drapery falling in lush white folds. Accenting the fatal severity of his condition, they hung from his beaten body like loose skin.

Even a blind man could see he was on the threshold of death. Both hands were cuffed and suspended midair. Resembling the sacrifice of Christ with uncanny precision, his limbs were out-stretched and fastened tight—both arms embracing his dark fate.

Two chained corpses rested on either side of him. Each one

stared forward, seeing nothing. Indeed, their decapitated heads laid at his heels, strewn carelessly about, the stumps of their necks clotted with blood.

The prisoner's head collided with the stone wall as it fell back in a rush of despair. Blood leaked from the corners of his eyes, cascading down his sallow cheeks. They looked remarkably like crimson tears. And he was not alone. The Marquis de Boury was seated across the cell waiting for his fate to be sealed.

The captor knelt on the ground and tore the prisoner's robe aside. His flesh glistened, fresh punctures marring his body from head to toe. A pectoral crucifix dangled against the thin expanse of his chest. The gold was dingy and stained with blood, the beauty of its sovereign likeness tarnished beyond recognition.

The captor clamped onto the pendant and lifted it to his eyes. The prisoner breathlessly struggled, groaning and battling his chains.

A diabolical chuckle swelled the darkness. "Where is your God now, my good archbishop?" The captor heaved a melodramatic sigh, released the crucifix, and rose to his feet. He appeared as no more than a demonic silhouette, the hilt of his blade alive with a sparkle.

Keys jangled as he crossed the cell. He unlocked the marquis's cuffs, grabbed onto the scruff of his collar, and shoved him to the floor. Marquis de Boury was old—well into his seventies—and nearly unconscious. Unsheathing the weapon, the captor aligned it to his neck and held it beneath the arch of his chin. He slowly drew it away, engraving a faint line of blood in the sweat-lined skin.

The archbishop shut his eyes and bowed his face in silent prayer. He murmured incoherent words of salvation for Marquis de Boury.

The captor raised his blade in a majestic gesture and positioned it adjacent to the Marquis de Boury's neck. After a brief moment of silence, he pulled his arm up and back—swinging the blade, full force, like a bat ...

•

Deep rumbling and the roar of cannons echoed overhead like thunder. A blood-curdling scream shook the Commune's base. Just as quickly, the sounds choked off and faded into dead silence.

Sofia cringed at the familiar refrains and tugged at her restraints. Trembling, she cried out as the rusted cuff sliced her wrist. A stream of blood trickled down the slope of her elevated arm. Her curls were severely tangled and heavy with mud, her hairline clotted. The material of her chemise was stained, drenched in a mixture of blood, sweat and dirt.

Sofia parted her chapped lips with a groan. Despite a few of the men's half-hearted persuading, she had continually refused a drink of water. Disoriented, clearly drugged, and zoning in and out of consciousness, Sofia had proceeded to tell each man precisely what she thought of his pestering—a nasty charade that had earned her two ice-cold splashes to the face.

But she regretted all of that now. Why had she been so very stubborn?

Her tongue seemed to have grown to the roof of her mouth. Coated by a thick white film, it felt impossibly swollen and bone-dry. She had awakened in this hell a few hours ago—chained to the wall, shivering, and beyond nauseated.

A thousand questions bombarded her thoughts, each one more desperate than the one before. What was the last thing she could bring to memory? Where was she? For what purpose? Who were those gruff brutes? Was she to be raped? And what, pray, had been the cause of all that terrible screaming? Was she to suffer the same fate?

Was Alek in harm? She felt herself begin to panic. The music of bombs resounded every so often, causing all of Paris's underground to tremble.

"Monsieur?" The deep voice snapped Sofia from her whirlwind of thoughts. She inhaled a sharp breath and searched her surroundings.

No one was in sight.

With a tinge of fear and ache in her gut, she studied the wide selection of weapons that were ceremoniously arranged before her. Guns, daggers, and the like had been propped up against a parallel wall. They stood as the one proof she had not been abandoned and left down here to rot and die, only the sewer rats for company. Above the weapons, a crimson flag hung like a mural. *Vive la Commune!* was printed across its canvas, each letter prouder than the one before it.

The rhythmic clink of approaching boots anchored her attention. "Monsieur?" came the rugged voice once more—now sufficiently closer. "Is all well?"

"Daft idiot! I have been absent little more than two hours. In Christ's name, what have you done?" Sofia's ears pricked and eyes widened. That voice! She knew that voice ...

"Carried out the orders, monsieur."

"Orders? Whose orders?"

"Maurice—Maurice Lupont. He—"

"Maurice Lupont? Fool! You answer to me and only me!"

"Yes. Yes, 'course, Monsieur Cleef."

Cleef—Christophe Cleef. Her dark stranger. A veteran of war and Aleksender's dearest friend.

A dozen or so men surrounded Christophe, enveloping him within a loyal ring of followers. Tan, gruff, and clearly members of the working class, they appeared ready for anything. It seemed that the Dark Ages had returned to Europe, and lawlessness was king. Only through the embrace of death and decay would things again be righted. Only after conditions worsened would they be allowed to heal.

Regardless, Sofia's heart sang in swift relief. Surely, he meant to aid her from this mess!

Surely, the noble Christophe Cleef was not the enemy?

•

"You did this to me."

Brimming with a devil-may care attitude, Christophe eased toward the small and helpless voice. His lost humanity resurrected as he was struck with the faintest trace of pity. Chained and defenseless, the chit resembled a virgin sacrifice, entombed within a crypt and strapped to the altar. But no—he knew this girl was no blushing virgin. Chastened by the thought and returning to his sardonic nature, Christophe exhaled a breath that he hadn't known he was holding. Grinning wide, he knelt beside her and thoughtfully cocked his head.

"Well. Not entirely." Blue eyes pierced the dark as Sofia peered up at him. She was emotionally and physically drained, half-drugged, and weaker than a baby fawn. There was little to no fight left in her. "Could not have done it without Monsieur le Comte's cooperation ... or, shall I say, lack of ..."

Sofia revived with a bolt of energy. Blood crept down each wrist as she tugged on her restraints. "N-No! What have you done! That screaming—was that him? Where is he? Where is Alek? Answer me! Answer me now!"

Christophe lowered himself to his knees, almost in slow motion, eyes softening. He pressed his index finger to Sofia's lips, demanding silence. She jerked away and inhaled a strangled gasp. The back of her head collided with the wall in an attempt to escape his touch. Her breaths grew shallower as Christophe cradled her cheek in his palm.

"No, please. Don't touch me. Just leave me alone." Her voice sounded far away, distant and surreal, spoken through the filter of some lucid nightmare.

"Shh. There is nothing to be afraid of. You are under my protection now, my little Sofia."

My little Sofia.

He withdrew a cigar and matches from his coat and lit a smoke. Sofia eyed the blazing tip with an unnatural fear and shrank against the wall. Sweeping away the tangle of curls, Christophe clenched the cigar between his teeth and laid a hand upon her shoulder. The countless burns were painful to behold. He gave a dull grunt as he snuffed the cigar with his heel.

"Christophe ..." Their eyes joined together at the whispered sound of his name. "I know you. I know you are a good man. I know you have a soldier's heart." A dull silence weighed heavily in the air. Burned by her words and rendered speechless, Christophe swallowed deeply as his hand fell from her skin.

"Please ... Why are you doing this?"

"I was left no other choice."

His words were no more than a tragic sigh. For an iridescent moment, Sofia believed it had been the wind weeping.

And it was weeping for the three of them.

•

Aleksender lay in bed, sleepless and still. His mind and body felt numb and detached. He was soulless ... far more dead than alive.

A tentative touch whispered across the unfertile terrain of his back, stroking the various crevices and scars. After a moment Elizabeth's voice broke the silence. "What happened to you?" The words were soft, serene and empathetic. How could they be any different? He was broken.

What dark secret was locked in his heart? What was eating away at his mind and body—consuming her husband from the inside out?

The questions were a conundrum and the answers a paradox. And Aleksender found that all his frustration, guilt, love and sadness could be eloquently expressed through a single word: "Defeat."

•

A shaft of light split the floor as Aleksender eased into his father's study. He turned the knob of a kerosene lamp and flooded the room with a warm glow. Nostalgia filled the darkest and most delicate crevices of his heart.

This had been his father's most treasured room. The smell of brandy and whiskey still hung in the air. Aleksender inhaled his father's memory with a heavy heart. He hadn't dared step foot inside Philippe's domain since his return from the war. The memories, the resentment for his loss, had simply been too great.

Now he felt only contentment within his father's presence among his belongings and precious keepsakes. Philippe de Lefèvre had been a connoisseur of knowledge and the arts. Telescopes, globes and other worldly trinkets filled his study like toys fill a nursery.

Aleksender wandered over to a towering bookshelf. Stroking his father's memory, he ran a fingertip across the dusty bindings, leaving railroad tracks wherever he touched … Descartes' *Mediations on First Philosophy*. Novels of all genres. *The Happy Prince and Other Tales.*

Oscar Wilde's masterpiece protruded farther than the others; it seemed to beckon Aleksender's attention. He obliged as he breathlessly slid the slender book from its home in the shelf. Dust clouded the air as he tossed it open. A folded piece of parchment was tucked inside, bookmarking page thirteen—the beginning of *The Nightingale and the Rose.*

Aleksender unfolded the note, instantly recognizing his father's elegant penmanship.

Dearest Aleksender,
I fear I may not live to see your return.
It is for this reason I'm compelled to write you. I meant to tell you the truth years ago, but could never quite find the courage. Now,

I fear that time has run out. I shan't tell you here, nor do I need to.

Above all things, I owe you an apology. I only wished to protect you and your brother. I yearned to replace the darkness with beauty. But the truth has always been there, buried beneath the surface of your consciousness, clawing to break free. I have seen it in your eyes.

Perhaps it is time that the illusion is lifted. You need only to look inside of yourself.

I love you dearly, my son.

The wailing babe, glinting knife, sloshing water—the shattered memories simultaneously bombarded Aleksender.

He remembered. A grand crash resounded. Aleksender collapsed to the floor as his legs failed him. Barely able to breathe, his entire body convulsed, eyes seeing varying shades of red. Beads of sweat poured from his hairline and slid down his flesh in strides, the salty liquid distorting his vision.

Elizabeth found him in this state—curled up on the floor like a young boy, shuddering, a volume of incoherent words slewing from his lips.

"Aleksender!" He latched onto her forearm as she knelt to help him up. His gaze was wild and detached; it seemed he was watching something unfold within his mind.

Yes. In a single rush of despair, he remembered everything.

Those loose puzzle pieces, which had longtime floated inside of his awareness, came together in a glorious epiphany. The terrible memory was at last unveiled—a memory Aleksender immediately wished had stayed forgotten.

"Aleksender, speak to me! Please! What—"

"I remember."

"What? What do you mean? What happened?"

Staring down at his father's words, Aleksender sagged against the bookshelf, the frantic beat of his heart booming in his ears.

"I killed her. I killed my mother."

CHAPTER TWENTY-SIX

Twenty-six years earlier …

Comtesse Victoria de Lefèvre paced through Paris's sleeping streets. Her heels melodically clinked as the elegance of her beauty contrasted against the vast night. A little boy of ten years clasped her hand as he struggled to keep up stride, three of his steps matching one of her own.

"Maman," Aleksender piped, a full-blown pout fixed upon his lips. "My feet are sore. I'm cold. And my tummy hurts something terrible."

"Hush now, my son," came his mother's soft reply. "We are nearly there."

Aleksender's chest constricted into a tight ball. Her composure was strangely haunting.

Victoria had always been prone to elaborate tantrums; more often than not, Mother appeared to be composed of two separate personalities—one being society's darling and its counterpart a rather melodramatic fool. Both individuals were susceptible to the consequences of extreme emotion. But Aleksender had never witnessed anything quite like that evening. She'd been sobbing since dusk, madly pacing Father's study and whispering biblical passages through freely flowing tears.

And now, not two hours later, she resembled the picture of serenity—perfectly calm, perfectly content.

The calm before the storm.

A humble home rose into sight as they rounded a corner. Constructed from a fortress of sleek bricks and slate, it was inviting and wonderfully storybook. Beguiled by the sight, Aleksender's lips curved into a smile.

"Are we here?"

Victoria stopped to smooth down her bright and bubbly skirts. "Indeed. It's awfully drab, is it not?"

"Non! I think it's purty." The sanctuary was as charming as can be. How could Mother perceive anything other than its beauty?

Shaking her head in disapproval, Victoria exhaled a sigh that marked her aggravation. Raven coils cascaded down and over her cheeks, each one falling in a bountiful swirl. She bent forward and gazed into Aleksender's eyes. "You have much to learn, sweet thing."

Once more, the chime of heels resounded as she resumed pace and headed for the structure's entrance.

"Where are we, Maman?"

Silence was her response; she fished a skeleton key from inside her bodice and turned the lock with a startling click. As if in warning, the door gave a defiant creak as mother and child entered.

In contrast to the cheery exterior, the inside was empty, lonely, and nearly pitch black. Shadows snaked through the corridor and crept up and down the plain walls. Aleksender rooted his shiny boots into place, emerald eyes widening.

"I-I don't wanna, Maman. It's frightfully dark."

"Why, there is nothing to fear, amour."

Of course there was not. He was being more than a bit silly. Sobered by her words, Aleksender squared both shoulders and bravely followed after his mother, a surge of comical male pride empowering each step. He raised his chin and stiffened his upper lip—just as Father had often instructed him to do so—pushing aside the terrible premonition that had inflamed his gut.

"Why we here? Where are we?"

"You mustn't speak, chérie," Victoria gently chided. She splayed a fair hand upon Aleksender's lower back and gave a firm nudge. Gesturing a nearby chaise, she murmured, "Be a good boy and go rest. I shall be but a moment."

"But why? Why must you leave me?"

"Please—no more questions. I will call out for you."

Steps dragging and mutinous, Aleksender obliged with a small grumble as he ushered himself further into the home. He plopped his bottom onto the chaise and watched with growing uneasiness as his mother's silhouette was swallowed up by the shadows. The flesh on his arms tightened and crawled. The endless corridor resembled a mouth into hell.

Several minutes of eerie silence crawled by. Bored out of his mind, no longer afraid of the engulfing darkness, Aleksender swung both legs back and forth, to and fro, animated with youthful impatience as he awaited the sound of his mother's voice.

After ten minutes it finally came. "Aleksender, dear."

"I'm comin', Maman! I'm comin'!"

In a burst of energy, he leapt down from the chaise, brushed a swarm of locks from his eyes, and sprinted in the direction of her calling.

Hollow footfall pitter-pattered against the floorboards with the audacity of a drum roll. The home was exceptionally small, allowing Aleksender to reach his destination in moments. Light oozed from under a partially open door panel, beckoning him inside. He followed after the illumination and his mother's gentle voice— quickly finding that the shaft of light had been far from holy.

The bedchamber was distinctly feminine. A cluster of candles was arranged on the vanity, emitting a collective glow. An oval bathing tub lined one of the far walls, all copper and finely sanded oak wood. And a water basin sat at the tub's heels, tin lips gaping with the charm of a Glasgow grin, a film of rust marring its appearance.

Both of Victoria's hands were demurely folded and clasped together, presenting the pretense of a lady. The front of her gown was damp, her coiffure uncharacteristically disheveled and thick with sweat. The beauty of her eyes was dull and tarnished as she gazed hypnotically forward.

A Windsor-style rocking chair was stationed directly in front of her. And, within that chair, was a woman's slumped form.

She was unconscious, each slender limb falling unceremoniously at her sides. A drenched scarf was wrapped around her head like a bandit, its fine silk covering both her mouth and nose. The sullied material polluted the air with a musky scent ... a potently foul scent.

"M-Maman? Who is she?"

Victoria's mouth quavered as tears coated her pale cheeks in harsh streams. An unsteady hand came to her lips, commanding her son's silence. "Shh ... She is sleeping. We mustn't wake her."

Aleksender caught the glint of a knife for the first time.

The seductive glint of a knife.

Indeed—a slate of gleaming metal was cradled in his mother's palm, the blade pulled back into a toothy snarl. Envious and seemingly competing for attention, her wedding ring sparkled against the expanse of black.

"Maman, I'm scared. I wanna go home!"

"Why, there is nothing to fear, love." Those identical words of only a half-hour ago were equipped with a venomous undercurrent, and they were anything but comforting.

Aleksender felt himself drowning.

Victoria untied the scarf with surprisingly nimble fingers. With a slick twist of her wrist, she drew the material away—moving with a magician's suaveness. Aleksender had nearly expected her to cry out, "Ta-da!"

It was a rather pretty face that lay beyond the veil. The woman appeared wonderfully peaceful in her sedated state. Worry etched in his brow, Aleksender cocked his head to the side and inched toward her still form. Although her eyes were presently shut, he knew them to be carved from a rich mahogany. He studied every detail of her face, marveling how he possibly recognized her.

Who was she? And why was Maman doing this?

Victoria inclined the knife toward Aleksender with a feral hiss, tears falling hard and strong.

Empty and burning tears.

"Why are you doing this, Maman?" Aleksender's flesh constricted around his bones. "Why?"

She seemed not to hear nor see him.

"Look away, my son! You must save yourself from earthly temptation before it is too late." A flash of burning emotion inflamed her stare. "Alas, it is too late for him, too late for my beloved Philippe! 'When lust hath conceived, it bringeth forth sin—and sin, when it is finished, bringeth forth death.'"

An acute and stinging terror he hadn't known to exist pooled deep inside of Aleksender. Drained of their youthful brilliance, the rounded apples of his cheeks turned sallow and pasty. He was paralyzed with disbelief and an aching fear—virtually unable to move or utter a sound—perceiving everything through the filter of a dream world. His mother's words were remarkably surreal and far away.

The reality of the moment was lost to a boy of ten years.

Astonishingly vulnerable and childish, Victoria sniffled and swiped mucus from her nose. The timbre of her voice softened to its customary whisper. "Life is pain. Love is a pretty lie. Do not love the world or anything in it. The world and its desires pass away. Do you understand me, child? Do you?"

Aleksender nodded as the tears finally came forth.

"And make sure you never forget it. Never forget the truth. Never forget ..." Victoria's breasts heaved in deep pants. The ball of her knuckles whitened as she clasped onto the knife's hilt with a lethal death grip. "Come closer, Aleksender dear, you mustn't be afraid. Together, we shall cleanse our family of this unholy temptation." Aleksender shuffled forward a few meager inches, legs unbearably heavy and tears blurring his vision. Lost in the solitude of her prayers, Victoria's eyes fell to half-mast as crystal drops clung to each spike of her lashes.

"Maman, no ... don't do this."

A distorted prayer.

"'And the ten horns which thou sawest upon the beast, these shall hate the whore, and shall make her desolate and naked, and shall eat her flesh, and burn her with fire ... God had put it into the hearts to carry out his purpose, and those who do the will of God shall live forever.'"

Both hands were held high and proud as she centered the blade above the swell of the woman's cleavage.

"Please don't hurt her! Stop scarin' me!"

"Be not afraid of those who kill the body. Fear him who destroys both body and soul in hell."

Steel, cold and rusted, plunged into a slate of creamy flesh.

A flash of steel descended in one graceful swoop. The woman would never again wake.

"Amen."

A crimson ring seeped through the woman's nightdress—its incalculable circumference widening at a leisurely pace—encircling the hilt like the Red Sea. Only the dying refrains of Aleksender's scream shattered the silent din.

Then the world split into two as a wailing babe cried out. Victoria brushed a film of sweat from her forehead and hastened to the blubbering sound. Frozen in time, Aleksender set his gaze upon the woman's fallen face. A ribbon of blood seeped from the corner of her mouth and sensually flowed down the curve of her chin.

Aleksender followed the morbid trail. For the second time, he wondered who she was.

Yes, he had seen this woman on occasion. Marianne Moreau ... the mom of his infant brother.

The wrath of a lover scorned.

Richard's wailing escalated, each cry amplified by his tin prison. Water sloshed out of the basin as Victoria dragged it across the floor in an effort to bring it within arm's reach of the tub.

Fight or flight instincts took hold. No longer thinking, Aleksender latched onto the knife's hilt and gave a firm tug. Nothing. It refused to budge. Indeed, it was lodged deeply—too deeply. The blade had been swallowed up by flesh and muscle.

Victoria hovered above the tub, morbidly beautiful, looking every bit like an Angel of Death. She gazed down at the babe's blotched face and flailing fists with an uneven sigh. The blanket had come unraveled in the midst of Richard's tantrum, leaving him victim to the elements. Victoria knelt forward, cooed some incoherent nonsense, and blessed him with the sign of the cross. "In the name of the Father, Son, and the Holy Spirit ..."

Aleksender struggled with the hilt in vain. The blade was sheathed within a shell of ivory—encaged between two parallel ribs. They gripped onto the steel like the devil's own hands. Alas, the knife was the Sword in the Stone and Aleksender was unfit to fulfill its prophecy. With an uttered cry of defeat, he turned away from the woman's limp form. Each passing moment it became more difficult to breathe, more difficult to think. Tears and bile clogged his throat by turns. His pulse pounded loudly in his ears.

Surely, he was only dreaming. Surely Maman didn't mean to kill his brother!

"He has your father's eyes," Victoria's monotonous voice cut through his thoughts. Still as death and entirely composed, she stared down at the fussing child who lay beneath her. "There's nothing of me in him." She looked over her shoulder and studied Aleksender's features with a small, sad smile. "You, sweet love, are the both of us."

"What are you going to do to him?"

"He is a bastard, born of sin and uncleansed, destined for the depths of hell." Victoria inhaled a shaky sigh and smoothed back her coiffure's loose coils. "God will make him pay for the sins of his father. Such a thing cannot do." She nodded her head as if reaching some inward decision. "First we must baptize him."

"No! Don't … don't hurt him! Please."

"My child," she assured through her glowing smile, "have you not learned anything I've taught you? We are doing nothing of the kind. We are granting him salvation."

"You're not well, Maman." Aleksender's slender chest rose and sank with erratic breaths. His throat had closed up minutes ago, making the tight chamber strangle each of his words. "You're sick."

Victoria knelt before Aleksender. Her touch was tentative and ironically gentle as she wiped away his tears. "My sweet son, it pains me to see you weep."

"Then stop. Stop d-doin' this."

She shook her head. "You must harden your heart. If not, the world shall crush your spirit one day."

"I will! I will do anything, I swear it! I won't tell anyone. I promise I won't. Just take me back home. I wanna go home. I wanna see Father."

Victoria straightened out, a scowl marring her pretty features. "Father is not here." She shook her head. "But you want him to be."

"Yes," Aleksender said, wishing for his father's comfort more than anything else.

"Then help me bring him back to us."

Everything seemed to happen at once.

Water spilled over the basin's sides, sloshing within, as Victoria struggled to lift it from the ground. Distorted laments poisoned the air. Aleksender pulled at his mother's skirts, sobbing—drowning in tears. Water was transferred from basin to tub. Richard wailed out as he was slowly submerged, first his tiny bottom, both pudgy legs, flailing arms …

The water level rose and rose … soon inches from completely submerging him.

With every ounce of his strength, Aleksender shoved his mother. A loud crash resounded as the basin slipped from her grasp and drenched the smooth floorboards below her feet. Mother and son instantly lost balance. She spun on her heels and fell to her death, a sickening crack efficiently snapping her neck. In the same breath, the side of Aleksender's head collided with the tub, rendering him unconscious.

And then the darkness descended.

•

There had never been a carriage accident, spooked mare, or unhinged wheel. Philippe de Lefèvre and his wife had never shared true love. All of the fluffy stories and sparkling fairytales had been carefully woven illusions. And each thread had existed as a sentiment of a father's affection for his son. Indeed—the fabric of Aleksender's childhood had been fashioned from pretty lies.

Elizabeth knew she could never offer Aleksender what he truly needed. And she was strangely at peace with the realization.
She met her husband's eyes with a new compassion and understanding. Everything, all of his tragic flaws and mishaps—his detached and resigned nature, his strange connection with Sofia— suddenly fell into place. The truth had been boiling inside of him, and now, countless years later, it had finally surfaced. As a boy, Aleksender de Lefèvre's youth had been spirited away. He'd lived through unbelievable trauma and horror. And, whether he was able to remember them or not, the memories had been planted deep within his soul.

Aleksender had been raised on lies that had never quite fit together. Shattered remnants and torn memories had existed inside his heart, creating an emptiness which was not all together empty. On some level, within some plane of consciousness, he'd always known the truth. And now, nearly twenty-six years later, the memories had crashed down with the force of an avalanche.

A landslide.

And what more is a landslide than the accumulated pressure of stress and time?

Aleksender propped a hand against the bookshelf and stabilized his body weight. His face fell forward as he stared down the burgundy wallpapering with an unsettling attentiveness, memorizing every small imperfection, every splintered hairline and every faded patch.

He could not bring himself to face the world. He was afraid to see Elizabeth's eyes. He was afraid of himself. For the first time in thirty-six years, he would be acquainted with his true character.

And the truth was painful, impossible to stomach ... even more so than his emptiness. Perhaps his father had done him a noble service after all. The greater part of his life had been constructed from blissful oblivion, a cocoon of charming lies.

But no—everything had not been a complete lie. His father's stories had held a passion, a beautiful and delicate adoration, which could not be faked. He'd been deeply in love. Only not with his mother.

"Marianne Moreau." The name pricked the roof of his mouth and tasted bitter on his tongue. "His mistress. Richard's mother. My father had loved her, and all of those stories—"

"They had been real." The heat of Elizabeth's body whispered against his back as she drew near.

Aleksender shook his face, overcome with a rush of anger, guilt, sorrow and resentment. "He tried to protect me, to make me forget what I had seen, what I had done. And look what he created. I've become a monster. An empty monster."

"Listen to me. He loved you. And he loved Marianne." She gently draped a hand over his shoulder, her touch tremulous and full of sympathy. "We all do what we must. Sometimes, we hurt the ones we care about most."

With a strangled sound, Aleksender jerked from her reach. "Don't. Please. Don't touch me."

"I'm sorry. I am so sorry," she said.

"Just go. I need to be alone."

Elizabeth collected the volume of fairytales and Philippe's note from the floor with a sigh. She placed them on top of the writing desk, side by side, and absently traced the book's cover. "Should you need me, someone to speak with ... I shall only be a room away."

Elizabeth picked up her skirts and moved to the door. But she stopped in her tracks and slowly turned toward Aleksender. She met his eyes with a small, sad smile. "If you don't come to me, if you must leave ... I shall understand." Aleksender stared at her, mute and motionless. "She needs you more than I do. And you ... you need her more than I need you."

CHAPTER TWENTY-SEVEN

May 23, 1871
La Semaine Sanglante, Day Three

Filth and corpses carpeted the walkways, collectively forming the stench of death. For the first time, the full extent of Paris's suffering came into focus for Aleksender. It was as if he'd been lost to a deep slumber and was just awakening.

He rode through the wreckage in stunned horror. Above head, the mutilated corpse of a Versailles solider hung from one of the gas lamps. Cradled by a delicate breeze, it swayed in a subtle motion and eerily moved from side to side. Aleksender cringed at the makeshift gibbet and everything it represented—ultimate desperation and despair.

Amidst his hibernation, the world had collapsed.

Cannons thundered as the shells of firearms buzzed through the air. The barricades were alive with hollering men and sparks of fire as the red Commune flag glowed in all of its crimson glory. Somewhere off to the side, a pair of gendarmes patrolled in a miserable attempt to retain peace.

Aleksender's flesh crawled like a living thing and hugged his bones in a deathly embrace. Where were the eagerly awaiting clientele? What had ever happened to the whistling baker? Where was that hollow clapping of hooves, the creaking of carriage wheels?

Where had those sounds of life vanished to?

Nearly all the shops had been abandoned since the massacre, equipping Paris with a haunting appearance of a ghost town. Dozens of dead bodies were piled off to the side in the hopes they might be claimed by loved ones. And the streets were literally stained, the gutters overgrowing with blood.

Aleksender rode alongside the fallen with a heavy ache in his heart. He tugged on Juliet's reins, demanding her to a halt. She obliged with a mutinous snort and pawed at the cobblestones.

Nearby, a lone gas lamp winked, emitting a faint ring of light. Aleksender lifted the rim of his bowler hat as he gazed down. Down below, he stared into the face of a boy no older than seventeen years. In a quick and decided movement, he dismounted and lowered to his knees. Respectfully Aleksender pulled the hat from his head. His heart stirred. With a sweep of his palm, he urged the boy's eyes shut.

Christophe Cleef was right; he'd been oblivious to everything but himself.

To have so much potential for power, for change. To throw it all away is unforgivable. Unredeemable ...

Aleksender shook away his comrade's words. He wearily rose to his feet and withdrew the note. Writing had been scrawled on each side of the parchment, its latter reading: *Join me for a toast to Paris.*

•

Aleksender tethered Juliet to one of Cafe Roux's wooden columns. Praying she'd not be spirited away by some lecherous horse thief, he whispered a tender farewell before heading to the entrance. A pair of Versailles soldiers strolled by on horseback, their gaits slow and steady. Each man tipped his hat in a ritualistic greeting.

It was Aleksender's fine clothing that distinguished him from members of the Commune and working-class. Playing the role with ease, he returned the nod, more than a bit thankful for the hat that concealed his identity.

The first thought to cross Aleksender's mind was the deadness of Cafe Roux. The place was empty and eerily still. Streams of moonlight poured through the shattered windows and danced across the countertops. Dust motes fluttered midair like snowfall. Broken glass crunched beneath Aleksender's boots as he searched the length of the room.

Where in God's teeth was Christophe?

Easing toward the bar, Aleksender removed both gloves and stuffed them deep inside his satchel. A thick film of dust covered the countertop like a blanket.

And then he saw it.

A note had been placed on top of a stool. Aleksender unfolded the parchment, staring down at that clumsy and familiar cursive:

Do not fear. This is nothing more than a godsend.
If any man's work shall be burned, he shall suffer great loss. But he himself shall be saved yet so as through fire. — C.C.

Aleksender crumpled the paper in his palm and hung his face. This was no simple note. He understood Christophe's game. It was a clue. A step closer to whatever fate his comrade was plotting for him.

The hours of fireside ramblings had thoroughly paid off. Christophe knew of Aleksender's stories, his hopes, his dreams and his greatest fears. And now, damn him, Christophe was leading Aleksender on a journey.

Alas, hand it to his dear friend to send him on a scavenger hunt—and in the midst of a civil war nonetheless.

•

A young whore was stationed outside Bête Noire's entrance. Face bowed down in shame, an abundance of curls cascaded over her body and hid her features like some secretive curtain. The ill fitted bodice drooped from dangerously slim shoulders in harsh and irregular folds, flaunting her deprivation rather than sensuality. Judging by the gawkish shape of her figure, she was clearly not a day over sixteen. Aleksender felt the compelling desire to sweep away those curls, look into eyes that were undoubtedly filled with sorrow, and reassure her that everything would be all right. Instead, he hustled past the pitiful creature without a second glance.

A tiny, trembling hand grasped onto his sleeve. Delicate fingers curled into the material in a desperate pull. When she finally spoke, the tremor in her voice overpowered any hope for obtaining sensuality. "Care to have your bed warmed on this lonely night, monsieur?"

A rigid breath escaped Aleksender. "Mon Dieu—"

In an attempt to flee, the young whore inhaled a strained breath and instantly pulled away. Aleksender latched onto her shoulders and realigned their bodies. Three of his gloved fingertips pushed against the curve of her chin, forcing her face up and back. He felt his eyes sharpen as they bore into her own. "Elise. What are you doing? What have you done to yourself?"

The servant girl stared forward for several weightless moments. Aleksender gave her a firm shake and increased the pressure of his grip. "Elise?"

Her eyes widened in horror as she appeared to see Aleksender for the first time. Then she broke down without warning, bursting into a jumble of tears and incoherent words. "No! Not for me, Monsieur le Comte! Maman has taken a t-turn for the worse. Without a proper bed, she shall die within the month! What would you have me do? I cannot lose her, monsieur! Surely you can understand?"

Aleksender looked away and swept fingertips through his hairline. He paced in front of Elise for several moments, too shocked to speak. "You should have come to me."

"I didn't wish to impose. I know you've been terribly troubled as of late."

Aleksender froze in his tracks and returned her stare; an unexpected pang of sorrow filled his heart. Eyes swollen and curls plastered to her cheeks, Elise looked remarkably like a little child.

Deeply shamed, her shoulders shook with silent sobs. Aleksender mumbled something beneath a ragged breath and collected Elise in his arms. He held her close, offering his warmth and comfort.

"You have always been good to me." She sighed the words into his chest.

Aleksender said nothing as he gently massaged her back, easing her pain in the only way he knew how.

Elise misread the gesture.

Both hands slid around the circumference of Aleksender's waist in slow, caressing strokes. Trembling fingers slipped to the front of his trousers. She nuzzled deeper into his chest as her eyes fluttered shut. Nervous and clumsy hands sought passage to Aleksender's masculinity. He inhaled a hissed breath at the explicit assault and stepped backward. His hands shot out, quick as lightning, ensnaring each of Elise's wrists and pinning them at her sides.

"No, child."

Her mouth fell open in stunned horror. Humiliation stained her cheeks. Hiding her face within the shelter of her palms, she took several steps backward and rotated out of eyesight. "Oh, God ... I thought ... I'm so stupid." Her hands coiled into fists and repetitively punched either side of her head. "I cannot believe it. I—"

"Stop. Stop harming yourself." Aleksender grasped onto her fists and lowered them with a sigh. "It's not safe here. You must return to the chateau at once."

"But—but le Vicomte—"

"What? What of Richard?" Silence. "What did he say to you?" More silence. "Tell me, Elise."

She swallowed, eyes slowly rising to his. "He dismissed me. He's been quite mad ever since I overheard ... in the veranda that day ... since your luncheon. He—"

"Has no right to interfere or make decisions in my stead," Aleksender spat. Again, he paced and back and forth, fuming from the inside out. Then he came to an abrupt stop, latched onto Elise's shoulders, and curled his fingers around the slender blades. "Listen to me. You shall stay at Chateau de Lefèvre. You and your mother. Do you understand?"

Elise nodded as the beginnings of a soft smile curled her lips.

"Good." Aleksender tore away his cloak and draped it over her body. "Go straight to the chateau and order a carriage. Fetch your mother at first light. Talk to no one. Leave now—I trust you know the way."

Her chin dipped into a subtle nod. Swept with emotion, a few tears tumbled down her cheeks. "Thank you."

•

Moonlight oozed through Bête Noire's shattered windows. Overhead, the chandelier was as black and as grim as the surrounding night. Shadows crawled across the splintered floorboards and materialized in an array of shapes.

Aleksender's heavy footfall echoed in the silence. He examined the dreary atmosphere as he approached the service desk. After several steps, he pounded at the golden bell and awaited Madam Bedeau and whatever clue she might bring.

A pistol was clutched to her breast when she finally appeared. "Stay back, monsieur! I'm not afraid to spill your blood."

Aleksender tore away his bowler hat and stepped closer, revealing his identity. Madam Bedeau tilted her head, lowering the firearm as she studied his features.

She inhaled a sigh of relief and smoothed down her coiffure. "Ah, Monsieur le Comte. Forgive me. Here—" She dug a hand inside of her bodice and withdrew a folded piece of parchment. "I was asked to give you this. Not to worry. I didn't read a word of it. Even if I'd wanted to, I can't understand the letters."

Madam Bedeau passed the note into Aleksender's hands. Worry was etched into her brows. "Forgive me for saying—but you should not be here. It's only a matter of time before you're slaughtered like the rest of us. Perhaps by the Commune and Guardsmen, if not Versailles."

"I have a personal war that must first be won."

Aleksender unfolded the parchment to read: *Faith is a passionate institution. — C.C.*

Madam Bedeau nodded as her eyes grew heavy with pain. She pressed a hand against her heart, easing an unseen ache. "Yes. I understand. I was a mother. Did you know that?" Aleksender carefully shook his head and waited for her to continue. A whimsical smile spread across her worn features. In that moment, the countless years of pain eased from her face. Aleksender saw the little girl she'd once been. "Charles was a good boy. Seventeen years, handsome as can be. He had his father's heart. We were out looking for food when he was shot in the back—damned coward!"

"I'm sorry."

Madam Bedeau shrugged, dabbing away her tears with a handkerchief. "It's a terrible time for us all. Tell me … would you like a room till morning? You'll do better on a night's sleep." She gazed at him with caressing eyes and leaned across the counter. "And perhaps we can keep each other warm during this hard time."

Aleksender shook his head. "Just a room will be fine."

Madam Bedeau paused before continuing. She gestured at the parchment in Aleksender's pocket. "He was quite mad with grief."

Aleksender swallowed and nodded. "I imagine he was."

"And what audacity! The fool threatened to close down Bête Noire … said such a place was a mockery of the law. Mockery, indeed! From the looks of it, I daresay he's tumbled more whores than all my clientele put together." Madam Bedeau picked up her skirts and inched forward. With a graceful wave of her hand, she signaled Aleksender to follow. "Well. That's enough talk. Come along, then, monsieur."

CHAPTER TWENTY-EIGHT

Beers in hand, Christophe and Elliott sat side by side as they found a moment of refuge from the war. They drained bottles and balanced cigars between their lips as a comfortable silence hung in the air.

The catacombs, in all of its macabre and demented glory, weren't nearly as grim as the streets of Paris. The above ground had transformed into a cemetery of awakened horrors, and it lay as a far darker realm.

Christophe surveyed the endless wall of gawking death heads with a monotonous expression. Black and bottomless, those eye sockets were vats of dark secrets and twisted terrors. As if challenging Christophe's tolerance for death and decay, each skull grinned wholeheartedly and without mirth.

Would his own head join these lonely souls by the week's end? The thought was disheartening and all too real. Despite his facial disfigurement, Christophe rather liked his head.

He inhaled a swig of his cigar and drowned the smoke with a mouthful of brandy. "Once we're all dead and buried—whether we're a pauper, prince or whore," Christophe said, gesturing at the skulls. "We all look the damn same."

Elliott nodded in agreement. "Obscenely happy, I take it?"

Christophe surrendered to a small, rolling chuckle. "Very good. I should like to drink to that."

He stared into Elliott's eyes as an unexpected pang of affection tugged at his heartstrings. Apart from Aleksender, he'd never felt such compassion for another. This protective instinct—this need to recompose the world for an orphaned soul—must have been how Aleksender had felt all those nine years ago. Alas—Sofia and Aleksender's relationship had begun as no more than an impulse and paternal need. For the first time, Christophe understood his comrade's affection for the little blue-eyed ballerina ... and, for the first time, a chord of guilt struck his conscience.

And now, like some sentimental fool, he was overcome with the compelling need to remap Elliott's destiny—to order him to take the first ship out of this wretched land and sail away to America—to forget martyring himself, forget the notion of becoming just another death's-head upon a wall. To simply live life, have painted whores by the dozens, and grow old to see the birth of his grandchildren. Once the barricades fell, he and Elliott would be forgotten. Their sacrifices would fade away with time, and their corpses would be brushed off to the side like a bad joke.

Neither of them would be claimed by loved ones.

Indeed—they'd merely add another layer to the catacomb's vast tunnel. They would exist as two nameless, faceless casualties. His father had declared his patriotism back in 1848, only to die drunk as a skunk while wrapped in the arms of some decadent harlot. Christophe, in all of his brandy guzzling and wenching glory, was destined to follow in his father's footfall.

He ached to steer Elliott away from this doomed fate. Instead, Christophe heard himself murmur, "This week may very well be our last."

Elliott nodded and tapped his bottle against Christophe's. "Then I shall count myself blessed to die at your side."

•

Persistent knocking filled Chateau de Lefèvre in the mid-afternoon. Appearing pristine and righted, the first footman thrust open the massive double doors. In the same breath, Elizabeth soared down the winding stairwell, a silk shawl clasped about her shoulders. Its airy material flowed behind her, fluttering with the delicacy of wings.

"Is it him? Is it truly Aleksender?"

"No, madame—it's not he." The first footman stepped aside and allowed Paris's vicomte to enter. Elizabeth's eyes widened at the sight of Richard. She flew down the remaining steps at record time and soared within his reach.

"Richard! You came!" she cried, looping both arms around his neck without thought. "Oh, thank the lord you are here!" A dashing smile formed on his lips. He returned Elizabeth's embrace and held her close for several moments.

Elizabeth hesitantly stepped backward and glanced into his eyes. Richard tucked a loose curl behind her ear as their gazes tentatively came together.

"How have things been?" she asked with a slight tremble. "Very awful?"

"Yes. I'm afraid so," he said. "But you are safe. That's what matters most." The shawl sagged from Elizabeth's shoulder and nearly slipped to the floor. Richard massaged her bare flesh, rubbing life into her skin. "You've nothing to worry about. I shall stay with you till the end."

Elizabeth nodded, a small smile at her lips.

"But it is urgent that I speak with Aleksender." Richard turned to the first footman. "Call him down for me at once—"

"No—he is gone," Elizabeth interrupted.

Richard twisted in the direction of her voice. "What? What do you mean he is gone?"

Elizabeth nodded at the first footman, subtly dismissing him from the room. "Something happened. Something terrible."

Richard's entire demeanor darkened as he humorlessly chuckled at her words. "You speak of terrible? Madame, have you even read Thiers's latest statement?"

Elizabeth shook her head, flushed at the cheeks and a bit shamed. Richard fished a folded newspaper from inside his coat. "It was posted several mornings ago." He flattened out *Le Figaro's* pages and read aloud. ""Citizens of Paris: The government wished that you might free yourselves independently of the tyrants who scoff at your liberty and life. Since you cannot, it has become our task. We are an army that has come not to conquer but to set you free. You outnumber the Commune sectarians. Regroup. Open the doors that they have shut on law and order. Should you not, the government will be forced to take the swiftest and surest means available to set you free.'"

Elizabeth snatched the paper from his hands, her own trembling, eyes frantically scanning over the print. "Lord. This is worse than I ever imagined."

"Tell me. Where is he? Where has Aleksender gone off to?"

Elizabeth lowered the paper. "He wasn't exactly sure. To meet Christophe Cleef. At the cafe, I believe—"

"God in heaven! Has Aleksender lost his damn mind? Falling straight into his trap?"

"I don't understand?"

"I shall have you know that his dear comrade is heading the revolt. The Commune will kill him, I tell you—just as they killed three others in the dungeons only days ago."

"No! You are wrong. You know Christophe! He and Aleksender—they are close to brothers!"

Those words wounded Richard far more than he dared admit. Of course, he'd known them to be true for some time—he and Aleksender were as opposite as day and night. But to hear them spoken aloud was a rude awakening. It shook him to the very core. He wandered farther into the foyer and leaned up against the banister. His head fell forward in a rush of pain. Massaging his temples and speaking more to himself, he rambled, "I'll never understand him. Weeks ago, I tried to open his eyes. Why now? Aleksender has never shown the slightest interest in Paris. Why? Why the sudden change of heart?"

A long silence passed. "The woman he loves has been taken. By Christophe, I believe."

Richard stared off, his mind visibly turning. "Then he is helpless."

"Please, you mustn't be angry with him. He had no choice."

"There is always a choice. I am growing quite tired of his excuses. And how can you defend him after all the heartache he has caused you?"

"You speak of heartache?" she teased, mimicking Richard's tone of several minutes ago.

As if working out some great mystery, Richard shook his head and inched toward Elizabeth. "There is just something about you so remarkable." Two fingertips wound about her chin. He deftly lifted her face and brought their gazes together. "Yes. There's something about you I can't quite place my finger on ... something I wish my brother could see."

They were mere inches apart. Elizabeth's heart fluttered, skipping several beats.

"Richard." She gave a weak smile and curled her fingers around his forearm, directing him to follow. "Come with me. Come, and I shall explain everything."

•

Sofia nibbled at a stale loaf of bread. Her gut ached with pains that had nothing to do with hunger. The morsel scratched at her throat and clawed like nails as she swallowed. Bile seared her insides. Forcing herself to eat was utterly useless. She'd already tried with little success. A chain of painful, dry heaves had overcome her the last time. She cringed at the recollection—tasting the acidic flavor all over again. Hours later, remnants of vomit still soured the air.

She laid her meal aside, inhaled a deep breath, and adjusted her leg with a groan. Metallic clinking echoed across the Commune's base as she wiggled her ankle, urging circulation back into her foot. To her relief, the cramp slowly faded into a dull ache.

A day ago—had it only been a day?—Christophe had traded the two chains for one ankle cuff, granting her the slightest cut of freedom. The chain was an impressive twenty pounds and a good twenty-five feet in length. She'd been quite content at first, cherishing her new mobility and immediately plotting some elaborate form of escape. Perhaps, she would seduce Christophe—play him for the fool he was and steal the key from his trousers. Or, should she be fortunate enough to come in reach of a rock, she could smash her way to freedom. How about one of the men's swords or daggers? Surely it could bust through the metal?

After dragging the dreaded chain for an hour the burn had begun to sink in. Her foot had grown numb. And, a moment later, it seemed to absorb every prickle of pain known to mankind. The realization was terrifying; what if she lost all feeling in her foot? What if it had to be amputated? What if she lost the ability to dance forever?

Approaching footfall resounded and clipped her thoughts short. Sofia tensed and eased against the wall. She winced as the rugged stone grated her flesh. The footsteps grew louder, closer. Could it be her Alek? Had he come to rescue her?

But it was Christophe who appeared, weary and stained with blood.

Dieu. Had he been shot?

"Sorry to disappoint you—but no, chérie, I have not been shot. You must be terribly devastated."

It was too strange for Sofia to wrap her mind around. Christophe consistently joined her during his lowest moments. Before she could further ponder the meaning of his calculated visits, he interrupted. "You would barely recognize Paris. One glance and your poor little Christian heart would freeze over."

Christophe dug a hand beneath the neckline of his shirt and withdrew a pair of dog tags. Transfixed and hypnotized, he dangled them midair and willed them to dance. They glimmered beneath the sconce lanterns, spinning in free-fall, tossing shards of light along the walls. Studying the lettering, he rotated a token between his thumb and forefinger:

ALEKSENDER R. DE LEFÈVRE
38097645
PARIS, FRANCE

After a moment, he dropped Aleksender's dog tag and clasped his own in a tight fist.

CHRISTOPHE G. CLEEF
38010729
PARIS, FRANCE

"Your God has abandoned you."

Sofia's blood drew cold at his words, though her face remained flat and expressionless. A man with nothing left to lose—nothing left to believe in—was a dangerous man, indeed.

"Will you return to the barricade soon?" she asked.

"No. Not now. Not till he arrives."

Keep calm, Sofia's mind warned, *you must keep calm. If you wish to see Alek's face again, you must remain calm and collected.*

With each passing day, it was becoming more evident that earning Christophe's trust was her one hope for escape. In all of his power and clever scheming, the man was painfully transparent.

In the end, his vulnerabilities would inevitably be his downfall. Christophe Cleef was in obvious need of comfort and companionship. And, much like an avalanche, his façade was gradually crumbling away and revealing the damaged soul beneath. It was only a matter of time before he caved. Something that felt remarkably like pity slammed against Sofia's conscience. Surely she was going mad. He was a murdering monster—nothing more!

Wasn't he?

"So what are you going to do? When you see him, I mean?" Her voice was perfectly casual, perfectly conversational.

The chain slipped through Christophe's fingers as his brows knotted together. The dog tags swung like twin pendulums. Shaking his head, he bellowed an eerie laugh. "Strange. Truth be told I haven't even thought on it." Two of his fingertips pinched the necklace and glided down the cool metal in a tentative caress. "I suppose it shall depend on him." He sighed and stared off, eyes settling on Sofia's ankle cuff. A twisted smile curved his lips—a smile that took Sofia back to that afternoon in Père Lachaise.

For a fleeting moment her dark stranger had returned.

"It seems we're both imprisoned by chains," Christophe said. He cupped the dog tags within his palm and held them tight. "Except mine are harder to break."

CHAPTER TWENTY-NINE

May 25, 1871
La Semaine Sanglante, Day Five

Paris was burning. In a mad fit of revolutionary fervor, the rebels had set fire to the Palace of Tuileries, Hotel de Ville and the Council of State. Debris rained onto Paris and monuments exploded as they were gutted from the inside out. Black smoke, swollen and sinister, ascended, clashing against a paisley spring sky. Ashes of all forms littered the ground and fluttered through the air like snowflakes. A murky, yellowish haze poisoned the atmosphere and swallowed up the city. In the midst of this apocalyptic despair, the Commune's red freedom flag flew high and proud.

A small secretary's desk was arranged on one of the far ends of Rue de la Paix's alleyways. Versailles soldiers stood by, rifles cocked and ready, as they questioned handfuls of Parisians by the dozens. The citizens had been rounded up like herds of cattle—and each "insurgent" was to be systematically butchered and thrown into the gutter. Men, women and children were lined up against the stone wall and tied at the wrists. Two soldiers patrolled the rebels. They walked the length of the alleyway, maintaining a semblance of order.

Speaking in a unified voice, the citizens of Paris chanted a war cry: *"Vive la Commune! Vive la Commune! Vive la Commune!"*

"Shut your filthy mouths!" The hollers only intensified. One of the soldiers slammed the butt of his pistol across a man's face. Blood erupted from his mouth and curled around the slope of his jaw.

"Never! We will never be quiet!" cried a young woman of nineteen years. She stood several feet away, frail body defiantly erect. A little boy clutched onto the hem of her skirts and hid his face within the filth-ridden folds. "Wretched sod!" she said. "You are scum! Scum!"

The Versailles soldier grasped onto her shoulder with a muttered curse. In response, the little boy cried and leapt forward. The other soldier restrained him, shoving him flush against the wall. The crowd went wild at the show of villainy.

"Maman! Maman! Where you takin' my Maman?" he shouted as his mother was dragged away without mercy.

Hands tied at the wrists, she lost balance and fell face first into the cobblestones. Blood clotted her hairline and streamed down her cheeks like scarlet tears. The soldier latched onto the scruff of her dress and yanked her onto her feet. "Up with you!" The rifle's nozzle came down against her back—a nasty trick that sent her straggling forward. "Come along, whore."

The woman—who, indeed, was a whore—spun on her heels and spat in the soldier's eye.

"Try that trick again, putain," he sneered, "and I shall personally take care of your son."

"Monster! Murdering monsters, the lot of you!"

And with that, she was brought in front of the secretary desk to undergo a mockery of a trial. "This one's worse than the whole of them," the soldier said. "Got the rest all riled up. You can hear 'em now."

Nearby the drone of angry cries and lewd obscenities filled the alleyway. Not seeming to hear them, the seated gentleman nodded. Eyes fixed on the parchment before him, he drawled, "Name?"

The rifle was shoved into the small of her back when she refused to speak. "My name is Clarice Rochelle—you pathetic filth!"

"What did you do for the Commune?" he asked in a monotonous and painfully flat tone.

"Everything! And I shall die for the Commune!"

"Very well."

The seated man signaled to his fellow soldier with a magical wave of his hand. On cue, the woman was pushed against a nearby wall in a ritualistic fashion. The soldier raised his rifle, leveling it to her chest. "I shall enjoy this. But not half as much as I'll relish killing that bastard of yours."

•

The sun was swallowed up by a crimson sky as nighttime came to Paris. Over the course of a single week, night and day, dark and light, had become entirely indistinguishable from one another. Everything had been bruised and branded with the mark of despair. Even the most devout atheists could no longer deny the truth. The Day of Judgment had arrived and there was no escaping its wrath.

The walls of chateau de Lefèvre shook with the force of the civil war. Richard and Elizabeth stood on the balcony as red clouds of smoke cloaked the sky. The sunset, normally so beautiful and vivid, was lost to shooting flames and echoed cries. Elizabeth shuddered at the morbid spectacle. "I wonder if he is all right, if he is safe."

Richard swallowed before allowing himself to speak. "Aleksender is a survivor. He has a way of detaching himself from everything, from everyone … a way of seeing only what's in front of him and shutting out the world. Both a blessing and a curse, I've always thought."

Elizabeth shook her head and inhaled a shaky breath. "Not Sofia. He has never been able to separate himself from her. And Christophe knew—he knew his weakness. He knew how to break through his barrier and reach his heart." She sighed. "I still can't understand. They were great friends. Why is he doing this? Why would he be so … so cruel? What does Christophe want from him?"

"If I were to guess, I suppose he wants his friend back."

Elizabeth smiled at that. She pressed her folded arms against the railing and glanced at Richard. How very handsome he was. His features were gently chiseled, those eyes carved from a rich mahogany. Days ago, Elizabeth had delicately explained all that she knew to Richard—Victoria's insane outburst, Aleksender's loss of memory, and everything in between. Afterward, Elizabeth had taken Richard within her arms and offered whatever semblance of comfort she could provide. Since that time, a soothing calm and new understanding had washed over Richard.

He reflected her smile. Moonlight lightened the auburn waves of his hair. Rotating on his boots, he aligned his body with Elizabeth's. "Fate is a strange thing. Imagine the possibilities if things had been different." Richard lifted his hand in a deft movement and grazed the slope of her cheek. Unspoken words and withheld confessions transpired between them … words as concrete as they very breaths they shared. "It makes me wonder," he tentatively resumed. "What we could have been."

Time stood still as he leaned into her warmth. He cupped her face with his other hand, tilted her head onto its side. Elizabeth's lashes grew heavy and fluttered shut. The heat of Richard's breath swirled against her skin. Ever so carefully, his lips brushed across her cheek. The caress as soft and sure as a butterfly's wings. Overwhelmed with emotion, tears pricked the corner of her eyes and slid down her face.

Richard pulled away and returned to the banister. In his absence, the chill returned to her bones. Glancing into the crimson night sky, he shook his face and murmured, "Damn our fate. And damn the stars."

•

Sacred Heart was the last thing that remained of Paris's innocence. Aleksender held his breath as the storybook structure crept into sight. A breeze stirred, tickling the flowers of May and infusing the pond's glassy surface with life.

In contrast to this sliver of serenity, cannons sounded in the distance and roared like caged beasts. Gunshots peppered the ambiance every now and then—and each one shook Aleksender to the very core.

He tied Juliet to the weeping willow and made way for the convent. Aleksender rapped at the little wooden door and awaited Sister Catherine's greeting. A groan of wood and metal resounded as she unhinged the latch—something she'd never bothered with during his past visits. Her eyes and the black hood of her habit were visible through the slate. After a moment of recognition, the door was unlocked and thrust open.

Aleksender's heart constricted. She appeared to have aged a good twenty years. Maybe more. "Monsieur le Comte," Sister Catherine said. A tinge of panic made her voice quaver. "You have seen no trace of her?"

Aleksender swallowed and shook his head.

A cluster of beaming faces crowded around Sister Catherine's skirts before she was able to respond. A chorus of overlapping girlish chatter filled the air.

"I tell you it's him! Sofia's black knight."

"Nu-uh! Impossible! See—he's riding a white horse, not a black one!"

"He's so very handsome!"

Sister Catherine blushed like a young schoolgirl as she struggled to hold the children back. "Ladies! That's quite enough! Back to your prayers. Right away." She turned to Aleksender and exhaled a dejected sigh. "You must forgive them, monsieur. They are not accustomed to receiving gentlemen and haven't been allowed outside the walls for days. I'm afraid their terribly restless."

His lips curved into a small, crooked smile. "No worries. They are quite charming."

Miriam pushed to the front, cradling her dolly, cheeks rosy and stained with tears. She sniffled and swiped at her nose before speaking. "Is Miss Sofia c-comin' back-k?"

Aleksender playfully ruffled her golden locks with a gloved hand. "Not to worry, ma petit. She'll be here before you know it."

"Oh, yay!" Miriam giggled and swiped at her nose once more. Her voice dropped to a secretive whisper as she motioned Aleksender close. He was forced to kneel in order to hear the words. "Are you really, truly magical?"

"Hm. You tell me," Aleksender said as he reached behind Miriam's ear. When he withdrew, a yellow rose—that had been carefully tucked beside his heart—was balancing between his fingertips.

Miraculously it hadn't wilted since the evening on the rooftop.

"Oh, wow!" Miriam squealed, clasping her hands together with delight. Then, a second later, "Oh, look! A horsey!" Miriam raced out the door, heading straight for Juliet. Aleksender scooped the little one into his arms. "Whoa, there, chérie. Let's be more careful." He set Miriam down and ruffled her hair once more. "I suppose that someday I should take you out riding. Would you like that?"

"Oh, yes! Yes, yes, yes!"

Aleksender peered at Sister Catherine. The slightest grin had settled into her lips. "Very good. Go back inside now and mind Sister Catherine. Can you do that for me?"

Miriam nodded, pecked a kiss onto Aleksender's cheek, and waltzed past Sister Catherine's skirts. Aleksender came to his feet. He tracked a gloved hand over his lapels and smoothed down the fine material. "You have enough food, Sister? And fresh water?"

"Some of the Communards delivered a fresh supply days ago.

Food, water, and an assortment of medical equipment."

A silence whisked by.

"You have something for me? A note, I reckon?"

"Dear me and my old mind. I nearly forgot. A moment, monsieur ..." Sister Catherine vanished inside of Sacred Heart and returned with the note. It was predictably folded, *Comte de Paris* inscribed across the front.

"Tell me ... the man who delivered this—did you recognize him? Or did he have any distinguishing marks." Aleksender traced an invisible line from ear to cheek. "A scar, perhaps?"

"Sister Marie-Joie received it, monsieur. I can fetch her for you if—"

Aleksender gracefully raised a hand and ordered Sister Catherine's words to a halt. "That won't be necessary. I haven't the time."

Sister Catherine stared into his eyes for several moments. Then she did the unexpected. She unclasped the crucifix and fastened it around Aleksender's neck. Blessing him with a wave of her hand, "In the name of the Father, of the Son, and the Holy Spirit ..." Sister Catherine continued with a serene smile, "The love I have witnessed between you and Sofia has often brought me to tears. The night Elizabeth had her stillborn, I found Sofia out in the garden, weeping into her palms." Aleksender paralyzed at her words, complexion paling. "Should I live to be a hundred years, I shall never forget her words. When I asked what was troubling her, she said that you and Elizabeth had just lost your child. I inquired how she could possibly know such a thing. Sofia shook her head and whispered, 'I don't know. I don't know for certain. I just feel it.'"

Aleksender swallowed and managed a weak nod, head spinning and unable to speak.

"I'm sorry. I didn't mean to startle you or open old wounds," Sister Catherine said in a slow voice. "I only wished to reassure you. You and Sofia share a connection that is not easily broken. I have faith you will bring her home." Sister Catherine closed her eyes in prayer. "I feel it."

•

Père Lachaise was as silent as the grave that night. The wind blew in all directions, rushing through the mausoleums, tombstones and statues in a ghostly breath. Stone crosses appeared as silhouettes against the bleeding skyline. And a decapitated angel stood off to the side, withered and infected with moss.

Chilled to the bone, Aleksender held his breath and gazed down at Christophe's next clue: *For the Love that is perfected by Death. For the Love that dies not in the TOMB. —C.C.*

Crumpling the words, Aleksender's nails dug into his flesh as he curled his hand into a fist. Crescent moons formed from the pressure and stained the parchment an unforgiving red.

Comte Philippe de Lefèvre's mausoleum towered before Aleksender, impressive and almighty, a fortress of stone ascending into infinity. An oversized crucifix decorated the building's facade like some Christmas tree ornament. Jesus hung from the cross, head lolled onto its side, those eyes expressing all of humanity's sorrow. Situated above the archway, *DE LEFÈVRE* was printed in bold and proud lettering, each one engraved below Jesus's heels. Aleksender's heart roared against his ribcage as he drew closer to his beloved father's resting place. With each step he took, a whirlwind of memories raced through his mind.

Father's countless love stories. How he and mother met. Their first kiss, stolen beside the River Seine on a warm summer's night. In their younger years, how'd they observe the sunrise each morning from the garden. The way in which they'd read stories before the blazing hearth, wrapped solely in the warmth of each other.

Entwined within those stories was a web of lies.

Even now, it was difficult to distinguish truth from illusion, deception from actuality.

Aleksender ran his fingers over the mausoleum's smooth stone walls and stroked his father's memory. As he'd expected, the door was firmly sealed shut. He glanced in every direction, ensuring that he was alone, and headed around the structure. Stained glass windows were situated on each side. He stared up at a remarkable depiction of the Virgin Mary. Alas—it was as though she could see the truth, as though she could see into his heart's secrets.

And they both knew what had to be done. Aleksender had no choice but to continue on this journey—this carefully constructed and haunting journey—no matter where it might lead.

There was no turning back. He'd come too far, and there was far too much at stake.

Aleksender balled both hands into fists and struck at the glass—once, twice, three times—smashing away Mary's eternal features.

He swept away the remaining shards and climbed through the portal, dropping inside of the mausoleum.

Aleksender rose to his feet in breathless wonderment. Blood from his knuckles dripped onto the flooring below, the sound unnaturally loud within the silence. Two shafts of moonlight poured through parallel broken windows. Aleksender's inclination was correct. Christophe had been here.

The separate illuminations mingled together like a diva's spotlight, highlighting Philippe De Lefèvre's casket.

The sight was too much to bear. Bile rose inside Aleksender's throat, hot and churning. His legs failed as he crumpled at his seams and fell to his hands and feet. Body positioned in a mock bow, he laid a foot away from his father's resting spot.

Like a tangible force, he could sense his father's spirit all around him. And, a moment later, a haunting but not altogether unpleasant calm washed over him. Aleksender held his breath and crawled toward the casket. He knelt before the monument and clutched his chest, head sunken forward, eyes stinging with a wave of unshed tears. Trembling hands rose from his sides and rested on top of the meticulously carved slate. When he at last spoke, the tone of his voice was strained and impossibly heavy—each word weighed down with years of inner torment and heartache.

"Father. I'm so sorry. So sorry I wasn't at your side. It haunts me. Every day. And now, without you here the entire world is collapsing. And I cannot help but think that it's all my fault. You would have known what to do. You always had. I miss you, Father. I miss you so much—" His words broke off into a soft cry.

Aleksender searched around the dark crevices, seeking answers. He was at a total loss … defeated. His eyes returned to the casket, heart as empty as before. What now? What was he to do now? What did Christophe possibly want from him?

And then it struck him. Follow the light. The illuminations from the two broken windows.

Aleksender curled his fingers around the sides of the casket. Rugged juts of stone bit into his flesh like teeth. He was paralyzed. Mon Dieu. What had become of him? What if he was terribly mistaken? Was this truly Christophe's intention? Could he bring himself to look upon his father's features?

Somehow, someway, he knew. Aleksender's face fell forward in pained agony. Time had run out. He would have to follow his gut.

He couldn't risk questioning himself. He inhaled deeply, not quite believing what he was about to do—what he was about to see. Grunting from the exertion, his muscles quivered and broke out in sheens of sweat. Aleksender summoned every ounce of his considerable strength and slid the massive slab of stone away.

His heart instantly contracted.

His father looked remarkably like a porcelain statue. Cold, pale, and perfectly still. Aleksender grazed a fingertip along the curve of his cheek in a tender caress. Laugh lines creased the corners of his eyes—a testament to the gentle spirit he'd once been. Both of his father's weathered hands were folded together and positioned over his chest. Sparse, gray hair was combed neatly back, his lips chaffed, eyes fastened shut.

Aleksender shuddered at the sight. He hovered above his father's corpse, studying his peaceful features. Then his eyes narrowed in disbelief. Clasped between his father's pasty fingertips was a note. Head spinning, Aleksender slid the parchment from his father's grasp.

Alek,

He is lost to eternal slumber. Yet your pain reminds and warns you that you are very much alive. Take care: Love is not the only thing perfected in death.

Embrace yourself and return to the living.

Come, Desmond. Venus is shining. It's time for a night out at the OPERA. — C.C.

The sensation came in one fell sweep—an overwhelming blend of closure and peace lightened his spirit. Aleksender pressed a kiss to his father's forehead and murmured words of love beneath a hushed breath. He lifted the stone slate and covered the casket, tucking his father into bed for the night.

CHAPTER THIRTY

May 26, 1871
La Semaine Sanglante, Day Six

As it happened, one of Paris's underground tunnels led directly to Opera Garnier. The queer passageway had been deemed as the "Communard's road" over the past weeks. Snaking through the catacomb's eerie bowels, it had granted the revolutionaries a secure hideaway and a clever means of transportation. The nearly completed opera house, which loomed high above, had been transformed into a storage facility and infirmary. Standing as a strange warehouse-hospital hybrid, weapons, gunpowder and the like were mended inside of the walls and kept at bay. In other sections, dismembered and bloodied Parisians were nursed to life and cared for by an assortment of nuns, nurses and volunteers.

Sofia crouched at her heels as she knelt amidst the sea of battered bodies and tangled limbs.

"At least let me be of some use," she'd chided Christophe a day earlier, wearing a smile that could melt the most frigid of hearts. "Please—allow me to tend to the wounded. Sacred Heart taught me much about patient care. Why … I've already gone half-mad down here, and you have my word I won't run off." In spite of herself, Sofia had inwardly grimaced at her deceit.

But it'd only been half of a lie.

And so, as most men are wont to do, Christophe had fallen for her doe eyes and hopeful smile. The weight of the world seemed to have lifted from her shoulders as the cuff was unlocked. Unable to suppress a laugh of relief, she'd swiveled her ankle and rubbed at the swollen skin, nursing her circulation back to life. A sudden and unwanted guilt had swelled her gut as her eyes rose to Christophe. His stare was utterly trusting of her intentions.

"I hope it's nothing too serious," he'd murmured, gesturing her ankle. "But fine. Do what you will, only take care—there shall be eyes on you, chérie. And too many to count."

Sofia had nodded as she felt the numbness ease from her foot. "You have my word. Thank you."

All it took was a single glance at the outside world and the inevitable had been confirmed: she was a prisoner. And neither Christophe nor the Commune were her true captors. Paris, in all of her embittered and malicious agony, held the key to her captivity.

One step onto the street and it would be her last. That much was also pristinely clear. Versailles soldiers occupied every corner—perhaps, sixty thousand in total—and, within the span of a heartbeat, she'd be marked as a Communard. With an aching fear, Sofia knew such a thing was not so far from the truth.

Yes, Christophe had gone to an extreme (a sentiment which comes with obsession and losing one's sanity, she very well assumed), and many of his followers were slacken with bloodlust. But the underlying principle, that crimson freedom flag, was nothing but noble.

Desperation was a terrible thing.

Sofia's thoughts quickly turned to Aleksender. She only prayed—God, she prayed—that Christophe would do him no harm. Over the past few days, she'd witnessed a goodness in the man, a transient gentleness and compassion, which could not so easily be ignored.

Sofia tended to a wound as she executed her infirmary training from Sacred Heart. A chunk of debris had fallen onto the man's chest, leaving him with a nasty second degree burn. She drenched a cloth and pressed it against the inflamed flesh. The man groaned and lolled his head onto its side. He was only half-unconscious, which proved to be a small mercy. "I'm sorry. It hurts something terrible, I know."

"In God's teeth, how would you know?" The words were spoken between clenched jaws and full of cynicism.

Sofia swept away a mass of curls and exposed her scars. "They're not quite as severe as yours, but—"

"I'm sure the memories make mine pale in comparison," he finished. "I can see the pain in your eyes."

She smiled weakly and felt the sting of tears. "Yes, well ... that was long ago. Now. Let's get you all wrapped up, shall we?"

•

Blacker than pitch, the darkness enveloped Sofia inside a suffocating cocoon. Within this windowless prison, no stars were to be found. She was a little girl again—helpless, frightened, and alone.

The flared end of a cigar sears my skin like a brand. I cry out and fight to run away—far, far away! But long fingers snake in my hair and tug at my scalp. A weak protest emerges from my lungs. Maman sobers me with a stinging slap to the face. I slide across the floorboards like some wounded mongrel ... through the winding hallways and into that impenetrable darkness ...

Maman tosses me into a blackened pit. It is the faint click which confirms my fears. I am locked inside.

Beyond the walls of my prison I hear thunder ... deep, growling thunder. I pound and pound ... thrashing against the wood till my fists ache and blood seethes from each knuckle ...

Sofia woke with a scream that could resurrect the dead. Slowly she caught her breath and tugged on her restraints without luck. Once more, she'd been chained to the wall and left unable to stir a limb. Her head rolled backward in despair. It could only mean one thing. And her heart nodded in rapid agreement.

He was near.

•

Apollo, the God of Music and Art, balanced his lyre high above his head as he'd done for so many years. Strings spun from gold jutted against the horizon and kissed the metallic sunrays. Aleksender briefly thought of Moses standing atop Mount Sinai, two stone tablets in hand, as he sought to bring order and peace to his people. But the Hebrews had grown impatient during his absence and had fallen into a state of chaos and immorality. Angered by what he'd seen, Moses had smashed the tablets at the foot of the mountain upon his return. Only after his people had paid for their sins was order again restored.

Up until this moment, Aleksender had always scoffed at the tale and turned his cheek in apathy. But everything had changed. He was involved now—and, as a result, his understanding of the world had become recomposed.

Aleksender adjusted the burden of his satchel, carefully survey-ing the monument that loomed before him. He'd abandoned his beloved Juliet to the carriage house only moments before, which had been no easy feat. Without her comforting nickers and playful nudges, he felt anything but heroic.

A rush of hopelessness engulfed Aleksender in a dense, black haze. All of Opera Garnier's entrances were barricaded off and suf-ficiently guarded. The red flag of the Commune covered the opera house's facade like a security blanket, branding the house as a sanc-tuary and place of rest.

The leather satchel eased its grip as he slipped to the ground and pressed his back against one of the cracked walls. The fate of Paris flashed before his eyes as he watched the doom of his home-land unfold. From crevice to crevice, gunfire, brutal fist fights and wailing children swarmed every inch of the square. Blood and corpses littered the streets. Hoping to strengthen the barricades, furniture had been tossed from the windows days earlier. Thou-sands of cobblestones had been torn from the ground and utilized as deadly weapons.

And all the omnibuses had been either discarded or flipped over. It was chaos and total anarchy.

Aleksender's eyes grew heavy and fluttered shut. Nestled with-in the haven of his inner thoughts, he saw her face and smile, heard the melody of her voice, watched the gracefulness of her steps. The world fell away, leaving only the two of them. Aleksender groped his chest, massaging his heart in steady circles, easing the pain within. Mon Dieu. He missed his little Sofia. He missed his darling ward more than he could bear to comprehend. And he had saved her once, nearly ten years ago.

Could he do the same again? Or was his quest purely in vain? Maybe this was Christophe's ultimate revenge, his last laugh. May-be Sofia was already long dead and Christophe was sending Alek-sender into the grave for no other reason than to mock his weak-ness, much like the little nightingale who vainly sacrificed herself for a rose ...

What now?

Aleksender couldn't risk being recognized. He'd be marked as an enemy of "the people" without a doubt—which wasn't so far from the truth. And this place had to be the endpoint of his journey. Alas, this was one of the Commune's central bases, and Christophe was inside.

But how in God's name was he to sneak past the watchmen? The opera was thoroughly guarded from wall to wall. And only recognizable figures belonging to either the Commune or National Guard held any chance of gaining entrance. Indeed, the security was the finest that Paris could buy.

Aleksender lolled his head against the impressive stonework. Zoning in and out of his thoughts, he studied the towering architecture and black night sky. Carved angels hovered above him by the masses, intricate columns perched upon their backs.

Sofia was beyond those walls. Of that he was certain. Aleksender nearly laughed at the realization. The message of his journey was borderline poetic. Over the past days, he'd seen and lived the horrors of Paris.

Christophe had forced Aleksender to become a part of the bloodshed—a part of the revolution.

Aleksender climbed to his feet without further thought and barricaded himself behind one of the jutting columns. He stripped away his coat and hat, throwing them into the surrounding wreckage. In decided movements, he disregarded any giveaways of his social standing or identity, keeping only the satchel on his person.

Aleksender eased back into the crowd and searched the distressed faces.

In moments, Aleksender was sucked into the surrounding combat. His fighting instincts took over as he dodged the wild shells with a fantastic show of agility. He clasped a hand to either side of his head, warding off the resounding gunfire and cries. Alas, he was back on the battlefield and near to panicking.

He needed out.

Nearby, Aleksender spotted a National Guardsman who was presently yelling orders rather than fighting. A pair of civilians dragged a wounded man over, muttered some quick incoherent words, and escorted him inside the opera house. Aleksender inhaled a shaky breath, knowing precisely what had to be done. A nearby angel, who held a column upon his mighty back, seemed to suddenly slump—as if he'd realized the gravity of his fate.

Heart pounding in his ears, Aleksender scaled the side of the building until he found a corner of privacy. Squeezing his eyes shut, he sagged against one of the towering walls and held his breath. Aleksender's words from the rooftop echoed his mind and rekindled his perseverance. *Pain is in the mind. And, in my mind, ma chérie—*

Detaching mind from body, he dug the muzzle of his shotgun into his shoulder and—*bang*!

A rush of excruciating pain overcame Aleksender. His scream was last to the overwhelming ambiance, camouflaged within the cries of fallen men, women and children.

Clutching onto his arm, Aleksender fought to retain every ounce of his strength. He had been stabbed and shot before, countless times, and this was no different.

Mon Dieu. The entire journey would be useless if he fell. But the military of Versailles was on the brink of breaching the opera house. In a matter of hours—perhaps less—everyone inside would be slaughtered like a flock of sacrificial lambs.

Your pain reminds and warns you that you are very much alive.

Aleksender shook away Christophe's voice and continued his pursuit. He fought for consciousness at every step as he stumbled through the dead and wounded. Bloody faces and amputated limbs paved the walkway. Grasping onto his satchel, he squared both shoulders and stood before the National Guardsman.

"My shoulder. I—I've been shot." Aleksender's words emerged in a strained gasp. Excruciating pain shot through his body and spirited his breath away. Praying he wouldn't be identified as Paris's comte, he dropped his face as the guard surveyed his body. For once fate was in his favor. The man merely latched onto Aleksender's hand, tugged it aside, and gave the wound a thorough once over.

"Don't worry, monsieur. They shall aid you well. There— through that door."

With a sharp nod, he called out to another guard and directed Aleksender beyond Opera Garnier's forsaken walls.

CHAPTER THIRTY-ONE

"By and by thou shalt come unto a river of hell, whereas Charon is ferryman, who will first have his fare paid him, before he will carry the souls over the river in his boat, whereby you may see that avarice reigned amongst the dead, neither Charon nor Pluto will do anything for nought: for if it be a poor man that would pass over and lacketh money, he shall be compelled to die in his journey before they will show him any relief ..."

—The Marriage of Eros and Psyche

Aleksender maneuvered through the maze of flesh and weapons, unsure of where precisely he was to go. The pain in his arm had settled into a dull and throbbing ache. No one cast him so much as a second glance, completely absorbed and dedicated to their tasks. Off to the side, men, women, and children labored before melting pots as lead was casted into bullets.

Aleksender ventured deeper into the opera house, moving past the excitement and activity, tracking through endless corridors. The surrounding commotion gradually faded into an eerie and detached silence. Searching for answers, he continued his quest.

Aleksender quickly discovered that Opera Garnier was the Goliath of Salle Le Peletier. It contained over six thousand doors, secret passageways, and more gold than the king himself. Many of the rooms were bare, unfurnished and unlit.

Then—

A shadow moved across one of the walls in quick and decided motions. Aleksender followed after it, tracing the steady footfall. He quickened his steps—shadowing the shadow. He rounded a corner and caught a glimpse of whomever or whatever he was pursuing; the shadow now appeared as a mere silhouette. A ball of light bounced off the dark walls and carpeting.

As he suspected, the silhouette was clutching a lantern and a chassepot rifle. Aleksender strained his eyes. The felt brim of the silhouette's hat was barely visible, but he could see enough to identify the man as a member of the National Guard. Indeed, the guardsman was moving with purpose, never breaking stride. He'd obviously walked this path many times before now—the path of the Communard's road.

A low creak resounded and a door swung open. The man entered one of Opera Garnier's rooms—a library or parlor, Aleksender took notice—and approached the towering bookshelf. Just as Aleksender was certain he would collide straight into the fortress of books, the thing came to life. The rosewood shelf moaned, groaned, and gave a sharp pivot—sweeping the silhouette out of sight. Aleksender stormed across the room. He fumbled and pressed at the shelf, willing it to life.

Magic. In a single flash of movement he was swept to the other side.

Darkness blanketed everything. The lantern was yards away now and growing further—a winking star amongst a false horizon—slowly bobbing out of eyesight …

Without the lantern, everything fell pitch black within moments. Aleksender's erratic breathing swelled the small space to its limit. A sense of claustrophobia took hold, wrapping his throat like a fist.

Aleksender had seen enough to know that he was standing in a hallway approximately three feet wide and infinitely long, which curved this way and that, twisting like a serpent … a hallway that was lined with human remains. Millions of them.

Aleksender blindly outstretched his good arm and groped onto his surroundings. His index finger curled into an eye socket. The heel of his palm wafted across a humorless grin. The pad of his thumb skirted up and over a slight protuberance—a nose, by Aleksender's estimate.

He continued in this way, wading through the dark emptiness, only the love he felt for his ward guiding him. What if he was going the wrong direction? That was quite likely. What if he became stuck down here—down in this labyrinth of death and decay—

alone in the darkness? That was even more likely.

As he snaked through the endless corridor, blind and alone, the pastor's emotionless drawl echoed his mind. *Yea, though I walk through the valley of the shadow of death, I will fear no evil, for thou art with me. Thy rod and thy staff comfort me. Surely goodness and mercy shall follow me all the days of my life, and I will dwell in the house of the Lord forever.*

The pain returned to his arm with brutal force. Aleksender cried out and clasped onto the drenched material of his dress shirt. His legs failed him in the same breath—sending his body slamming against a cluster of skulls. He collapsed like a sack of bones and was forced into a fetal position. Indeed—the length of his form spanned wider than the hallway by a good foot. Lying in the darkness, engulfed by death and multitudes of pain, Aleksender felt himself begin to surrender. Yes, his mind throbbed against his skull. The walls seemed to shrink, closing in on his mind, body and spirit.

I should just do nothing. Do nothing and die here. It will be a matter of days—at most, a week—before the wound infects itself. It will redden and swell. Pus and other sour smelling fluids will mingle with my blood. I will vomit my guts out. Defecate myself a half dozen times, maybe more ... and eventually either starve to death or be swept with infection. Perhaps, I can bash my head in—these skulls certainly feel sharp enough—and surrender much, much sooner.

Aleksender's eyes slipped shut as a veil descended, sweeping him to a different time and place. In his mind's eye, he was seated before a blazing hearth and she was sprawled before him, chin in hands, her youthful features perfectly relaxed, perfectly content.

Damn it to hell. Aleksender would never find his way out of this maze.

His voice echoed the haunted cavern of his mind, distant and foreign to his ears:

Ah, but you are wrong, ma chérie. You see, this is built as a labyrinth. It's only an illusion designed to appear as a maze.

He'd come so far—he and his little Sofia had come so far. No—a few dark halls would not be his downfall. Aleksender had lived a lifetime of darkness. An underground labyrinth would not best him.

•

Nearly an hour had passed before Aleksender could make out the faint hum of voices. He snaked through the walls with squinted eyes, barely able to decipher his surroundings. Hints of grinning skulls and mildew-covered stones came into vision. In this section of the catacombs, torches and sconce lanterns hung from the walls and cast faint streams of light. The illuminations tossed thick shadows along the skulls and stone flooring, enhancing the deathly aura. Every so often the pathway would veer off in one direction and continue in another.

Aleksender froze in his tracks as a pungent scent flooded his nostrils. The scent reeked distinctively of death and decay.

God's teeth, what was that smell?

A terrible vision of Sofia's beautiful, limp form flashed behind his eyes. Aleksender splayed a wrist over his nose, bit back a curse, and followed a slight curve in the path.

The dangling sconces harmoniously throbbed, threatening to wink out. Aleksender blindly clung onto the damp wall for guidance and steadied his body. Condensation covered the skulls in a slimy film, making them feel remarkably like brains. The floor turned and slanted as he descended deeper into Paris's underground—deeper, deeper still.

The pitter-patter of a rat fled past his boots with the audacity of a drum roll. His battered limbs tangled in one of the low hanging spider webs.

After what seemed an eternity, Aleksender encountered the makeshift prison cell. Three decapitated corpses were sprawled across the floor, their limp bodies nearly overlapping. Swarms of maggots clogged the stumps of their necks as hundreds of hungry mouths consumed the rotten flesh. All of it became too much. Far too much. The war, the carcasses, his throbbing bullet wound, the underground labyrinth, his father's uncalled death. Richard's words, *Father would have never denied them such a thing ... you could be named next.* Sofia's kidnapping.

Aleksender's stomach tightened, clenched, and sunk, broken out in a chain of dry heaves. Relief came in a fell swoop as lukewarm liquid bubbled from his gut—mostly brandy, he assumed—and splattered onto the stones below. Gasping for breath, he swiped away the vomit and conjured an image of Sofia inside his mind.

Aleksender regained a semblance of composure and knelt beside the corpses.

A note poked out of one of the coat pockets, its parchment faintly dribbled with blood. Aleksender collected it, eyes running over the familiar writing: *That which doesn't burn must pass through fire to be made clean.*

Two men materialized from the shadows without warning. Aleksender was violently seized, arms folded behind his back and fastened together at the wrists. A foot of rope rendered him entirely defenseless. He cringed in an explosion of pain as the satchel was ripped from his shoulder. Agonized curses flew from his lips. A hand grasped at the seething wound with the force of an iron manacle. Aleksender felt the air gush from his lungs. He bellowed a low groan and nearly collapsed to the ground. Keeping him upright took the conjoined effort of both men.

"Ah. Been shot, have we?"

Aleksender jerked, easing the torturous pressure of their holds. Sweat rained from his brows and blurred his vision. Fighting for consciousness, his words emerged in erratic and twisted gasps. "Where is he? Where the hell is Christophe Cleef?"

"Ah, you mustn't fret, Monsieur le Comte," the first man said.

"Indeed. They've been waitin' for you a couple days now," offered the other. "Both Christophe and the girl. But I'd reckon you already know that."

CHAPTER THIRTY-TWO

Aleksender arrived at the Commune's base to find his comrade leaning against the farthest wall. Reeking of despair, death and filth, Christophe Cleef appeared as just another dark secret ... just another lost and broken dream. Two tarnished silver chains twinkled within the bottomless expanse, each one reflecting the sconce lanterns' wavering lights. An assortment of weapons was propped in a corner—daggers, muskets, chassepot rifles and the like. The Commune's crimson flag proudly hung above the artillery.

Christophe was consumed by deep thought and entirely unaware of Aleksender's presence. In fact, he appeared to be unaware of everything outside of his own inner torment. A paralyzing chill settled deep inside Aleksender's bones.

Where had his friend gone to? This—this was not his noble comrade. This was not the great Christophe Cleef. Only a poor imitation.

This man was far more dead than alive, teetering on the brink on sanity. And he stood as a mere shell of the solider that he'd once been. The navy material of his coat was covered in filth and a full size too large. It draped from his limbs in harsh and irregular folds. In spite of all the torment he'd undergone at Christophe's hands, a distinct sadness shadowed Aleksender's heart.

"Alek!"

Sofia's cry dispelled any remaining compassion he'd clung to for his friend. Alarmed by the noise, Christophe twisted his face back. He pocketed the dog tags and took a clumsy step toward his hostage.

"Ah, Sofia ... mon amour ..." Christophe slurred through a grin, hovering above her body. Mon Dieu. He could barely hold himself upright. "Why, it seems your hero has come to save the day."

Sofia was fastened to the wall, resembling some mystical virgin sacrifice, each limb completely immobilized. Aleksender's chest stirred as he surveyed the raw scabs that decorated her flesh. He briefly thought of Eros and Psyche. Beautiful Psyche, lost within the vast Underworld, waiting for her dearly beloved's return.

Aleksender jerked forward and struggled to break free of his captors' holds. With each movement, the rope dug a little deeper, the pain burned a little more. Ragged pants inflated his lungs as his flesh was bloodied and severed. Wounds and fresh blisters circled the rope, tinting it red.

"I'm here, Christophe," he grated between clenched teeth. "I played in your little farce. Now let her go."

Christophe barked a sharp laugh and lulled forward till he stood a foot away from Aleksender. A putrid stench radiated from his body and polluted the air. Aleksender wrestled with the desire to take several steps backward. Instead, he straightened out his posture and returned Christophe's leveled glare.

"That how you greet your ol' friend, eh?" Christophe drawled as he meddled with Aleksender's shirt lapels. His breaths were stale, rancid and heavy. Grime covered his teeth, staining them an unforgiving yellow. "Not so much as a 'how do you do?'"

A loud thud resounded as one of the Communards threw Aleksender's satchel to the ground.

"What's this?" Christophe questioned.

"His things, monsieur."

Christophe nodded, knelt, and probed through the belongings. Glazed eyes drew to the pistol. His fingertips gently grazed the carved handle, tracing the calligraphic words *de Lefèvre*.

"This is between you and me," Aleksender grated between clenched jaws. "Release Sofia."

"Ah, very well." Christophe climbed onto his feet and rotated in Sofia's direction. He fished a tarnished skeleton from the confines of his trousers and spun it between two fingertips like a baton. A dark smile formed on his lips. "That's fine by me. She's an awfully good girl."

Click. Click. Click.

Sofia exhaled as the chains came undone. She gracelessly teetered onto her feet, weak at the ankles and plagued with pain.

Christophe grasped onto Sofia's shoulder and steadied her body. "Careful, there, ma chérie ..."

"Get your hands off her." Aleksender growled as he struggled against his restraints. "I said now."

Christophe spread his palms wide and held them over his head in an elaborate show of surrender. Sofia straggled forward till she was inches from Aleksender. Tears streamed down her pale cheeks. Christophe grumbled and scratched the back of his head, suddenly rather uncomfortable and at loss for words.

Sofia wearily glanced at Christophe as she undid Aleksender's bindings. Making no attempt to stop her, he swallowed and stared at Aleksender's bloodied wrists and hands, his hanging, wounded shoulder. Poorly hiding his discomfort, he shrugged and gave an off look. "Might as well make this a fair fight, eh now?"

Any peace was short lived. The thunder of thousands of boots and hollered commands resounded overhead. The military of Versailles was coming.

Christophe muttered a curse and scrubbed a hand over his features. Turning on his heels, he addressed his followers. "Both of you—return to the ranks. I reckon you'll be of more use up there. We're out of time. They're breachin' the house." His scar twisted, manipulated by his smirk. "A broken veteran and wee paragon shouldn't be much trouble. Now go—go finish what we started."

Moving with a sudden haste, Sofia tossed the rope aside and collapsed within Aleksender's arms. He stroked her hair with trembling hands. Sister Catherine's crucifix gleamed against his dress shirt, shining like a beacon. "Sofia, you are all right. Dieu, thank you."

"We must hurry," she deftly murmured into his chest.

Aleksender cringed as he was encircled by her arms. Sofia gasped, struck by the realization. Her face whitened to a ghostly hue. She eased backward and studied the hazy depths of his eyes. "No! Alek—your arm ... You are shot!"

He cupped her cheeks, lips lifting into that dashing and crooked grin. "Ah. It's but a scratch."

"A scratch!"

Blood stained her hands.

"Come—we must find you help right away. Upstairs—there is—"

Christophe's booming voice cut through the air like a knife. Cruel laughter followed after. "Upstairs? There is no more upstairs, stupid chit. And you really think I've had him come all this way only to waltz on out of here?"

"His arm has been shot! Surely, you—"

Aleksender arched his brows, threw Sofia a commanding look, and rotated toward Christophe. He edged through the shadows, moving with the grace of a panther.

"Tell me—what do you want?" The timber of his voice was low, husky, and seething with venom. "What the hell do you want from me, Christophe? Want to see me die? Is that it?" Silence filled Paris's underground. Aleksender throbbed from head to toe and perceived varying shades of red. "Or was this just your elaborate way of making me suffer? You despise me. You always have despised me." He glanced at Sofia from the corner of his eye. "You are angry because you have no one to love. No one to love you."

At that moment, two members of the Commune flew inside the base. Horror was etched in their youthful faces, blood artfully splattered across torn shirts. Refusing to meet Christophe's eyes, they collectively swallowed and exchanged glances. "Monsieur Cleef."

Christophe shot a narrowed stare and examined each of their faces. "What? And be quick about it."

One of the boys stepped forward and slid the cap from his head. A swarm of greasy, red locks shone beneath the lanterns. "You wanted us to tell you right away if anythin' should happen to Elliott."

Christophe froze in his tracks. "What? What about Elliot?" Nothing. "Answer me!"

"He fell, monsieur," answered the other man. "At the barricade."

Overcome with a wave of nausea, Christophe swallowed and swayed on his feet. "Where is he?" His voice was a whisper and barely audible. He lunged forward, latching onto the redhead's lapels, eyes blazing. The Communard struggled against his hold. Christophe's fists turned to steel, preventing any chance for escape. "No. Don't you turn from me, fool! Now where is his body, damn it? Speak up!"

"He'll be placed out on the street, monsieur, to lie with the others. So that a family member might claim him."

Christophe threw his shoulders back in a wild roar. He groped at the mangy tendrils of his hair and slid backward till he was swallowed up by the shadows. "So that a family member might claim him, you say? How ingenious! I applaud the both of you!" Christophe balled his hand into a fist and pounded at the side of his face. Tears finally came to his eyes, hard and strong.

Aleksender seized the chance for escape. Careful on their feet, he and Sofia eased away from Christophe. "He had no family! He had nothing! Nothing!"

Blinded by the darkness, Sofia tripped and gave herself away with a hushed *oomph.*

Christophe instantly twisted to the sound. The fire of hell blazed from his eyes. "No. You are not running away. Hear me? Not this time. Not now. You'll pay for this."

Aleksender stopped dead in his tracks.

"Where were you all this time, eh?" Christophe yelled to him. "With her, I suppose? Now tell me—how does it feel knowing you could have put an end to this death?"

Aleksender rotated on his boots and stepped cleanly in front of Sofia. Trembling with emotion, Christophe withdrew a flintlock pistol from his trousers' pocket and leveled it to his friend's chest. "His blood—it is on your hands! You hear me, Alek?"

Sofia surrendered to a soft cry as Christophe cocked the pistol. The Communards stepped backward, stunned into silence by the sudden turn of events. Young and impressionable, they were in a state of shock from the horrors and reality of a civil war. And each boy was clearly torn at the seams, aware that the great Christophe Cleef was well beyond their reach. But no help was to be found. Only more agony and suffering lay above—and every corner of the opera house had transformed into a death trap. The morbid sounds of screams, gunfire and thundering boots stood as unshakable proof.

"Listen to me," Aleksender said in a slow, calm voice. He eased back several feet, palms outstretched, eyes never leaving Christophe's scathing expression. "This isn't who you are. You have gone mad. You have gone mad and you're not thinking any longer."

"No. That's where your wrong, mon ami. For the first time, I'm thinking clear. Real clear. And I think I'd rather enjoy blowin' you to hell. How 'bout it, ol' friend?"

Aleksender eased back several more steps. "It's over." He turned and guided Sofia away from Christophe at a spry pace.

"Running away again, I see? You're a damned coward, Alek! And that's all you've ever amounted to. I wonder what your father would think of your desertion? You do him proud."

"This place is about to be swarmed from roof to cellar. We don't leave now, and we're all dead." He grasped onto Sofia's arm, enunciating each word. "All of us."

Infused with the slightest touch of pity, Sofia glanced over her shoulder and stared into Christophe's eyes.

Yes—this is how it felt to fall from grace ...

Bang!

She uttered a choked cry and reeled around Aleksender's body—collapsing on top of him as metal tore through layers upon layers of flesh, blood, and muscle.

CHAPTER THIRTY-THREE

Aleksender and Sofia instantly lost balance from the brutal force of the impact. The sensation of ripping flesh slammed through both their bodies. Sofia's fingers curled around the lapels of his shirt as she bit back a sharp scream. In the same breath, Aleksender bellowed a groan and plummeted onto the cold stones—taking Sofia's body down with him. The extent of their shared agony was blinding. Blood seeped onto the stones in a slow, lazy circle.

Time seemed to stand still as Sofia lay on top of Aleksender's motionless form.

Varying degrees of pain shot through her veins and numbed the length of her body. She couldn't stir a limb. Couldn't think. Could barely draw breath. The pain was excruciating—unlike anything she'd ever felt before. It splintered through her bones and crashed down with all the pressure of an avalanche.

"Oh, Alek, I can hardly breathe." No response. Tiny, trembling fists grasped onto the material of Aleksender's shirt. She instantly recoiled—discovering that his shirt was as sullied as her shoulder. With an uttered cry, she summoned her remaining strength and fumbled off Aleksender's form. She spread her fingers wide and held them up to the light.

A scream roared inside of her throat. Blood—Aleksender's blood—seeped down her wrist at a leisurely pace and dripped onto the ground below.

Sofia's heart clenched against her ribcage as the realization sunk in. Positioned on her hands and knees, she crawled over to Aleksender and met the glassy depths of his eyes.

"God, no. Please, no. Alek, my Alek," she sobbed, curling against the heat of his chest. "I love you. I love you so much ..."

Aleksender ran his fingertips over Sofia's wound with an exasperated groan. "My little fool, why would you do such a thing?"

Sofia grasped onto Aleksender's dress shirt and tugged him closer. Their foreheads came together as tears coated the sallow curves of her cheeks. "Because we are one. And nothing could ever change that. Always and forevermore."

•

Christophe withdrew his Prussian dagger and unsheathed it from its leather cocoon. Indecisively he scanned the discarded flintlock pistol, the assortment of firearms, a chassepot rifle? No, not a rifle—a rifle was much too clean, too quick, and far too merciful.

He emerged from the shadows and inched closer, barely able to sustain the weight of his body. Everything was spinning—physically spinning like a toy top. With each movement, gallons of brandy rolled inside his gut. And he could feel it. He was drowning, barely hanging onto this haunted precipice.

The two Communards exchanged hushed words and eased away from Christophe. So be it. He didn't need their help or anyone else's.

The bittersweet taste of vengeance was tangible—it was on his tongue, in his heart, embedded deep in his very marrow. One person and one alone was responsible for his suffering. And yes, he would pay in blood. How sweet it would feel plunging the blade deep into his chest.

Feelings of scorn and resentment were amplified as he observed Aleksender and Sofia's interaction. Alas, it was better than an opera, far grander than any love ballad. And damn them both. Aleksender and Sofia remained ignorant of his looming presence—completely lost in each other, within the potency of the moment.

Aleksender groaned and lifted his hand, guiding it across the curve of Sofia's cheek. She cupped it within the heel of her palm and held him soundly against her.

"Sofia ... you are hurt. You need to get out of here."

Heat from a nearby torch danced across Christophe's features and drew sweat from his brow. No. This torment wasn't nearly enough—not by half. He burned to unleash the full extent of his hatred and wrath. Damn it to hell—he bore so much hatred. Christophe quivered with emotion as he steadied the dagger against his palm. The blade's toothy snarl edged into his flesh, slicing his skin with ease. The sting was a welcomed sensation, as was the sweltering liquid that welled his palm.

Your pain reminds and warns you that you are very much alive.

A cloud of despair shadowed what remained of his heart. This was it. This was the end. In the back of his mind, he saw the Vendôme Column crashing down, heard the people's unified cry: "*Vive la Commune! Vive la République! Vive la Résistance!* Death to the Empire." Napoleon's lifeless stare bore deeply into his own, all-seeing and perceptive.

Yes, Aleksender was right—it was over. And Christophe yearned to hurt the person who'd caused him so much pain, so much misery and loss.

Snapping from his thoughts, Christophe focused his glare on the two lovers. Sofia shook her head as tears streaked her cheeks. They streamed from the brilliant blue of her eyes in a fierce storm. "I shall be perfectly fine." Her lips curved into a weak smile. The sullied material of her nightdress strained in time with her labored intakes of air. "See?" She gasped, adjusting her bleeding shoulder. "It's but a scratch."

Sofia and Aleksender's forehead came together in a gentle and tentative touch. Struggling to breathe, she peppered kisses over every inch of his face, not daring to leave an inch of him unloved.

No one to love you. No one to love you. No one to love you.

The words swirled inside Christophe's mind until he grew dizzy. And those mocking refrains continued to echo until he could perceive nothing else.

"Alek, just don't leave me. Don't you dare leave me. Promise me. Promise you'll fight through this."

"Sofia, I'm sorry. So sorry." Holding her cheek within his palm, he drew invisible circles along her flesh, worshiping everything that was his beloved Sofia. "I fought for you, for us. For nine years I fought. This wasn't supposed to happen. It's all my fault."

Each word was a dagger in Christophe. He muttered a curse and continued his pursuit.

Sofia froze. He stood mere inches away, a looming eclipse of torn emotion.

She glanced over her shoulder and leveled her stare upon his battered features. With an intake of breath, she eyed the rusted dagger cradled in his hand. The cross engraved upon its tarnished handle was anything but holy.

Blood-lust pumped through Christophe's veins as a cruel smile stretched his mouth. He felt his scar twist and tighten, wreathing in agony. Alas—that cross seared his flesh, branding his soul.

"Please," Sofia pleaded in a fleeting voice. "Please, Christophe. I beg you. Enough blood has been shed. Enough."

He mutely shook his head and narrowed his eyes upon the dangling crucifix. It hung against Aleksender's chest, encircled by his comrade's life's blood.

The all-consuming question rose to Christophe's lips before he could stop it. "What have I become?"

The dagger was thrust into the air. Torches and sconces reflected off the blade in a blinding flash of light.

Christophe squeezed both eyes shut. Giddy anticipation, a strange sense of peace and finality, ignited his soul. In a clean swoop, he plunged the blade straight into his own chest. An unstoppable cry fell from his lips as it tore through cloth and flesh with ease. Then satisfaction inseparably mixed with pain. Yes—the vengeance was every bit as sweet as he'd fantasized it'd be. Muscle, bone and flesh devoured the metal to its hilt. Behind his eyes, a thousand gawking death-heads shared a laugh and jeered at his suffering.

With a great grunt of effort, Christophe twisted the dagger, urging it a little deeper. He angled it snugly between his ribs … felt as an organ was impaled. It ruptured at the assault, painting his insides a brilliant red. Then he withdrew the sullied blade and stabbed himself once more—branding the exact spot where Aleksender had taken his bullet all those months ago.

Sofia turned away with a cry and buried her face in the folds of Aleksender's shirt.

A resonating pang sounded out as the weapon fell from Christophe's numb fingers and tumbled onto the stones. A second later, he weakened at the knees and collapsed face first, joining the dagger on the ground. The bridge of his nose shattered on impact and issued a choked scream from his throat.

Side by side, Aleksender and Sofia watched the scene in pained silence.

The Communards crossed the base, rushing to Christophe's aid in a collective panic. "Monsieur! Mon Dieu. Monsieur Cleef!"

Christophe's chest rose and sank with labored, uneven breaths. He clasped onto a seething wound and rolled onto his side, barely retaining consciousness. Vats of blood welled both nostrils.

And he could feel it below him—a dark puddle was vastly blossoming. With a muttered curse, he shoved away the hands of his men as they wrestled to inspect his injuries.

"You're bleeding out, monsieur," observed the redhead as he struggled to appear calm and remotely collected.

"Ah, is that what happens when you jam a blade in your gut, eh?" Christophe scoffed, his voice dripping with that predictable sarcasm. "I wouldn't ... wouldn't have ever guessed."

The Communards ignored his remark and continued their investigation. "Please, monsieur! Let us help you. We really must—"

"No, damn you! Let me alone! Devil take me." They exchanged a desperate glance as their hands uniformly froze midair. "Now listen and listen close." Christophe's voice choked off into silence.

He groped at his chest, breathing drawing more and more shallow. A ribbon of blood leaked from his jawline and curled around his thickly bearded chin. His head lolled onto its side as he stared over at Sofia and Aleksender's embracing forms.

"I have a last order ... for the two of you fools." He turned away from Aleksender and Sofia, unable to stomach the sight of their affection.

Loneliness and a fierce self-hatred swelled Christophe's gut.

"Get them help. Now." Trembling hands clasped onto the Communard's collar and tugged him near. Wiry, red strands fell across his brow in a flurry. Christophe's dusty breaths seared the youth's sodden cheeks. "Don't let them die. Hear me?"

"Yes. Yes, I hear you."

"Good." Christophe's hand fell back down to the stones, leaving a bloody print in its wake. He stared at the image, strangely transfixed. He prayed—merciful God, he prayed—that religion was nothing more than an elaborate hoax. Salvation wasn't in the stars for a man such as himself. He'd burn in hell till kingdom come.

Shouts, cries, and pacing bodies intensified overhead. "Hurry. Sneak ... sneak out through the Rue de Scribe exit ... Versailles ... won't find you ... those miserable dogs." Staying true to his nature, Christophe finished with an irritated grumble and absently waved off both boys. "Now get the hell out of here and let me die with a damn shred of dignity."

One of the Communards began to rise to his feet—only to be steadied by Christophe's hand once more. "Wait. One more ... one more thing. Here ..." With a deep groan, he lifted his neck and withdrew the dog tags. *CHRISTOPHE CLEEF* and *ALEKSENDER DE LEFÈVRE* gleamed beneath the lanterns, each one equally vivid. Wincing, he tucked them in the boy's palm. "Want ... want my comrade to have 'em."

"Yes, m-monsieur."

The stained emblems vanished as the Communard curled his hand into a fist. He smoothed down the torn material of his coat and staggered to his feet. After a moment, he signaled his fellow comrade to follow suit. And, without exchanging so much as another nod, they tended to le Comte de Paris and his ward.

Christophe's death-rattle split the silence like a knife. His skin grew impossibly pale. His eyes lost their remaining sparkles. The gurgling intensified, loudened, overpowered. Blood crawled across the stones at a steady pace. Eclipsed by sounds of death, his final words were muted. Overwhelmed with a deep and undeniable ache, Aleksender met his comrade's vacant eyes. "Christophe," he whispered, "mon ami ... You are not alone."

CHAPTER THIRTY-FOUR

May 27, 1871
La Semaine Sanglante, Final Day

Aleksender groaned as he teetered on the brink of consciousness. He was steadily losing blood, descending into that eternal, dark emptiness.

All around him Paris was devoured by flames. He could feel the sweltering heat flash across his face, searing his neck with the bite of a cattle brand. Sweat clotted his hairline and trickled down his temples. His lips were chaffed, overgrown with blisters, his tongue inseparable from the roof of his mouth. Both bullet wounds throbbed, twisting his body in a raw ache.

One of the Communards secured Sofia's limp form against his chest and cradled her bridal-style. Two others dragged Aleksender's body. His heels slid across the pavement, each massive arm propped over their shoulders.

Muffled snippets of conversation cut through his hazed mind:

"Everything's burnin' to the ground."

"Nothin' left."

"It's all gone—gone."

Hopelessness engulfed them as the infirmary seeped into sight. The three Communards stopped dead in their tracks and marveled at the spectacle. Fire consumed the structure in a hungry blaze and tinted the horizon in crimson shades. Flames licked at the sky like the devil's tongue, lapping up a multitude of screams and dying breaths.

The man holding onto Sofia hung his face and searched the

surroundings in growing despair. "God above, what are we to do now?"

With a low groan, Sofia stirred in his arms and harnessed back a flash of pain. She fought for consciousness, her voice breathy and dangerously hollow. "Sacred Heart. Please—go to Sacred Heart Convent."

•

Persistent knocking resounded inside of Sacred Heart's walls. The latch surrendered to a defiant creak and was thrust aside. A second later, a pair of ancient eyes beamed from within the slit. Then the sound of a jingling knob and creaking followed.

Sister Catherine gasped as she tossed the door open.

"Monsieur le Comte! Sofia!" She lifted a hand to her lips, jarred by the sight of their mangled bodies. "What has happened to them?"

The Communards briefly bowed their heads and shuffled forward. They adjusted their grasps on Aleksender, stabilizing the burden of his weight. "They've been shot, Sister. And with the fires there's nowhere left for us to go. The infirmary's burnin' to the ground."

"Mon Dieu." Sister Catherine stepped aside and ushered them across the threshold with a persistent wave of her hand. "Through the hallway and to the left. The door has been left open, messieurs." An assortment of faces crowded Sacred Heart's interior. From wall to wall, the citizens of Paris were packed tight. Men, women, and children huddled in a comforting circle. Hands clasped together, they chanted a prayer as tears of remorse fell from their eyes. Tension snaked through the shadows like a living entity. And beyond Sacred Heart, the brutal sounds of war boomed for miles around—a vast contrast to the home's hushed din.

Weaving in and out of the men, women and children, Sister Catherine raced through the surrounding faces, scanning each one. Indeed, many of the people had found refuge within the sanctuary of the home. Sacred Heart Convent was one of the only places that had been left untouched by Paris's revolutionaries.

Sister Marie-Joie stood before the hearth, the young girls of Sacred Heart gathered about her heels. She read to the children, calming them with the absolute sureness of her voice. Sister Marie-Joie instilled a wisdom well beyond her thirty years. Her eyes were whimsical and strangely omniscient—the eyes of an elder woman in a young woman's face. Cued by Sister Catherine's entrance, she set the book aside and scrambled to her feet.

"Don't move, children," she whispered as she eased toward the head nun, her matronly skirts rustling. "Sister Catherine? The wounded gentleman—heavens, is that le Comte?"

"And his ward," Sister Catherine finished. "Is there anyone who can help them, I pray?"

"Come with me this way." Following Marie-Joie's lead, Sister Catherine swallowed and clutched her chest.

She exhaled a choked breath as she was brought before a hand-ful of doctors. "Oh, gracious Lord." All three gentlemen donned wired spectacles, whiskers and deep frowns. Had circumstances been different, Sister Catherine might have laughed. Instead, she crossed herself, murmured words of thanks to Sister Marie-Joie, and grazed one of the men's gangly forearms. "I'm in need of your help. Please, messieurs—quickly now."

In a uniformed motion, they rose from their seats and followed Sister Catherine into the bedchamber. Unusually clumsy, she fumbled to the door and closed it, allowing them privacy from prying eyes.

Aleksender shuddered, not bothering to suppress a moan as his large form was arranged across the mattress. "Non, non. Don't elevate him," the eldest doctor interjected, taking control of the situation. "Elevation shall only worsen the bleeding."

At the same time, a blanket was spread across the floorboards. The Communard hustled over and gently arranged Sofia's body across the coarse material. "Careful now," urged the doctor. "Stay clear of her shoulder."

"Sofia …" Aleksender whispered to Sister Catherine, his voice dangerously shallow. She approached the weak sound. Struggling to make out his words, she shoved the wimple from her head and leaned in close. "Where is Sofia?"

Sister Catherine grasped onto his hand with a reassuring smile. "She is right here at your side, monsieur." She patted the sweat from his brow and brushed away the heavy forelock. "Just relax now. You're in God's good hands. For the both of you—you must have faith."

Aleksender nodded as his eyes blinked shut. Tears formed at

the corners. Deeply touched by his vulnerability and sacrifice, Sister Catherine's chest gave a painful lurch. "Whatever happens to me, take care of my Sofia—it is all I ask." The tragic meaning of his words sent chills down her spine. Her gaze slid from his face and descended to his bloodied, battered wrists. Thoughts of the Lord and Savior empowered her spirit.

"Of course. She is dear to me, as well, monsieur." And with that, Sister Catherine turned to the doctors, offering whatever aid she could provide.

They took a moment to survey Aleksender and Sofia. The eldest man pushed the spectacles up the bridge of his nose, squinted, and leaned in close. He examined Aleksender and Sofia's wounds at length, lips tightened into a thin line. The wiry tufts of his hair stuck out in every direction, gleaming beneath the faint light. "Mm. It's urgent that we extract the bullet from his chest. Remarkably, it doesn't appear to be very deep, but may have fragmented on impact. Tending to the girl shall be quite simple enough. A couple linens and some alcohol should clean her up nicely." With a groan, he straightened out and addressed the other two doctors. "Have you any tools about?"

The youngest of the three men stepped forward. He shook his balding head, eyes darting between the two wounded patients. Sweat gathered where his hairline might have been a good twenty years ago. "Non, monsieur. We haven't our equipment, I'm afraid."

"Tell me—what shall you be needing, monsieur?" Sister Catherine quickly interjected. "We are well supplied here."

The doctors exchanged a brief word before naming off a list of items.

Sister Catherine fetched fresh linens, a pocketknife, gauze, iodine, alcohol, an assortment of sewing tools, two water basins and a candle from her vanity. A faint ring of light glowed as she struck the match and urged it to life.

Willing her hands not to shake, she arranged the items across the nightstand. The doctors nodded their gratitude and softly conversed amongst themselves. Sister Catherine held the candlestick over them as they collectivity labored. Aleksender's dress shirt was unclasped from throat to stomach, exposing his seething wound. The flame quivered, shaking in time with Sister Catherine's movements.

Sinking in and out of consciousness, Sofia groaned from her spot on the floor. Sister Catherine knelt at her side and dabbed her brow with a wet cloth, washing away the dirt and grime. The sight of Sofia's battered appearance was difficult to endure. "Shh, petit, relax. You are in good care."

"Alek?" Sofia strained, attempting to lift her head from the blanket. "Is he all right? Where—"

"He is here with you," Sister Catherine consoled. She gently pressed on Sofia's chest, coaxing her back into a reclined position. "You mustn't exert yourself, my dear, brave girl." Brushing away a swarm of curls, voice heavy with emotion, "You, Sofia Rose, are the daughter I never could have." Clearly touched by those words, Sofia nodded and managed a weak smile.

"If I may see to her now," the youngest doctor interrupted. As he came to Sofia's care, Sister Catherine nodded and rose from the floor. Nerves dancing, she warily approached the bed. "Are the wounds fatal?" Her voice was little more than a whisper.

"The girl shall be quite fine," one of the men answered.

"And what of him?" Sister Catherine demanded, her skin turning impossibly paler. "What of le Comte?"

"He's already lost a lot of blood and is suffering from not one but two injuries." The doctor mutely hung his face. The spectacles slid down his nose, wired frame glittering in the candlelight. "I'm afraid that only daybreak shall tell." Aleksender's dress shirt was completely stripped away. Sister Catherine's heart lunched, jarred by the sight of his scars. Where was the mercy? It seemed that Aleksender had suffered far more than his own share of original sin.

Her thoughts were cropped short. "You may want to look away, Sister."

Pocketknife in hand, the doctor angled the blade, heating it with the candle's flame. "Some assistance, if you would, messieurs."

The other men held Aleksender still as the point was lowered to the chest wound. Alcohol was poured inside the marred flesh in a blistering inferno. Probing for bullet fragments, the tip dug into the gaping hole ... raking ... searching ... scraping the raw and painfully tender skin. The wound instantly gushed at contact, blossoming in a burst of scarlet. Executing decades of medical knowledge, the doctor maneuvered the knife with precise and graceful movements.

Aleksender trembled and cried out, teeth chattering with the audacity of tin cymbals. The men increased the pressure of their holds and steadied his flailing body. Unable to stomach his pain, Sister Catherine whispered a prayer and fixed her gaze upon the dangling crucifix.

CHAPTER THIRTY-FIVE

A week after the horrors of La Semaine Sanglante, the following announcement was published in the *Époque*:

> *Only a week ago, power was seized from our provisional government. The National Guard, recruited from the honorable men and women of Paris, had replaced Thiers's army of Versailles. A new day had finally dawned.*
>
> *But the liberty had been short-lived.*
>
> *On the twenty-first of May at two PM, over sixty thousand troops were inside Paris by nightfall.*
>
> *No one was spared from the brutal massacres. The barricades fell quickly and the defenders were summarily executed. The dead littered our streets and homes. Every crevice of Paris overflowed with corpses and dying men, women, and children.*
>
> *The killing continued for eight days and nights straight. Every Parisian pavement was a battlefield and every home a fort. On the twenty-eighth of May, the Communards were driven to a last stand at Père Lachaise cemetery where they were executed against the ancient wall.*
>
> *With heavy hearts, we include amongst the deceased the archbishop, le Comte de Paris, and his beloved and talented ward, Sofia Rose.*

•

Sister Catherine arrived at Chateau de Lefèvre almost two months after the announcement was posted. Dusk had broken fifteen minutes earlier, drenching the horizon in various shades of orange and pink. The sun was swallowed up by the skyline and the first stars had begun to creep into sight.

Sister Catherine smoothed a palm over the coarse material of her habit, mentally confirming the note's placement. Indeed—it was nestled safely against her breast, just as it'd been for the past four and a half weeks. Nerves dancing, she eased toward the enormous double-doors and collected the brass lion head within her palm. The metal felt unbearably cool—as hard and as relentless as steel. She tapped lion against wood, stepped backward, and waited in mounting suspense.

Several moments passed without any sort of answer. Sister Catherine turned away, head hung in defeat, and began her descent. On the third step she paralyzed in her tracks. The door thrust open with a resounding creak. Flooded with relief, she turned on her heels and ascended the steps once more.

Regarding her with a curious expression and arched brow, the first footman returned her leveled gaze. "Yes, Sister? How may I be of service?"

"Is the madame of the house able to receive company?"

His head sank into a curt nod as he stepped aside, welcoming Sister Catherine across the threshold. "Of course. Just allow me a moment to fetch her."

"Please—take your time, monsieur. I'm in no rush."

The chateau was as beautiful as she'd imagined it might be. Sister Catherine felt infinitely small as she entered the foyer. Columns lined the walls and swept at the domed ceiling. The de Lefèvre coat of arms was engraved in the stonework more than four and a half dozen times.

With a courteous bow the first footman took his leave. Sister Catherine idly wandered the length of the foyer, studying the countless hanging portraits. One picture stole her breath.

The man was dressed in military garb. His hair was black as the night, body strong, lips curved into a knowing grin. And those eyes—those emerald eyes appeared jarringly alive, alert, wise and calculating. No matter where Sister Catherine positioned herself, Aleksender's gaze seemed to trace her every step.

"Sister Catherine? Is that really you?" Elizabeth's voice jolted her from her thoughts. Richard de Lefèvre stood mere inches behind, appearing proud and wonderfully aristocratic. The sureness of his posture shouted authority and commanded obedience. A small, secretive smile tugged at Sister Catherine's lips. His likeness to a nearby portrait of Comte Philippe de Lefèvre was startling to behold.

Sister Catherine took a moment to observe Elizabeth and Richard's closeness—the way his hand rested upon the arch of her shoulder, his protective, all-seeing stare—something not unlike his father's portrait. After a moment, she bowed her face and withdrew the folded parchment from inside her habit.

Bewildered, Elizabeth's hand froze midair. "I don't understand?"

"He wanted to be sure you received it. Read it well. The both of you." Sister Catherine glanced from Elizabeth to Richard, then studied them together.

Elizabeth slid the parchment from Sister Catherine's fingers and held it against her breast. She nodded, tears swelling her almond eyes. "Thank you. Thank you for everything."

Wrinkles appeared at the corner of Sister Catherine's eyes as she surrendered to a faint smile. She reached for Elizabeth's face and caressed her cheek with a reassuring and gentle touch. "May happiness follow the both of you. Good luck."

With a last glance, Sister Catherine was gone.

Hands trembling, Elizabeth unfolded the note and rotated in Richard's arms. She swallowed, willing herself not to shake. He steadied Elizabeth's hands with his palms and gave an encouraging smile. "Don't worry. I am here with you."

Elizabeth inclined her chin and smoothed down the parchment. Basking in each other's warmth, she and Richard read the familiar cursive.

Dearest Elizabeth,

No amount of words can undo the pain I've caused you over the past years. But I am not a coward—and I refuse to become a mere casualty.

The first stirrings of daybreak have begun to pour through Sacred Heart's windows. I lay here shot but far from defeated. I am very much alive. In rescuing Sofia I have rescued a part of myself. And in Christophe Cleef's death, a part of my soul has resurrected. If I survive this day—which I'm confident that I shall—I have vowed to reinvent my destiny, to start anew, to leave Paris.

As hollow as the words sound, as inferior as they appear scrawled upon this scrap of paper, I care for you, Elizabeth. I have always cared for you, and at times, I'd cared for you as much as I was ca-

pable of caring for anyone. I know it is wrong to request anything of you, but I ask that you do likewise.

Do the same as myself. Free yourself and start a new life free from binds. In a way, is this not the very message our martyrs bled for?

I have witnessed Richard's affection for you throughout the years. He can care for you in ways I cannot. He can love you fully, as you deserve to be loved.

I shall write to you and Richard within the next few months. I trust that Sister Catherine will ensure my words have reached you.

Always yours, Aleksender De Lefèvre

EPILOGUE

Summer of 1875

Slow and steady, *The Nightingale* skimmed across the pristine waters of the Pacific Ocean at a leisurely pace. The sails swelled as gusts of wind whistled through their linens, carrying the vessel through an endless glassy haze.

Resembling something out of the pages of a storybook, the view was beyond breathtaking. Shades of orange and red illuminated the horizon. Blankets of white clouds mingled with the surrounding colors, artfully swirling in every direction.

And up above, tucked high in the crow's nest, a couple intimately embraced.

Sofia sighed as her lashes fluttered shut. Flooded with pure contentment, she settled deeper into the beloved arms of her husband. They'd wedded two years earlier, and had been traveling the vast ocean ever since. Evenings were spent on Coney Island's gilded stages, while the nights were reserved for Aleksender's embrace.

The divorce had not been by any means easy to come by. But, in the land of America, with the proper circumstances and finances, such a thing was far from impossible to obtain. Elizabeth and Aleksender had concluded their fifteen-year partnership on understanding if not delicate terms. A year and a half after, hand in hand, she and Comte Richard de Lefèvre had joined them on board for the ceremony. And a bundle of unsent letters had accompanied their presence.

Granted, Elizabeth hadn't been entirely forgiving of Aleksender's ways. She'd rather taken a decadent satisfaction in granting herself the freedom to love openly. Likewise, witnessing the pains of love and war firsthand had allowed Richard to open his mind and disregard his insecurities.

During La Semaine Sanglante, Aleksender de Lefèvre was reported as a casualty of the fires and mayhem, and only those whom mattered had known the truth. Thanks to Sister Catherine and some strange stroke of fate, he'd survived that final night in Sacred Heart Convent. Marked as a widow shortly after, Elizabeth had managed to live free from the stigma that came with divorce. And, for the four of them, it had been the beginning of a new life. A fresh start and redesigned destiny.

In all likelihood, one of the noblest things Aleksender de Lefèvre had ever done was run away.

Standing intimately near to Sofia, his raven hair danced freely in the wind's breath and skimmed the wide expanse of his shoulders. Condensation curled the tips and sparkled like teardrops, dampening the lush forelock across his brow. His cotton dress shirt fluttered about, whipping with the audacity of a high-flying flag. Half of the claps had been left undone, exposing strong slates of bronzed, sun-kissed muscle. A pair of dog tags and Sister Catherine's crucifix shone beneath the sunrise.

Breasts molded against the silky material of his dress shirt, Sofia rotated within the circle of his arms. She set a long kiss upon his chin as her fingertips whispered across his flesh. Aleksender returned her smile. His eyes blinked shut. Pure contentment flooded his body.

Sofia's lips curved with devilish intent. She undid the clasps of her dress—snap, snap, snap—allowing the material to slide from a pair of scrunched shoulders. It fell down to her belly, exposing a sheer layer of cotton. She flexed at the knees and crouched before Aleksender's form.

The front of his trousers was in view. Rows of golden claps were kissed by the morning's sunrays. The material puckered and strained, manipulated by the impressive bulge that lay beneath. Sofia caressed him through the linen. Aleksender stiffened as a wild moan escaped from his throat. One hand fisted in her curls. The other grasped onto the wooden railing to better stabilize his weight.

"Yes, chérie."

Sofia unfastened the clasps at a maddening pace and released

Aleksender from his confines. He was magnificent wrapped in her little fists. She moved both hands up and down, up and down, coaxing a melody of groans, moans, and pleas from his lips. Her tongue joined in the dance, swirling and licking, skimming his length from base to tip, tip to base. Aleksender's head lolled back in acute pleasure.

"Take me in, darling," he demanded in a silky smooth baritone. "Take all of me." Sofia relaxed her throat and obliged with a complimentary moan. With a firm tug, the final clasp of his trousers came undone. Sofia ran her fingertips up and over his finely sculpted thighs as they fell to his knees, claiming her prize, teasing him with the heel of both palms.

Consumed by overlapping sensations and the surrounding beauty, Aleksender went feral and loss control of his body. His fingers twisted against Sofia's scalp as his breaths shortened to erratic grunts. Splinters that were embedded in the wooden railing bit at his flesh. Sofia increased her tempo and massaged the smooth planes of his chest, moving down the broad length of his back, caressing the endless scars that had branded him for so long.

Far, far too long.

Climax claimed Aleksender in a sudden and sweet rush. Trembling from head to toe, he chanted her name like a sacred prayer.

Sofia rose to her feet and embraced Aleksender in the circle of her arms. Her nude breasts molded against his chest as they held each other for countless moments. He recuperated from his spent passion as his breathing steadily grew more regular. Staring into the limitless horizon, Sofia brought her lips against the column of Aleksender's neck and whispered, "I am with child."

Shuddering within Sofia's arms, he increased the pressure of his hold. His head spun with a pinnacle of emotions.

"And should it be a boy, well, I'd like to name him Philippe."

Sofia stepped back and swept the forelock from Aleksender's eyes. She was startled to find he had begun weeping. Surrendering to a smile, he sprawled an unsteady hand across her lower abdomen and brought her impossibly nearer.

Fierce passion ignited both of their souls—a passion nearly fourteen years in the making. Sofia gasped as he pinned her body against the jutting pole. Aleksender drowned her beneath his kisses, caressing every curve of her body, his arms strong, steady and sure. Sofia sagged against him as she grew weak at the knees.

"My Alek, my beloved ..."

He whispered the eternal vow, his voice beautiful and soothing, every word spoken like a lullaby, "I am yours and you are mine."

•••

Rachel L. Demeter

Rachel L. Demeter lives in the beautiful hills of Anaheim, California with Teddy, her goofy lowland sheepdog, and her high school sweetheart of ten years. Rachel holds a Screenwriting BA from Chapman University's School of Film and Media Arts. She enjoys writing dark, edgy romances that examine the redeeming power of love.

RachelDemeter.net

CPSIA information can be obtained
at www.ICGtesting.com
Printed in the USA
BVHW031039140223
658482BV00005B/63